Surviving the Dead Volume 7:
The Killing Line

By

James N. Cook

COPYRIGHT

Also by James N. Cook:

Surviving the Dead Series:

No Easy Hope

This Shattered Land

Warrior Within

The Passenger

Fire in Winter

The Darkest Place

Savages

ONE

Heinrich peered through his binoculars and tracked the caravan as it crossed the Kansas plains.

"I count thirty-two," Carter said. "All armed, a few women and children, eight Blackthorns. The rest look capable."

Heinrich grunted assent. The two men lay prone on a wooded hillside where they had spent the last several hours waiting for a target to present itself. At this juncture of the trade route they knew someone would come along sooner or later. In this case, it was sooner.

Heinrich lowered his field glasses. "They're headed for 160."

"Probably going to Tennessee or Kentucky. What do you think they're carrying?"

"Hard to be sure. Whatever it is, it must be valuable to hire eight of Jennings' men."

1

Carter frowned at the mention of Tyrel Jennings and his mercenaries. He'd encountered them in the past, and his experiences had invariably resulted in lost comrades and permanent scars.

"I'd take 'em just for that."

Heinrich grinned. Two teeth were missing on the left side of his face, courtesy of an elbow strike from one of Jennings' men. "Any excuse to take on the Blackthorn Security Company, eh?"

Carter's battered face returned the smile. "You know you want 'em."

"You know me too well, old friend. Let's get back and round up the others. Make a plan."

Heinrich turned his head to one of the men waiting farther down the hillside with the horses. "Locke. You and Rourke follow the caravan. Stay out of sight, but keep a visual. Leave the usual signs."

The two men acknowledged and swung into their saddles. Heinrich gazed out over the plains. Eight Blackthorns. The rest armed, even the women and children. People did not survive on the road long if they could not defend themselves, meaning the caravan was a hard target. Heinrich and his raiders would be outnumbered, and eight men trained by Tyrel Jennings was enough to tip the scales of any fight. Hell, four men would have been enough. Maybe it would be best to leave off, find an easier target. Heinrich almost convinced himself until he looked down and saw his left hand. The first two knuckles of his ring finger and little finger were missing, the product of a swipe from a Blackthorn's kukri. Heinrich would have died that day if Carter had not ran the mercenary through from behind with his cutlass.

No. This one is mine.

They would need the element of surprise, which meant a night raid. His men would not like it, but then again, they didn't like anything except ambushing people foolish enough not to travel in large numbers. Heinrich would bring them around. Hurl the usual insults, call them weak, call them cowards, tell them they didn't have to join the raid, but they would get no share of the spoils. And they had damn well better be in camp when he got back. If they weren't, he would hunt them down and kill them slowly. That would goad them. They had all seen what happened to deserters. Signing on with Heinrich was a commitment. His people either fought, or they died.

Carter slid back down the hillside, staying low. Heinrich gave the caravan one last look, then followed.

*****

They had made camp in an abandoned farmhouse on the north side of what remained of Liberty, Kansas. Feral chickens and goats roamed the surrounding fields, providing an easy food source. The well on the property had a hand pump, giving them access to clean, potable water. There had been a few infected when they got there, but Heinrich and his men had dealt with them. All told, it was a good place to hide out.

The scarred raider chieftain looked out over the wide expanse of Kansas and thought how ironic it was he should be grateful to the Army. Despite the trouble they had given him over the years, he had to admit that Operation Relentless Force had been an unequivocal success. Kansas was as close to a revenant-free zone as existed in the continental United States. And the resultant boom in farming, ranching, and trade had created ample pickings for those with the will to take what they wanted.

Heinrich looked back toward the barn, his raiders' temporary barracks, and saw Carter talking to the men. Good. Between his height, bald head, shovel of a beard, heavy build, and the gruesome keloid scars on his face, he was an intimidating sight. Precisely the reason Heinrich had made him his second in command.

He would let his enforcer snarl at the filthy dogs for a while, then step in and calmly lay out the plan. A reasonable voice and commanding presence would reassure them, get them thinking about the rewards and not the risks. Then, when the time came, the three who had best acquitted themselves in the last raid would get to remain behind, still receiving a full share of the loot, while the rest went forth to do the fighting. And the best of those would sit out the next fight, and so on and so forth. Those were the rules. Heinrich was very strict about the rules. Without rules, there could be no discipline, no unit cohesiveness. He had learned all about such things in Marine Corps Force Recon. Offenses needed to be punished, and exemplary performance rewarded. That was how he kept them hungry, ready to fight.

When Carter had finished whatever tirade he was on, Heinrich strode to the barn entrance, gave his second in command a nod, then addressed his men. "Is there a problem here?"

The men glanced sidelong at one another, but no one spoke.

"Come on, you dogs. What's the issue? You have my permission to speak freely."

One of his squad leaders, Maru, a stocky Maori with a tattooed face and thick New Zealand accent, stepped forward. "We're just worried about the odds, Chief. Thirty-two is nine more than we have, and eight of those are Blackthorns. Got to be an easier mark out there."

Heinrich nodded slowly. "A valid concern. We all know firsthand just how capable the Blackthorns are." He held up his diminished left hand for emphasis. "But do we let that stop us? Are

4

we suddenly afraid of a hard fight? Did you all become scared little pussies when I wasn't looking?"

He paused to let the question sink in. After a few seconds, he said, "Ask yourselves this. How much would it cost to hire eight of Jennings' men?"

Another silence. Maru nodded, eyes thoughtful, seeming to grasp the point immediately. Heinrich approved. If anything happened to Carter, he knew who his next second in command would be. "Something on your mind, Maru?"

"Yes sir. I see your point. Eight Blackthorns would cost a small fortune. Whatever that 'van is haulin', it's got to be worth it."

"Exactly."

"But that doesn't solve the problem of the Blackthorns."

Heinrich put his hands behind his back and began pacing. "I'm reminded of two quotes from Sun Tzu's seminal masterpiece, The Art of War. Have any of you read it?"

He stopped pacing and looked. There was a general shrugging of shoulders and shaking of heads.

Figures.

"The two quotes I'm referring to," Heinrich continued, "are as follows: First, 'opportunities multiply as they are seized'. Second, 'let your plans be dark and impenetrable as night. And when you move, fall like a thunderbolt.'"

He stopped pacing and waited to see if the quotations had any effect. A few heads nodded, faces pensive. The rest were either blank or confused. *Well, I didn't hire them for their towering intellects.*

"What it means," Heinrich said, "is when you spot an opportunity, you take it. But you don't go rushing in half-cocked.

You make a plan, and you stick to it. In this case, since we're outnumbered, we'll need the element of surprise."

"You're talking about a night raid," Maru said.

Heinrich nodded. "Exactly. And before anyone starts whining, I know the risks. I've survived the Outbreak as long as you have. We need to remember this is Kansas, not Kentucky or Missouri. There aren't nearly as many infected here. Hell, this whole town only had a little over a dozen when we got here, including crawlers. Night ops here aren't nearly as dangerous as most other places. Additionally, there will be a full moon tonight. Add that to the fires the traders will have in their camp, and there will be plenty of light to see by."

"And the dumbasses in the caravan will ruin their night vision looking into the fires," Carter said. "It'll be hard to see us coming."

"The Blackthorns won't make that mistake," said Slim, another one of Heinrich's squad leaders. No one knew his real name, he just went by Slim. The name was a joke; Slim was a hulking monster of a man. "They'll be on the perimeter, looking outward. And them fellas got sharp ears. At least one or two will have NVGs."

"That's where I come in," Heinrich said, smiling. Between the missing teeth and the scar that turned his mouth downward on one side, the smile put his men ill at ease. Even Carter took a step back. The raider chieftain slid his sniper rifle around and held it at port arms. "Knight's Armament M-110. Suppressor equipped. One of the most advanced sniper weapon systems ever created. I'll watch, and wait, and take out their night-vision boys. And when I've done that, I'll radio the others' positions, Carter and Maru will lead you in, and we'll slaughter the fuckers like babies in a blender."

The raiders started getting into the spirit, heads bobbing, grins appearing, yellowed teeth bared in the dim light of the overcast afternoon. Filthy, scarred hands strayed to weapons, guns and blades and bludgeons of all kinds.

"We'll take out the men, capture some Blackthorns, kill 'em slow. And when we're done, we'll take stock of the women."

Fierce laughter, the sounds of eagerness and bloodthirst in rough voices. Heinrich knew he had them now. "And whatever it is they're hauling, whatever's worth hiring *eight* fucking Blackthorns to protect, we'll divide it up and set out for Parabellum. And there'll be booze and brawls and gambling and as much pussy as we can fuck."

Then men had drawn blades and other weapons and were clanking them together, sending forth a steady chant, *Heinrich, Heinrich, Heinrich*, each syllable punctuated by the clash of metal on metal.

"But first." Heinrich held up a hand for silence. The chanting and clashing stopped. "We have to prepare. Squad leaders, see to your men. Set up the panels and start charging radios. Carter, ride out and get a report from Locke and Rourke. We need to start mapping our route in."

"Yes sir." The big brute headed toward the barn, and his horse.

The raiders broke up into small groups, squad leaders checking their men's weapons and makeshift armor. Some were lucky enough to have ballistic vests taken from dead soldiers, while others had made their own armor from whatever they found lying around: scrap metal, leather, nylon, plastic, wood, books, bone, anything that could stop one of the Three Bs: bites, bullets, and blades. Or at least slow them down.

Heinrich walked to the farmhouse and climbed the stairs to his quarters in the master bedroom. He felt no pity for his men sleeping in the barn. Rank had its privileges, and he was the only one strong enough to hold these men together, the only one with the will to keep them from killing each other. He controlled them by redirecting their aggression, by giving them something they wanted more than watching each other die.

He gave them a purpose.

And that purpose was to raid, to take from others, and to use what they gained to indulge their vices. Which were many and varied, and, even to John Byron Heinrich's loose sensibilities, downright detestable. But he did not judge them openly. Doing so would start a fight, and his men were far more useful alive and motivated than lying dead on the ground with one of Heinrich's blades protruding from their throat.

He put his rifle on the bed, disassembled it, and gave it a thorough cleaning. When it was reassembled, he counted his ammo. Two-hundred twenty three rounds of 7.62 remaining. Four magazines, each holding twenty cartridges. He would have eighty rounds on hand when the fighting started, not counting the bullets in his pistols. Heinrich had other rifles, but he elected to leave them behind. Once Carter and Maru led the men in, it would be all up close and personal, pistols and blades and looking into a man's bloodshot eyes as he died. He anticipated losing a few men in the coming violence, but that was all right. He could always recruit more from the ample supply of murderers and thieves at Parabellum.

Heinrich sat on the bed and stared out the window as the sun went down. When the last red traces of daylight barely hovered above the horizon he lit a candle, smeared black grease on his hands and face, shouldered his rifle, and left the farmhouse. Moments later, armed with a detailed report from his scouts, Heinrich consulted a map, plotted his course, and set off. The raiders in his band held their weapons high in a gesture of respect, the sound of metal clashing against metal receding in the distance as he rode steadily eastward.

*****

Midnight.

The moon was high, illuminating the valley two-hundred yards ahead. Heinrich watched as the men on guard duty grew bored waiting to be relieved. All except the Blackthorns. Those bastards never got bored.

It was a good spot for a camp, he had to admit. Nestled between two shallow hills, low-banked fires fed by nearly smokeless bio-mass logs instead of wood that could be smelled half a mile away, and guards rotating on two-hour shifts. All precautions taken on the advice of the Blackthorns, no doubt. The camp would have been invisible to anyone approaching from the north, south, or west. Hardly anyone was headed east this time of year, least of all raiders and marauders, so the traders' probability of being spotted was low. If Heinrich had not seen them on the road, he never would have found them. But he had. And the time to strike was growing near.

"Strike Bravo in position," Carter said over the radio.

"Strike Charlie, ready to go." Maru this time. The other two squads checked in as well.

Heinrich keyed his mic. "Hold position and stay the fuck quiet. Wait for my command to commence."

A round of affirmatives. Heinrich's pack lay on the ground beside him. He slowly and carefully opened it and took out his secret weapon, a FLIR infrared scope. He had found it in an abandoned house in Missouri a few months after the Outbreak, along with the M-110 rifle he now carried. Its former owner had been a soldier bitten by one of the infected. The doomed man had holed up in the empty house and later turned. But before he turned, the soldier had propped the rifle in a corner and there it had

9

remained until Heinrich happened along. A swing of an axe later, and Heinrich had himself a brand new sniper rifle and state of the art optics complete with rechargeable lithium-ion batteries. Shortly thereafter, he'd found a twenty-watt solar trickle charger and a USB connecter, giving him virtually unlimited ability to recharge the scope.

In the following years, as his band of raiders and his reputation had grown, he had kept the scope a closely guarded secret, never allowing any of his men to see him using it. In so doing, he had achieved legendary status among them for his skills as a sniper. In a land with no electricity, nights were extremely dark. His ability to shoot accurately at long rang in pitch black conditions had led some of his followers to believe he had supernatural abilities. Heinrich did nothing to discourage this thinking.

He mounted the scope, activated it, and scanned the interior of the camp. Most of the traders slept in their carts or in small tents, fires banked low. A few of the men sat on low stools around warm embers, conversing with their heads close together. Smart. Kansas had a very low infected population, but people knew better than to make more noise than necessary. Not if they wanted to live.

Next, Heinrich searched the perimeter. There were six men on watch, the warmth of their bodies glowing bright white through his scope. Four were hiding in patches of trees and long grass, while two others lay prone on hilltops, clad in ghillie suits.

Counter snipers.

Heinrich dialed up the magnification on his scope, and sure enough, both of the counter snipers had the tell-tale shape of night vision scopes on their rifles. Heinrich smiled. His men were far enough away and sufficiently hidden that the Blackthorns would not be able to spot them even with night vision. Not that it mattered, really. The snipers would be the first to die.

He radioed the positions of all the guards, settled over his rifle, and spent a few moments gauging the distance between hides. The first two shots were the most important. Hit the first sniper, transition to the next target, and fire again. Two shots, two kills. No room for error. The M-110 was equipped with a suppressor, but its muted crack would still be audible down in the camp. Sound carried very well at night, and the hills would form a natural echo chamber. He would have less than two seconds from the first kill to the second. Any longer, and he would be firing at a moving target, greatly reducing his chances of getting them both.

So he aimed at one sniper, imagined himself pulling the trigger, then quickly moved to the second. After four practice runs, he figured had the timing down. Maybe it was perfect, maybe it was not. In Heinrich's experience, the longer he waited to engage the enemy, the worse his accuracy. Better just to clear his head, focus on the process rather than the result, and get to killing.

The reticle settled on the first sniper, half a breath left his lungs, and he squeezed the trigger. The figured jerked, his brain and skull collapsing in a white mist through Heinrich's scope. Less than a second later, Heinrich aimed center of mass at the second sniper and fired three times. Three jerks. The figure rolled onto his side, shuddered, and then tumbled halfway down the hill.

"All stations, move in and engage."

The gunfire started immediately. Automatic weapons chattered from the north and west, catching the traders and Blackthorns in a crossfire. The men in the camp scrambled for cover, reaching for rifles as they went. Some of them went down screaming in the darkness.

The Blackthorns on watch turned in the direction of the shooting and began returning fire. Unlike the panicked traders, they stayed low to the ground, presented the smallest target profile

11

possible, and aimed for muzzle flashes. Heinrich saw two of his men fall in the first few seconds of the exchange.

Back to work.

He trained the IR scope on a Blackthorn edging toward cover. The first shot went wide, but the second did not. The mercenary was not dead, but he soon would be. Heinrich shifted his aim toward the throaty roar of a heavy machine gun. A trader had thrown back the cover on a tripod-mounted M-240 bolted to the deck of an open wagon, and was strafing Heinrich's men to the west. The raiders returned fire, to no avail. Bullets impacted the low wall of the wagon but did not penetrate.

Armored wagon, Heinrich thought. *These bastards are getting smarter.*

Meanwhile, the hail of automatic fire had forced Heinrich's raiders to keep their heads down. With their enemy unable to advance on the western flank, the Blackthorns organized the traders into a skirmish line and began advancing northward, laying down suppressing fire as they went. If they reached the firing line, Heinrich's men would be outnumbered two to one. Heinrich was tempted to let the fight play out to see how they would fare, and would have if it was just the traders, but it wasn't. Each Blackthorn was worth three men in a stand-up fight.

Heinrich's raiders were no good to him dead.

A quick assessment told Heinrich what he had to do. For a few seconds, just long enough to allow the Blackthorns to close to within a few meters of the northern flank, he let the machine gunner live. Then, when the two lines of defenders were sufficiently far apart, he fired three rounds and dropped the gunner where he stood.

A roar sounded from the western flank. Above it, he hard Maru ordering his men to charge. Heinrich's lips pulled back from his teeth.

12

Now for the fun part.

The raiders fell upon the caravan defenders left behind by the Blackthorns before they had time to form a proper line. Bellowing, frothing madmen clad in outlandish armor smashed into them, burying blades into bodies and firing at point blank range with pistols. One defender managed to avoid a slash from Slim, countered with a vicious kick that snapped one of the big brute's knees, and followed up with a bullet to Slim's head. The trader turned to look for another opponent and ran face first into Maru's machete. The force of the blow opened the defender's head like a flip-top lid, his severed cranium bouncing off his back as he fell.

Now Maru's path to the machine gun was clear. The Maori warrior leapt into the cart, checked the weapon, and swung it northward.

Heinrich keyed his radio. "Carter, fall back and hug the dirt. Maru got himself a chatterbox."

"Copy."

As much as Heinrich was enjoying the show, the fight was not yet over. He returned his attention northward, where the Blackthorns and their men were still advancing. The reticle of his scope found the leg of a man in the Blackthorn's distinctive uniform and fired. The round passed through the man's calf muscle and shattered his shin bone on the way out. He fell screaming to the ground. Less than a second after he went down, Maru opened up with the M-240, cutting the Blackthorn's line like a scythe through wheat. He kept his aim high, keenly aware that he was firing over the heads of Carter and his people.

It was over in seconds. Heinrich keyed his radio. "Carter, move in. Kill any men you find and bag up the women and children. Be advised, there's a wounded Blackthorn in front of you. He's gimpy, but still dangerous. Watch yourself."

"Right. On it, boss."

13

Heinrich stood, stretched, and began making his way toward the camp.

*****

The Blackthorn's screams echoed long into the night.

Heinrich watched dispassionately as Carter worked, firelight flickering malevolently over his ugly, vicious face. The big raider grinned with sadistic pleasure as he slowly peeled skin from the doomed mercenary's back.

"So what's the tally?"

"Most of the dead are men," Maru said. "Got six women and four kids alive. Put up a bit of a fight."

"How are the women?"

"Five are useful enough. One's too old."

"Never stopped these animals before."

"True enough."

"And the kids?"

"Two girls, two boys. One of the boys is a bit defiant."

Heinrich laughed quietly. "That won't last long."

"It'll hurt his price."

"Not if we break him nice and docile before we get to Parabellum. Put Rourke on it. He's into that kind of shit."

Maru grimaced. "Right, Chief."

Heinrich walked away from the fire and the ring of raiders laughing and taunting the Blackthorn as he died slowly. His steps carried him past the ten trussed-up prisoners, some plainly

14

terrified, others glaring at him with naked hatred. He did not care. They were cargo, nothing more. He would take first pick of the women and let the men have the others. The good old days of the Midwest Alliance were gone, but slaves were still valuable in the hell-pits where raiders, marauders, and other assorted outlaws gathered to do business. And, quite often, fight amongst themselves.

He stopped at one of the wagons, threw aside a canvas cover, and stepped up onto the tailgate. Sixteen steel barrels roughly the size of beer kegs stood in orderly rows, held securely with hemp rope and padded from one another with compressed hay. A good configuration. Keep them still, keep them from rattling. It was hard enough to keep the infected away under the best of circumstances, much less with giant steel cans clanging against each other.

He undid a clasp and opened one of the barrels. Inside was a coarse white powder. Heinrich reached in, lifted out a handful, and let it sift through his fingers. Afterward, he touched his tongue to his palm.

Salt. Holy of holies.

Heinrich now understood why the caravan had hired eight Blackthorns. With this much salt, they could have hired a hundred and still turned an enormous profit. But that kind of display would have told people like him what they were hauling was worth forming alliances with other tribes for, assuming they did not immediately try to murder one another after they seized the shipment. Which happened more often than not.

The scarred raider picked up another handful and let it fall. He could not believe his luck. Just one barrel of this stuff would be enough to keep a man warm, fed, safe, and awash in as much hired flesh as he could indulge in for several months. But here, firmly in his possession, were eight carts carrying sixteen barrels each. Not to mention the food, guns, ammo, livestock, slaves, and other trade he had just seized.

He would announce the shares in the morning after his troops buried their dead. Each man would receive three barrels of salt and a full share of the lesser trade. They would like that. It was more than any of them had possessed since the Outbreak. Enough to last them for years if they were careful, which they would not be.

Heinrich sat down atop a barrel, glanced toward his raiders as they enjoyed the evening's entertainment, and wondered what to do with his newfound wealth. He had never made a score like this one; 128 barrels of salt was a kingly fortune. He might even have to kill a few of his own men to keep them from insisting on a higher share. This simply would not do. Heinrich was the chief, and the chief decided the shares. It was one of the unspoken laws of being a raider. If a man didn't like it, he could leave. Or if that was not an option, challenge for leadership. Heinrich was not worried. There was not a single scumbag under his command who could defeat him in a duel, and they all knew it.

What to do, what to do, he pondered. First thing would be to hire more troops. If word got out what he was worth, he would be fending off attacks from all sides. *Yes, more troops. Good ones, preferably with combat experience.* He would also need to set up his own base of operations now that he could afford to build one. He looked down at the salt. With this much trade, he could build a fort to rival Parabellum. Hell, maybe he could even take Parabellum for himself.

Yes. That seemed like the easier option. But first, he needed troops.

TWO

The blue-eyed soldier with the scarred face said examinations were mandatory for all visitors. Sabrina pointed to her clothes and asked if she looked like she had been bitten.

"No," the young man said. "But it's not my call to make. You want in, you have to go through the exam. No exceptions."

A moment of silence. "Do I get my stuff back?"

"Yes."

"Weapons too?"

"Yes."

Huh, Sabrina thought. *That's unusual.*

"Okay. Whatever it takes."

She was then led to a small wooden building just inside the gate. There was another, similar building across the street, and a pair of manned guard towers overlooking both structures. *Smart. Maybe these people aren't as useless as they look.*

The woman who came into the little wooden room with her was older, possibly as old as sixty. She was tall and severe looking, but with an understated compassion in her eyes. She pulled a green curtain across where Sabrina sat and said, "Please disrobe. Let me know when you're finished."

Sabrina looked around. There were windows in the little building, but they were high on the walls and covered with thick white blinds. Enough to let light in, but still opaque from the outside. The door was closed and bolted.

Fuck it. If she wants to smell me, let her.

As she took her clothes off, Sabrina wrinkled her nose at a wave of pungent body odor. She did not usually mind her own stink, but when she was ripe enough to offend even herself, she knew it was time for a bath.

She stood her rifle up in a corner followed by her ammo belt. The four-hundred or so rounds of .22 caliber cartridges rattled as they settled to the floor. She found the noise comforting.

Her first layer of clothing hid two karambit knives in her coat pockets. The karambits were deadly little things, easy to conceal, constructed of a slim, wickedly curved blade designed to be wielded underhand, a steel finger loop to keep the knife from slipping when wet, and a narrow wooden handle with finger grooves. She had been forced to use them many times over the years, each instance resulting in a kill before her attackers had even known she was armed.

She placed the karambits on the bench, pressed her hands together, and bowed over them. It was less a gesture to her knives than to the man who had taught her how to use them.

Always respect your weapons, she remembered Manny saying in his thick Filipino accent. *They don't care who they kill, so never let your opponent know you have them. The first indication they should have that you are armed is when they feel your knife cut into them. By then, it will be too late.*

She missed Manny. He had been one of the good ones. And, true to her word, she had not let him become one of the infected. He would have done the same for her.

Next came the second layer of clothes, the nine-millimeter pistol recovered from a dead soldier, the .38 revolver taken from a would-be rapist she had killed, a two-shot .22 caliber Derringer-style pistol she kept up her left sleeve, and most of her trade goods. She had made the clothes in this layer herself, and had included plenty of pockets, some visible, some hidden. The pockets held ammo of various calibers, sugar packets, little bags of instant coffee, wads of toilet paper and paper towels, tampons, cotton balls, small bricks of homemade soap, baking yeast, pre-Outbreak painkillers, half an ounce of marijuana, a pouch of baking soda, petroleum jelly, and a few other light, easily portable trade items.

The next layer was mostly buckskin. It was hot, heavy, and uncomfortable, but it did a damn good job of stopping ghoul bites when reinforced with normal fabric. Last was her undergarments, which she had also made herself. They smelled worse than she did, which was not surprising considering she had been wearing them for nearly a month.

Each layer of clothes was folded carefully and placed in small piles. She put her pack down beside them, and said, "Okay. I'm naked."

The old woman opened the curtain, made a face, and took a step back.

"Good lord, sweetie."

Sabrina couldn't help but grin. "Hey, you asked for it."

A nod. Donning of a surgical mask. *Nurse, maybe?*

"Been on the road a while?"

19

"Yes."

The old woman began looking her over, eyes roving, hands moving Sabrina's arms and hair aside. "How long?"

"Why do you want to know?"

The woman met her eyes and saw the suspicion there. "You're a Traveler?"

"Yes."

Back to the exam. "That explains a lot."

The nurse, as Sabrina assumed she was, finished looking her over. She asked no further questions. At the end, the nurse said, "You can get dressed now. I would suggest you hire a laundry service to clean your clothes if you're going to be in town for any length of time. Or burn them and buy new ones."

With that, the nurse left.

Sabrina looked at her clothes and realized she did not want to put them back on. It had been over six months since she had been in a town with laundry service and she fully intended to take advantage. She dug in her pack, removed a brown pullover and a long linen skirt, and put them on. They were the nicest clothes she owned. In the past, she had found they helped her blend in among townies.

Next was her jacket, in which she hid her knives and the .38 revolver. Last, she put on her only clean pair of socks, her boots, and the elastic armband that concealed the Derringer. Her pack was not big enough to hold all her remaining possessions, so she settled for making a haversack out of her blanket and tying it across her chest. She left out the shirt with all her trade items and put it in the front pocket of her small rucksack. Her hair felt tangled, but she did not have a comb. Sabrina spent a few minutes working the knots out with her fingers and smoothing it down as best she could. At least she had straight hair. She could not imagine how much worse untangling it would be if it was curly.

Finished, she stepped outside into the bright morning. The exam room had been dim, and the light hurt her eyes. She stood blinking for a few seconds to let her vision adjust. When the burning stopped, she looked around and assessed her situation.

The nurse must have given the guards some kind of signal because they no longer seemed interested in her. Judging by the multitude of human and animal prints on the ground, she guessed the gate to her right was subject to heavy traffic, which meant this town was on a trade route. Sabrina smiled. She needed to resupply. If her suspicions were correct, this would be a good place to do it.

A guard from one of the towers called down to her, "Need directions?"

"Yes," she replied, looking up. "There a market around here?"

The guard pointed down the road. "One block that way. Most places don't open until nine in the morning, but a food stall or two should be up and running. You can also try the general store."

"Where's that?"

The guard gave her directions. The town was laid out in a grid, so she figured the store would be easy enough to find. Sabrina thanked the guard and headed toward the market. She smelled it before she reached it, her stomach growling at the scent of cooked meat, roasting vegetables, and pork fat. She quickened her pace.

Past the guard shacks and newly-built caravan registration booths, the street widened out into a broad plaza. There was a brick building ahead that could only be the local city hall, and in the space between, hand-built stalls lined both sides of the road. Most of them had their shutters closed, but two were open. One advertised meat for sale, the day's cuts listed on a blackboard out front. Goat legs, whole chickens, eggs, pork belly, loin, heads, feet, and smoked ham. Quantities limited. First come, first served. Federal credits not accepted. No refunds.

The second stall was the source of the smell. Sabrina walked over to it and stood for a moment, eyes closed, breathing in the scent of fresh food. She had eaten only road food for the last six weeks, and nothing at all for the last three days. She could have stopped to hunt or fish, but had not wanted to waste time. Finding her father was too important. She did not want to miss him because she had taken too long getting here. But now that she *was* here, and she knew her father was in town, she saw no harm in taking a moment to fill her empty belly.

As she approached the stall, a blond girl behind the counter smiled at her. "Mornin'," she said, her Southern accent very thick. She looked to be about sixteen or seventeen, curvy and overfed like most townies, but still very pretty. "I'm Kari. What can I do for you?"

"I need something to eat."

The smile broadened. "Well, you come to the right place. What'll it be?"

Sabrina leaned forward and peered over the counter. "What do you have?"

"You never been here before, have you?"

"No."

"New in town?"

Sabrina hesitated. She did not like answering questions from strangers. But then again, in a town this small, everyone probably knew everyone else. She decided the question was less an inquiry than a confirmation. No harm in answering.

"Yes."

"Figured. You a Traveler?"

"Yes."

"With a caravan?"

Sabrina frowned. "What do you serve?"

An embarrassed pause. "I'm sorry. I didn't mean to pry, I was just wonderin' is all. Things get busy when caravans come through. I might need to send for more supplies."

Sabrina sensed no deception, so she said, "I'm alone."

"Oh, Lord. All by yourself? Isn't that dangerous?"

Sabrina rolled her eyes. "Listen, I haven't eaten in a while."

"Sorry, sorry. Of course. Sorry. We have eggs, roast chicken, barley soup, flatbread, lettuce, tomato, grilled squash, pickled cucumber, and fresh venison."

"Got any bacon?"

"No, sorry. Sold out yesterday."

"That stall over there is selling pork belly."

"Yes, but we buy our meat wholesale. Those folks over there won't sell us any unless they can't unload it at higher prices."

Sabrina frowned, disappointed. "Well, in that case, I'll take eggs, tomato, and chicken on flatbread."

"Comin' right up."

Sabrina watched Kari put a small dollop of lard in a skillet resting atop a grill over an open fire. Into the lard went two eggs and a handful of pulled chicken, dark meat by the look of it. Good. Dark meat had more fat. The lard smelled wonderful. Kari began slicing a tomato.

"You travel far to get here?"

Sabrina had to swallow before she could speak. "Yeah. Pretty far."

"Where you comin' from?"

"Last place I stopped was down in Mississippi."

"Mississippi? Goodness gracious, what were you doin' way down there?"

"Staying the hell away from the Alliance and their marauders."

"Oh. Yeah, I heard things were pretty bad up north."

Sabrina almost snorted. *Pretty bad. Talk about understatements.* "You have no idea."

"Well, here you go. Enjoy."

Sabrina took the sandwich. Juice from the chicken and tomato slices dripped onto her hand, hot against her callouses. She did not care. She took a step back from the stall window and began wolfing it down. After a few bites, she waved a hand at Kari.

"Got any water?"

Kari was watching her with wide eyes. "Um ... yeah, sure." The water came in a plastic cup. "I'll need that back."

Sabrina gave a thumbs up, took a few long pulls from the cup, devoured the rest of her sandwich, drank the rest of the water, and wiped her mouth on her sleeve.

"That was good. Thanks." She handed back the cup.

"You must have been hungry."

"Yeah. Been three days."

"Three days?"

Sabrina smirked at the girl's innocent expression. "Three days since the last time I ate."

Kari's eyes went wide. "My God, three days with no food? You must be starving."

Sabrina could not hold back a laugh. *Soft little townies.* "Three days is nothing. Three weeks, yeah. But three days? No."

Kari kept staring, but did not reply. Sabrina asked, "What do you take for trade?"

"Um … what do you have?"

"How about ammo?"

"Sure. That rifle looks like a twenty-two. Four rounds ought to cover it."

"I'd rather keep these for myself. How about this?" Sabrina produced a single 30.06 cartridge. Kari shook her head emphatically.

"Oh, no, that's way too much. You could eat for two days with that thing. Got anything smaller?"

Sabrina blinked. She had meant the offer as a joke; 30.06 was practically worthless on the road. To big, too heavy, too loud. No one used rifles that powerful unless they had no other choice. "Okay, how about nine-millimeter?"

"That'd be fine. Three rounds should do it."

Sabrina stood aghast. "*Three?* You're telling me a 30.06 can feed me for days, but you want *three* nine-mils for a goddamn *sandwich?*"

Kari held up her hands defensively. "Look, now, that's the going rate around here. Okay? Nine-mil is pretty common."

Sabrina went still. "Common? Nine-mil?"

"Yes."

"How's that?"

Kari pointed northward. "There's an Army FOB not far from here. Fort McCray. They trade ammo all the time. Lots of nine-mil."

25

An Army base? Way out here? Interesting. Sabrina dug around in her pack again and produced two shotgun shells. "Twelve gauge," she said. "Double-ought buck."

"Just one will be fine."

Sabrina handed over the shell. She was amazed it was worth anything at all; road people preferred small caliber guns, but townies seemed to enjoy heavier ordnance. "Thanks for the sandwich."

"You're welcome. Come back and see us anytime."

"I'll be sure to do that." Sabrina started to walk away, then stopped and looked over her shoulder. "Hey, any place I can get a bath around here? Laundry?"

"Go two blocks that way and take your first right. Three houses down you'll see a sign for Elena's Inn. She'll take care of you."

"Thanks."

*****

Elena's Inn was exactly where Kari said it would be.

The house was a large two story colonial, wide front porch, fluted columns soaring to the upstairs balcony, wrought-iron fences, flowers along the verge, and a few large-leafed plants rounding out the garden setting. The exterior was well maintained, the grass cut low, the paint fresh. Sabrina wondered where people in this town acquired something as rare as paint. Maybe they made their own.

She ascended the stairs and tried the doorbell. To her surprise, it actually rang. For a few seconds, no one answered. Then there was a swish of motion near one of the windows, the thump of footsteps approaching, and the front door opened.

26

"Hello," a small, redheaded woman of middle years said, standing inside the foyer. "What can I do for you?"

"I need a bath and a room for the night. Got any vacancies?"

A gentle smile. "As a matter of fact, I do. Come on in, we'll get you fixed up."

Sabrina took three steps inside, glanced at the room to her left, and stopped. The room was one of those chintzy spaces where people display China cabinets full of antique dishes, figurines, and furniture not meant to be sat upon. But the décor was not what grabbed her attention. What stopped her was a set of LED light fixtures in the ceiling and the illumination pouring out of them.

"You have electricity," Sabrina said.

Elena stopped and turned around. "Oh, yes. This whole part of town is connected to set of biomass generators. The Phoenix Initiative representative here in town, fella named Ishimura, real smart young man, he set it up. Wired all the houses to run on twelve-volt. I can operate the control panel he installed, but other than that, I'm not quite sure how it all works. It's certainly not the most reliable system in the world, but it's better than nothing."

Sabrina grunted. She had been to places with electricity since the Outbreak, mostly solar, wind turbine, or hydro-electric setups, but never a functioning grid.

"Impressive."

"Would you like to look around?"

"Not now. Maybe later."

"Well then, if you'll follow me, I'll show you to your room."

They went up a flight of stairs, richly stained hardwoods creaking beneath ornately woven carpets and runners, past landscape paintings of fox hunts and rolling green hills, LED bulbs mutedly lighting the way in stained-glass lampshades, and stopped in front of a door on the second floor hallway. While Elena flipped through keys on a large ring, Sabrina looked around and decided she liked the feel of the place. It reminded her of the historical homes she used to tour during her childhood in Maryland. It was clear someone wealthy had lived here once, and had spared no expense to project a sense of opulence.

"Here you go." Elena opened the door and stepped back. Sabrina walked in and looked around. It was a medium-sized room with a bed, small writing desk, wardrobe, washbowl on a high table, and a dark wooden trunk at the foot of the bed.

"Nice," Sabrina said. "How much?"

"What do you have for trade?"

She produced the same 30.06 round she had offered Kari. "How much will this get me?"

Elena asked to hold it and looked at it closely. "One night's stay and a bath."

Sabrina almost laughed. Here she was in the nicest inn she had seen since the Outbreak, and this lady wanted trade no Traveler would have given a second glance. She took out four more rounds. "And this?"

Elena's eyes locked to the cartridges in Sabrina's hand. Sabrina had seen that look before, and knew she was in a good bargaining position. "Well, five bullets will get you five nights."

"How about seven, a bath each night, and laundry service. Which would include the bedsheets, if needed."

Elena narrowed her eyes. "Besides the sheets, how much laundry are we talking about?"

Sabrina indicated her pack and the small bundle wrapped in her blanket. "Not much."

"Deal." Elena held out a hand. Sabrina closed her fingers around the bullets.

"On deposit," she said. "I get the balance back if I leave early."

"If you leave early, I'll have to charge you one round per night."

Sabrina thought it over. They were trading in bullets, so it was not as if the old woman could give her change. Nevertheless, Sabrina was alone, and in her experience, taking someone at their word was asking to be fleeced. And being alone meant she would have very little leverage if Elena decided not to honor the trade. Then again, one of the gate guards had said he knew Sabrina's father, and that he was a big deal in this town. So she decided to take a gamble.

"Fair enough. But if you try to stiff me, my father might have something to say about it."

Elena looked offended. "I run an honest business, young lady."

"I'm sure you do, but look at it from my side. The road is not a kind place. Just about everyone you meet will smile to your face and stab you in the back. I'm not accusing you of anything, but when I trade with someone, I like to make sure they know where we stand."

Sabrina handed over the cartridges. Elena took them and said, "I understand."

No you don't, you weak little townie.

The innkeeper turned to leave, and Sabrina began sorting her belongings on the bed. Behind her, she heard the old woman stop and turn around.

"Just out of curiosity, does your father live around here?"

"Yes."

"Anyone I might know?"

29

Sabrina looked at the innkeeper. "His name is Gabriel Garrett."

By Elena's open-mouthed surprise, Sabrina could tell her gamble had paid off. "Oh. Well then." The old woman recovered her dignity and gave a polite little bow. "I'll just go warm up the water for your bath."

The door closed gently. Sabrina walked over to the window, looked out over the well-maintained houses and gardens along the street, and wondered where to begin looking for the father she had never met.

THREE

Eric

Across the street from the Hollow Rock Church of Christ is a rather nice piece of acreage that was once a trailer park. It consists of a wide, rolling field surrounded by a verdant forest of pine, maple, cedar, and elm. The trailers are gone now, replaced by a cluster of thirty-six homes, all built by my good friend Tom Glover and his construction company. Tom's crew is a small outfit, boasting only eight employees, not counting Tom himself, but most of the new construction in Hollow Rock has his stamp on it.

The houses now occupying the former trailer park are all made of hand-cut lumber, asphalt shingles on tarpapered roofs, scavenged Tyvek cladding, scorched cedar siding, and foam insulation I found on a salvage run. This by itself would have made Tom's homes popular, but he went the extra mile by putting them

31

up on twelve foot pilings, installing retractable ladders to keep the occupants safe from infected, building hand-filled water towers for each unit, installing rain cisterns, and crafting a brick wood-fired stove in each kitchen.

Each house was built with three bedrooms, a fireplace that extends all the way to ground level, including a standard pit for indoor use, and a larger, more open pit for outdoor cooking. The outdoor cooking pits were built away from the homes, not underneath them, to prevent fires. Tom made the house's screened windows wide to allow air in during the summer, and fitted them with shutters to keep out the cold in the winter. The glass in the windows was salvaged from old office buildings in nearby Bruceton, and how Tom had managed to cut the glass precisely to size with simple hand tools without shattering them was a secret he would not divulge despite many askings on my part.

The development was a joint venture between the two of us. I bought the land, and Tom's company provided the labor. We took everything that was useful from the existing buildings and sold the scrap to the federal government. They were paying top trade for scrap metal at the time, which by itself made the land grab a profitable venture.

Tom built the first model home on my dime, which I planned to keep for myself, and I used some of my paper reserve and Mayor Stone's office printer to print some brochures. The mayor thought it was a waste of resources, so I reminded her the toner I was using to print the brochures had been donated by G&R Transport and Salvage. At this, she relented.

The brochures went into a box in the town square beneath a hand-drawn billboard announcing:

PROPERTIES FOR SALE:

High-quality new construction in the perimeter expansion zone, built by Glover Builders. Model home available for viewing. Lots will be marked and auctioned, with reserve. All sales are final upon contract signing and receipt of down payment. Terms of trade negotiable. Open house August 1st.

I had expected a small crowd, maybe twenty or thirty people. The development was outside the wall, after all, so I expected to sell maybe one or two properties on the day of the open house, and hoped to offload the remainder over the next year as construction progressed on the extension to the wall. Which, I might add, was the reason I decided to invest in the land in the first place. Property values have a way of skyrocketing once someone erects a sturdy barrier to keep out the infected. Ergo, I was not worried how long it might take. It was, after all, already a profitable venture.

So imagine my surprise when more than half the lots sold on the first day.

The crowd had been huge, over two hundred people. Some were Hollow Rock's more affluent residents, while others were well-to-do farmers who wanted a place in town. The rest were real-estate speculators from other communities along the trade routes that connected Hollow Rock with the rest of the country.

Most buyers seemed skeptical at first, but when they got a look at the quality of Tom Glover's work, skepticism quickly turned to excitement. Very soon, the madding crowd was howling for the auction to begin.

Interspersed amongst the well-heeled were a number of hard, sun-browned faces in simple clothes, many with wives and/or children in tow, staring around at the obviousness of wealth and influence. These hardscrabble folk were looking at the people they worked for, paid rent and owed debts to, people who held sway, in one form or another, over their lives. The properties were being sold at auction, after all, so the hopeful souls who had come here looking for something more than a shack to live in knew immediately they could never scrounge enough trade to outbid the contemptuous faces and sneering eyes looking down on them.

Nevertheless, most of the poorer folks stuck around for the open house. When it was over, they filed out and began walking dejectedly back toward the south gate. I told my assistants, Johnny Green and Miranda Grove, to start writing up letters of interest and getting signatures and set out on an intercept course.

The deal I offered was simple. I would set aside six of the units for the families to share as a co-op, and in exchange, they would mortgage off the value of the homes by clearing and farming a large tract of land I owned behind the development. Part of the land would be set aside for subsistence gardens and raising livestock, while the rest would be used to grow cash crops such as wheat, barley, potatoes, beans, cotton, and hemp. I figured three or four years' harvests would be sufficient to pay off the mortgage, and afterward, I would take thirty percent off the top of whatever the land produced and split the rest among the families in even shares. The interested parties conferred briefly, then accepted the deal. We shook on it.

So, putting it all together, I now owned a housing development that produced monthly income of various trade—hand-made bows and arrows, crossbows and bolts, hand-forged weapons and tools, greenhouse vegetables, chickens, goats, lumber, grain liquor, hemp, a vast array of pre-Outbreak salvage, and so on—a farming co-op, and a fifty-percent interest in G&R Transport and Salvage, a portion of which I was thinking very seriously about selling to Lincoln Great Hawk.

In short, I was a very, very wealthy man, and likely to grow wealthier in the not-too-distant future. Hard to believe, considering I had started out with a single weapons cache the Army missed after dealing with an insurgent militant group. The yields of hard work and sound investments never cease to amaze me.

34

And now, on a cold late November morning, I sat on the roof of the model home I still owned and had no intention of selling, the pounding axes and roar of heavy equipment from the people building the perimeter expansion echoing across the fields, helicopter rotors thumping in the distance toward Fort McCray, and stared across the crumbling street at the Hollow Rock Church of Christ. I could hear voices raised in song. *Amazing Grace*, unless I missed my guess.

The congregation had grown in recent months. Most people had lost interest in religion after the Outbreak, but here in Hollow Rock, safety and prosperity had led to a resurgence of the faithful. The town had weathered many storms and come out of them better than most. Our greatest threat, the Midwest Alliance, no longer existed. Hordes of infected were growing markedly less numerous. Food was abundant. We had plentiful access to clean water. The drought that had plagued the region when I first arrived seemed to have broken. The nuclear winter that had, until recently, made life so difficult was slowly but noticeably abating. Crime within the city limits was almost non-existent. Trade caravans passed through regularly. Raiders and marauders knew better than to try our defenses, especially with Fort McCray nearby. Life was not exactly easy, but it was, in most respects, good.

I did not like it. I looked at the people around me and saw once-hardened survivors growing soft. I saw a lack of vigilance and discipline. I saw guardsmen dozing in their towers during the long watches of the night and no one kicking them in the ass about it. I saw kids not being properly trained to survive if Hollow Rock suddenly became uninhabitable. I saw people who did not have to engage in regular physical labor growing fat, something unheard of in the first three years after the Outbreak. I saw people concerned too much with petty societal squabbles and not nearly enough with making sure this town was not only safe, but a going concern. In other words, I saw a whole population of Outbreak survivors

35

beginning to forget just how dangerous the world still was, and how vulnerable our place in it.

My inner grumblings were interrupted when a multi-fuel generator, donated by the Phoenix Initiative, coughed to life across the street behind the church. It spent most of its time at the towns' only schoolhouse, but on Sundays, it was used to power the church's lights and the preacher's PA system. The singing of many voices stopped, and the unnaturally loud tones of Reverend Griffin began to reverberate through the walls. Why the good reverend needed a microphone, amplifier, and two large speakers in such a small church was beyond me. If a mouse squeaked under the altar, you could hear it in the back pews. My only assumption was he believed his sermon would have more impact, and thus better assure the ultimate destination of the souls of his flock, if it reached the intended recipients with enough volume to rattle their teeth.

I shuffled my feet for better purchase on the roof shingles, put a different part of my butt on the crown of the house, and turned my head to stare back toward the south side of town. My other house lay in that direction, the one I shared with my wife and son.

Allison Laroux Riordan was not home that morning, but Miranda Grove was there with little Gabriel while my wife was busy tending the sick and injured at the clinic. I'd told Miranda I needed to run some errands and left her with the baby. She had offered no argument, as she was too busy cooing over the little guy. She did that a lot.

I thought about the mission I had participated in over the summer, the one that had eliminated one threat to the Union and galvanized another. I thought about my part in it, and how hard it was to listen to people talk about how much better things were now that the Alliance was no longer the Sword of Damocles dangling over our heads. I thought about the people who argued with me when I worked at the store, how they moaned at the slightest sense of disadvantage in a trade, and how I often wished I could show them the demons in my head, shake them by their ears, and scream at them to look at what they made me give.

But I couldn't. Officially, the mission in Illinois never happened. I did not travel to Alliance territory with Gabriel Garrett, Caleb Hicks, and Lincoln Great Hawk, and we did not meet up with a special ops group codenamed Task Force Falcon. We did not slaughter a group of marauders, capture their leader, and discover a secret initiative by the Alliance to secure their supply routes while they launched an offensive against the Union. We never travelled to the Alliance's capital city, never met with an intelligence asset who happened to be enemy nation's vice president, and never carried out an assassination mission against said nation's highest officials. I was not in a helicopter crash, I did not spend days alternating between running from and ambushing fanatical Alliance troops led by a murdering psychopath named General Randolph Samson, and I most certainly had not watched through a rifle scope while Gabriel Garret put a bullet through the general's head.

Nope. Didn't happen.

Officially.

Unofficially, I'd just about had my fill of warfare for one year. Maybe next year I might take a mission or two, but not now. I had businesses to run, a son to raise, a wife to love, and 3000 watts of solar panels, associated control equipment, and sealed, deep-cycle batteries to install on my house. More than enough to power my eight-cubic-foot refrigerator, a 10-gallon water heater, furnace, and other household appliances.

The panels had not come cheap. In fact, it would not be inaccurate to say I spent a small fortune on them. The caravan leader I traded for them had been hauling the system around for months, unable to find a buyer who could pay what it was worth. I gave him the asking price, no haggling. The man told me I should be canonized by whatever was left of the Catholic Church. I told him if he found any more solar equipment to swing by Hollow Rock and look me up.

Allison had balked at the expense, initially, but calmed when I told her how much power the system could generate.

"So … we could have a refrigerator again?" she said.

"Yes. And an icemaker, and hot water, and working fans, and a lot of other conveniences we've been doing without."

"And you haven't installed it yet … why?"

"It's on my list."

"Move it to the top."

"Aye, aye, captain."

That was a week ago. Time to stop procrastinating. I climbed down through the roof hatch, closed it, locked up the house, and headed toward home.

*****

At the North Gate, Caleb Hicks was just getting off watch. He spotted me, waved, yelled at me to hold up, and when he had finished speaking with the oncoming guards, jogged over to where I waited.

"Man, you're never going to believe what happened this morning," he said.

I went immediately on alert. Anything momentous enough to stir Caleb Hicks from his usual silence into a state of excitement was cause for worry. "What happened?"

"I might be wrong, but I think Gabriel has a daughter. And I think she just came into town this morning."

I blinked. Twice. Then I asked him to repeat himself to make sure I had heard him right. He did, and it was the same as before. I said, "But Gabe doesn't have any kids."

"That's what I thought too. But when she came through, she showed me a picture of Gabe and said he was her father."

"You're sure it was him in the picture?"

"Yep. He was a lot younger, but it was definitely him."

I felt a strange tingling in my hands and along the edges of my face. My pulse picked up, and there was a weight in my stomach that had not been there before. "What did she look like?"

"She looked like Gabe, if he was a fourteen-year-old girl. Spittin' image. Even had the same eyes."

I did the math in my head, counting from the year Gabe had told me he had gotten divorced. It added up.

"Holy shit on a stick."

"No kidding."

"Where is she now? Did she give a name?"

"Not sure, and Sabrina. Got here early, just after seven-hundred hours. Heard her ask one of the guards where to find the market. Probably stopped for something to eat. Might want to start there."

"I will. How about a description?"

He gave me one. I doubted there would be too many tall, black haired, gray-eyed girls running around in an old Army field jacket with a rucksack, Marlin rifle, and salvaging tools.

"Thanks for the heads up."

"No problem." I started to run toward the market, but stopped when Caleb called out to me.

39

"Hey!" he said.

"What?"

"Let me know how it goes, will you?"

"Next time I see you."

He gave me a two-fingered salute. I jogged toward the market.

I talked to four different food venders, the last being Kari Cooper at Cooper's Country Kitchen. She said a girl had come through fitting the description I gave her not long after seven that morning, which meant she had passed through just over two hours ago.

"Any idea where she went from here?"

"Why do you ask?" Kari said. "She in some kind of trouble?"

"No, nothing like that. I just want to talk to her is all."

"Well, she asked if there was a place around here she could stay, and I recommended Elena's."

"Why Elena's? Why not somewhere less expensive?"

"She had some pretty good trade on her. Tried to pay for her breakfast with a thirty-ought-six round. I figured she could afford to stay somewhere nice."

I processed that. A dozen questions flew circles in my head, but there would be no answering them until I found her.

"Do you think she went there? To Elena's, I mean."

"I think so."

I reached in a pocket, pulled out a little pouch of instant coffee, and slid it across the counter. "Thanks for the info."

The packet disappeared. "Anytime, Mr. Riordan."

I covered the distance to Elena's in just over two minutes. Outside the entrance, I stopped to catch my breath, wipe sweat from my brow, and compose myself. Once I felt centered again, I rang the doorbell. A few seconds later, Elena answered.

"Well hello, Eric. What can I do for you?"

"There may be someone staying here I'd like to speak with. She says her name is Sabrina Garrett. She's about five-foot-ten, black-"

"I know who you're talking about," Elena interrupted. "Normally I don't give out information about guests, but knowing how close you and Gabe are, I'll make an exception. Come on in, but keep your voice down."

I followed the little woman inside. She led me through the lobby, down a hallway to our right, and into her office. The room faced a back garden with a large French door which, during the spring, offered a spectacular view of flower beds, hedges, large green plants I could not identify, towering oak trees, and a small, gravity-fed fountain. Now, in late autumn, the garden was mostly brown.

"What business do you think this girl has with Gabriel?"

I sat down in one of the plush leather chairs in front of her desk. Elena did business with Gabe and me on a regular basis, and anything that might affect us could potentially affect her. "I don't know," I said. "That's why I need to speak with her. Don't want Gabe getting blindsided. By the way, is she still here?"

"Yes. She just finished bathing a little while ago. Her clothes are being laundered as we speak, and judging by how they smelled, I'd say she's been on the road for quite some time."

"She come here alone?"

"Near as I could tell, yes."

I wrapped my fingers around my chin and pondered. What were the odds that Gabriel had a daughter he never knew about who survived the Outbreak despite the fact she would have been no

41

older than eleven at the time and somehow managed to stay alive, searched for her father, found out where he lives, and came all the way here to see him? Not very strong, in my opinion. But then again, the odds of *anyone* surviving the Outbreak were pretty slim. And if the Blackmire incident had taught us anything, it was Gabe's name was known far and wide, and that was not necessarily a good thing. The girl could have heard about him from any number of people between here and Colorado. Hell, there were probably people in the Nevada outposts who had heard of him. Maybe the chances weren't so slim after all.

"Is there any chance you could ask her to meet me in the lobby?"

"I can ask. But I'll warn you, she's a suspicious soul. Expect her to be armed."

"Duly noted."

Elena stood up from her chair. "Go wait in the lobby. I'll send her down."

"What are you going to tell her?"

"Your name, affiliation, and the fact that you have information about her father."

I nodded. "That should do it."

Elena went upstairs while I waited in the lobby. The only weapon I carried was a nine-millimeter Beretta pistol, which I moved from my hip to the small of my back and concealed beneath my shirt. Better not to appear threatening.

A minute or two later, Sabrina walked down the stairs to meet me. Her pace was quick and graceful with just a slight hint of teenage awkwardness. She wore an ankle length terry-cloth robe and slippers, both provided by the inn. Her hair was still wet from her bath, long and dark black just like Gabriel's. By the angles of her hands as she held them in her pockets, I could tell she was carrying a pair of knives up her sleeves. Cautious indeed. Finally, my eyes moved to her face.

I could not speak for several seconds. I could only stare.

Caleb had not been kidding. If Gabe had been born female, I was pretty sure I was looking at his visage at age fourteen. The lines of the girl's face were hauntingly similar, albeit softened and distinctly feminine. She was not pretty, but neither was she ugly. The mouth was wide, the lips thin, the cheekbones high and sharp, the jaw broad and softly curved. A familiar shallow line bisected her chin. The resemblance alone would have been enough to convince me, but what really struck me were the eyes. Slightly almond shaped, set wide apart, deeply sunken, and the exact same wolf-gray as Gabriel's.

No paternity test necessary. This girl was, without a doubt, Gabriel's kid.

"Hello," I said with a slight smile, keeping my hands where she could see them. "I'm Eric Riordan."

She stared at me and did not move. We were about ten feet from each other, but I had the feeling she could cross that distance very quickly if I gave her reason to.

"Okay," she said.

"I understand you're looking for Gabriel Garrett."

No response. I waited a few seconds, but she did not budge.

"I can tell by looking at you that what you say is true. You're his daughter."

She shifted her head slightly, the eyes blazing to life. "So you know him?"

"Yes. He's my business partner and a very close friend."

She hesitated, chewed her lip for a moment, and said, "Do I really look like him?"

43

"Yes."

Another pause. "I only have one picture of him, but I think I do too."

I gave a nod. "Would you like to talk in the café? They have tea and instant coffee. My treat."

She looked me over, saw no weapons, and relaxed slightly. "Sure."

"You think you could take your hands off the knives while we talk? Just to be polite?"

I smiled while I said it. Sabrina's face told me she was reassessing me.

"Okay," she said. Her hands came out of the pockets, but the knives stayed. I could see their weight sagging the fabric. The girl indicated for me to lead the way. I did, although I kept my ears sharp for sounds of sudden movement.

We crossed to the back of the inn and sat down at one of the tables in the small dining area. One of Elena's employees, a girl in her early twenties named Darlene, came out in her black-and-white waitress uniform.

"Hello ma'am. Mr. Riordan. What can I get for you?"

I looked at Sabrina. "You hungry?"

"No."

"Me neither. Darlene, do you still have any of that tea I sold you?"

"Only the Lipton stuff, sir. I'm afraid the rest sold out last week."

I breathed a small sigh, genuinely regretful. "Oh well. Lipton it is, then. Make it two, please."

"Right away." Darlene disappeared into the kitchen.

44

Sabrina watched her go, looked back at me, and said, "They really have tea here?"

"They better. I'll give Elena an earful if they don't."

"Where did they get it?"

"From me."

Sabrina tilted her head again. The gesture reminded me so much of her father I almost looked away. "And where did *you* get it?"

"It's a little early to be handing over the secrets of where I source my salvage, don't you think?"

She smirked, again reminding me of Gabriel. Same impishness, same dark humor. "Can't blame me for trying."

"I can't, but hopefully at least now you know I'm not stupid."

"No. I didn't figure you were. Some people you can tell, you know? It's in the eyes."

"I know exactly what you mean."

She leaned forward a little, looking at me intensely. "You have nice eyes. Dark blue. I like that. You're a good looking guy, Eric Riordan."

"I'm also happily married," I said, giving her a level stare. "And you're my best friend's daughter. I'm afraid you'll have to bark up another tree."

The heat of her smile increased by about a hundred degrees. "I don't care if you're married. Never stopped me before. Maybe you've heard about Traveler women? We don't have hang-ups and inhibitions like townie women. We see something we want, we take it. Including men. Or women. Or both."

I noticed one of her hands was invisible beneath the table and repositioned my feet. If she attacked, I would spring backwards, push the table over, and hope there was nothing to stop me from rolling into a fighting stance. "One small problem," I said.

"What's that?"

"You're not a woman. And I'm not idiot enough to buy into your slutty little act. So knock it off. I'm not a kid, and I'm not apt to be led around by my dick."

The lascivious smile left as quickly as it came. The hand reappeared, and I relaxed. "I'm impressed."

I wanted to say, *don't flatter yourself,* but figured that would get us off on the wrong foot. Instead, I said, "What is it you want from Gabriel?"

The measured stare again. "Why should I tell you?"

"Because he's my friend, I'm buying you an exorbitantly expensive cup of tea, and I asked you nicely."

Darlene came out of the kitchen bearing two steaming cups on little saucers. The teabags were still in them, the aroma sharp and acrid to my post-Outbreak nose. When one goes long enough without smelling the comforts of the old world, they tend to stand out.

Sabrina looked down at her cup. "Holy shit that smells good."

"I concur."

"Sugar, Mr. Riordan?"

I looked at the waitress. "Brought my own. But thanks anyway."

Darlene smiled and gave a little curtsy before leaving. When I returned my attention to Sabrina she was staring at me hungrily. "You have sugar?"

"Yes."

"I haven't had sugar in two years. Too valuable to eat."

46

"You know, I often wonder about that. Most people say the same thing, it's worth too much to actually use. But if no one consumes it anymore, what makes it so valuable?" I reached into a shirt pocket, removed four little packets—equivalent to a week's wage for a farm worker—and slid two across the table. "Wait until the tea finishes steeping. It'll taste better."

"How much longer?"

"I'll let you know."

We sat in silence while I counted down two minutes in my head, then I took the teabag out of my cup and motioned for Sabrina to do the same. She did, squeezing the bag with her fingers and wincing at the burn of the hot water. If she was like most people, she would keep the teabag, dry it, and reuse it. Or sell it. Even used, it was still valuable.

I watched Sabrina hesitate with her hand over the sugar packets before she picked up one and stuffed it into a pocket. She looked at me when she did it, but I just gave her a shrug.

"A gift freely given, Sabrina. Do whatever you want with it."

The steady gray eyes grew a little less suspicious, and a little more confused. "Thank you."

"You're welcome."

I poured both packets into my tea, stirred, held the steam under my nose to breath in the scent, and sipped. Even for someone of my means, it was a rare indulgence. I intended to enjoy it. To my amusement, Sabrina mimicked my actions.

"I see you appreciate the finer things."

She smiled a little. It brightened her face, softened the hard eyes, and made her look more like a girl and not a world-weary woman trapped in an adolescent body. "This is really good. Better than anything I've had in a long time."

47

I nodded. "Glad you like it. But you still haven't answered my question."

She put her cup down and let out a breath. "Did you have a family before the Outbreak?"

"Not really. Just an uncle I hadn't seen in years. I have no idea if he's still alive."

"If you had reason to think he was, would you try to find him?"

She was touching on something I had thought about before, at length, even going so far as to make a few inquiries with some of the caravans that traveled back and forth between Colorado and Tennessee. I had a picture of Uncle Roger, but it was over ten years old. A person's looks can change a lot in that time. So far, I'd had no luck. "I think I would, yes."

"Then you see what I'm getting at."

"I think I do."

She sipped her tea again, eyes downcast. "He's the only family I have left."

"You're mother, she ..."

Sabrina shook her head. "She got bit protecting me."

"I'm sorry, Sabrina. I lost both my parents before the Outbreak. I know how bad it hurts."

She wiped a tear from her left eye as if its presence made her angry. I'd seen enough crocodile tears to know what they looked like, and this was not it. She was genuinely upset. I felt inwardly angry at myself for pushing and making her cry. Maybe after I was finished here I could find a few puppies to kick, or old women to threaten.

"So do you understand, now? Do you understand why I want to see him?"

48

"Yes, Sabrina. I do."

She spun her teacup on its saucer, an absent gesture. "What's he like?"

I leaned back in my chair. "He's big. That's the first thing people notice about him. Big and scary looking. And he *is* scary if you cross him, but he's not usually quick to anger. Quick to irritation, maybe, but not anger. I've never seen him raise his hand against someone who didn't earn it first. He's also highly intelligent. And I don't mean normal smart, I mean, like, genius smart. If you lie to him, he'll know it. Best if you're honest. If he asks you something and you don't want to answer, just say so. He won't push. But you should expect him to ask you things only someone who lived with his ex-wife should know. He's a suspicious man by nature. He'll want to make sure you are who you say you are, although I think one look at your face should be plenty convincing."

"Do you ... do you think he would even *want* to see me?"

"Sabrina, I know for a fact he's going to be thrilled to meet you. In fact, I'm actually glad you found him and not the other way around. If he knew he had a daughter out there not under his personal protection, he would leave a trail of destruction between here and wherever he had to go to find you."

The girl looked up. "You say that, and it makes me nervous. I don't want to meet him if he's going to be violent toward me. I've seen plenty of that out on the road, and I want no part of it."

"He won't be. He's not like that. Maybe toward anyone who tries to hurt you, but not to you personally."

She stopped spinning her cup. "So you can take me to him?"

"If that's what you want."

"I'd like that."

49

I reached out slowly and patted the back of one slender, long-fingered hand. "Finish your tea first, sweetheart. This shit is expensive."

She smiled again. Not small like before, but a full one, broad and genuine. It made her beautiful.

FOUR

I walked Sabrina to my house and introduced her to Miranda. She stared at Sabrina in confusion for a moment, then realization dawned and her mouth fell open.

"Is she?"

I nodded. "I believe so."

"But how?"

"Probably the usual method."

A frown. "You know what I mean."

"Sure. Is Gabe home?"

"Yeah, I think so."

"You mind waiting here a little longer?"

"Not at all."

Sabrina looked uncomfortable as she stared at little Gabriel snoozing in Miranda's arms. "Is that your kid?"

"He is," I said. "His name is Gabriel."

Sabrina looked at me. "Like my father?"

"Yes. He's named after him."

The gray eyes left me and settled on the baby again. "You two must be really close."

"We are. Wait here. I'll be back shortly." I started walking toward the door, then stopped. "Hey, you still have that picture of Gabe from his wedding day?"

Sabrina reached into a pocket of her shirt and produced a small plastic bag. The photo was inside. "Be careful with it."

I held the picture up and studied it. Yep. That was Gabe all right, holding the waist of a pretty young woman with a bright smile and dark brown hair. He stood tall in his Marine Corps dress uniform, hair buzzed short, face still mostly unscarred. It was hard to believe my big, gruff friend had ever been this young.

"Mind if I hang onto this for a few minutes? I want to show it to Gabe."

"Why?"

"I think it'll make breaking the news a little easier."

"Fine. But I want it back undamaged."

"You have my word."

I walked the short distance to Gabe's house slowly, mind racing, trying to think of what I was going to say. My feet stopped just short of his front porch. A minute or so passed. How was I going to do this? I looked up at the glass panes in the top half of the front door, rubbed a hand across the back of my neck, and took a deep breath.

"Just get it done."

I knocked on the door.

"Hang on a minute." Gabe's voice was muffled. At this hour, he was probably in his office going over inventory logs and trade requests. His approach was quiet, boards creaking gently, telling me he was wearing the fur-lined moccasins Great Hawk had made for him. He had made a pair for me as well. They were warm and comfortable, perfect for wearing around the house on a cold day.

The door opened. "Hey, Eric. Come on in."

He vacated the entrance and walked back inside. I entered and shut the door behind me.

"What brings you by?" he asked from the kitchen.

I walked into the living room and stared through the open doorway. Gabe was squatting in front of the woodstove feeding split sections of cedar into the fire.

"There's something I need to talk to you about."

A glance over his shoulder. "Sounds serious."

"Yeah. It is."

He stood up and gestured toward the table. We sat down.

"So what's on your mind?" Gabe asked.

I removed the picture from my pocket and slid it across the table. "Recognize that?"

He picked it up and stared at it. At first his face was blank, then his eyebrows slid down and I heard him mutter, "What the hell?" The cold eyes grew distant, as though seeing something far away, the look of someone dusting off long-ago memories. Finally, he came back to the present and stared intently at me over the photograph.

"Where did you get this?"

"There's someone at my place you need to meet."

"Who? Did they give you this?"

"Yes."

Sudden hope dawned on Gabe's face. "Is it her? Is it Karen?"

I shook my head. "No, Gabe. I'm sorry."

"What do you mean, you're sorry?"

"I think Karen died in the Outbreak."

The big man's face began to flush. "Eric, you need to tell me what the hell is going on. Who gave you this picture?"

"Come over to my place. I think all will be made clear."

Now he looked confused. "All right. Fine."

He followed me to my front door, where I stopped and faced him. "Do me a favor."

"What?"

"Calm down. Try not to look so angry."

"Eric, I'm getting real tired of this mystery shit."

I put a hand on his shoulder. "Please, Gabe. I'm asking you as your friend to trust me."

He let out a long breath, white mist fogging the air around his head. "Okay. I'm good. Can we get on with it now?"

"Gabe, this is going to be difficult. Whatever happens after today, don't forget you're not alone. You have help whenever you need it."

The confusion returned. "I appreciate that. But right now, you're making me nervous."

I tried to think of something else to say, something to smooth the road. Nothing came to mind. The only thing left to do was take the leap. I opened the door and led Gabe inside.

Sabrina was sitting on the couch with Miranda, leaning over my son, face shining with the smile all women seem to instinctively

54

exhibit around babies. She noticed us come in and stood up quickly. I stepped aside and studied Gabe's face. First came a narrowing of the eyes, then a jaw-drop not unlike Miranda's a few minutes ago. Sabrina pointed at the picture in his hand.

"You look different than I thought you would."

Gabe stepped forward on numb feet. He held up the photograph. "Where did you get this?"

I winced a little. He was in denial, his mind refusing to admit what the eidetic memory was undoubtedly telling him. Sabrina backed off a step. Gabe realized what he was doing and stepped back as well.

"Mom gave it to me when we had to evacuate," Sabrina said. "It's the only thing I have left from before."

"Karen gave this to you?"

"Yes." Sabrina stepped closer to him. From my angle, the resemblance was downright spooky. Even their expressions were the same. "You're Gabriel Garrett, right?"

He nodded slowly.

Tears stood out in the young girl's eyes. Her voice was a whisper, hands trembling as she clasped them in front of her. "My name is Sabrina. I'm your daughter."

Gabe reached up a gentle hand and ran two fingers down her cheek.

"But how?"

"She was pregnant with me when you left, but she didn't know it yet. She never told you."

"Why not?"

"She said she was afraid of you."

Gabe closed his eyes and put a hand over his mouth. He seemed to collapse into himself. "Did she survive?"

"No. She got bit outside of Morgantown in West Virginia." Sabrina reached up and took her father's hand. "When it happened, before the soldiers took her, she told me to give you a message if I ever found you."

Gabe looked up, his eyes red.

"She said she never stopped loving you, she just couldn't stand to watch you lose yourself anymore. She was sorry she never told you about me. She told me to do whatever it took to find you. She said if there was anyone in the world who could protect me, it would be you."

The big man blinked and tears fell down his cheeks. He tried to speak, found he could not, and reached out for his daughter. Sabrina's hardened mask fell away and she began to sob, her arms going around Gabe's midsection, the tension of long, painful years draining away in a flood. Father and daughter held each other tightly, Gabe crying silently and Sabrina like the child she was. Miranda looked at me, and we both left the room. Neither Gabe nor Sabrina seemed to notice.

*****

The passage of two weeks found me muddling through December. The winter's first dustings of snow fell on the roof of Stall's tavern as I walked up the stairs and left the cold winds behind for the warmth of a hot woodstove.

Solar panels on the roof powered a series of fans that blew hot air from the stove through tubes located around the periphery of the tavern. The result was a comforting heat evenly applied throughout the premises. Mike Stall, owner, proprietor, and executive bottle washer, once told me his profits tripled during the winter. Judging by the crowd on a late Tuesday evening, I believed it.

At the pool tables were were the usual bachelors who would rather part with a bit of trade than cook their own dinner. They snacked on bread and roasted chicken and sips of Mike's grain liquor between bits of conversation and whacking balls around with sticks. The tables in the dining area were mostly full, a low roar of conversation hanging like a cloud among the couples and families and the occasional loner. At the bar was the singles scene, people in their twenties regurgitating the same old pick-up lines and awkward flirtations I once reveled in but now found exhausting.

The far left end of the bar broke off in an L shape. A long table stood next to it with a sign overhead that read 'STAMMTISCH'. A few regulars occupied the table, so I took a stool at the bar. The seats on this side were painted red to notify patrons that this area was reserved for people Mike had dubbed VIPs. I was one of them. I did not usually sit there, but it was late, cold, I was tired, and the only thing I had to look forward to was going to bed and praying my son managed a few hours' sleep before he woke up screaming for milk. Allison and I took turns feeding him, and tonight was my shift. Being able to operate a breast pump and store milk in the fridge were two of the many unintended consequences of installing solar panels on my house.

"What's goin' on," Mike said as he approached. He pronounced 'on' like 'own'. He was old, tall, lean, and hell on wheels in a poker tournament. His two greatest passions were distilling liquor and his rather majestic handlebar moustache. He was never seen without his trademark cowboy boots, ten-gallon hat, and large gold belt buckle he won riding bulls back in some far distant juncture of his youth.

"It's cold. That's what's going on."

57

"Little something to warm you up?"

"Please."

The old cowboy poured me a double of the good stuff—pre-Outbreak bourbon. Maker's Mark, to be exact. It cost a small fortune per bottle anymore, but God, was it worth it.

"You're looking a might out o' sorts Mister Riordan."

"You're a perceptive man, Mister Stall."

He leaned an elbow on the bar and pushed back his hat. "What's botherin' ya?"

"Lots of things, great and small."

"Care to elaborate?"

I took a long pull of bourbon, let it rest on my tongue a few seconds, and sent it down. The burn was warm and comforting. "Well, for starters, there's my son. I don't think he's capable of sleeping for more than three hours at a time. And after the sun goes down, it's more like two."

Mike chuckled. "I know the feeling. Had three girls, all born close together. Was about seven years there I don't think I slept at all."

I looked at Mike with renewed interest. One of the many unspoken rules of the post-Outbreak world was you did not ask people about their past. I'd seen fights break out over that sort of thing. So for Mike to volunteer personal information was a profound show of trust.

"Heard anything from them since … you know."

"Not yet. But hope springs eternal."

My problems suddenly did not seem so bad. "Sorry to hear that, Mike."

He waved a hand. "What else is botherin' ya?"

58

I shrugged. "Business stuff. The perimeter expansion is taking forever, which makes it hard for my farm co-op to get anything done. Tough to work when you have to scan the horizon for infected every ten seconds."

"Not much farming goin' on right now. It's winter, in case you didn't notice."

"Right, but they have other projects. Clearing land, cutting timber for boards and firewood, making charcoal, harvesting eggs, building greenhouses, that sort of thing."

"Gotcha."

"And then there's Allison. She's supposed to be working part time, but it doesn't feel that way. She's almost never home before sundown. Seems like every woman in town is either pregnant or about to be, and they all want Allison to take care of them."

"I have noticed a surge in the number of large round bellies and swollen bosoms. Guess now there's no TV, folks are finding other ways to entertain themselves."

"So it would seem. I might be the only man in town not getting any action."

"How long she makin' you wait?"

"At least another week. There was some tearing when the baby came out."

Mike winced. "I've always been glad men ain't the ones gotta have the babies. Don't seem like no kind of fun at all."

I downed the rest of my drink. "Truer words and all that."

"How's Miranda doin'? I ain't seen her in a month of Sundays."

"She's doing busy. Between working at the shop and babysitting for me, she doesn't have a lot of spare time."

"Ever think maybe you're working her too hard?"

"All the time. But a couple of weeks ago she told me if I mentioned it again she'd slap me with a frying pan. I don't want to get slapped with a frying pan, so I've been keeping my mouth shut."

"That is wise."

"Indeed."

Mike leaned closer and spoke in a low voice. "How's Gabe gettin' along with his daughter?"

I'd known the question was coming sooner or later. In a small town, word travels fast, and Gabe, being something of a local hero, was the star-du-jour of the rumor mill.

"Well enough, I guess. It's been kind of awkward between them, but I think they're happy to have each other."

"Glad to hear it. Gabe is a good man. He deserves a little happiness."

"Yes he does."

A hand came up farther down the bar. "Hey Mike! How 'bout another round?"

"Just a second," Mike called over his shoulder. He poured me another drink and took my empty. "Duty calls."

"Go forth, my friend, and tend the huddled masses."

A snort ruffled his moustache as he walked away. The little birds chirped, and Mike fed them booze. Waitresses made their way to and from the service stand next to me, some of them giving me short greetings before hustling away with drinks to serve. The noise at the bar and the pool table grew steadily louder as I sat and nursed drinks. The chill I brought in with me faded and I settled into a kind of dim hypnosis. The stove was warm at my back. The drinks loosened me up and helped me relax. I felt good for a little while.

But then, as always happens, the noise of the crowd began to sound like the howling of ghouls. When people slapped their hands to the bar while laughing at some joke or another, I flinched. The fire began to smell like the large pits outside of town where the infected were burned to prevent them spreading disease. Drunken revelry became the shouts of injured and dying men. Men who had died at my hands. Men whose faces I'd seen through a rifle scope as they twisted with pain and disbelief and muttered last-minute prayers that expired on their lips as their eyes went blank and they settled into that long, final sleep. Full dark. No light.

So when a hand slapped down on my back, startling me enough to spill some of my drink, it was all I could do not to break the arm attached to it.

"Hey, Riordan," A voice said from behind me. "How come you get to sit over here in the VIP room? What's a guy gotta do to get this kind of treatment around here?"

I turned and recognized the guy talking to me. His name was Silas Montgomery, and he was a pain in the ass. Gabe had once tossed him out of the general store for being a little too aggressive flirting with Miranda. He rarely worked, instead making his way through the beds of various single women who took care of him until they wised up and kicked him out. One particular bed he'd occupied had belonged to a married woman, whose husband had taken exception to Silas violating the sanctity of their marital union. He'd confronted Silas in the town square, and before Sheriff Elliott could get there to stop it, Silas had just about beat the ass clean off him.

I pointed a finger at Mike Stall. "Ask him. He's the one told me I could sit here."

Silas stepped closer so he was leaning over me. He was tall, broad through the shoulders, and had curly black hair and light blue eyes. His forearms were thick and ropy and he probably tipped the scales at about two-twenty—thirty pounds heavier than me and a couple of inches taller. His success with women had a lot to do with his appearance, but that particular shine always faded once his victims saw the selfishness beneath the veneer.

He pointed at my drink. "I notice you're drinking alone."

"Yes. And I'd like to keep it that way."

He sat down in the stool next to mine. "Come on, man. Nobody should drink alone."

"Hey," Mike called out. "That's reserved seating, Montgomery."

"Come on, Mike. I drink here all the time."

The old cowboy started to walk over, but I stopped him with an upraised hand. "It's all right, Mike."

"You sure?"

"Yeah. Let him be."

Mike glared, but walked away.

"That was nice of you, man. Really." He held out a hand. "Name's Silas."

I kept my hands around my drink. "I know who you are."

His lips peeled back with all the warmth of stainless steel. "Yeah, I do have something of a reputation."

"Listen, Silas. No disrespect to you, but I'm not in the mood for conversation. If you don't mind, I'd like to be alone."

The smile sharpened. I let out a sigh because I knew where this was headed. Some people never learn to distinguish kindness from weakness, or patience from fear. It was the fourth time in the last couple of months someone had decided to test me. I guess that's what happens when a man becomes wealthy, well known, and influential. People get jealous.

"Did Allison ever tell you we dated in high school?"

"Allison has never mentioned you at all."

He leaned closer. "Then she didn't tell you why I broke up with her."

"No. Or about any of the other guys she dated before she met me."

"And why do you think that is?"

"Because they, much like you, are of no consequence to her. Or to me."

"Oooh. Getting touchy, are we? I can understand. I mean, look at me, and look at you. What guy in your position wouldn't feel a little threatened?"

I laughed quietly. "Silas, you're no threat to me. Or to my marriage. Now do yourself a favor and fuck off before something bad happens to you."

The blue eyes took on a note of cruelty. He leaned in so close I could smell the liquor on his breath. "She wouldn't suck my dick. That's why I dumped her. She'd let me fuck her, but wouldn't give me a blowjob. What kind of a bitch thinks a man's dick is good enough for her pussy, but not her mouth?"

Silas must have seen the coldness in my gaze, because when I turned to look at him, the smile faltered and he leaned away.

"Listen carefully, you little flea. You need to get out of my sight, and you need to do it now."

His face closed to within inches of mine. "What happens if I don't?"

He made it easy for me. Big, cocky guys always think they can intimidate people. Except some people are very difficult to intimidate, especially when they have seen and done the things I have. So when I slid off my stool, grabbed him around the throat

63

with both hands, and slammed him backwards hard enough to rattle the floorboards, it was no wonder he was surprised.

While Silas struggled to draw a breath and clear the stars from his vision, I picked up his stool and calmly put it back in its place.

"Goddammit, Montgomery!" Mike stormed toward us holding a truncheon. "I told you-"

I held up a hand. "It's okay, Mike. I got this."

The old cowboy's eyes were bright with anger. "Fine. But take it outside. There's kids around."

"I know. I apologize for the disturbance."

Mike let out a long breath. "Hell, I know it ain't your fault. That little shit causes trouble everywhere he goes. Go on back to your drink and I'll send for the sheriff."

"Won't be necessary." I hauled Silas to his feet, wrenched an arm behind his back, clamped on a wristlock, and began walking him to the door. "Might want to notify the clinic, though."

"Ah hell. Robbie!" Mike called out to one of his kitchen staff. "Get in here. I need you to run a message."

Every eye in attendance followed us as I led Silas Montgomery outside. A hush fell over the tavern as people stopped eating or talking or shooting pool or whatever they were doing. I ignored them. I used Silas' face to push the door open, walked him down the stairs, and tossed him face-first to the ground.

The cold must have revived him, because he was on his feet in seconds. When he turned to face me, the predatory smile had returned. "That was good. You're quicker than I thought. Caught me by surprise."

I slipped off my jacket and hung it over a rail. Then I set my feet and waited, hands at my sides. People began to emerge from the tavern and congregate on the wide porch, eyes wide with anticipation. I ignored them.

Silas held his hands out at his sides and began walking slowly toward me. "Listen, Riordan. We got off on the wrong foot. How about we go back inside and-"

The kick came at my groin. If it had landed, it may well have been the end of the fight. But it did not. I saw it coming, sidestepped, caught his leg, stiff-armed him back a few steps, and kicked his other leg out from under him. He made a pained shout as the small of his back met the corner of the curb.

I could have finished it right there. A stomp to the balls would have gotten the job done. Or, if I really wanted to hurt him, I could have heel-hooked him and wrenched his knee out of socket. Hard to fight when your lower leg is on backward, all the tendons and ligaments popped like old rubber bands. But I was not looking for a quick victory. I did not care if somebody sent for the sheriff and I ended up in jail. My blood was up. The Irish devil in me was spoiling for violence. The little shit-worm on the ground in front of me had insulted my wife, and it was high time he learned a lesson in humility.

Silas struggled to his feet and looked at me with venom in his eyes. The smile was gone. The beast behind the bluster had finally revealed itself, fangs and all. I took an open-handed stance and circled left toward his weak side. Montgomery switched to southpaw and tried to angle in on my right. He faked a jab, then charged in with a straight left that would have taken my head off if I'd stood still for it.

The punch went over my head as I slipped it, shuffled left, and popped him in the ribs with a left-right combo. Silas grunted and tried to counter by clinching. I slipped his arms, caught him in a head-and-arm tie-up, and sent him flipping over my hip. It was a good throw. His legs pointed straight skyward at the apex and I landed solidly on top of him. Whatever air was left in his lungs came out in a rush.

Not knowing how good his ground game was, or if he was armed or not, I wasted no time transitioning to side control. Popped the ribs with a couple of hard knees. Pushed the head sideways with the near side shoulder, hip switched, and transitioned to the full-mount. Left, right, left, and the arms covered the face. Gripped the wrist. Pushed the arm across the throat.

Now he knew he was in trouble. If he had known what he was doing, he would have bucked upward with his hips, forcing me to use my free arm to keep from getting reversed. It would not have improved his position, but it would have kept me from hitting him. But he did not know what he was doing. Silas was a savvy brawler on his feet, but like most street toughs, he was helpless from his back.

The crowd on the porch had gotten into the spirit of the event. Silas Montgomery was not well liked. Voices urged me on with such pleasantries as, *fuck him up Riordan*, *beat his ass*, and *stomp a hole in that motherfucker*. I looked at them, and then down at the desperation in Silas' eyes, and in a flash, the anger went out of me.

I did not want to be here anymore, rolling in the dirt with this viscous imbecile. If Allison had been there, she would have been screaming at me to stop. So instead of smashing Silas Montgomery's face into hamburger, I let him roll over, hooked in with my legs, and applied a choke hold. Counted backwards from ten. At three, he went limp. I held on a couple of seconds longer than I needed to, then released and got to my feet. Silas did not move. I rolled him over on his side and vigorously rubbed my knuckles into his chest. The motion revived him enough to get him breathing again.

I left him lying in the snow-dusted street, slipped my jacket on, and walked home.

FIVE

At first glance, Parabellum looked like any other far flung wilderness settlement. A double-layered wooden palisade roughly a quarter mile in diameter ringed the outer perimeter, deep berms had been dug around the defenses, and the interior of the fort was accessible only via a heavy-duty lifting platform connected to a complex system of ropes, gears, swing arms, and pulleys. No gates, just the lift. Anyone who wanted in had to hail the guards. If the guards were in a good mood, and someone had something to trade, they might let them in. Or, if they deemed them sufficiently weak, open fire and loot the corpses.

Heinrich heard Carter key his radio. "All stations, report."

A moment passed, then Carter said, "Copy. Stay alert." He turned to his chief. "All clear, boss. No infected in sight."

"Good."

Heinrich glanced over his shoulder at his raiders. Each man carried a crossbow and a plentitude of bolts purchased on their way out of Kansas with trade from Heinrich's own personal treasury. Many of those bolts now resided in the skulls of neutralized infected. The crossbows had proven invaluable on the long trek from Kansas to Northern Arkansas. Heinrich's men knew how to travel quietly, but one gunshot could draw every infected for miles. Consequently, they only used firearms against living assailants, or if there were too many infected to deal with by other means. Luckily, they had run into no resistance from the living, federal or otherwise, and had made minimal contact with the undead. The trick, as Heinrich once explained to Carter, was to stick to high ground.

"To people in our line of work, this might sound counterintuitive", he had said. "But remember, ghouls tend to follow the path of least resistance. They stick to valleys and hollows and low-lying areas. They'll climb a mountain to get to your ass if they hear you, but otherwise, they're lazy."

"What about feds?" Carter asked. "Skyline yourself, makes it easy to spot you."

"So? You ever seen a caravan take the low road? Hell no. They use the same methods I do. That's why we do our damnedest to look like traders when we travel. Don't give them an excuse, the feds leave you alone. You think they like fighting? Shit. I know how soldiers think. They're even lazier than the ghouls."

Heinrich raised his hand as they came within a hundred yards of the lift. The area around the wall was bare of trees and littered with the bones of infected left to rot where they were killed. The last fifty yards approaching the berm was a maze of ghoul-trippers fashioned from sticks, vines, logs, cables, and anything else the people behind the wall could find to do the job. The scattering of bones grew much thicker closer to the perimeter. Some of the corpses were still fresh.

Heinrich resisted the instinct to wrinkle his nose. The constant reek of death in the air was something for which Parabellum was well known. Most outlaws who frequented the place thought the fierce people encamped within were merely too lazy to clean up their own mess, but Heinrich knew better. They left the corpses in the field because nothing sends a clearer message than the smell of rotting flesh. And that message was simple:

Leave. Get you gone.

Heinrich did not leave. He urged his horse forward. Carter, Maru, and a few other men followed. They rode single file along a narrow path through the ghoul-trippers leading to the lift. When they were within twenty yards—point-blank range for a capable marksman—an armored head appeared over the wall and aimed an RPK machine gun at Heinrich's party.

"The hell you want?"

"Name's Heinrich, chief of the Storm Road Tribe. I'm known here."

"Good for you. Answer the question."

"I'm here to trade. Ask the Khan. He'll vouch for me."

A silence. "Stay where you are. Gotta check you out."

The head and the RPK did not move, but Heinrich knew a runner was being sent to the registry. He sat patiently on his horse, breathing in the miasma of stinking meat and thinking how enjoyable it would be to throw the leader of this place into a pit of flaming ghouls. A few minutes passed before the armored head yelled again.

"Okay, we're sending down the lift. Tell your men to advance along the path."

Heinrich nodded to Maru, who turned his mount and headed back where the others waited. The cracking of whips split the air,

70

followed by horses snorting and nickering in protest. Gears turned and thick ropes moved through pulleys as the two cranes supporting the platform creaked and groaned and the large wooden rectangle made its slow way to ground level.

The platform was large enough to accommodate six loaded wagons. Heinrich knew this because he had seen it happen. He also knew the mechanism operating it was capable of lifting far more than just wagons and livestock. One needed look no further than the hijacked military vehicles within the encampment for proof of that. Heinrich waited until the screeching and rattling of the lift ceased before ordering his men to dismount and board the platform.

Another shout, more cracking whips, and up they went. At the top, they led their horses down a steep ramp and emerged into the central square. In the center of the square was a tall platform topped by a torture rack and a gallows. Crows and buzzards crawled across its surface, occasionally dipping their heads to snap up dispersed bits of bloody meat.

"Must have been an execution recently," Carter said.

Heinrich grunted and surveyed the interior of Parabellum, eyes scanning rooftops and windows and doorways. Nothing looked out of the ordinary. Same muddy streets, same bustle of hard-looking men and women crowding the square, same hum of voices bartering and arguing and cursing and laughing, same wretched slaves scurrying from one place to another, same haphazard, low-slung buildings built of wood cut from the surrounding forest, and above it all, the same palpable sense of danger in the air. Lantern light burned through shuttered, glassless windows, tired-looking whores stood on the porches and balconies offering their wares to passersby, and peddlers of every stripe pushed carts along the edges of buildings where the mud was shallowest. Heinrich smelled shit and blood and fire and cooking food. Discordant hums of despair and revelry competed for dominance in the permeating atmosphere of smoke and cold.

All was as it should be.

A man in a guard shack near the end of the entrance ramp emerged and approached Heinrich. When he drew close, the two men exchanged a nod of greeting.

"Wasn't expecting you back so soon," the man said. He was a giant, standing nearly seven feet tall and easily weighing close to four hundred pounds. His face was broad and cruel, a mohawk of bright red hair streaked his scalp, and a dark orange beard hung in braids down to his chest. His voice sounded like wagon wheels crunching over old bones, and he was dressed in pre-Outbreak biker attire of black leather, metal studs, hidden weapons, and a pair of tanker's boots that had stomped enough people to death to fill a graveyard.

"I missed your pretty face, Ferguson."

The big man laughed. Heinrich was reminded of rocks tumbling down a mountainside.

"Heard tell you were in Kansas a few weeks ago. Must have found something good to hump it all the way back here."

"Wouldn't you like to know?"

An amused grunt. "Fine. Be mysterious. Not like I won't get a cut anyway." Ferguson turned and looked up at the men operating the cranes. "They're on the level. Let 'em in. And move your asses, I want this caravan inside before nightfall."

The men shouted acknowledgment and set to with urgency. A foreman cursed them for their laziness and demanded they work faster.

"Come on. The Khan will want to see you."

Heinrich motioned for Carter to follow, then glanced at Maru. "You're in charge. Get the men settled, remind them to stay alert, and tell them no more than three drinks tonight. First round is on me."

"Right, Chief. Any women?"

Heinrich began walking away, following Ferguson. "They're rich men, now. They can buy their own women."

"Right, Chief."

*****

Necrus Khan sat in a chair upholstered with goose down and human flesh. Heinrich and Carter sat across from him in similar chairs. A desk carved from a single, massive oak tree squatted between them, ornately carved with depictions of damned souls writhing in agony, unspeakable acts of torture, naked bodies in every sexual position imaginable, and at the top of each corner, a human skull. Only the skulls were not carvings, but the remains of four of the Khan's enemies. The room smelled like a week-old corpse. The walls were stained wood boards festooned with shelves covered with more skulls, organs, and genitalia suspended in fluid-filled jars. There were mounted animal heads, skins, furs, and an assortment of demented carvings. At the back of the room, incongruous with the macabre décor, was a large metal safe and a filing cabinet.

The Khan leaned back in his chair, his tooled Italian leather boots atop his desk. The only hair visible above his neck was a goatee and a pair of thick dark eyebrows. His skin was brown and swarthy, his bare scalp gleamed in the dim lamplight, his teeth shone perfectly white, his custom-tailored suit would have looked at home on a wealthy rancher from the late nineteenth century, and everything from the clasp of his bolo tie to the tips of his boots bore the shine of flamboyant silver inlay.

Heinrich was reasonably certain Necrus Khan was not the name the man was born with. Before he had killed his predecessor and taken control of Parabellum, he'd simply gone by Necrus. Why he called himself a khan instead of a chief or governor was a mystery. Perhaps it had something to do with his ethnicity, which Heinrich could not quite place.

"So," Necrus said. "Salt. Interesting. Wonder where it came from?"

"Don't know," Heinrich said. *And I wouldn't tell you if I did.*

"Come on, Heinrich. Don't expect me to believe you didn't keep a few alive."

"Just a Blackthorn and a few slaves. None of them could tell us where the cargo originated."

The Khan glanced at Carter with a wry expression. "I'm assuming you handled the interrogations?"

Carter said nothing, his expression neutral. Necrus laced his fingers behind his head. The arms of his suit jacket bulged with knotted muscle.

"Well, we both know salt is too valuable to turn away. And even though I could just kill you and your men and take it for myself, I'd lose more than half my number in the process. Can't afford that now can I?"

"No, you can't. And we both know you won't try. So can we cut the shit already?"

Necrus laughed, his voice deep and genuinely entertained. "A confident man. I like you Heinrich. I might have to kill you someday, but I like you."

Heinrich felt himself growing impatient. The tough talk was just that—talk. Necrus no more wanted him dead than any of the other marauder chiefs who brought him trade and kept him wealthy. The Italian boots returned to the floor and the Khan pulled his chair closer to the desk.

"I'll set the tariff at ten barrels."

"Two."

"Don't insult me, Heinrich. Eight, and my choice of ten of your seized guns and a thousand rounds of ammo."

"Don't insult *me*, Necrus. That's the same price. Make it three."

"Eight."

"Four."

"Seven, five guns, half the ammo."

"Five, and no more. You sure you want guns and ammo? I told you I brought slaves."

The Khan raised his eyebrows. "Interesting. Mr. Ferguson?"

The door opened and the giant poked his head inside. "Sir?"

"Do we have a manifest on Mister Heinrich's slaves yet?"

"Yes sir. Just came in." Ferguson disappeared for a few seconds, then came back and handed Necrus a sheet of rough parchment half covered in charcoal writing.

"Hmm. Says here you have a nice blond girl. Green eyes. Not quite sixteen yet."

"Five barrels and the girl."

"How about the barrels, the girl, and five hundred rounds of my choice?"

"Only if I get use of the auction hall for two days, starting tomorrow morning."

"That can be arranged."

Heinrich pretended to think about it. The tariff was far lower than he'd expected, confirming his suspicion that Necrus did not realize how valuable the salt really was. *Spends too much time holed up in this place. Losing touch with the wider world.*

"Done."

The two men stood up and shook hands. Necrus Khan had a grip like a pipe wrench. It was a useless gesture, Heinrich knew, just Necrus reminding him of his physical prowess. It was also stupid. It showed weakness. A smart man wants his enemies to underestimate him. Only an apprehensive fool would make a show of strength when none was needed.

"A pleasure as always, Heinrich. If you'll accept my hospitality, Ferguson will show you to your room."

Only if I were suicidal. "I'll arrange my own accommodations."

A shrug. "Suit yourself."

Heinrich and Carter followed Ferguson through the building, down a set of hallways, through a large room full of naked women chained to the walls, and out the front door. As they walked away, Carter said, "I'm going to skin that bastard alive one of these days."

Heinrich smiled. "You'll have to get in line."

*****

The next morning, Heinrich's men cleaned out the refuse from the last group that had used the auction hall. The building was the largest in town, had a rectangular floor space of over twenty thousand square feet, and came equipped with tables, chairs, booths that could be put up by hand, chains, locks, meat hooks, and iron rings driven into the floor for slave auctions.

Necrus Khan arrived early while Heinrich's men were still setting up and wheeling in the inventory. The slaves were already chained in place, awaiting their fate. The Khan examined his girl, found her satisfactory, and thanked Heinrich on his way out. The girl's mother cried out and lunged for her daughter as she was led away, only to be laid low by a swift strike from Maru's club.

"Stay down, you, or I'll break your legs and leave you for the ghouls."

Heinrich paid no attention.

His men set up two booths, laid out the merchandise for perusal, and established a perimeter in short order. Their flow of movement was well coordinated, no confusion, no wasted effort, minimal conversation. Maru barely had any work to do keeping them on task. Heinrich liked what he saw. His men had come a long way under his tutelage, and they would go even farther in the days to come. The problem, as he saw it, was there were simply not enough of them. He planned to change that.

Word had spread overnight what was for auction. The start time was early in the morning with reserve set for all items to prevent syndicates from driving down the price. It was an old tactic—the parties bidding on a certain item collaborate, decide who gets what, and only one of them makes a lowball bid. If no one else bids, the syndicate wins. By setting a reserve price, syndicate bargaining power was minimized. If that failed, Heinrich generally employed more forceful and bloody tactics. The last group who had pulled such a stunt were probably still nailed to the trees where they had been left to die.

The slaves were auctioned first, followed by guns and ammunition Heinrich did not want to keep. Then came the salt barrels. When the reserve was announced—a list of the things

Heinrich was willing to trade for and the minimums thereof—more than a few auction goers cursed, spit on the floor, and departed. Some complained the price was higher than the value, others grumbled they wanted to bid but could not afford the reserve. Heinrich cared not in the least. There were still plenty of bidders on the floor.

There were only fifteen barrels up for auction, but the bidding went on well into the evening. The sun had set and the auction floor was awash in lantern light by the time the last barrel was sold. Heinrich had deliberately displayed his remaining forty-seven barrels in plain sight. He wanted every hired blade in the compound to see his wealth, and what it could buy.

That night, after a watch was set and the rest of the Storm Road Tribe's wagons, livestock, and trade were secured in a warehouse under heavy guard, Heinrich turned his men loose on the town. His purpose in doing so was twofold: first, they needed to cut loose. Too much time on the road with no booze or women was bad for discipline. Second, he wanted them to spread the word he was recruiting. Not hiring, recruiting. There was a difference.

At noon the next day, the buyers showed up at the auction house with their trade. Men looking to sign on with Heinrich had been lining up since dawn. Heinrich set the time for the recruiting drive to start two hours after the trade exchange. He wanted the hopefuls to see, and fully understand, what they could earn fighting for him.

Wagon after wagon pulled up to the auction house. Some unloaded and left, but most stayed, livestock and all. A stir of excited conversation rumbled through the men in the recruiting line as the trade piled up outside the hall. Bags of feed for the horses, barrels of clean water, dried meat and fish, ammunition, guns, vegetables preserved in jars and cans, and most tellingly, nearly two tons of hard-tack bread. It was soon all too obvious what Heinrich was planning.

He was going on the march.

SIX

Gabriel

Sabrina sat on a stool behind the counter while I haggled with an old woman over the price of eggs. The woman seemed to think a dozen eggs should be enough to purchase a pound of dried fish from Kentucky Lake. I explained dried fish weighs next to nothing, meaning a pound of it is actually quite a lot, and with the proliferation of chickens in Hollow Rock, eggs simply did not command the same price they used to. Preserved meat, on the other hand, was highly prized. We settled on two dozen eggs for a quarter-pound of fish. After I weighed it, the old woman said it was a lot more than she thought it would be. I did not say 'I told you so'.

"I don't know how you put up with that shit," Sabrina said after the woman left. She was staring out the window beside the counter at a robin perched on a limb of the old maple tree next to the general store. Its song was barely audible through the double-paned glass.

"It's a living."

"Like hell. You're the richest man I've ever met. You don't need this place. You don't need these people."

I scraped a hand over the three-day stubble on my face. "Sabrina, we've been over this."

"Sure we have. Doesn't mean I'm wrong."

Before I could say anything else, she slid off the stool and left through the back door. I leaned against the counter and closed my eyes.

Teenagers.

Things had gone well between us the first couple of weeks. She moved into the spare bedroom in my house. We talked a lot. She told me about her childhood in Maryland where her mother moved after we divorced. She remarried when Sabrina was three. The husband's name was Patrick. He was a mild, jovial dentist with a big house and a wide green lawn and horses boarded out in the country and a BMW 7-series. He was nice. He liked to cook. Sabrina wasn't sure she'd ever heard him raise his voice.

Karen took a job as a public relations coordinator with a small software company. I always figured she would end up doing something like that; she had an engaging personality and a smile that could light up a room. I told Sabrina that was what made me fall in love with her way back when. I asked her if she had been happy, and Sabrina said yes. Karen loved Patrick well enough, and Patrick was enamored with the both of them. The years they spent together were good ones. Sabrina had a happy childhood.

But that childhood ended the day of the Outbreak. They were in Baltimore at the time visiting her stepfather's parents. They left when the riots started and fled to a small town where FEMA had set up an emergency relief camp. Two days later, the camp was overrun by infected and the Army was forced to evacuate. Patrick got bit protecting Karen and Sabrina. When the soldiers came the next morning to take him away, he said a tearful goodbye and left without protest.

Later, at another camp in West Virginia, they were overrun again and it was Karen who became infected. Same story, same ending. I took some small comfort in the knowledge she died quickly, and though it shames me to admit it, I felt a sense of closure, that it was okay to move on. Part of me still loves Karen and always will, and I know I will mourn for her in time. But knowing she is gone, not just wondering, but knowing, put the final mark on that chapter of my life.

Sabrina, for her part, took the loss hard. She hated the soldiers for killing her mother even though she knew it was necessary. And now that she had no one to protect her, she worried what some of the men in the convoy might try to do.

The day the president declared martial law was the day Sabrina abandoned the convoy. No one tried to stop her, and no one came after her. Everyone was running. Everyone was afraid. Nobody cared if people wanted to leave. Fewer refugees meant fewer people for the Army to look after, and fewer mouths to feed.

Sabrina spoke in vague terms after that. She said she ran for a few days until she found an abandoned town. At the time, she was starving and near death from dehydration. The houses she looted yielded food and water and the .22 rifle she still carries to this day. She decided to stay in the town for a while. That afternoon, not long after she had collapsed on a couch and passed out from exhaustion, she was awakened by the unmistakable howling of infected. She climbed up into the attic and pulled the ladder after her and heard a voice speak to her with a strange accent.

"You need to stay quiet," the voice said.

Sabrina turned and saw a smallish man with black hair, brown skin, and eyes with epicanthic folds at the corners. He was aiming a pistol at her. She reached for her rifle, only to realize she had left it downstairs.

"Don't worry," the man said. "I won't hurt you." Slowly, he laid the gun aside. "What's your name?"

"Sabrina."

"I'm Manny. We'll talk later."

They said no more for the nine hours it took the infected to break into the house, moan and howl and grunt with impotent rage, realize there was no one to eat, and finally wander off. It was hot in the attic. They had only a liter of water between them. Nevertheless, Manny made Sabrina wait another four hours after the last of the thumping and scraping and growling stopped and they could no longer hear the undead screeching in the distance.

"They have good hearing," he told her. "If we come down too soon, they'll hear us and come right back."

Sabrina had been too terrified to argue.

They stayed in the town a few more days living off what they could scavenge. Manny decided to leave and told Sabrina she was welcome to come with him. She had just turned eleven years old. She went along.

And so the pair of them traveled together for over two years. Manny had been a full-time diesel mechanic and a part-time martial arts instructor before the Outbreak. He was raised in Manilla and trained in Kali, Escrima, and Silat his entire life. He moved to the United States in his early twenties. Manny taught her how to use a blade and gave her the twin karambits that were her primary weapons against living opponents.

I asked her if she had ever killed anyone. She laughed and told me of course she had. At least twelve, maybe more. She was not

83

certain of the exact number. When she cut someone, she didn't stick around to see if they bled to death. She was usually too busy running.

I was relieved to find out she had never been raped or forced into prostitution. People had tried, but she had always managed to defend herself. I have met far too many women over the years who cannot say the same. Sexual assault was an enormous problem long before the world fell apart, and the lawless years since the Outbreak have done nothing to improve things.

As time went on, Sabrina became reluctant to give any more details about her life since the Outbreak. I asked her where she went while traveling with Manny, and she shrugged and said, "All over the place." I asked her what happened to Manny, why they no longer traveled together, and she said, "Got bit. Had to put him down."

"That's tough. Sorry to hear that."

"Thanks."

And that was the last we spoke of it.

So the weeks passed and Christmas came. We had a feast at Allison and Eric's place. Elizabeth joined us after she finished her duties with the town's official celebration. We sat around Allison's antique dining table, all twelve feet of it, and ate roast chicken and bread stuffing and squash and peas and homemade gravy. Eric gave Allison a wedding ring with a diamond the size of a blueberry. I had no idea where he found it, but it fit perfectly and Allison said she loved it.

I gave Elizabeth a pair of sapphire earrings and a matching pendant. Even though such things aren't worth very much anymore, she seemed genuinely pleased. Sabrina rolled her eyes and shook her head and muttered something about spoiled townies. I shot her a look but otherwise let it go.

My gift was a framed four-by-eight photo of Sabrina and I standing on a hillside overlooking the town square, the landscape around us covered in snow. We were backlit by a dark pewter sky and the bare branches of oak trees in winter, both of us laughing at some joke I had made. I remembered Elizabeth taking the picture with her big digital camera, but never thought I would see it in print. Where she'd found the ink and photographic paper, I could only guess. Such things are rare and very expensive. When I looked at the picture, something tightened in my chest and I had to clear my throat before I could speak.

"This is perfect. Thank you."

Elizabeth's hand covered mine. Her brown eyes were warm and reflected the golden light of candles on the table. "You're welcome."

Sabrina leaned over. "Can I see?"

I showed it to her and felt warm inside when my daughter's rare smile appeared. She asked if she could have a copy, and Elizabeth said yes.

Now it was mid-January, two months to the day from when Sabrina came into my life, and I had learned a few things about her in that time. Namely, despite the fact she never knew me growing up, we had several personality traits in common. For starters, she had a temper. Not a hot, boiling one that could get her into trouble, but the kind of low, simmering anger that can last for days when roused. Something I know a thing or two about.

She did not talk much. When she did, she said exactly what was on her mind and did not mince words. If she thought a question was stupid, or the answer should be obvious—even when it was not—she simply ignored the questioner. She was not a trusting soul. Her gray eyes, so much like mine, constantly scanned her surroundings, checking rooftops and windows, gauging distances, looking for exits and escape routes, assessing whether or not people were armed and with what.

Despite a bit of physical awkwardness, she did not have the demeanor of a child. She spoke and acted like a grown woman, and for reasons I cannot put easily into words, this pained me every time I noticed it. Which is saying something because, at this point in my life, not many things affect me anymore.

So I sat and listened to the silence in the store in the early morning hours and wished it was six o' clock so I could go home. I wanted to talk to Sabrina. I wanted to explain why I was reluctant to talk about the future just yet. I wanted to tell her I had some plans in the works that might interest her, but I needed to make sure of a few things beforehand. The first of them being a caravan due to arrive sometime that afternoon, and a man named Spike.

*****

It did not take a great deal of imagination to figure out where he got his name.

A morningstar mace, forged from what appeared to be a tangle of sharpened railroad spikes, hung from a loop on his belt. It had an ironwood handle and a trailer hitch for a pommel. He wore leather armor riddled with sharp metal studs on the shoulder pauldrons, gloves, elbows, shins, toes, and the bottoms of his forearms. The helmet he carried under his arm looked like something from ancient Greece, only instead of a horse-hair crest on the crown, he had welded a short, wickedly sharp spear point. There were dark brown stains on the spear that looked like rust until I realized it was made of stainless steel.

"Good to see you alive, Garrett," he said as he walked in.

I offered him a hand and he shook it. "Same to you. Run into any trouble on the way in?"

"Nothing I couldn't handle."

"Come on back. I'll make us some tea."

"On the house?"

"Of course."

Spike smiled and motioned for me to lead the way. "Just making sure. Stuff is pricey these days."

I turned the sign on the door to the side that said CLOSED, put the hands on the little red clock to indicate the store would reopen in half an hour, and went into the back room.

Spike pointed at a small refrigerator in the corner. "That's new."

"Yep. Put it in a few months ago. Runs on twelve-volt. Found an old Windstream trailer about twenty miles south of town. Had a hundred-sixty watt solar rig on the roof, this fridge, and a ten-gallon water heater. Stripped them and sold the trailer at auction. Young couple moved here from Michigan bought it. You should see what they did with it."

"I hear Windstreams are popular. Easy to ghoul-proof."

"Yep. Folks that bought it from me riveted sheet metal over the windows, installed escape hatches on the floor and roof, put in a composting toilet, and ripped out the dining table and benches and built a rocket stove. Even rigged a manual pump to the water tank. There's a little plastic thing you step on and water comes out of the kitchen faucet."

"Sounds like a nice setup."

"A little cramped, but yeah. I've seen a hell of a lot worse."

I cut the power to the fridge and plugged an electric kettle into an inverter. The deep-cycle battery connected to the solar panel was a wonderful convenience, but it only had enough juice to power one appliance at a time. When I had the tea steeping in cups, I unplugged the kettle and diverted power back to the fridge.

Spike accepted his cup and sipped it carefully. At five-foot-eight and two-hundred solid pounds, he looked about as delicate as a battle-scarred pit bull. Fought like one too.

"You got it pretty good here, Garrett."

"That I do."

"Maybe one day I can retire some place like this."

"I doubt you'll live long enough."

Spike grinned. "Fuck you, jarhead."

"Sorry, you're not pretty enough. And I figured you were here for business, not pleasure."

The grin faded. He put on his business face. "That I am."

"What did you bring me?"

"Salt. And lots of it. Just like you asked."

I stared at him flatly. "I *asked* for delivery two months ago."

"Yeah. About that." He put down his cup and crossed his hands on the table. "We lost that shipment."

"Seriously?"

"Seriously."

"I thought you hired Blackthorns to guard it."

"I did. Eight of 'em. And five other merc types, and an armored wagon, and a goddamn heavy machine gun. It wasn't enough. Found their remains in central Kansas."

"Jesus."

88

"Don't think he was around that day."

Neither of us spoke for a few seconds. *Eight Blackthorns,* I thought, shaking my head.

The Blackthorn Security Company had been in business for only a year or so, but had already garnered a reputation as the best mercenary outfit around. They were fierce, fearless, highly trained, and when they signed a contract, they pinned their lives to it. They had armor, weapons, explosives, night vision equipment, the works. Pound for pound, the rival of any pre-Outbreak security outfit. Maybe better. I had heard that Tyrel Jennings, the company's founder, who happened to be an ex-Navy SEAL, utilized a cadre of special warfare operators from every branch of the Armed Services to train his men.

"Must have been a hell of a fight," I said.

"Lots of bullet casings. Lot of dried blood. Some of the bodies were marauders. My people didn't go down easy."

"That's something, I guess."

Spike tapped his thumbs against his mug. "Yeah."

"Can you absorb the loss?"

"Most of it. Shipment was insured. FTIC."

The acronym stood for Federal Trade Insurance Commission, a public-private venture established to keep trade, the lifeblood of the new barter economy, flowing. Any trade going in or out of Colorado Springs and the surrounding communities had to be insured. If it was not, caravan operators faced steep tariffs that were usually more than the FTIC's insurance premiums. The commission hired agents in most of the large settlements in the new Union—including Hollow Rock—which allowed contracts to be purchased by just about anyone. In the event of a loss, the commission paid out in the various commodities the government always seemed to have in ample quantities—fuel, bullets, and medical supplies.

"Won't get back what I spent on security," Spike went on, "but I don't really care about that. I lost some good people, Gabe. People with families. There were women and children in that caravan. We never found the bodies. I don't have to tell you what that means."

I would have liked to tell Spike it meant there was still hope, but we both knew better. Even if they survived the attack, the captured traders faced a fate worse than death. Few people rescued from marauders lasted very long. Most committed suicide. And those who had the strength to go on had to live with the memories of what happened while in captivity every day of their lives. I stared at my hands and breathed out slowly.

"Any clue who did it?"

"Yeah. Guy in my outfit, ex-Army fella, recognized the symbol the raiders drew on their weapons. Skull with crossed lightning bolts beneath. Said they call themselves the Storm Road Tribe. If I ever find them, they'll be the fucking Storm Road Corpses."

"You report it?"

Spike nodded. "When I went looking for them, I had to bring along a rep from the FTIC. Bastards wanted verification. Tried telling the rep my people wouldn't have hijacked me, not with the Blackthorns around. Guy said I wasn't the first person to say that. Shit world we live in, huh?"

"Most of it, yeah."

I finished my tea and let Spike brood quietly for a while. The little refrigerator hummed comfortably in the corner, reminding me of better days when life seemed bright and shining and hopeful. Sometimes I would come in the back room after closing the shop and sit with my eyes closed and listen to the refrigerator hum and imagine I was back in the house my father built, dozing on the couch and waiting for dad's truck to crunch the gravel in the driveway. Time was, I found the hum of appliances annoying. Now it sounds like home.

"Well, guess we better get down to business." Spike pushed his cup away.

"Yeah. Your crew through the gate yet?"

"Going through inspection. Be a few hours."

"In that case, I'll meet you at the caravan district tomorrow morning."

Spike raised an eyebrow. "You can't take possession today? Costs trade to stay overnight, and I got customers in other towns waiting on me."

"Take the expense out of my shipment."

Spike dipped his head. "Fair enough." He stood up and yawned expansively, arms stretched behind him, leather armor creaking from the strain. "Christ, if I'm honest, a hot meal, a few drinks, and a night behind a well-guarded wall sounds like just what the fucking doctor ordered."

He started to walk toward the door, then stopped and snapped his fingers. "Shit, almost forgot. I got something for you."

"What?"

He stepped closer, reached under the armor on his right forearm, and removed a small plastic tube. "Letter from Mr. Hadrian Flint, director of operations for the Blackthorn Security Company. I can vouch for its authenticity."

I reached for it. "He deliver it in person?"

"Yep. Said it's for your eyes only."

"You didn't read it?"

91

"Check the seal."

I did. It was intact, the signet of the Blackthorn Company pressed into red wax. No way Spike could have opened it and resealed it, not without a signet ring. And the Blackthorns guarded them jealously.

"Thanks."

"I'll consider the tea my tip."

He left through the back door. I locked it behind him, sat down, and opened the tube. The letter was brief and to the point. It could not have come at a better time.

I rolled the letter up, put it back in its tube, and stuffed it in a cargo pocket. I thought about the salt I had purchased, how it was one of the best ways to collapse a large amount of wealth into a small, portable volume of trade. I thought about how salt was once less than a dollar a pound, and how that same pound today was the equivalent of half a month's wage for a farm worker. I thought about the trade routes between Hollow Rock and Colorado Springs, and the upcoming election, and how nice it would be to have Elizabeth in my bed every night and wake up next to her every morning and finally have the family I thought God or fate or whatever turns the gears of the universe had seen fit to deny me.

My eyes closed, the fridge hummed, and I decided to close the shop early.

SEVEN

Eric was exactly where I expected to find him—picking a fight. Or a sparring match to be more accurate.

The Ninth Tennessee Volunteer Militia has its own training facilities at Fort McCray just outside of town. I rode my horse there, left him in the public livery, and proceeded to the militia's corner of the base.

The gymnasium is a far cry from the empty field where Eric and I once held unarmed combat training for the men and women who risk their lives serving their town. The facility has mat space, punching bags, free weights, and an honest to God boxing ring. Where the guys who built the place found the ring, I have no idea. But I don't mind using it from time to time. Neither does Eric.

I climbed the corner, leaned on a turnbuckle, and said, "Keep your hands up, Riordan."

Eric looked my way for a bare instant and caught a right hook from Manuel Sanchez. He managed to slip the follow-up overhand left and circle out.

"You're an asshole, Gabe."

I laughed quietly while the two men finished their round. Sanchez was winning, as usual, but that did not surprise me. Prior to the Outbreak, he was a top-ten ranked welterweight about two or three fights from a title shot. Eric has fast hands, and is the bigger man, but Sanchez is a pro. And there no substitute for pro. My old friend looked relieved when the guy keeping time called for a break.

"If you want to watch me get beat up, strap on some gloves," Eric said as he walked over to my corner.

"I don't know. You're getting pretty good these days."

He eyed me to see if I was kidding him. I wasn't.

"Yeah, well, Sanchez is a good boxing coach."

The Pride of Hermosillo looked over his shoulder. "I heard that."

"You're also a dick. You hear that too?"

"Smartass."

I flicked a finger at Sanchez. "You in a nutshell."

Eric stripped off his gloves and squirted water into his mouth with a white squeeze bottle. His longish hair dripped with sweat and his shirt was soaked through. "You here for a reason, or you just like busting my balls?"

"Got plans this afternoon?"

"You're looking at them."

"Sarah's putting together a volunteer sweep. Still not too late to sign up. Figured with all the time you've been spending at home you could use a little recreation."

Eric looked over his shoulder at Sanchez. "You know, I do feel like shooting something."

"Good. Clean up. I'll wait outside."

"Right."

*****

"Christ's sake, Eric. You stink."

He sat up straight in the saddle, tilted his head at what he thought was a rakish angle, and said, "I smell like a sporting man possessed of good health and vigor."

"Really? I didn't realize sporting men of good health and vigor smelled like sweaty butthole cheese."

"Oh, quit your bitching. Everybody stinks these days. No such thing as deodorant anymore. You're not exactly a spring lily."

The wind picked up, blowing a dusting of snow across the field. Red tossed his mane and rumbled in irritation. I patted his neck and tightened my scarf around my face.

"There's normal stink, and then there's post-workout stink. When I told you to clean up I meant more than just changing your shirt."

Deputy Sarah Glover turned around in her saddle and cut the air with an angry hand. "Will you two shut it," she hissed. "We're on a sweep for Christ's sake."

We shut it. Sarah glared a few seconds more and then went back to scanning the treeline with her field glasses.

Around us were five other riders, all heavily armed, with Sarah out on point. The day was the gunmetal gray of winter overcast, a strong wind blowing heavy clouds fast across the sky. Loose powder on the open field surrounding Hollow Rock skidded across the ground in streaks of billowing white, ghostly in the afternoon dimness. Red's hooves sent white puffs of snow cascading in front of his legs with every step, making the already difficult going that much worse. He didn't like it. The other horses didn't like it either, and their riders were not any happier.

Ahead, Sarah held up a fist and leaned back in her saddle. Her mount came to a halt. She turned, pointed two fingers at her eyes, and gave a signal to hold position. Everyone complied. A minute or so passed while Sarah adjusted the lenses and looked through the binoculars again. Finally, she rode back to us and spoke in a low voice.

"Jackpot. Good sized horde, about two hundred yards north beyond the treeline, moving slow."

There was a general nodding of heads. The fact the infected had been slowed by the cold was no surprise. A few degrees colder, and they would have been immobilized completely. Winter may be tough on food production, but it's a bonanza for ghoul hunters.

"We'll let them move halfway across the field," Sarah went on, "then ride in and circle clockwise. Everyone got your hand weapons?"

I patted my falcata. Eric patted his military issue MK-9 Anti-Revenant Personal Defense Tool. Which, a thousand years ago, would have been wielded by conscripted Chinese peasants and called a da-dao. Meaning, 'big knife'. The MK-9 is designed for one thing, and one thing only: chopping. And at that, it excels.

The other volunteers made similar motions. "All right," Sarah said. "I'm on point. Riordan, you're second. Coleman, Morris, Jones, Haynes, and McCoy, in that order. Gabe, you're on anchor."

I let out a breath and cursed silently. The role of anchor was to keep a little distance and be ready to ride in and lend assistance to anyone finding themselves in trouble. Lost weapons, injured horses, thrown riders, that kind of thing. It did not happen very often, especially with experienced guardsmen like the five who had ridden out with us. Which meant I might not see any action today, thereby defeating the purpose of my presence.

96

"Sure, Sarah."

A curt nod. "Standard tactics. Ride and halt on my command, fall out if your gun jams, and for God's sake, don't forget to stake your horses before we move in on foot. Everyone clear?"

We were.

"Stay loose, gentlemen. Be ready to go."

Sarah adjusted her M-4 on its sling and checked the chamber. I did the same. Made sure the magazine was seated. Safety off. Suppressor screwed on tight. Then we waited. The wind died down somewhat. The groaning of ghouls became gradually louder until the first of them emerged from the treeline.

Your average ghoul, assuming their legs work properly, moves along at about two miles an hour. Under the current conditions, with thirty-something degree air clutching at their necrotic tissues, they moved at maybe half that.

Step by halting step, the horde took shape on the field. After ten minutes of watching and waiting, more than two-hundred ghouls marched disjointedly across the white plain in the now-familiar teardrop formation, the fastest ghouls in the lead, the slower ones in the press behind. They were spread out loosely, perhaps ten feet or more between one walking corpse and another. This was both good and bad. Good because targeting would be easier, bad because it was farther for the horses to travel.

Riding a horse is not like in the movies where the animals run and run tirelessly. Horses are living things that need oxygen, water, food, and rest. Their muscles get sore. They are prone to injury. When they run, they get tired. And just like people, some are in better shape or more athletic than others. That said, the hard part of riding in formation is not keeping pace, it's preventing the horses' instinctive herd mentality from letting them bunch together in a cluster. Doing so is great for confusing predators, not so much for fighting the undead. In this case, I was not worried. Red was a

97

good mount, and I had worked with the other guys before. They, and their steeds, were reliable.

"Okay, looks like we're ready," Sarah said, lowering the field glasses. "Everybody good?"

A round of affirmatives.

"Ten yard intervals, fellas. Let's move."

The good deputy rode out first, Eric and the rest following behind. I went last and urged Red gently with my heels to maintain the proper distance. In less than two minutes, we reached the horde and rode a few circles around it at a slow canter. This caused the ghouls to attempt to follow us, thereby ruining their formation and causing them to collide and trip over one another. The effect was like dragging a magnet around a pile of iron filings.

By the time Sarah called a halt, the horses were steaming the air with perspiration. The smell of death and sweaty horse filled my nose as I rode a short distance away from the main formation. At least it was cold. The odor would have been twice as bad in the heat of summer.

Red's flanks heaved slowly beneath me, but not hard enough to cause worry. He was just catching his breath; he'd be good in less than a minute. I sighted down my rifle and estimated the distance to the horde at twenty to twenty-five meters. Dangerously close in warm weather, but at the rate this horde was moving, it would be a full five minutes before they reached us.

Sarah patted her horse's neck, stood up in the saddle, shouldered her rifle, and turned to look at me. "Gabe, eyes on."

"Roger that."

She aimed her weapon. "Fire at will."

A staccato chorus of muted cracks filled the gusting air. We were all armed with M-4s on loan from the Army, equipped with suppressor's and ACOG sights. Our ammo had been purchased by the City of Hollow Rock during the summer with trade from tax revenue, not a small amount of it collected from G&R Transport and Salvage. The fact that I was sleeping with the mayor did not exempt me from the responsibilities of citizenship. I did not mind. I knew my taxes were being used wisely.

On the firing line, Eric was racking up the highest tally, as per usual. I took a small amount of pride in this. He learned almost everything he knows from me, after all. His keen eyesight and cool head under pressure have saved the lives of many of Fort McCray's soldiers. And while they do not entirely accept him, the troops at least respect him.

The five guardsmen with us, regulars who did the job full time, conducted their work with casual efficiency. These were not military men, or former law enforcement, or anything like that. They had been farmers and tradesmen and laborers before the Outbreak. But what they lacked in formal training, they made up for in courage and perseverance. Hard necessity had taught them the merciless lessons of survival. They learned marksmanship on the fly. Most of them had never stood next to a horse in their lives before civilization collapsed. But now they all knew how to ride, and shoot, and set up a perimeter, and sweep for ghouls and marauders, and do the dangerous, grinding work it takes to keep their homes safe. They were not professionals yet, but they were learning fast.

One of the men stopped firing. I sat up a little straighter in the saddle. He canted his rifle to the side and worked the charging handle. A round ejected and disappeared into the snow. The rifle came up and he tried to fire again. Nothing.

"Jones," I called out. "You good?"

He ejected another round, aimed, and squeezed the trigger. Same result.

"Damn thing ain't working."

He wheeled his mount and exited the line. "All yours, buddy."

"Got it."

I took his place, maneuvered Red into position, and leveled my M-4. The ACOG reticle settled on a ghoul's forehead. A gray, this one. I hate grays. Not just because they look completely inhuman, but because I don't know what is happening to them. I know they started out as human beings, then became infected, and afterward underwent some kind of change where they shed their skin, exposing dead, grayish-black muscle tissue—hence the name—and my experience with them has led me to develop some disturbing theories regarding their capabilities.

First, they seem to be able to heal. Most ghouls are covered in bite wounds. They wouldn't be ghouls otherwise. It takes a bite or some other kind of fluid transfer to spread the Reanimation Phage. And when the infected get their hands on prey, they never stop at one bite. Some of the undead are so badly mangled they can barely move. Some are completely immobilized by the injuries that killed them, little more than animated skeletons held together by strips of gristle. But the grays, for the most part, do not have injuries visible on their bodies. I am not the only one who has noticed this.

Second, their skulls are far more difficult to crack than normal infected. I know this from experience. My falcata is sharp enough to shave with, and made from very high quality steel. With most ghouls, I do not have to swing very hard to make a cross-section out of their craniums. With the grays, however, a swing with the same force results in my sword lodged two inches into dense, fibrous bone. I have learned it is better just to decapitate them.

Last, and perhaps most disturbingly, they are faster than normal infected. Not as fast as a living person, but fast enough they are at the vanguard of every horde I've seen for the last several months. This could be a result of their healing ability. Or it could be an indicator of some kind of long-term metamorphosis. I don't know. I'm not a biologist, and even if I were, I don't have enough information to say anything conclusively. What I do know is this: the more grays I kill, the better I feel.

A squeeze of the trigger made one less of them in the world. I shifted aim to a man of middle height, clothes worn away by time and the elements; mouth a rictus of dried blood, shredded lips, and blackened teeth. I fired again and he fell out of sight.

The next target appeared. I did my best not to look at it too closely, especially the eyes. The eyes are the worst. Wide, bloodshot, and whitish in appearance. The bleached out irises are always dilated and fixed with malevolent intensity on whatever prey they happen to be pursuing.

In this case, me.

Unlike many people, I do not hate the infected. They did not ask to be what they are. In fact, most of them fought tooth and nail to avoid their fate. But they didn't. And now they are trapped in a half-existence of mindless rage and unending hunger. When I kill them, I do not feel vindicated. I feel no elation or sense of revenge satisfied. I feel a small swell of pity, and I feel I have done the person they once were a kindness.

"Cease fire," Sarah called out.

We complied. The horde was only ten meters away now.

"On me."

The riders in front of me followed Sarah as I gave Red a light kick. He stopped sniffing through the snow, raised his head, and set off after the horse in front of him. I had to tug the reins to keep him from getting too close.

We rode westward around the horde until we were directly in their center. Sarah called a halt and we reset formation. I fired the last few rounds in my magazine, dropped it, drew a fresh one, and stowed the old one. A short time later I had to reload again. *Four left*, I told myself.

We had whittled the horde down by half when Sarah called another cease fire and repositioned us. Jones followed along at a distance, one hand resting on a battle axe that looked like something a Viking would carry on a raid. I wondered where he'd gotten the trade to afford something like that. Custom-forged hand weapons are expensive, and guardsmen aren't paid all that well.

The next halt came at the northern side of the horde. The ghouls in front of us were in full disarray, stumbling in the snow and bouncing off one another and tripping over their fallen brethren. I had noticed during the excitement that Sarah and the guardsmen were focused primarily on the front ranks of undead, so I had shifted aim to ghouls farther in the back, anticipating we might have to come at them from the other side. My forethought was paying off.

No grays remained, all of them having died permanently at the outset of the fight. The ghouls still in play were all slower ones, crippled to varying degrees by damaged limbs. And not all of the damage had occurred when they died. Ghouls are clumsy. They tend to trip over things, step on unstable objects, and attempt to cross terrain they simply lack the wherewithal to navigate. The results are dislocated ankles, broken knees, compound fractures, and other severe mechanical injuries. Ghouls feel no pain, but the human machine relies on its component parts for ambulation. Consequently, even in warm weather, these remaining infected would have moved at a snail's pace. In the cold, they were proverbial sitting ducks.

"Open fire."

I was already sighted in and waiting. A ghoul dropped. Then another. And another. And another. Half a magazine emptied itself seemingly of its own volition. I was squeezing the trigger on the sixteenth round when I heard Jones call out behind me.

"Garrett, on our six!"

I turned and my gaze followed where he pointed. A small knot of a dozen or more infected were straggling from the treeline behind us, still over fifty yards away.

One of the duties of the anchor is to watch the team's back and warn of any encroaching hostiles. Jones had done his job. I mentally commended him as I shouted to Sarah. She gave a thumb's up and kept her concentration on the task at hand, trusting me to handle things. I had no intention of letting her down.

"Need a hand?" Jones asked as I rode by.

"No, stay on anchor. Good looking out, by the way."

If he acknowledged, I did not hear it. I slung my rifle across my back and drew my falcata. The wind picked up and drove streamers of stinging white against my eyes, forcing me to stop long enough to don my goggles.

Should have done that from the beginning, numbnuts. You're getting sloppy in your old age. Screw your head on straight and focus.

The voice in my head sounded remarkably like Gunnery Sergeant Tyrone Locklear, the tall, whipcord thin drill instructor with dark black skin and fearsome eyes who, all those years ago on Paris Island, took a raw, oversized eighteen-year-old kid and turned him into a Marine. I shook my head to clear the memories and gripped my sword.

"Come on, Red. Get up."

A light kick, and the horse stretched his legs to a light gallop. I pulled the reins just a bit to slow him down. Red is big and long-legged, not unlike his owner, and when he gets a mind to, he can

103

build up a head of steam. I wanted him moving quickly, but not so quickly I could not swing accurately. When Red slowed to the right speed I loosened my hold on the reins.

We had done this enough times Red knew what to do. Without prompting, he angled toward the infected coming up ahead of us so that we would miss him by less than three feet. I dug my feet into the stirrups and whirled my sword overhead in anticipation of the blow. The blade spun toward my right side, a reminder of a lesson learned the hard way: always swing *away* from your horse.

Not long after acquiring Red, I had been on a patrol not unlike this one. I had ridden him close to a rank of ghouls and swung my falcata in the usual cross-body pattern that I had grown accustomed to. It worked very well when I was standing on the ground with my feet planted. On that day, however, cruising and bouncing along at close to fifteen miles an hour, my aim had been off and my sword glanced off the top of the ghoul's head. I had put too much force in the swing, I realized too late, and could only watch helplessly as the out-of-control blade swept toward my horse's shoulder. Thankfully, the angle was such that the only injury was the last few millimeters of sharp edge drawing a thin line of blood on Red's skin. He barely noticed.

I, on the other hand, had been horrified. A couple of inches lower, and the thick, heavy blade would have buried itself in my horse's shoulder tissue and probably sent us both hurtling and tumbling to our deaths. It was a mistake I had vowed never to repeat.

So as we reached the ghoul, I made sure to swing out, down, and back up on the follow through. I did not look back to see if my aim was true. I could tell by the way it felt: the crunch, the twist of blade through soft brain matter, the way the sword cleared the skull easily and drifted back up to shoulder level without noticeable friction. If I had done it wrong, the blade would have gotten stuck and been wrenched from my grasp. The fact I was still holding it was all the reassurance I needed.

I had just enough time to reposition and swing at the next ghoul. The top half of its head sailed off like a Frisbee, dripping blood and blackish-red brain matter as it flew. The sparkle of my blade's polished steel reminded me of a haiku I read long ago:

The bright blade flashes,

inscribing the final arc

on all tomorrows.

I kept my arm in motion and hit four more undead before hauling the reins to the left and circling for another pass. If my left hand were still fully intact, I would simply have switched grips and reversed direction. But my left hand was not fully intact. A bullet from a Kalashnikov wielded by a piece of marauding scum, who happened to be part of a group calling themselves the Crow Hunters, had taken my left ring finger off at the second knuckle. All that was left was a small nubbin I could wiggle around a little. I had been working on strengthening the hand to compensate, but was not yet confident enough to trust my life to it. I was beginning to wonder if I ever would be.

So I rode back to the other side of the encroaching undead, turned Red toward my targets, and kicked his flanks. Another pass reduced the number of infected to three. Red was showing signs of fatigue, so I let him rest, slid my rifle around, and clipped the last few ghouls with headshots.

Back at the formation, Sarah and the others had cut the horde down to no more than two dozen. Just as I arrived, she called a cease fire.

"All right, that's enough," she said. "Stake your horses and draw hand weapons. Gabe, we good on our six?"

"All clear."

"Good. Get ready to move in on foot. Make sure you cover your eyes and mouths. Riordan, I want you on overwatch."

He looked disappointed. "Will do."

I dismounted, and, from a saddlebag, removed a stake and a short length of rope with a spring-loaded hook clip on one end. The rope had a lanyard spliced into it so it could loop around the stake, which I drove into the ground with the back of my hatchet. Finished, I connected the hook clip to Red's halter.

"Hang out here, big guy. Be right back."

He snorted and lowered his muzzle to root in the snow for dead grass.

The others fanned out at five yard intervals, Riordan still atop his mount with his rifle at the ready should any of us get into trouble. I moved to put my hatchet back in the saddlebag, then looked at it and thought, *why not? It's just a hatchet. If I lose it, I have plenty more. And if I can't hold onto it, I drop it and rely on my sword. Be no worse off than I was before.*

Riordan saw the axe in my left hand and raised his eyebrows as I walked by, but said nothing. I took my place at the end of the line next to McCoy. He held a long, crude cleaver that looked to have been forged from leaf springs. I had seen quite a few of them around lately. A blacksmith had set up shop in nearby Brownsville and was turning out effective, if not aesthetically pleasing weapons and selling them relatively cheap. The others down the line held mostly wood-cutting axes, with the exception of Jones, who hefted his battle-axe with the enthusiasm of a child with a new toy.

Sarah held up a hand. "On my command."

We all looked at her.

"Advance."

We approached the horde at a steady pace. I was tempted to start singing cadence, but knew the distraction would not be appreciated.

The hatchet felt heavy in my gloved left hand. I had cut the ring finger on the glove to size and sewed it shut so it would not interfere with my grip. In fact, I had done the same thing with all my gloves. The first time Allison saw me wearing a pair, she'd said, "Aw, that's so cute. A nubbin sock." I was not amused. She looked at me a moment after speaking and saw something in my eyes that made her face go blank.

"Sorry, Gabe. That was inappropriate."

I grunted and shrugged it off.

To my left, Jones was the first to make contact. There was no whoop of satisfaction, no belligerent shouting, no colorfully worded challenges. Just a grunt of effort, a meaty *thunk*, and the sound of a body collapsing.

I drew close to my first target. She had been a teenage girl, once. Probably had been pretty before a ghoul bit off half her face. A shriveled length of nerve tissue dangled down her cheek, leading me to guess an unsocketed eye once dangled there. Something, somewhere along the way had sheared it off. As I swung my sword into her cranium, I wondered where she had left it and if it was still there, or if it had rotted away.

There was not time for further pondering. Another ghoul, a big one, appeared in front of me. He stumbled on the body of the girl I had just killed, giving me a clear shot at his throat. A swipe of my arm, and his head tumbled to the ground. Immediately to my left, I heard McCoy curse.

"Riordan! Sword's stuck."

"Got it."

Eric's rifle cracked a few times as he covered McCoy. I heard the man grunting and mumbling as he worked to free his weapon, but I did not turn to look. There were too many infected headed my way.

My next two targets were practically tripping over one another. I would not have time to hit one and then the other with just my sword. Time to use the hatchet.

I let them get almost within lunging distance, than sidestepped and lashed out with my hatchet. The sharp blade bit into a skull, crushing the bone as it entered. I gave it a twist and it pulled free. My grip remained firm all throughout the process. I had expected it to slip in my grasp, but it did not. Maybe all those hours spent squeezing a rubber ball were finally paying off.

There was no time to celebrate, however. No sooner than the first ghoul fell, the second was on me. Its hands reached out and latched onto my MOLLE vest with frightening strength. But this was not my first fight. I knew better than to try and dislodge it. Plenty of people had died over the years because they panicked and did exactly that. Rather, the best thing to do was to remain calm and use my natural advantages over the ghoul. Namely agility.

From the corner of my eye, I saw Eric swing his rifle my way. "Gabe, you all right?"

"I'm fine," I shouted.

The first thing I did was cross my left hand over and stick the head of my hatchet in the ghoul's mouth. It bit down on instinct, its jaw muscles flexing hard enough to chip several of its front teeth. The second thing I did was glance behind me to make sure the way was clear and quickly backpedal a few steps. This stretched the ghoul's arms and forced it to struggle to keep up. Now that it was off balance, it was a simple thing to twist my body and sweep the legs from beneath it. I put a knee on its chest, reversed my grip on

108

my sword, and plunged the tip into the ghoul's sinus cavity at the same moment I yanked my hatchet free. Bone crunched and thick blood ran out of the ghoul's face, but its grip did not loosen. I dropped the hatchet and, using my left hand as a hammer, bashed the pommel of my falcata until the tip penetrated through the back of the infected's skull. The grip relaxed and the hands fell free.

I retrieved my hatchet and got back to my feet. Someone else shouted and Eric's rifle gave two muted cracks. The others were hard at work, steadily reducing the infected's numbers. I waded back into the fight, swinging two handed. My arms began to spin in a familiar figure-eight pattern, each swipe sending a ghoul to its final rest. The diminished left hand held up to the strain, fingers one and two and the thumb maintaining grip strength while the little guy in the back assisted with direction and aim.

Finally, there were only two undead left. McCoy decapitated one with his cleaver and Sarah cut down the last one with her long-handled hatchet.

We stood in a loose knot, chests heaving, weapons dripping with gore. Sweat dripped down the center of my back. My core temperature was up, but it would soon drop. And when it did, the biting wind would set me to shivering unless I could get someplace warm. I doubted the others were in any better condition.

"Okay," Sarah said between deep breaths. "Good work. Mount up and let's ride a circle. Make an assessment."

We walked back to our horses, cleaned the brains and bone from our weapons, and got back on our horses. It took another twenty minutes to assess the damage. There were to three-hundred infected down, and no one injured. The horses did not seem the worse for wear. All told, a successful sweep.

"I don't know about you fellas," Sarah said. "But I'm freezing. How about we head home?"

We all agreed this was a good idea.

EIGHT

The bad weather moved out overnight and a clear, bright morning greeted Eric and I as we entered the caravan district.

Sabrina came with us. When asking if she could tag along, she had claimed she wanted to learn more about the business, get a clearer idea of how we conducted operations and who with. But I knew better. Two months with me had not fundamentally changed who she was—a Traveler, one of the tens of thousands of people who stayed alive by staying on the move. She'd had no news from the road in all the time she had been with me, and despite her professed lack of interest thereof, I had no doubt she was curious. I did not blame her. I was curious too.

It was cold that morning, down in the low twenties. Every breath was a white cloud, exposed skin became dry and itchy and red, and ungloved hands quickly numbed until one could not touch pinky finger and thumb together at the tips. The sun was a lemon colored explosion in the sky, its brilliance sharpening the edges of high cirrus clouds on the outskirts of the horizon. A dendritic sprawl of leafless trees lined the distance like a cloak, patches of light skewering the gaps between dark gray limbs. I took a deep breath. The air was clean and bracing.

At least until we reached Spike's caravan.

The air no longer smelled clean. It smelled like horses, cook fires, hot animal fat, and above all, dung. Thankfully, Spike ran a good camp, or it would have been a lot worse. The cook fires were communal, a few people around each one preparing breakfast for more than a dozen others. The animals were corralled in a space provided by the city for the purpose. The wagons were neatly organized, spaced a reasonable distance apart, and covered in case a storm blew up. The tents were also well situated, women and children in the middle and the men on the perimeter. Not that men, women, and children did not spend time together—they did. But when it came time to sleep, the men left the center and took position on the fringes. If a woman wanted to follow her man back to his tent, which happened a lot, she had other women watch her kids until she came back. And they always came back, at least while on the road. Spike was adamant about that. He relaxed the rule in places like Hollow Rock, but made sure everyone knew it was only temporary. I once asked him about it, and he explained his philosophy.

"It's not sexist or anything," he'd said. "The women are armed. They know how to fight too. It's just that they're more valuable than men, you know? A man dies, big deal. There are plenty of other guys in the world. But women, they're important. Kids even more. Women can have children. Kids grow up and carry on our work so there's actually a tomorrow to worry about. So that's how I prioritize it. If it comes to a fight, the men are shock troops. If someone gets past them, God help 'em because the women won't. And if that don't work, the kids got guns too. And I can tell you with authority they ain't afraid to use 'em."

"I believe it," I said.

"I think they got it worst, the kids. They ain't old like we are. They seen too much, too early. They don't remember how things were before. They can be such sweethearts sometimes. But when they have to be, there ain't nothing more ruthless."

I looked at a few small, dirty faces as I walked through the camp. They looked back with hard eyes glittering with distrust. As Spike had said, all but the smallest of them were armed with hand weapons, the older ones with firearms. And 'older' seemed to mean anyone over the age of twelve.

Their mothers hovered nearby, eyes watching, hands going through the routine motions of people who live their lives outdoors and have grown accustomed to the hardships of the road. Meals were made quickly and efficiently. No food was wasted. When people burn an average of five-thousand calories a day just going about their business, leftovers are not a problem. Dishes were cleaned with the minimum water necessary, and what was left was used to douse the cook fires. A gaggle of kids between the ages of five and eleven darted around the animal pens with buckets and small shovels gathering droppings. Most folks in town found this strange, but I knew why they went to the trouble. It was the same reason Sioux children used to gather buffalo turds; dry them out, and they make an excellent fuel that gives off minimal smoke.

"Nothing gets wasted," I muttered.

Sabrina turned her head. "What's that?"

I pointed. "Efficient people."

"Yeah. Have to be. Can't waste things on the road. Got to make the most of everything."

I looked down at my daughter and felt a surge of anger at how much time she had spent on her own. "I'm sorry you had to go through all that, Sabrina. I wish your mother had told me about you. I would have found you. I would have kept you safe."

113

She put her hand in the crook of my arm and held it as we walked. "I know. But what happened, happened. No changing it. We're here now. Best just to move on."

"Yeah."

She looked up at me. "I get the feeling you really do understand what it's like for Travelers. Most people don't."

"I'm not most people."

We found Spike near the edge of the district sitting beside a fire and eating some kind of porridge from a metal bowl. A few others sat around him, men and women with travel-stained clothes and hard, sun-browned faces.

"Mornin', Garrett," Spike said without looking up.

"It certainly is."

His eyes strayed to Sabrina. "Who's the lovely young lady?"

"My daughter, Sabrina."

A moment of silence. "You have a daughter?"

"Apparently so."

"When did this happen?"

"A little over fourteen years ago," Sabrina said. "And stop talking like I'm not fucking here."

The corners of Spike's mouth twitched. "I like you already."

"Everything set?" I asked.

"Yeah. Ready to go." Spike stood up and motioned to two of his people. "Let's get this done. We need to be on the road in two hours."

Eric and I split up and spent the next hour examining the cargo. I knew it was largely a ceremonial thing—Spike had a good reputation for a reason—but in my experience, traders are only as

114

honest as they are forced to be. Just because Spike and I had a good working relationship did not necessarily mean he wouldn't stiff me if he thought he could get away with it.

That said, there was not much to examine. The barrels were all sealed, filled properly, and in good condition. The time consuming part was weighing them. Sabrina helped by keeping a running tally on a notepad, and when the final barrel came off the scale, I glanced at the total.

"You're three pounds light, Spike."

"You told me to take lodging expenses out of the shipment."

"I know what it costs to camp here, even for a caravan this size. A pound and a half should have covered it."

"I bought food as well."

"Not my problem. You're responsible for feeding your people. I never said I would pay for that."

Spike glared a moment, but finally relented. "Fine. Saul, give him back a pound."

"And a half."

"Goddammit, Gabe. It took me twelve weeks to get here."

"For which you were well compensated. Pound and a half."

Saul measured out the salt with Spike looking on in discontent. I think he was less mad about the lost trade than he was about the fact he tried to pull one over on me and got busted in front of his people. I did not feel sorry for him. I run a business, not a charity.

Spike's people unloaded the barrels onto the ground, struck camp, and left through the north gate. Spike did not speak to me, but told Eric to use the usual channels if we wanted to hire him again. They shook on it.

"I think you hurt his feelings," Eric said while we waited for the transport to arrive. The caravan district was empty now, the scents of beasts, wood smoke, and shit still clinging to the air.

"Fuck his feelings. We agreed on a price and he tried to get more than what he negotiated for. These traders see a fortune and think they're entitled to a piece of it just because they did what the hell they were hired to do. I have no patience for that kind of thing."

"You are turning into a cynical, mean-spirited old miser."

"Says the guy who screws the Army like a cheap whore every chance he gets."

"It's not the Army *per se* I like to rip off. Just Captain Harlow."

"Amounts to the same thing."

"We'll have to agree to disagree."

The throaty rumble of a multi-fuel engine cut off the argument. Johnny Greene was in the driver's seat of the transport.

"Sorry I'm late," he said. The brakes squealed as the big all-terrain truck came to a halt.

"What happened?" Eric asked. "You're never late."

"Last guy with the transport was late turning it in."

"Fair enough," I said. "Let's get this stuff loaded."

Johnny pulled a ramp from beneath the cargo hold, opened the bay doors, and wheeled down a pallet jack. Eric and I began loading barrels onto it.

"Hey Dad?"

I looked at Sabrina. It was the first time she had called me 'dad'. I didn't hate it.

"Yeah?"

"Can I drive?"

"Do you know how?"

"Sure."

Eric looked skeptical. "Ever driven anything before?"

"Not exactly."

"So no, you don't know how to drive."

She shrugged.

Eric turned his attention my way. "Gabe?"

What the hell. She called me dad. "She's gotta learn some time."

A shake of the head. "This should be interesting."

*****

"So when are you going to tell me why you bought a metric shit-ton of salt?"

I closed the transport's bay doors and latched them. "Maple syrup was too hard to come by."

The engine rumbled to life and Johnny drove sedately away. The trip to the warehouse had been, as Eric predicted, interesting. It had also taken about five times as long as it should have, and I was reasonably certain Sabrina had reduced the service life of the transport's clutch by at least fifty percent. Eventually, however, she got the hang of it.

"That was fun," my daughter said. "Can I drive next time?"

I smiled at her. "Maybe you should practice on something a little less valuable."

"Like what?"

"Like a horse," Eric said.

"I already know how to ride a horse."

I patted her shoulder. "We'll work something out."

Eric locked up the warehouse and we began ambling back toward home. None of us were in any kind of a hurry. Miranda had little Gabriel, Allison was at the clinic, Elizabeth was doing whatever the hell she does all day, Great Hawk was minding the store, and Johnny Greene would soon be taking over for him.

I tried to keep the Hawk out from behind the counter as much as possible. While he has proven to be a valuable addition to our business, his customer service skills leave something to be desired. Not that he is rude or anything. He is always perfectly courteous. But a six-foot-three Apache with a mohawk, broad shoulders, a gaze that could intimidate a rabid Kodiak, and a minimum of three edged weapons on his person at all times—including a tomahawk forged during the French-Indian war—does not exactly put people at ease. For the most part, he sticks to running our salvage operations. Which is good because it frees Eric to spend more time with his family.

"So what's the deal?"

I glanced at Eric and frowned. "You're not going to let up about this, are you?"

"Nope."

"Figured."

"Why the salt, Gabe? And why so much of it?"

"Let's get home first. This is best discussed over a drink."

We were quiet the rest of the walk. I opened the door and went in first, lit a tallow candle in the kitchen, and fed some wood into

118

the stove. The kettle was already full, so I put it on the stovetop and waited.

Sabrina and Eric took a seat at the table. "You're stalling."

"I'm putting the kettle on. Want some tea?"

"Sure."

"Then shut up and wait."

I could almost feel Eric and Sabrina exchange a glance. My daughter was still a little unsure of herself around me, but she and Eric got along just fine. In fact, they had hit it off from the get-go and had been in cahoots ever since. Even worse, somewhere along the way, they had drawn Elizabeth into their conspiratorial little circle. I was now hopelessly outnumbered, and I did not hold the belief this situation would amend itself any time soon.

The kettle started to whistle while I deposited little white bags into ceramic mugs with the names and skylines of extinct cities on them and poured in the water. Sabrina got Seattle, Chicago went to Eric, and I settled for Los Angeles. I always hated Los Angeles.

"I always wanted to see Los Angeles," Sabrina said.

I grunted disapprovingly. *Figures*. "Trust me, sweetie. You're not missing anything."

"Yeah, I guess. It's overrun now."

"It wasn't much to see *before* it burned to the ground. In fact, L.A. is probably the one place the Outbreak actually improved. It was already full of the walking dead. The Phage just made things official."

"Can we stay on topic?" Eric said. "You're not weaseling out of this one, Gabe."

I waited until my tea finished steeping. Eric sat back in his chair and stared placidly. He was getting good at waiting me out, and Sabrina was starting to pick up the trick as well. I pulled the tea from my cup and set it on the counter. Even used, it still commanded a good price.

"First thing you should know, both of you, is Elizabeth will not be running for reelection this year."

Eric blinked twice and leaned forward. "Are you serious?"

"Yes."

"Why not?"

"Because she doesn't want to."

Eric went through a few false starts and gesticulations. "So who's going to be the mayor?"

"Will Laurel will probably run."

"The captain of the guard?"

"Only Will Laurel I know."

"Who else?"

"Sarah Glover mentioned she might be interested. I doubt she would win, though. Will has lived here a long time. But I think she'll be the next sheriff when Walter Elliott retires. Either one is a good choice. Town can't go wrong whichever way they vote."

Eric's mouth hung open. He tilted his head to the side like a confused dog and wrinkled his brow. "Okay. As interesting as that is, what does it have to do with the price of salt in the wasteland?"

I sipped my tea. "Clever, Eric. I see what you did there."

"Just answer the fucking question."

I let out a long breath and did my best not to stare at the table. "Sabrina, you ever been to Colorado Springs?"

"No."

"Shit," Eric said, drawing the word out. "You gotta be kidding me."

Contrary to popular belief, he really is a bright fellow.

"I think it's time, old friend."

"Why now? After all this time, after all we've done, why now?"

I glanced meaningfully at Sabrina. She looked confused.

"Does Elizabeth know?" Eric asked.

"It's why she's not running for reelection."

"So she's going with you."

I nodded.

Eric said another four-lettered word and inclined his head toward Sabrina. "Might want to discuss it with her."

Sabrina looked at Eric, then at me. "Would someone please explain to me what the hell you two are talking about?"

"I'm leaving Hollow Rock and Elizabeth is coming with me."

Sabrina went still. She did not speak for several seconds. "Okay. Where does that leave me?"

"Wherever you want to be. If you want to stay here, you can. This house will be yours, I'll give you enough trade so you won't have to worry, and you can work for Eric. You'll be safe here."

There was a tremor in her voice. "And if I don't want to stay?"

"You can come with us."

The relief on her face hit me like a thrown knife. She began to tremble. I stood up and walked around the table so I could kneel next to her. When I gathered her into my arms, she did not resist.

"You know, Gabe," Eric said, "not to criticize your parenting style, but you probably should have led off with that last part."

I held my daughter as she put her face against my chest, squeezed her arms around me, and worked to control her breathing. "Yeah. Sorry about that, sweetheart."

"You scared the shit out of me. I thought you wanted to leave me here."

I closed my eyes and shook my head. "Never."

Eric stood up. "We'll talk later."

NINE

One of Eric's better qualities is that he never stays angry for long.

He was calmer the next day, having discussed the situation with Allison, and questioned me at length as to what led me to my decision.

"We got a good thing going here, Gabe," he'd said.

"I know."

"So why walk away?"

"It's not so much walking away as branching out. I'm going to retain my half of the business, less the ten percent interest I'm selling to Great Hawk."

"He told me about that. He's buying part of my stake as well."

"Good."

"But you're leaving town."

"Yes."

"After all we've done to make Hollow Rock a safe place to live."

I did not answer.

"You've got a lot invested in this place."

"I know."

"I can't leave. Allison likes it here, and the baby is too young to travel."

"I know."

Eric stood up and began to pace around his living room. I sat in the recliner and stared at the blank, empty face of the big-screen TV. Now that Eric had electricity, he had connected a DVD player and we had watched a few movies on it. *The Usual Suspects* was one of my favorites. It was refreshing to see the pre-Outbreak world as I remembered it.

"We've been through so much shit together I don't even know where to start," Eric said.

"I think the day I bought the cabin from you would be a good place."

He stopped pacing and put his hands on his hips. "Yeah. I guess it would."

"We made the right decision leaving."

"Yes. Despite everything that's happened since, I agree. It was time to move on."

"So maybe you get why I want to move to the Springs."

Eric's hand rasped across his beard stubble. "No, I'm afraid I still don't. What's the Springs got that Hollow Rock doesn't?"

I reached into my inside jacket pocket and handed him the tube with the letter in it.

"What's this?" He opened the tube and unfurled the letter.

"A letter from Hadrian Flint, director of operations for the Blackthorn Company."

Eric read the letter slowly. I watched his eyes go back to the top of the sheet and he read it again.

"Is this authentic?"

"Spike gave his word it came from Flint himself. Check the signet seal."

Eric pressed the two broken pieces of wax together and let out a low whistle. "Looks pretty authentic to me."

"It's a good opportunity. Perfect, in fact. No more salvaging, no more covert missions, no more risking my neck every time I turn around. My entire adult life, all I've known is fighting. I'm tired, Eric. I'm not getting any younger, and I want what you have—a family."

"You already have a family."

"Not officially. I want to make my adoption of Sabrina legal, and I want to marry Elizabeth."

"You can do that here."

"True, but I can't train Blackthorns from Hollow Rock. It's a good, steady job they're offering me. Good pay. The salt I own is only about a third of my net worth. I can have the rest shipped over in installments. But the salt alone will be enough to buy us a nice house, invest in a few businesses, buy some farm land, that kind of thing. The work will keep me busy while I build wealth and influence."

"I have a concern."

"What?"

Eric looked at the letter again. "Says here you were recommended to Flint by a major client. The only guy we know in the Springs who fits that description is General Jacobs. And out of all the people Jacobs could have recommended, he picked you."

"And?"

"And Jacobs has wanted you to be his personal attack dog for years now. You don't think he's doing this just to get you closer to him, try to exert some pressure?"

"I'm a big boy, Eric. I can handle Jacobs."

"He can make a lot of trouble for you if he wants to."

"Let him try. I'll bury his ass."

"You're serious? You'd kill the head of Army Special Operations?"

"If I have to. I've done worse things."

Eric shook his head and gave me the letter back. I rolled it up and slipped it back into my jacket.

"I hope you know what you're doing."

I flashed a smile. "Nah. I just make shit up as I go."

*****

I had to concede to a few demands.

Elizabeth wanted an actual wedding, not just the announcement and small celebration most people do these days. I told her that could be arranged. She then said she wanted a spring wedding. I said that was fine, but we would have to do it in Colorado.

"Can't we postpone the trip until after the wedding? Maybe mid-April?"

"Sure," I said. "Long as you don't mind dodging infected and marauders all the way across Kansas. Spring is the high season for both. Whereas, if we leave in mid-February, the undead will be frozen and most marauders will be hunkered down for the winter."

"Good point."

Sabrina, for her part, wanted a custom-forged, two-handed minasbad sword and her own M-4. I told her the rifle was not a problem, but I had no idea what a minasbad was. She found a picture of one at the public library and showed it to me. Turns out it is a traditional weapon found in the Philippines—which makes sense considering her background in Kali—basically a medium length sword with a profile similar to my falcata, only straight rather than forward-swept and boasting a sharper tip. Good for both chopping and stabbing. I told her I'd commission the weapon, but I was taking the expense out of her allowance.

"What allowance?"

"The one you won't be getting for a couple of years to pay for that sword."

Her eyes widened and she tilted her head to the side. "But what about all the birthdays and Christmases you missed?"

I tried not to wince. *Damn, she really knows how to twist the knife.* "Fine. But after this, we're even."

"Can I still have the rifle?"

"Whether you want one or not. And you're going to train with it under my supervision until I feel comfortable with your proficiency."

She kissed me on the cheek. "Thanks, Dad."

Elizabeth watched the exchange sitting in my living room with a little smile on her lips. She laughed quietly.

"What?"

"You are in so much trouble."

I watched my daughter walk away and thought, *Yes. I am in a lot of trouble. And I don't care.*

The last person I had to appease was Eric. And by appease, I mean listen with growing frustration while he told me what he was going to do whether I approved of it or not.

"I'm going with you," he told me. We were at my house, it was late evening on January 19th, and he had brought over a bottle of the pre-Outbreak stuff. Jameson's Irish, to be specific.

"That's not necessary, Eric."

"No shit. Tell me something I don't know."

"You have a wife and son. It's going to be a dangerous trip."

"No shit. Tell me something I don't know."

"Spike's caravan is one of the biggest and most heavily-armed running between here and Colorado. There will be plenty of guards, all capable people."

"You know, I'm getting tired of repeating myself."

"Then don't."

Eric took a slug of whisky, breathed deep, and let it out through his nose. "Also, I hired Caleb to come along."

"Caleb Hicks?"

"You know another guy named Caleb?"

"Isn't he still on active duty?"

"For another eighteen months."

"And isn't Echo Company rotating back to Fort Bragg in the spring?"

"That's the plan, from what I hear. But you know how the Army is. Plans have a way of changing without notice or explanation."

I sipped my whisky and pondered that. "How'd you pull it off?"

"The usual method."

"So you bribed Captain Harlow."

"He is a greedy man, full of vice and iniquity."

"How much did he take you for?"

"Two pounds of sugar and fifty pounds of seed potatoes."

I wrinkled my brow and stared over my glass. "The sugar I get. But seed potatoes?"

Eric shrugged. "That's what he asked for."

"Is he starting his own farm or something?"

"Maybe. Makes sense, I guess. If he can feed his troops by farming, it would save him a boat load on expenditures. Which, I'm sure, he would find some way to launder into his own pocket."

"You really think he'd do that?"

"I know you haven't been paying much attention to what goes on at Fort McCray, but I have. And let me tell you, military service is rapidly becoming an entrepreneurial pursuit."

I drank some more whisky. My glass was now empty, so I motioned for Eric to fill it again. "That is monumentally depressing."

"Indeed. But, as in all things, there are opportunities."

"Where'd you get the potatoes?"

"My farm co-op."

"You buy 'em?"

"Didn't have to. First thing I had the co-op folks do when I set them up on my land was build a couple of greenhouses. Provided the materials and everything. They've been growing seed potatoes

129

since the first week of September. Just harvested the first batch a few weeks ago. About three-hundred pounds' worth."

"Impressive. From what I understand of potato farming, they don't grow all that well in greenhouses."

"No, they don't. We had to get creative."

"Don't they also need sulfur and fertilizer?"

"Yes. The sulfur was the easy part. Remember that home and garden place we raided last year?"

"Yes."

"Had tons of the stuff. Literally."

"What about the fertilizer?"

"Co-op folks had their own."

"Where'd they get it?"

"Let's just say nothing goes to waste with those people. Absolutely *nothing*."

"Ah. Understood. So why Hicks?"

"He volunteered."

"Excuse me?"

Another sip, another long breath. "Man this is good stuff. Anyway, we were having drinks a couple days after you told me you were abandoning me, and I was lamenting my woes to our mutual friend. When I mentioned the Blackthorns, and that you were taking a job with them, he got real intense all of a sudden. Like he took off that fake goofy veneer and I was seeing the real Caleb."

"I know exactly what you mean. Seen him do the same thing."

"Right. So he asks me if I'm going with you, and I tell him yes. He says is there any way we can work it out so he can come with us, and I tell him maybe, but it would be expensive. He says he has saved a lot of trade, and he can pay me back, whatever the cost. At this point I'm getting a little curious, so I ask him why he's so fired up about tagging along. Want to take a guess what he told me?"

I held my hands out in a 'how the hell should I know?' gesture.

"Turns out he knows Tyrel Jennings."

"*The* Tyrel Jennings? As in, the founder and managing partner of the Blackthorn Security Company?"

"The very same."

"How's he know that guy?"

"He was kind of mum on the subject—you know how he is—but I gathered Tyrel was a friend of the family, or something to that effect. Known the guy since he was six years old. Worked together for a while in the Springs doing salvage work. Then he got in trouble and had to join the Army. Hasn't seen Jennings since."

I shook my head and chuckled. "Small world."

"And getting smaller."

"Well that explains Hicks. What about you? Why do you want to come?"

"Several reasons."

"Such as?"

"For starters, I really want to see the Springs for myself. I've heard so much about it, but I've never been there."

"Okay. What else?"

"We do business via caravans with folks from the Springs all the time. But I've never met any of them face to face."

"Which is probably for the best."

"Maybe, maybe not. If I can get in good with them, which shouldn't be too hard considering how much trade they've made off of us, maybe I can find other opportunities. Expand operations, take on new lines of business."

"Like what?"

"Farming co-ops need capital. I have plenty of that to loan. And manufacturing is a lucrative field."

"If you can find the necessary resources."

"And the necessary people. Artisans are rare and valuable. But there are a lot of people living in Colorado, and I'm willing to bet with the proper training they could learn a trade."

"Such as?"

"Sawgrass Bowyers in Winfield, Kansas is a thriving endeavor."

"Yes they are."

"They're also small time, and they charge an arm and a leg for what they sell."

"Their stuff is worth it. Ever seen one of their crossbows?"

"I have. And sure, they're well made. But they use old-school methods. I'm willing to bet I could come up with a manufacturing process that produces crossbows and bolts of similar quality at a fraction of the price."

"How do you plan to pull that off?"

"The old fashioned way. Headhunting and economy of scale."

"So you're going to steal employees from Sawgrass?"

"Only if I can't find a good bowyer elsewhere."

I had to smile at Eric's audacity. "You don't do anything half-assed, do you?"

"Hey, if you're gonna dream, dream big. Which brings me to my next idea."

"And what's that?"

Another swig of whisky. "Great Hawk made some rumblings about starting his own private security company."

I was quiet a few seconds. "Did he now?"

"Yep."

"Hmm. Does he intend to compete with the Blackthorns?"

"Not necessarily."

"I don't follow."

"Well, we happen to know this guy who might be working for the Blackthorns pretty soon. Maybe we could leverage what you know, and what Great Hawk knows, and create some kind of strategic partnership."

"I doubt they would be interested."

"Only because they haven't heard my sales pitch."

I crossed my arms and leaned back. "Then let's hear it."

Eric sat up straight and used his Earnest Concerned Citizen voice. "How many men does the Blackthorn Company currently employ? Two hundred? Three? What's the attrition rate compared to the number of men who pass training and are selected to wear the uniform and take contracts?"

"Good question."

"And how much does it cost to hire one of these men? Let's say you're paying in ammunition; .22 long rifle and .22 magnum are always in demand. If I were to pay half of the fee with LR, and the other half with magnum, how much would it cost to hire a single Blackthorn for twelve weeks?"

"A hundred rounds LR and fifty magnum per week."

133

"A princely sum. Now convert that to other forms of trade, and you'll see the dilemma these prices create. Only the most prosperous of traders can afford that kind of protection."

"You say that like it's a problem."

"For you, no. There are plenty of people willing to pay those prices and then some. But what about everyone else?"

"What about them?"

"Have you ever heard the phrase, 'untapped market'?"

"I think I see where you're going with this."

Eric went on as if I had not spoken. "Did you know it's been almost four years since the Outbreak?"

"Yes. I know how to read a calendar."

"Of course, of course. Did you also know that during the first six months of the Outbreak more than two-hundred thousand survivors joined the Armed Services, and that most of them served in Army infantry units?"

"I was not aware. Where'd you find that out?"

"It's a matter of public record. You know those bulletins they read out over the radio every Saturday?"

"I am aware they exist. I generally choose not to listen to them."

"Why not?"

"Because they're as boring as they are depressing."

"Well, if you had listened to them, you would be armed with the facts I just related. Now, I'm sure you're asking yourself, 'how does that relate to the topic at hand'? I'll tell you how. Look at the timeline. In the next few months, those enlistments are going to expire. Now, I know a great many soldiers will reenlist, and I commend them for doing so. Our country needs soldiers. But quite a number will also be taking their walking papers. At a conservative estimate, let's say twenty percent decide to get out."

"I think it will be a lot more than that."

"Like I said, a conservative estimate. What is twenty percent of two-hundred thousand?"

"Forty thousand."

"Exactly. Forty thousand hardened, experienced soldiers. Men who have spent the last four years fighting infected, and marauders, and insurgents, and every other hellish challenge the wastelands could throw at them. And not only did they survive, they *won*. The Center for Revenant Extermination estimates that more than ninety million infected have been wiped out since they started using satellite data to estimate the undead population. And while individual citizens certainly account for a not insignificant amount of that, I think I can say unequivocally that without the Army's courageous efforts, that number would be far, far lower."

"Can't argue with that."

"The Midwest Alliance is no more. The Republic of California is hemmed in. With every passing month, more and more marauders are apprehended or killed. The roads are getting safer. Trade is on the rebound. The economy is beginning to recover. And none of it would have been possible without these soldiers."

"Can't argue with that either."

"Now one problem we still have, the same problem we had before the Outbreak, is when these troops leave the service, what do we do with them?"

"What indeed?"

"They're going to need work. But what can they do? Do they know how to farm? How to build? Maybe some do. But most probably don't have marketable job skills. So again, what are they going to do?"

"Resort to banditry?"

"You shouldn't make jokes. It is a very real possibility. But I have a better solution."

"And what's that?"

At this, Eric gave a broad, toothy grin. "They can come work for me and my associates at Great Hawk Security."

"Great Hawk Security?"

"Hey, it was his idea, so he gets to pick the name."

"Okay. Go on."

"We have the capital. We have a qualified trainer, a Navy SEAL like Mr. Jennings. And if we can establish a base of operations in Colorado Springs, we'll have access to as many troops as we desire. Great Hawk believes that if we select qualified, motivated candidates, we can prepare them for a career in private security in as little as three months."

"Three months?"

"Of very intensive training, utilizing seasoned troops, supervised by the Hawk himself. Of course, if anyone in the special operations community would like to apply to be an instructor, they are more than welcome to do so."

I felt my mouth stretch into a grin. "I gotta admit. I like it."

"And, if we were to operate as a subsidiary of the Blackthorn Company, well, that would only add to our prestige. And by making well-trained, armed security personnel widely available, we can decrease the costs involved significantly. This will allow us to take contracts from traders who ordinarily would not have been able to afford such services. And Gabe, let me tell you, there are a hell of a lot of them. It's the way retail works. To put it in pre-

Outbreak terms, you don't need a thousand customers to pay a hundred-thousand dollars each when you can get a million customers to pay a hundred dollars each."

"You make the same money either way."

"Exactly."

"Won't this undercut the Blackthorns?"

"Absolutely not. We'll offer tiered services, with the Blackthorns being reserved for the most elite clientele with the most sensitive needs."

"Elite clientele? Sensitive needs?"

"Hey, it's good advertising copy. Rich assholes like to feel important."

"*We* are rich assholes."

"*I* am merely rich. *You* are the asshole."

I tossed back the rest of my whisky and tapped the rim. Eric poured in two fingers. "You know, Riordan, you might be on to something with this."

"It's about time you admitted to being an asshole."

"Not that, idiot."

He held up a hand. "I know. And you're right. I think with the Hawk's know-how and my business savvy, we can make this work."

"It's possible. It's also academic."

"How so?"

"Your entire enterprise is contingent on us making it to Colorado Springs alive."

"Yeah, well, just because we're on step one doesn't mean I shouldn't be thinking about steps two through twelve."

I nodded. Eric finished his whiskey, stuffed the bottle into his coat, and bid me a good day. I sat in the stillness of my kitchen, looked out the window, and watched light flakes of snow descend from a dark iron sky. It would be cold in Kansas. The winds would be strong.

I went to my office, took out a pen and a notepad, and started planning.

TEN

The next month was a busy one.

I gave my list of supplies, gear, and other necessities to Eric and trusted him to see to the logistics. He's good with that sort of thing. I could have done it myself, but Eric was willing and I had more pressing concerns.

Sabrina turned out to be hell on wheels with a knife, but was not such a great shot with anything but her little Marlin rifle. She mostly used her pistols against the living, and only at close range. Anything beyond ten meters and her accuracy plummeted. So we spent two or three hours a day at the Militia's range at Fort McCray working on her marksmanship. She learned quickly, and by the end of the second week I was confident she had mastered the basics. From then on, we ran drills at the live-fire confidence course and the close-quarters combat facility.

I had expected some push-back from her during all this, but she surprised me by seeming to enjoy the experience. She had a keen interest in anything that increased her odds of survival, be it weapons training, wilderness survival, guerilla tactics, or whatever else. In working with her, I came to understand she possessed keen intelligence combined with cold, calculating ruthlessness. Rather than rely on intimidation, brute force, and superior fighting skill—otherwise known as my methods—she opted for deception and speed. During our few practice fights, I learned just how quick she was with those two little curved daggers of hers. And how lethal.

On the first day of February, Elizabeth held a town hall meeting to let everyone know she was not running for reelection. Further, she informed them she would be leaving Hollow Rock in two weeks and would be turning administration of the city over to the city council, who would elect a mayor pro-temp. This news was not well received.

In her farewell speech, Elizabeth highlighted how the town had gone from seven hundred residents to more than three thousand, and in a time when most of the country had been devastated, her city had risen to the challenge and not only survived, but prospered. She said this was not simply because of her leadership, but because the people of Hollow Rock were decent, honest, hard-working folks who were willing to work to build a future and willing to fight to defend it. She told the townsfolk she was not worried what would happen to them because she knew they were tough, self-sufficient people who could hold their community together regardless of who sat behind the mayor's desk. She also informed the townsfolk the city council was more than qualified to run things until November, being that they ran most of the city's day to day operations anyway. The only difference, for the most part, would be someone else's signature on the daily mountain of paperwork.

After the meeting, when all the hands had been shaken and all the goodbyes said, I commented that Elizabeth failed to mention the city council had known of her intentions for months and had plenty of time to plan accordingly.

"What difference does it make?" she said. "Do they really need to know? Will it help them sleep better at night?"

"Probably not."

"Well there you go."

Elizabeth came over the night before we left. She had sold or given away everything she owned that was not coming with us to Colorado Springs. Her worldly possessions barely took up half a wagon, including her savings, which, at my recommendation, she had converted to non-perishable marketable commodities including a ten-gallon steel drum of Mike Stall's high-quality moonshine, twenty pounds of sugar, ten pounds of water purification tablets, fifty pounds of dried beans, and fifty pounds of winter wheat seed, all locked in fiberglass crates.

"Why seed grain? Why not just buy regular wheat or flour?" she asked me. "Isn't that valuable enough?"

"The seeds I'm buying for you are heritage grains from organic growers donated by the Phoenix Initiative, not the genetically engineered pre-Outbreak stuff. In other words, after harvest, you can keep some of the grains and replant them to make more wheat. Can't do that with the grains we used in the old days."

"Oh. So they're sustainable."

"Exactly. Which makes seed grain far more valuable than harvested wheat or flour."

"Gotcha."

The night before we left, Elizabeth made dinner. The three of us, my soon-to-be wife, my daughter and I, ate together at the little table in my kitchen. I looked at their faces in the candlelight and watched them talk and smile and laugh and wondered at how natural it all felt. Like this was the way things should have been all along. I thought of Karen and wondered what might have happened if I'd just sought counseling and not gone off the deep

141

end with anger and depression and hard liquor. I may as well have sat there and wondered what would have happened if I hadn't joined the Marines. I would probably be dead, I never would have met Karen, and I never would have fathered Sabrina. I also never would have worked for Aegis Incorporated or learned of the Reanimation Phage. I never would have stolen that gold in Afghanistan, never would have smuggled it into accounts in Switzerland and the Cayman Islands, never would have bought that cabin from Eric, never would have met the best friend I have ever had. I was not willing to say things had turned out well since the Outbreak, but for me, they could have been a hell of a lot worse.

Sabrina turned in early, as she always does, and Elizabeth and I filled the tub with hot water and took a bath together. It was probably going to be a month or more before either of us would have another opportunity to properly bathe, so we decided to do so while we could.

I lay on my back in the tub, Elizabeth sitting astride me. We held each other for a while, and when she noticed how happy I was to see her, she sat up and kissed my neck. I made a noise deep in my chest and she pressed her lips over mine, our mouths opening, her soft tongue touching mine with an electric jolt. When the pressure became too much to bear, we dried off and retired to the bedroom. I lit a candle so I could see her.

At thirty-eight years old, she has the body of a much younger woman. She is tall, about five-foot ten, and broadly built. Not fat at all, just well-constructed. Her arms and shoulders are striated with muscle, there are small, graceful ridges in her abdomen, and the flare of her hips is wide and perfectly curved. Her breasts are probably not as firm as they were when she was younger, but they are still heavy and beautiful. I love the weight of them in my hands, the way her nipples become erect when I kiss them. She has wide-set brown eyes, dark wavy hair, and a full, sensuous mouth. Sometimes I lie in bed next to her at night and stare at her lips, marveling at how gorgeously shaped they are. It is a constant struggle not to kiss her every time I look at her. Sometimes I do not succeed. Thus far, she hasn't complained.

We made love quietly so as not to wake Sabrina. I took my time, not wanting the deliciousness of it to end. We started out with Elizabeth beneath me, and as always, she somehow wound up on top. I could not say exactly how it happened, as I was too lost in the process.

I knew she was close to orgasm when her nails bit into my chest and her hips ground forward and back at a frantic pace. Her eyes pinched shut, a red flush spread form her chest all to the way to her face, and her white teeth bit down on her lower lip. She did not cry out, but could not stop a low, repetitive moan from escaping her throat.

I held out as long as I could, but when she went over the edge, the grinding and the warm wetness and the little convulsions inside of her were more than I could take. I gripped her thighs and surged upward. I knew Elizabeth would have finger-shaped bruises on her legs tomorrow, but at that moment, I didn't care. All I could think about was the fire roaring through me, the clenching of muscles deep in my groin, and the satisfying sound of Elizabeth's ragged breath.

When it was over, Elizabeth collapsed on top of me, her soft skin damp with sweat. I ran my hands over her back and kissed the tops of her shoulders.

"That," she said, "was awesome."

I found I could not disagree. Neither of us had any trouble sleeping that night.

*****

There was nothing poignant about leaving Hollow Rock.

A stable boy came by that morning and collected Red and all his tack and said he would meet me at Spike's caravan. I tipped him a couple of shotgun shells. He accepted them gladly and said he would miss having me around, and good luck on the journey. I wished him the same.

"But I'm not going anywhere," the boy said.

"We're all on a journey, son. Just a question of how far it takes you."

It was a bitterly cold morning, the sun just barely beginning to stretch its golden fingers over the eastern horizon. The sky was clear and dark, the color of Rocky Mountain granite. A half-moon hung brightly in the sky, casting silvery light on the world below. Most of the town was catching their last hour of sleep, the promise of morning within reach. All was still and quiet, the air biting sharp against the skin of my face.

Sabrina and Elizabeth walked with me. We were dressed in warm travel clothes and carried rucksacks filled with a few items we had not yet delivered to the caravan. I had left behind all the furniture in my house, as it did not actually belong to me. The place I'd lived for the last couple of years belonged to Allison Riordan, who had inherited it from her grandmother. The furniture had been there when I moved in. I did not know who would live there next—Allison would probably rent the place out—but at least it would be fully furnished.

The stillness and peace of the morning ended when we reached the caravan district. Spike's people had already struck camp and were ready to leave. Lined up in front of the north gate were nearly a hundred wagons in orderly rows and twice again as many pack mules laden with supplies tethered to the backs of carts. The wagons contained mostly cargo, the accumulated trade of nearly three months on the road. Spike had turned a profit bringing his shipment out here, and he would turn another one when he returned to Colorado Springs with all he had acquired along the way. There would be numerous stops in towns along the trade routes to resupply and send messages.

Spike saw us coming and shouted something to one of his men. I was too far away to hear it, but guessed the meaning when one of his people kicked his mount and rode toward us. I scanned the setup as he approached. Most of the caravaners rode in the wagons, but there were thirty people on horseback, all men and all heavily armed. I noticed two of them wore the distinctive dark uniform of the Blackthorns. It appeared as if Spike had put them in charge of the security detail.

"Mr. Garrett?" the rider said as he reached us.

"That's me."

The man dismounted. He was medium in height and build, brown hair and beard, and a hard, tanned face with pale green eyes. The hand holding his horse's reins was dark, calloused, and criss-crossed with thin scars.

"Name's Weidman. Be showing you to your wagon."

I made a gesture. "Lead the way."

We walked abreast of his horse, a magnificent Arabian with a powerful look about him. Arabians are spirited animals, and can be difficult to manage for the inexperienced, but their endurance and toughness is virtually unmatched. I planned to purchase one for Sabrina once we reached Colorado.

Weidman led us to a wagon in the middle of the convoy. Like all Spike's wagons, it was custom built with a steel frame, wooden flooring and box walls, a dome-shaped cover lined with camouflage-painted tarpaulin, and large steel wheels treaded with hard rubber. Each wheel boasted its own independent suspension system consisting of springs and shocks cannibalized from scrap automobiles. I had ridden in many wagons like this one, and they were a damn sight better than the rickety shit-heaps the pioneers had taken to Oregon and elsewhere.

The wagon was filled with supplies, per my instructions. Red was also waiting for me, a blanket draped over his back and his halter tied to a steel ring screwed into the tailgate post. He clopped over when he noticed me and nudged me with his big, smelly muzzle. I scratched him behind the ears and said some low, soothing words. Mollified, he went back to snuffling the frozen ground.

"Everything in order?" Weidman asked.

"Good so far. Where's my cargo?"

Weidman pointed. "See the numbers painted on the sides of the carts?"

"Yep."

"Yours are forty-two through forty-seven."

"Mind if I take a look?"

"Better hurry. We leave in fifteen minutes."

"Will do."

I quickly saddled Red and rode him to the third rank of wagons lined up in front of the gate. The man driving number forty-two handed me a shipping manifest. I read it over, then looked into the wagons and counted the salt barrels. They were all accounted for, as well as the other trade I was bringing with me.

"All right," I told the driver, handing back the manifest. "Thanks for your time."

He grunted. I rode away.

Back at the wagon, Sabrina and Elizabeth had thrown their rucksacks in the cargo area and made themselves comfortable on

146

the bench. I unsaddled Red, tethered him to the tailgate post, and fed him a handful of grain from a feed sack. While he chewed, I climbed into the driver's seat and took up the reins. The animals pulling us were a team of four oxen. Elizabeth put a hand on my arm and pointed at the stinking, bulky creatures.

"Do we have to, you know, take care of those things?"

"No. Spike has people who'll do that for us when we stop for the night. All we have to do is drive the wagon and try not to steer them off a cliff."

"Oh. Well that's good."

"What if infected come?" Sabrina said. "This caravan is going to be loud."

"If we're on the road, we leave it to the security detail. When we stop, the wagons will be arranged in a two-layer square formation. Women and children will sleep inside the formation, men on the perimeter. No exceptions."

"So you won't be in the tent with us?" Elizabeth said. She did not look happy with this development.

"Not after nightfall."

"So who's going to keep me warm at night?"

I smiled at her. "You can snuggle up with Sabrina."

The girl snorted. "Not likely. I have a tendency to hit people who touch me in my sleep. No offense, Liz."

"None taken."

My fiancé still did not look happy. I reached out and held her hand. "It's only for a few weeks. Then we can go back to our usual tangle of limbs."

"I like our tangle of limbs. It's comforting and good for circulation."

147

"Among other things."

Sabrina rolled her eyes. "For Christ's sake. You know I can hear you two, right?"

I started to say something, then heard the creak and rattle of a buggy-for-hire pulling up in the row between wagons. A familiar voice called out to me.

"Looks like I caught you just in time," Eric said.

I turned and watched him pay the driver with a pair of .308 rounds. Caleb Hicks hopped out of the back. He was dressed in fatigues and carried a large rucksack on his back and a smaller go-bag in his right hand. There was a pistol in his chest rig, an M-4 hanging from a tactical sling on his chest, and on either side of his pack were lashed two long-guns. One was a Benelli combat shotgun and the other was a .308 SCAR battle rifle in sniper configuration. In his left hand he held his short-handled spear. Eric was similarly armed, although his sniper rifle was an M-110 I had given him a couple of years ago.

"Better hop in," I said. "We're leaving in a few minutes."

Eric clambered aboard, stowed his gear in the back, and sat on one of the short seats just behind the bench. Caleb took the seat on the other side. Sabrina looked at him a moment with brow furrowed, then pointed a finger.

"I recognize you. You were the guy at the gate when I first got here."

The young man held out a hand. "Sergeant Caleb Hicks, First Reconnaissance Expeditionary."

"Sabrina Garrett. I have no idea what an expedition whatever-the-fuck is."

For maybe the third time since I'd met him, Caleb laughed out loud. "I'm in the Army."

"Yeah, I kind of figured that one out on my own. What are you doing here?"

He nodded toward Eric. "Ask him."

Sabrina turned. "Well?"

"He's hired muscle."

"Can we trust him?"

"I do."

"I'll second that," I said. Sabrina turned her gray eyes toward me.

"Really?"

"Bet your life on it."

The suspicion left her gaze as she reassessed Caleb. Her eyes started at his face and traveled slowly down to his feet and back up again. Her head tilted to one side and I saw a ripple of something in her expression I was pretty sure I did not like.

"All right then, blue-eyes. Welcome aboard."

I glared at both of them. Sabrina did not notice. Caleb merely shrugged as if to say, *what do you want me to do about it*? Beside me, Elizabeth twitched convulsively and covered her mouth.

"You know what they say about Traveler women," she whispered.

"Sweetheart, I love you dearly, but please stop talking."

*****

We rode out the north gate in a cacophony of rattling and animal grunts and clopping of hooves. Once outside the wall, the noise wasn't so bad. No close buildings to reflect sound back at us.

149

The caravan swung westward along the crumbling remnants of the old highway.

I took a moment to look back at the place I had called home for nearly two years. It looked different than when I had first arrived. The wall had been reinforced with another layer of wooden palisade. The expansion was coming along nicely; in two or three weeks it would be finished. There were more guards on the catwalks and in the towers. Men on horseback patrolled the outer edge of the field surrounding town, eyes searching the forest for signs of infected. When we approached the edge of the wall on the western side, I caught sight of movement and looked toward it. Standing at the corner was Lincoln Great Hawk. We had already said our goodbyes and settled our business transactions, but it was nice to see the big Apache had taken the time to see me off. I waved to him, and he waved back. His expression did not change, but he gave a single nod of his head as I rode by. For the Hawk, that was practically wailing and throwing flower petals.

Then we were past the wall. The caravan plodded slowly forward and the town behind me grew smaller and more distant. Eventually, we topped a rise, went down the other side, and Hollow Rock disappeared from view. I did not look back, but I did wonder if I would ever see the place again.

A warm hand slid into the crook of my elbow and I felt soft lips press against my cheek.

"Everything's going to be fine," Elizabeth said. "We're making the right decision."

I looked into her eyes and felt I could drown in them, like being pulled into a dark, inviting ocean. "I know."

The sky was dark blue to the west. A cold wind picked up from the north and made the wagon sway from side to side. I stared into the distance and felt something within me fade and lighten, as if a part of me had come untethered and drifted off on the breeze.

150

It felt good to be on the road.

ELEVEN

Heinrich stayed with the wagons while his men rode forth to scout the road ahead.

He was dressed like a trader, heavily armed and wearing leather anti-ghoul armor over his arms, shoulders, midsection, and lower legs. His men were similarly attired, all two-hundred and thirty-four of them.

The raider chief had spent the last two months in the vast openness of northern Kansas training his new recruits. He had started out with two-hundred and seventy, but thirty-six had not made the cut. Some attempted to desert and were caught and executed. A few others died in training, something he had warned them could happen because of the intensity and harshness of what he was putting them though. The rest died from accidents and mishaps. Or, as Heinrich thought of them, idiotic mistakes. Not that he mourned the fallen—far from it. Rather, he found there was something appealingly Darwinian about weeding out the weak, the frightened, and the truly stupid.

Now what remained was a hardy fighting force led by the small number of veteran raiders Heinrich had started out with. He had retained the title of chief instead of naming himself a general, figuring it would be too confusing for the men who had been with him from the beginning. He had made Maru and Carter his two colonels, promoted the other squad leaders to majors, and assigned the rest of his original band as lieutenants. The twenty-six sergeants in the tribe, each heading up his own squad and answering to some lieutenant or another, had been promoted from within the ranks of the newcomers.

The rules were simple: Heinrich's word was law. The rank structure was strictly enforced. Everyone was to conduct themselves as if they were humble traders until told not to. When it came time to do their bloody work, everyone fought. Cowardice was punished with brutal permanence. Valor was richly rewarded. Anything more complicated than that, Heinrich theorized, would only lead to unnecessary confusion.

The day was waning, the last light of the low winter sun fading under the onslaught of nightfall. Heinrich waited patiently, hands loose on the reins of the team of oxen that had spent the day pulling his cart. Just as the first stars came out, his men returned to camp and rode over to Maru to make their report. The big Maori listened to them, then motioned to one of the riders and began heading in Heinrich's direction.

"What did you find?" Heinrich asked when they arrived. Maru told the man next to him to give his report.

"Caravan about five miles ahead, sir," the new recruit said. "Moving along Highway 56."

"Disposition?"

"I counted fourteen wagons, twelve men on horseback. Maybe forty people total, all armed."

"Any Blackthorns?"

153

"I didn't see any, sir."

Heinrich rubbed his chin. "Doesn't mean they're not there. What do you think Maru?"

"We should send a couple of scouts to trail them. Get a look at 'em in the morning. If it's like the man says, we get out ahead of them and set up an ambush."

"I concur. Send Locke. Have him take one of the new guys, show him how it's done."

"Right, Chief."

*****

Dawn brought with it the beginnings of a storm. The wind was cold and hard and unrelenting. Heinrich sat on his horse wearing a gray cloak sewn from a pair of wool Army blankets. The cloak's hood hid his face from view, only the dark brown of his scarf visible beneath the cowl. Heinrich could see the fires of the caravan he was tracking in the distance. They did not look far away, but out here on the plains, things were often more distant than they seemed.

Maru, Locke, and the newcomer scout he had spoken with the day before emerged from the treeline to his right, riding hard. Heinrich nodded to them when they arrived.

"Were you seen?"

"Don't think so, Chief," Maru said.

"What did you find?"

Maru jerked his head toward the scout. "Just like he said."

"Blackthorns?"

"Didn't see any. Or anybody who moved like 'em."

154

Heinrich nodded approvingly. "Go find Carter. Tell him to take two squads and block their road to the east. You and Fallon set up on their flanks. Make sure everyone stays hidden. Use your ghillie suits."

"Right, Chief."

"Do not fully engage. Take potshots on Carter's signal and keep them pinned down. I'll ride in with the rest of the men and nail them from behind. Try to spare the women if you can."

"Kids?"

Heinrich shook his head. "Slaves are small time. We're done with that. But the men haven't fucked anything in a while. Bad for morale."

"Right, Chief."

"Set radios to channel eight." With that, Heinrich rode back to the wagons waiting behind him.

Four hours later, everyone was in place. Heinrich keyed his radio. "Carter, commence the attack."

Two seconds passed. Carter acknowledged by shooting the driver of the lead wagon in the chest and then cutting the legs out from under one of the oxen pulling his cart. The confusion was immediate. The wounded ox thrashed helplessly on the ground, bleeding and mewling in agony. Shouts went up and down the line of traders as they floundered to rouse themselves from shocked surprise and circle the wagons. Before they could, more shots came at them from the north and south simultaneously.

Despite their surprise, the traders moved quickly once they knew what they faced. A few leaders took charge and organized everyone, getting them into defensive positions. As they did, the men on horseback rode fast circles around the wagon train, pouring suppressing fire in the general direction of where the shots were

155

coming from. Problem was, the shots seemed to be coming from everywhere at once.

"Ready for you anytime, Chief," Carter said into his radio.

"On our way," Heinrich replied. "Standby."

He had left the ambush location up to Carter, and as usual, he had picked a good one. Heinrich and his men waited inside the barn of an abandoned farmstead a few hundred yards off the highway. The flat, open terrain left them nowhere to hide, making the barn ideal.

Fifty men on horseback crowded flank to flank inside the barn while the rest of the Storm Road Tribe hid behind the barn, awaiting orders. There were not enough horses for everyone, so the rank and file would have to charge in on foot. Light infantry, Heinrich called them to their faces. They seemed to like the title. Inwardly, he knew they were nothing more than cannon fodder.

Heinrich keyed his radio. "Rourke, do you copy?"

"Lima Charlie, Chief."

"Proceed with silent charge. Stay low and quiet, and try not to let them spot you too far out."

"Roger that. On our way."

He heard the sound of boots pounding over cold earth and frozen snow as the infantry departed. "Carter, let me know when the infantry is engaged."

"Copy, Chief."

Then Heinrich waited. The popping of gunfire and screams of wounded and dying men reached him despite the distance and the walls of the barn. He hoped there were not too many infected around. It did not occur to him to wonder how many men he was losing.

"Infantry is engaged, Chief."

156

"Roger. On our way." He motioned to a man posted by the barn door. "Open it up."

The door opened and the riders trotted out in orderly fashion. Heinrich rode up and down the ranks and dressed the men into a wide skirmish line. When they were properly arrayed, he gave the order to move out.

It took less than a minute to come within sight of the caravan. The infantry troops had spread out into two large units and had enveloped the wagon train in a classic pincer maneuver. The ambushers on the north, south, and east sides of the highway had ceased fire and were awaiting orders.

He ordered his men to charge. As his mount increased pace to a gallop and the thunder of hooves reverberated on both sides of him, he watched three of his men throw pipe bombs over the circled wagons and into the cluster of defenders within. He could not see how many traders were hit, but it was enough to allow the infantry troops to seize the reins of a team of oxen and drag them away from the circle. They did not make it far, however, because the brake on the wagon was set, forcing a raider to leap into the driver's seat to disengage it. He caught a bullet in the shoulder for his efforts and tumbled screaming to the ground. Despite this, Heinrich grinned as the wagon was pulled out of formation. He spurred his horse to move faster and rode beside one of his cavalry squad leaders.

"Blain! Take your men and ride for the breach!"

Blain nodded to show he'd heard the order and complied. Heinrich raised his hand and gave two signals, the first telling the cavalry to slow down, the second telling them to fall in with Blain's squad. The men did as they had been trained to do.

Blain's cavalrymen hit the wagon train like a hammer, tearing into the traders within and riding over any who got in their way. Heinrich broke off, signaled for the rest of the cavalry to follow him, and rode a circle around the wagons. As he did so, Blain led his men around the interior of the defenses and then rode back out through the breach. He exited just ahead of Heinrich, who led his squad of hand-selected raiders into the breach and hit the traders again. He quickly realized he should not have bothered. Only a few defenders remained. One tried to take aim at him, but Heinrich was faster. Two cracks from his pistol and the man fell over backward. A few of his other men fired pistols or swung hand weapons into the faces of people trying to pull them from their mounts. As Heinrich exited the breach, he signaled his men to leave off and ordered the infantry to move in and neutralize any remaining hostiles.

At a signal from their chief, the cavalry backed off. Heinrich found Blain and his men and commended them for their efficiency and competence. He told Blain to send two dozen men to set up a perimeter and patrol it.

"No one comes in, no one goes out. Understood?"

"Yes sir," Blain said.

"Good. Make it happen."

Heinrich smiled as the man rode off. He could tell by the look in Blain's eyes he'd created another convert. He'd given the man a chance to be strong, to be powerful, to prove himself. And he had. He'd absorbed Heinrich's praise like a sponge absorbs water. Now he would be loyal. Now he would be fearless. It would probably get him killed someday, but in the meantime, he would be very useful.

*****

"Can you believe the fucking luck, Chief?"

158

Heinrich smiled at Carter. "A few months ago I'd have said I didn't believe in luck. But now ..."

Carter picked up an RPG launcher and looked it over. "Two years. Two years of feed bags and junk and slaves and a little food and guns and ammo here and there, and now look at us. And all it took was two good scores."

Heinrich scanned the loot they'd won. Three of the fourteen wagons had been loaded with supplies obviously meant for the traders to subsist on during their journey. The rest, however, had contained trade goods. Food, grain, liquor, crossbows, bolts, and in the false bottoms of two wagons, they had discovered twelve RPG launchers and forty rockets. Just two of the launchers and ten of the rockets would have been worth more than the rest of the trade combined. But Heinrich had no intention of selling them. These weapons had a grander destiny.

Maru approached and tapped his machete against his chest by way of salute. "Finished the BDA, Chief."

Heinrich noticed a new guy standing nearby glance at Maru in confusion. "Stands for battle damage assessment," he told him.

"Oh. Thank you, sir."

Heinrich turned back to Maru. "What did you find?"

"Four women still alive. Not pretty, but serviceable."

"Good. What else?"

"Rest of the traders are dead except two. One of the new guys, fella named Wells, is interrogating them."

Heinrich looked at Carter. "Kindly go supervise. Make sure he doesn't kill them before we find out where they got these RPGs."

"Will do, Chief."

As he walked away, Heinrich asked, "How many men did we lose?"

159

"Two dead, one wounded."

"Wounded man the guy got shot in the shoulder?"

"Same one."

"What's the damage?"

"Not bad. Didn't hit any bones or arteries, medic got the bleeding stopped. Be out of commission a few weeks, though."

Heinrich stepped down from the wagon and began walking toward where his men were setting up a perimeter. "He still has one good arm. Tell him to help out around camp until he's ready to fight again."

"Understood."

"And give him first crack at the women. Tell him I saw what he did, saw him go down. Tell him I said courage like that deserves to be rewarded."

"Will do, Chief."

Heinrich stopped and watched his men work. Maru stood with him, a silent presence to his left. After the fight, they had loaded the dead into the wagons and moved everything back to the farmstead where it could be hidden from passersby on the highway. That done, they had hauled the dead into an empty field, set a burial detail for the fallen raiders, and went to work putting up a government-issue anti-revenant temporary settlement barricade. Or, as it was more commonly known, a cable fence.

The barricade consisted of galvanized steel posts standing nine feet tall, each driven into the ground eight feet apart, with enough half-inch steel cable to surround an eighth of a mile square encampment. His men used post-hole diggers and manually rotated augers to dig the holes for the posts, used sledgehammers to pack them in with dirt, then strung the cables up the posts eight inches apart from bottom to top. The cables were then tightened at various intervals around the perimeter using heavy duty turnbuckles and torque wrenches to ensure proper tension. The men would camp inside the main perimeter while a larger, less heavily reinforced cable fence was set up for the livestock. This one was designed not so much to keep the infected out, but to keep the animals in. If a large horde of ghouls showed up, the raiders would simply release the livestock. The animals knew where their food came from, so if released, no matter how spooked they were, most of them would eventually get hungry and follow their nose back to camp.

At three sides of the main perimeter, teams of men were putting together pre-fabricated guard towers. The towers were simple wooden affairs held together with nuts and bolts. They could be put up and taken down repeatedly, sparing the raiders the trouble of cutting raw wood and scrounging for nails.

Heinrich looked over the tents being set up in orderly rows and spotted his large command tent in the center. He turned to Maru. "Walk with me."

The two men entered the command tent. Heinrich returned a salute from the guard within and told him to inform the other guards outside to post up out of earshot. The man acknowledged and left.

"Something on your mind, Chief?"

Heinrich watched the guards walk away from the entrance, then closed it and sat down on a stool near a small folding table. "Have a seat."

Maru sat across from him. There was a combination lockbox on the table from which Heinrich produced a map drawn on graph paper.

"I was going to wait to tell you about this, but considering what we captured today, I think I'm justified in moving up the timetable."

161

Maru looked at the map. "Is that Parabellum?"

"It is indeed. Secret tunnels and all."

The big Maori grinned, still looking at the map. "Where did you get it?"

"Let's just say Necrus Khan is not so well liked among his men."

"Too bad for him. And for the fella who gave you this."

Heinrich chuckled. Maru's pragmatism was one of the many things the raider chief liked about him. "Yeah. He's not around anymore. Can't have any loose ends."

"'Course not."

"Any guesses why I went through the trouble of obtaining this map?"

"Tired of raiding on the dangerous highways of Kansas? Looking for a bigger score, something a bit more permanent?"

"Something to that effect."

Maru's smile broadened. "Carter know?"

"He helped me plan it."

A nod. "So what did you have in mind, Chief?"

Heinrich told him. Maru's expression grew serious as he listened. When Heinrich was finished, Maru sat quietly for a while rubbing his chin.

"It's a good plan. Hard part will be getting into position unseen."

"True. It'll have to be a night operation."

"Won't make things any easier."

"No. But it'll be worth it. Just imagine having Parabellum all to ourselves."

Maru rubbed his hands together. "That would be nice. What do you want me to do?"

Straight to the point. I like that. "We're going to need at least eight infiltrators to make this work. I want you to start vetting the men, find some likely candidates. Carter and I will do the same."

"Not a problem. Anything else?"

"For now, no. But be thorough, Maru. And be discreet."

"Right, Chief."

Heinrich thanked Maru for his work earlier in the day and dismissed him. When his colonel left, Heinrich sat down in the armchair and put his feet up on the ottoman that were part of the small number of luxuries he allowed himself. He rang a small bell and his steward, a teenage boy too young to fight but old enough to take orders, stepped into his tent. The boy wore a leather cord around his neck to which was attached a metal disk with the skull-and-lightning-bolt emblem of the Storm Road Tribe, an announcement to his men that he was the chief's servant and was not to be abused. Verbally or otherwise.

"Sir?"

"Whisky. Pre-Outbreak stuff. And something to eat."

"Yes sir. Right away."

The boy shuffled off. Heinrich put his hands behind his head, sank into his chair, and thought about Parabellum. How nice would it be if he could catch Necrus Khan alive, maybe turn him over to Carter? That would be a pleasant day indeed.

But not for Necrus.

TWELVE

"Chief, you awake?"

Heinrich opened his eyes in the darkness. A small sliver of gray appeared at the back of his wagon as the curtain was moved aside. A dark, head-shaped blob appeared in the middle.

"I am now. What is it?"

"Scouts are back. Say they want to speak with you."

"They say what about?"

"Yeah, but you should probably hear it from them."

"All right, Maru. I'll be out in a minute."

"Right, Chief."

Heinrich sat up and rubbed his face and looked at the pocket watch passed down his family line starting with his great grandfather. It told him he had only managed three hours of sleep. Whatever the scouts had to report, it better be good.

After tugging on his boots and rinsing his mouth with water he climbed out of his wagon and looked around, letting his eyes adjust. There was not much of a moon that night, the majority of light in the camp coming from small, low-banked fires. Knots of men coming off watch huddled around the fires and cooked meals of hard-tack bread, dried peas, and preserved meat. The wagons were arranged in a square, the tents in the middle. Two dozen men were on security patrol at all times. Everyone slept inside the square. Heinrich had foregone his command tent for the last few weeks, opting instead to sleep in his wagon. If any federal types showed up, or if his caravan was surveilled from a distance, he did not want anyone to immediately know who the leader was. The more closely he and his small army resembled legitimate traders, the less likely they were to run into trouble.

"Maru?"

"Over here, Chief."

Heinrich looked. His colonel stood a few feet to his right, eating a bowl of rehydrated camp rations.

"You're going to spill that walking around in the dark."

Maru gave his small, tight smile. "Nah. Used to it."

"You say so. Lead the way."

True to his word, on the walk to where the scouts sat around their cook fire, Maru did not spill a drop. Heinrich watched him and realized there was nothing particularly special about how he accomplished this. He kept his eyes forward, watched the ground in front of him, and let his hands and mouth go through the motions of eating automatically, as if on autopilot. The kind of thing anyone could do with concentration and practice. Heinrich had a feeling those two qualities, concentration and practice, had a lot to do with why Maru excelled at a great many things.

"Here we are, Chief."

The scouts began to stand as Heinrich approached, but he hissed at them and motioned them to stop. "What are my orders?"

165

The men froze, then sat down. "Sorry, sir. Won't happen again," one of them said.

"It damn well better not. Now what do you have to report?"

"We scouted out the settlements around the Wichita Safe Zone. Talked to our contacts there."

"And?" Heinrich said impatiently.

"The troops stationed there just rotated out last week," the scout said. "Got a bunch of new guys."

Heinrich looked at the scout closely and saw, beneath the beard and scraggly long hair, he was speaking to a kid in his early twenties. He made a motion for the young man to continue.

"Get to the point."

"Well, sir, the troops there are new to the place, don't know their way around. Still learning emergency drills and procedures, that sort of thing. And there's about half as many as there used to be. Won't be able to mount much of a force if someone hits a caravan near the safe zone."

Heinrich stared a moment in silence. He had an idea where this was going. "I'm waiting for the part where you tell me why you thought it necessary to wake me from my sleep."

The scout clutched his food bowl and shuffled his feet in the dirt. "There's a big caravan coming in soon, run by a guy named Spike. Informants say he's a rich man. Supposed to be eighty-four wagons, all hauling trade bound for the springs."

"What kind of trade?"

"Salt, ammo, guns, food, maple syrup from up north, rice from down south, salvage, candles, soap, all kinds of stuff. And lots of it."

Heinrich put his hands on his hips and considered this development. The Wichita Safe Zone was well-guarded by the

Army—infantry, artillery, air support, the works. But any army is only as good as its troops. Heinrich had been listening to the bulletins the president made every week. He knew a huge number of troops were finishing their enlistments and opting to leave the military, meaning most of the soldiers being sent to Wichita were new recruits. Probably never even seen real, pitched combat. If he could find this caravan, hit them well out of sight of the troops and other caravans, he just might pull it off. It would be taking a huge risk, but if what the scout said was true, well worth the reward.

"When is this caravan due to arrive?"

"Three to four days, sir. Depends."

Heinrich turned to Maru. "Put more scouts in the field at first light. I want this caravan found, and I want it tracked. Notify Carter first thing in the morning and get the senior officers together at the livestock pens by nine-hundred hours. Mandatory."

"Right, Chief."

He turned back to the scouts. "Who else knows about this?"

The senior scout shook his head. "No one, sir. Just you and Colonel Maru."

"Keep it that way. I mean it—you two keep your fucking mouths shut. You blab about this, you'll never blab about anything ever again. Do I make myself clear?"

"Yes sir. Very clear, sir."

"Good."

Heinrich bored into the scouts with his gaze, watching them wither under its heat. Satisfied they knew the score, Heinrich headed back to his wagon, smiling inwardly. He thought to himself that in the ongoing debate as to whether it was better to be respected or feared, he had always found fear the far more useful emotion. Respect was just a side effect.

THIRTEEN

Eric

Six weeks' travel from Hollow Rock found us a day's ride outside of the Wichita Safe Zone.

It was bitterly cold and overcast most of the way. We crossed the Mississippi on the western border of Kentucky and then began the long slog across Missouri. Or Misery, as the traders in Spike's caravan not-so-lovingly called it.

Wild game was plentiful, even in winter, but the weather and the harsh terrain made for slow, difficult going. By the second week, I was very, very tired of having to get out and put my shoulder to a wheel and push the wagon out of a rut or pothole or mud-slop or whatever crap we had become mired in whilst serenaded by the grunting and cursing of Gabe, Hicks, and Elizabeth. Sabrina did not have to push a wheel, being that she was the smallest and lightest of us and someone had to hold the reins and beseech the oxen to pull.

The road flattened as we approached the Kansas border, and though at first I was grateful, I quickly grew weary of the steady, unending, monotonous sheen of white overlaying what would be tall fields of wheat and barley come spring.

If not for the maps and GPS units we had with us, I would have been completely lost. The roads were invisible. The plains seemed to stretch on forever, broken up by the occasional patch of woodland or pitched roofs of houses, farms, and small bits of crumbing civilization. We stopped four times at settlements to resupply and send brief HAM radio messages back to Hollow Rock to let our friends and loved ones know we were still alive and as safe as could be expected. My sleeping bag was supposed to be rated down to -35 degrees Fahrenheit, but I still woke up shivering every morning. The only redeeming quality of the bleak Kansas winter was there were no infected to be found.

At night, when I lay alone and cold, I thought of my wife and son and missed them and wondered if I had made the right decision coming along on this trip. I certainly had done nothing of significant value thus far, and had encountered no opportunities to expand my business interests westward. A very loud, very persistent voice in my head was telling me I had made a mistake. I told the voice Gabriel was my friend, and we had been through too much together not to tag along with him this one last time. The voice asked if I really thought this was our last journey together, and when I answered in the affirmative, the voice laughed uproariously. I told the voice to shut up and resolved to ignore it from then on.

The day before we reached Wichita I sat in the driver's seat, reins in hand, with Sabrina riding shotgun. Literally—she was holding Hicks' Benelli. Gabe had ridden off somewhere to inquire where his cargo would be stored while we were in the Safe Zone. Elizabeth lay snoring gently on her bedroll behind me. Caleb was riding in a wagon with some ex-Army type he knew from the battle

170

of Singletary Lake. So, for all intents and purposes, Sabrina and I had the place to ourselves.

"You know a lot about business and trade and shit, right?"

I looked at the girl next to me. For the last hour, she had said nothing, just stared at the empty vastness of the snow-covered Kansas plain, lost in her own thoughts. It took me a few seconds to clear my throat and answer.

"Yeah. I know a bit."

She flicked a hand toward the beasts drawing our cart. "Where do the caravans get those things? I don't remember oxen being that common when I was a kid."

"You ever eat a cheeseburger before the Outbreak?"

A low, hungry sound. "God yes. Loved the things. Don't remind me, haven't had one since I was ten."

"Ever see a grocery store or a restaurant running short on beef?"

"No. What's your point?"

"My point is the pre-Outbreak cattle population in this country was massive. And oxen are cattle. Specifically, castrated bulls."

"Castrated? Why?"

"Makes them more docile, easier to train."

"Still doesn't tell me where they come from."

"They come from all over. Back four years ago, when it was obvious the government had collapsed and everything was going to hell, most ranchers turned their livestock loose. Figured they had a better chance roaming wild than starving to death in holding pens."

"The infected didn't get them?"

"Oh, I'm sure they got some. The sick, the old, the lame, the very young. But your average healthy cow is more than a match for even a large number of infected. You see, like all animals,

171

cows are immune to ghoul bites. They also have tough hides that are extremely difficult to bite through, they're very physically powerful, and they can run in excess of twenty miles an hour. When traveling in herds, they can fend off hordes thousands strong just by trampling them. So, since the Outbreak, cattle populations have boomed nationwide. An entire cottage industry has cropped up around them. Young bulls are one of the most valuable commodities a wildcat rancher can hope to find. Just cut their balls off and teach them to pull a yoke, and you've got yourself an ox. And oxen are not cheap."

"So there there's good trade to be made in ranching?"

I shrugged. "Sure. It's dangerous, brutal work, but if you can stay alive long enough and get some good people working with you, yeah. You can make a living at it."

Sabrina nodded quietly and did not speak for another hour. It had been this way with her for the last three months or so. The questions she directed at me mostly regarded the elements of post-Outbreak society she did not understand, and the questions she asked her father pertained to life before the Outbreak. What kind of car is this? Were there really billions of people, once? What does the Pacific Ocean look like? What was New York City like? Which war did you fight in? How do you say the word on that sign over there? How many languages do you speak?

One of the difficulties we encountered early on was, despite Sabrina's age and natural intelligence, she had only a fifth grade education. Worse, the nearly four years of day-to-day survival she'd endured since the Outbreak had done nothing to sharpen her recall of what few lessons she had learned.

She could read well enough, and could do basic four-function math, but her memories of history, science, civics, and everything else kids used to learn in school were spotty at best. When she wrote, she often misspelled words and substituted correct spellings

172

for what the word sounded like. For example, she'd once left a note on the store corkboard reading, "Jonny helpd me cleen the shop today. He is a good helpur."

She was not quite sure who John Adams was. She remembered Abraham Lincoln's name, but not why he was important. She regarded the wars our nation had fought like stories of great, mythical beasts repeated to frighten unruly children. She could not find England on a map. Or Hawaii, or Japan, or any number of other places. Oddly, though, she knew where to find Madagascar. Something to do with a kid's movie she watched as a little girl.

I remember the first week she was with us, I pointed to the night sky and said, "You can see Venus tonight."

She scrunched her eyebrows at me and said, "That's a planet, right?"

"Yes."

"Closer or farther than us?"

"What do you mean?"

"You know. To the sun. Venus is part of our solar system, right?"

"Yes. And it's closer. Mercury, Venus, then us."

It was at that moment I decided to have a nice long chat with Gabe about seeing to her education. He listened and took action.

Despite his efforts, however, there is only so much a kid can learn in three months, and only so much that can be learned about her. I knew she liked to read. She came over to my house often and sat alone on a chaise lounge in one of the guest rooms reading to herself, her lips moving over the prose of Steinbeck and Hemingway and Joyce Carol Oates, an old Oxford English dictionary close at hand for the difficult words. When she finished a book she wandered into Allison's office and hungrily perused her

173

small library of paperbacks for a new one. Sometimes she would read six or seven books a week.

Math, on the other hand, she did not like very much. She was good at it, she just did not enjoy it. I told her I did not enjoy it either, but it was necessary for her to learn. At this she shrugged—her go-to response for pretty much everything—picked up her math textbook, and set to work. And my God, did she work fast. In a week, she was caught up on junior high math. Two weeks later, she was ready for algebra. By the time we were three weeks on the road, she had mastered statistics while sitting in her bedroll at night and working problems under a little battery powered reading light. I spoke of this to Gabe and asked if he had done any testing of her mental acuity yet.

"She can't do what I can do," he replied.

"You tried already?"

"Yes. Her capacity for repeating quotes and pieces of information is remarkable, but she does not have an eidetic memory. Close, but not the same. That said, her ability to learn and absorb new information is far beyond what I can do."

"How so?"

"There's a difference between memorizing and learning. Memorizing comes naturally to me. Doesn't take much effort. Learning is taking that which is memorized and applying it in a useful way. Take her knife fighting, for instance. She only trained for two years, but her level of advancement is beyond that of some masters I've trained with. If somebody teaches me a new technique, I have to drill it hundreds of times, build muscle memory. Sabrina's not like that. I teach her something once, and she's got it. Barely needs to practice."

"Must be nice. What do you think it means?"

Gabriel poked a stick in the fire and looked at his daughter with a glimmer of pride. "It means she's barely reached a fraction of her real potential."

Without looking up from her textbook, Sabrina said, "You two assholes know I can hear you right?"

"Sorry. Thought we were being quiet," I said.

"Not quiet enough."

I frowned at her. "Yeah, well, do me a favor. Don't call your father an asshole."

Her eyebrows lifted enough for the gray eyes to fix on me. "Why not?"

"Because he loves you," I said flatly, "and he's been nothing but kind and generous and patient with you. And he's my friend, and I don't like it when people insult my friends. So knock it off."

She did not reply, but I had not heard her insult Gabriel since. Me, yes. Plenty of times. But not Gabe.

Ahead of us, the Wichita Safe Zone grew larger and more distinct. Having 20/10 vision, I was able to see it much better than most of the other people in the caravan. In this instance, I was not so sure my enhanced eyesight was such a good thing.

Wichita, like most major cities, was a burned-out wreck of what it had once been. The place reminded me of pictures of Hiroshima after the bomb: flattened buildings, rubble-strewn streets, bare patches of scorched ground where houses once stood, broken ruins of walls and foundations and columns stretching upward like fingers on a skeleton's hand, and covering it all, a thick layer of gray dust and black soot.

About a year ago, the Army had embarked on a mission the president had dubbed Operation Relentless Force. Over a hundred-thousand soldiers set out with tanks, artillery, and air support with

175

the sole intent of liberating Kansas from nearly three million infected. They had succeeded, but at great cost. Over ten thousand troops were lost to the infected, with another ten thousand dying of exposure, disease, accidents, and skirmishes with raiders and marauders. I suspected friendly fire factored into that number as well, but the brass at Central Command did not like to discuss such things. Not publicly, at least.

By the end of it, Kansas was as ghoul free as anywhere on Earth. Even in the spring and summer, if rumors were to be believed, one could ride for days without seeing a single walking corpse. I had my doubts about that. No one had built a wall around Kansas, and the last time I checked, the infected do not give a pinch of flying monkey shit about state borders. Ergo, I treated Kansas with the same level of healthy paranoia I treated every place else.

The military presence was light as we rode into town. Most of the ruins on either side of us had been bulldozed to allow the Army to lay down a broad concrete highway through the ruined city. Guard towers manned with light machine guns stood at staggered intervals on alternating sides of the unmarked gray road. Our caravan rode single file northward while people leaving town traveled southbound to our left. Ahead, I could see the sectioned square walls of the various districts rising out of the ashes, small figures of soldiers patrolling the catwalks.

"Security seems pretty light," Sabrina said. "Last time I was in a safe zone the place was crawling with troops."

"Yeah," I muttered. "Strange."

We continued bumping and rattling along until we reached a crossroads that branched off in eight directions. I had heard one of Spike's guards refer to this area as Eight Points, referring to the various avenues for caravans to go.

The caravan ground to a halt as the lead wagon reached a large security checkpoint. A low wall of concrete highway dividers barred the way ahead for a hundred yards on each side of the entrance, which itself was wide enough to allow four carts through side by side. Four forklifts loaded with additional highway dividers waited in a row not far away should the gates need to be closed quickly. I did not see drivers waiting in them, so I assumed the task had been assigned to designated soldiers nearby. It's what I would have done, anyway.

A semi-circle of five guard towers stood behind the checkpoint, all manned with M-240s and snipers carrying long guns. I spotted two M-110s, two bolt-action .338 Lapua magnums, and in the center, a big Barrett .50 caliber. There were additional machine gun nests at ground level laid out to create a crossfire on the highway, as well as numerous troops armed with everything from M-4s to LAW rockets. All in all, not the kind of place one wanted to get mouthy with the security staff.

Probably best if I kept quiet.

A discussion spanning perhaps two minutes occurred at the checkpoint, after which the officer in charge directed Spike and his men to take the caravan up one of the avenues headed northeast. As we entered the massive compound, I could feel dozens of eyes watching us, alert for the slightest indication of malfeasance. I kept my hands on the reins, my eyes straight ahead, and did my best to look disinterested.

"I hope they have baths," Sabrina said. "I could go for a bath."

"I think we all could."

"And laundry. My clothes stink. Smell like sweat and cow shit."

As she said this, the beast at the top right of the four-oxen team pulling us along voided its bowels less than two feet from the face of the animal behind it. It did not break stride, nor had any of its brethren the hundreds of times I had witnessed similar events in the last six weeks. It occurred to me a few days into the journey that anyone wanting to track the caravan's progress need not keep us in sight—just follow the trail of dung piles and they'd be on us in no time.

"You know what I miss more than anything?" I said.

"What?"

"Cars. I miss cars."

FOURTEEN

"Not so bad here."

I looked around the square we stood in. It had once been a residential neighborhood on the northeast side of Wichita. Now, it was a bulldozed patch of snowy ground dotted regularly with bare foundations of houses long destroyed. A twelve foot wall of concrete and steel surrounded the square, complete with catwalks and guard towers at the corners. I counted twelve troops on duty, two machine guns, and a single sniper in the northeast tower.

"How big you figure this place is?" I said.

"'Bout a quarter-mile square."

I looked northward and saw a long, dome-shaped building shaped like half a cigar planted into the ground. The roof peaked out at twelve feet or so with walls maybe thirty feet apart at the base. I had seen buildings like it before at Fort McCray. The soldiers called it a drill hall, but the civilians in the caravan called it a long house. The floor was bare concrete, the windows were horizontal and mounted eight feet off the ground, and the doors at either end were made of reinforced steel. The building's purpose

179

was to put a roof over people's heads and provide a layer of protection from the elements, nothing more. No heating system, no place to prepare food or do laundry, no fires allowed inside.

To the south, well away from the long house, were the livestock pens and the biggest damn latrine I had ever seen. Wooden buildings marked MENS and WOMENS straddled the latrine side by side. When our caravan left, an excavator would pour mulch over the latrine, then empty it into trucks and haul it to the edge of the city where it would be used to make the fertilizer the government provided as a subsidy to farms in the area.

To the east were bathing facilities, and to the west was another long house, this one with just a roof and support posts, no walls, with cooking stations and rows of picnic tables. A tangle of caravaners were already hauling bags of grain, beans, and boxes of preserved vegetables to the cooking stations. A team of two dozen men and women worked to haul the oxen and horses into the livestock pens where children were already emptying feed bags into large bins and pumping water into long troughs. Spike and a few of his men, including the two Blackthorns, spoke calmly with a quartermaster whose attention never seemed far from a clipboard in his hands.

"What do you think they're talking about over there?"

Gabe looked in Spike's direction. "Ordering supplies, applying for passes to the market district, that kind of thing."

"Where's the market district?"

"Not sure. This is my first time here, same as you."

"You know if they have hotels there?"

"They do. Laundry and private baths too."

I smiled. "You and your daughter think alike."

"Hmm?"

"Something she said on the way in."

Gabe's eyes tracked to Sabrina sitting in the wagon. She had her feet kicked up on the buckboard and was leafing through a paperback. As I watched, a few years seemed to drop off my old friend's countenance, the hard lines easing, the jaw less tense, the eyes softer and kinder.

"Maybe there's a nice place to eat," he said. "I bet Sabrina would like that."

I patted the big man on the shoulder. "I bet she would."

Elizabeth sat up from the back of the cart and rubbed sleep out of her eyes. "We there yet?"

"Halfway," Gabe said. "We're in the Wichita Safe Zone."

The former mayor of Hollow Rock stood up and climbed down from the wagon. Once on the ground, she raised her arms and stretched luxuriously. I tried very hard not to notice the line of stomach and navel her shirt revealed as it went up and the wondrous way her large breasts lifted under her wool sweater as she put her arms over her head. When I felt my eyes lingering too long in places they shouldn't, I looked away and told myself I was only human, it had been over a month since I had seen my wife, and Elizabeth was a very attractive woman. No shame in noticing a woman's beauty any more than appreciating a bright sunrise. Except pretty sunrises did not elicit a low tug in my groin.

Stop it.

"So what now?" Elizabeth said.

"Now I'm gonna go talk to Spike," Gabe said, "and get passes to the market district."

"For all of us?"

"Of course."

"I'll go with you," I said.

181

Gabe grunted acknowledgement and walked in Spike's direction. He was still in conversation with the quartermaster, who saw us approaching and pointed.

"Who's this?"

"Gabriel Garrett and Eric Riordan," Spike answered. "They're VIPs in this caravan."

A greedy twinkle appeared in the quartermaster's eye. He was a squat man, broad through the shoulders and narrow at the waist, pale skin, shaved head, wearing a neatly pressed uniform and clean boots. The nametag on his chest read, SWANSON.

"What can I do for you, fellas?"

"Need passes into the market district," Gabe said.

"For what purpose?"

Gabe's eyes narrowed. "Trade."

"And what are you trading?"

I looked at Spike. "He always ask this many questions?"

"No. He doesn't."

Swanson glared at Spike. "It's part of my job."

"Listen," Gabe said. "We already went through inspection. Spike is known here. I'm registered in the Archive and will sign a waiver of responsibility for the rest of my party. Last I checked, those were the only requirements to obtain passes in a federal safe zone."

Swanson's grin was as greasy as a skillet full of lard. "That and the approval of the quartermaster. So what are you trading?"

Gabe chuckled. "So you want to play that game? No problem. I'll just head over to the radioman and send a message to General Phillip Jacobs, head of Army Special Operations Command. He's a friend of mine. I'm sure he'd be thrilled to know one of his quartermasters is extorting traders in a federal safe zone."

The grin vanished. "Now hang on, no one is trying to extort anyone."

"Bullshit," Gabe said, pressing his advantage. "I know your type. You're a fucking worm. You abuse your position for personal enrichment. You bully traders and force them to pay bribes in order to access facilities and services they have every right to as Union citizens. And I'm willing to bet the poorer and weaker they are, the more you take. It's little shits like you that make it hard for honest traders to earn a living."

Swanson's face turned bright red. "Now listen here-"

"No, you listen. You're going to go to the guard shack and fill out five passes. You're going to bring them to me. I will pay the standard fee; the equivalent of twenty-five federal credits is twenty grams of salt. You will take it with a smile and a thank you. And if you don't, I'll call General Jacobs, and by the end of the month you'll be busted down to specialist and manning a watch tower in the Nevada outposts. Do I make myself clear?"

Swanson sputtered a few times, too enraged to speak. One of the Blackthorns flanking Spike rubbed his mouth to conceal a smile and said, "You better do as he says, Swanson. I've heard of this guy. He's got pull."

Swanson looked at the Blackthorn, then at Gabe, then turned on his heel and stormed off toward the guard shack. Through the window, I saw him sit down behind a desk and open a laptop.

"Probably checking your file in the Archive," I said.

"Yep."

"I wonder if we'll see the very moment he learns you're telling the truth."

A smirk. "Keep watching."

Sure enough, as we watched, the angered expression evacuated Swanson's face and was replaced by a wide-eyed, horrified realization. He closed the laptop, grabbed a box of small papers, and began writing furiously. Finished, he composed himself and returned to where we stood.

"Here you go," Swanson said, handing over the passes.

Gabe took them. "Where do I pay the fee?"

Swanson did not make eye contact. "Supply building, north gate. The green converted shipping container."

"Thank you. And do yourself a favor, Sergeant Swanson." Gabe leaned in close. "Be honest from now on. I'll be keeping tabs on you."

With that, we went back to our wagon. I managed to hold the laughter in until we were out of earshot, but it was a near thing.

"Gotta tell you, old buddy. It's a pleasure to watch you work."

Gabe did not answer, but I could see the amusement in his eyes.

FIFTEEN

When I hear the word 'marketplace' I generally think of the market in Hollow Rock near the north gate. I expect a vibrant, bustling place of smiles and laughter and haggling and good-natured shouts of merchants exhorting the value and quality of their wares. I expect the smell of food and wood-smoke in the air, the laughter of excited children, the sound of wagers being placed in gambling booths, the odor of marijuana smoke from head shops (which, in Hollow Rock, were conveniently located next to the food vendors in a mutually beneficial strategic partnership).

The market in the Wichita Safe Zone was certainly bustling, but it would have been ambitious to the point of disingenuousness to call it vibrant. There was no shouting. No one seemed good-natured. There was some smiling and laughing, but it was muted and conducted between members of the same caravan, not between traders and merchants. There were very few children present, mostly teenagers. This was not a place where people came to have a good time.

"Looks kind of dull," Sabrina said, echoing my thoughts.

"I hear it livens up at night," Gabe replied.

"So what's our first stop?" Hicks said. It was the first thing I had heard him say since rejoining us. I glanced his way and noticed him looking around curiously, eyes taking in everything.

"Local smithy," Gabe said. "Commissioned a blade for the little lady."

Sabrina shot him a glare. "Since you're buying me a sword, I'll let that 'little lady' shit slide."

"Oh for Christ's sake, Sabrina" I said. "He didn't mean anything by it."

"Now children," Elizabeth cut in. "It's a nice day and there's shopping to be done. Let's all play nicely, okay?"

I shook my head at the ingratitude of youth. Sabrina lapsed into sullen silence. Gabe patted her on the shoulder, but otherwise left her alone. Caleb, as always, looked indifferent.

The sound of the forge reached us shortly ahead of the smell. I could detect at least two hammers beating on something metal and wrinkled my nose at the acrid scent of charcoal burning at over fifteen-hundred degrees. The forge itself was a squat structure built from a patchwork of mismatched bricks and homemade mortar with several cylindrical steel chimneys jetting black smoke into the sky. A gangly, pimple-faced boy of no more than thirteen greeted us at the door.

"Welcome to Wichita Custom Fabricators. What can I do for you?"

Gabe spoke up. "Name is Gabriel Garrett. Commissioned a blade about two months ago. Message came via radio from Hollow Rock over in Tennessee." He produced a slip from his shirt pocket. "Here's your confirmation of receipt."

The boy read the slip, nodded to himself, and said, "Just a moment, sir."

We waited while the boy disappeared into the darkness of the forge. He returned a moment later smiling obsequiously.

"Do you have your method of payment with you, sir?"

Gabe patted an old Army messenger bag slung across his chest. The boy stepped aside and gestured for Gabe to enter. He did, followed by Sabrina. The rest of us waited at the entrance until, a minute or two later, Sabrina emerged grinning broadly. For a few seconds I had the feeling I was seeing what she may have looked like had the Outbreak never happened, none of the cynicism and suspicion and canned violence, the face of a happy teenage girl unmarred by trauma or tragedy. It was a bittersweet thing to see, and I had to remind myself not to dwell on things that could not be changed.

"You gotta see this thing," Sabrina said to me.

"Is it nice?"

"It's fucking badass."

I gestured to the cloth-wrapped bundle in her arms. "Let's see it."

"Not here," Gabe said. "Too many eyes. People might get funny ideas."

"Right. Well, I'm hungry anyway."

"Seconded," Elizabeth said. "I smell something good coming from up the street."

Gabe made a sweeping gesture with his arm. "Lead the way."

She did, and as she walked ahead of me, I could not help but notice the form-fitting cut of her pants and how trim and well-muscled her legs and butt were. I allowed myself a few moments of admiration and then stared at the ground for the remainder of the

187

walk and thought to myself that I really, really needed to get back to Allison.

*****

Two days later, it was time to leave.

The others were already back with our gear, our newly replenished supplies, and our wagon. I lingered a while that morning on the rooftop deck of our hotel, mug of tea in hand, staring at the Kansas plains stretching endlessly westward. It was warm that morning, nearly seventy degrees, with the first hints of spring whispering in the mid-March air. There was no reason for me to stay behind; Gabe and Elizabeth had seen to our supplies, and Sabrina and Caleb had taken care of our laundry. I was bathed, shaved, hair neatly trimmed, and I had done an outstanding job the last couple of days of holding down a barstool and paying too much for medium-quality hooch at the hotel's tiny bar.

I knew the day was going to move quickly, but I could not seem to work up the motivation to settle my bill and check out. And as underwhelmed as I had initially been with the newly-constructed wooden lobby and bare floors and creaky stairs of the Heartland Inn and Tavern, I had to admit I was going to miss the place. The beds were clean, the staff was friendly, and someone came by to empty the composting toilet every evening. Certainly beat the hell out of life on the road.

I sipped my overpriced tea and thought about Allison and my infant son and how, if I got home on time, I was going to have missed six months of my little boy growing up. Granted, I was missing out on the screaming and crying and soiled diapers portion of his upbringing, but I regretted not being there nonetheless. I didn't mind so much when he screamed and cried. It was gratifying to calm him down and feel him relax and fall asleep in my arms.

And while changing and cleaning cloth diapers a few dozen times a day—or so it felt—was no picnic, I found would rather be doing that than sitting here on this rooftop with a heavy feeling in the bottom of my gut at the prospect of climbing back into that goddamn wagon and spending another six weeks on the road. And that was not counting the journey back to Hollow Rock.

Maybe I could pull some strings with General Jacobs and get myself on a military flight back home. It would be ridiculously expensive, but getting there in a matter of hours versus a minimum of twelve weeks would be more than worth it.

A door opened on the ground floor and I heard footsteps on the stairs leading to the roof. A waiter stopped next to me and asked if I would like anything else. I drained the last of my tea and told him no, I'd be checking out in just a few minutes. He thanked me for no reason, the way hotel staff always do, and left. I put my cup down.

"Stop feeling sorry for yourself," I said aloud. "You started this with your eyes wide open. Now finish it."

I stood up, gathered my things from my room, paid my bill by measuring out four ounces of sugar into a small bowl on a scale in the hotel kitchen, and headed for the caravan district.

*****

There were three additional horses attached by lead ropes to the tailgate. Caleb sat atop a fourth one I had never seen before.

"What's with the extra livestock?" I asked as I slung my rucksack and duffel bag of weapons into the rear of the wagon.

"Weather's warming up," Gabe said. "Infected and marauders will be out and about. Figured we ought to take some sensible precautions."

I walked over to the horses and let them sniff at me. "Which one is mine?"

"The one trying to bite your ear."

The horse in question was not really trying to bite my ear. Horses have a way of probing at people with their semi-prehensile upper lips by way of greeting. Still, it tickled and I gently nudged the horse's muzzle away. He was a brown gelding, not quite as tall as Red but sturdily built, possessed of the confident, unhurried manner of a horse used to being ridden long distances.

"Seems friendly enough."

"Get used to him. You're going to be spending a lot of time together. Only one person in the wagon the rest of the way. I want everyone else on horseback, full loadout. So suit up."

I let out a sigh and wiped a hand across the back of my neck. It was probably pointless to argue with Gabe about this, but I had to try. "Don't you think you're being a little paranoid?"

"No."

"There are eighty wagons in this caravan."

"Eighty-four, actually."

"And no less than a hundred and twenty people, all armed, driving them. And an additional thirty guards on horseback, two of whom are Blackthorns."

"So?"

"So marauders travel in small bands, typically no more than twenty or thirty. And they're not known for negotiating strong alliances. You'd have to be nuts to take on this caravan with anything less than a hundred people on horseback."

190

"It could be done with less if they were well trained."

"Which most raiders are not."

"And your point is?"

I rubbed the bridge of my nose. "My point is this is unnecessary. Riding in the wagon is exhausting enough."

"Tell you what, Eric. When we get safely to Colorado Springs, I'll buy you dinner and as many drinks as you want, and you can say 'I told you so' until you're blue in the face. But until then, we do this my way."

As usual, his tone brooked no argument. "Fine. But you better set aside some serious trade. I plan to have many, many drinks on your dime."

"I sincerely hope you do."

"By the way," I said, climbing into the wagon and rooting for my MOLLE vest. "How much did the horses cost us?"

"Doesn't matter. I'm selling them as soon as we get to Colorado."

I found my vest and spare ammo and began gearing up. "Never let it be said you're not a practical man, Gabe."

"Glad you noticed."

SIXTEEN

Heinrich sat at his table, a plate of half-eaten food shoved to one corner, a map of Kansas spread out before him. He heard footsteps approaching his tent—a small one, not his command tent—and the flap was moved aside.

"They're here, sir."

"Send them in."

Maru and Carter entered the tent and sat down on the canvas and small rugs covering the ground. Heinrich spun the map around so they could read it.

"Just got word from the scouts. We move tonight."

Carter's perpetual snarl moved slightly under his beard in what, for him, passed for a smile. "What's the plan?"

Heinrich poked a spot on the map with a thick index finger. "They've stopped for the night here, near Haviland."

"Think I remember Haviland," Maru said. "Place is abandoned, right? We holed up there for a while last year."

"Right. Army stripped it for salvage, but the buildings are still standing."

Carter grunted. "Yeah. I remember the place."

"Good. That'll make things easier. So here's what we're going to do. Infantry will barracks in the school gymnasium, we'll hide the livestock and wagons at the old farm co-op on the south side of town. Plenty of barns and storage buildings, perfect place to deploy the cavalry."

"How far from town is the caravan camping?" Maru asked.

"Four miles, give or take."

Carter did the math in his head. "We'll have to ride hard tonight to get ahead of them."

"Nothing we haven't done before. We'll head overland, stay a mile north of them and then swing southward when we get to Haviland. Gives us three, maybe four hours' rest before the attack."

"Not much time," Maru said.

"Again, nothing we haven't done before."

"How sure are we they're following this route?" Maru asked, pointing at Highway 400 on the map.

"They've been following it since Wichita. Have to go overland to find another route. I doubt they're going to do that at this point."

Maru nodded.

"I'll have the men charge radios and NVGs," Carter said. "All the deep-cycles are maxed out. We're on straight solar at the moment."

"Use the batteries," Heinrich said. "Button up the solar rig and get it on a wagon. I want the tribe on the road as soon as possible."

"Yes sir."

"You two know what to do. Make it happen."

The two colonels acknowledged and left the tent. Heinrich instructed his servant to leave the tent and post a guard to make sure he was not disturbed. When the boy left to carry out his orders, Heinrich opened his pack, removed his infrared scope, and connected the battery pack to a Yeti charging station he had taken for his own personal use.

"One more big score," he muttered to himself. "And then on to Parabellum."

SEVENTEEN

Gabriel

Eric complained the first couple of days. But then again, Eric always complains.

I endured his bitching stoically and refused to relent making everyone not driving the wagon stay on horseback. Nor did I relax the loadout requirements. Everyone carried an M-4 as a primary weapon, Beretta M-9 as secondary, some kind of revolver as a backup, a hand weapon, knife, and camping axe, and in our saddlebags, we all carried five days' worth of food, four liters of water, survival and first aid kits, spare ammunition, radios, solar trickle chargers with inverters and charging ports, two changes of clothes, five changes of socks, spare boots, suppressors for both the rifles and the pistols, and whatever extra firearms each person wanted to bring along. For Caleb, it was his Benelli shotgun and SCAR sniper rifle; for Eric his M-110; Elizabeth and Sabrina had Ruger 10-22 rifles with short-range scopes (it took some

195

convincing to get Sabrina to part with her little .22 Marlin, but I eventually sold her on the Ruger's superiority); and for me, a classic Marine Corps M-40 sniper rifle and my trusty Desert Tactical SRS chambered in .338 Lapua magnum.

The weather continued to improve the farther west we traveled, but I did not regard this as a good thing. It was nice not to freeze my ass off at night, but I knew it was only a matter of time until we made contact with infected or marauders. According to Spike, raiders in the area were fond of late night strafing runs intended to nab a small bit of loot and ride off into the darkness. I thought about my infrared scope and goggles, and the NVGs a few of Spike's security crew possessed, and told Spike I felt sorry for the raiders who attempted such a thing against his caravan. He grinned and said, "I don't."

During the day, I watched the horizon. At night, I wandered out on foot and scouted the plains with my IR scope, alert for the slightest movement. By the fourth day, I was reasonably certain we were being followed, and whoever was doing it was no amateur. I expressed my concerns to Spike.

"So what else is new?" he said with a shrug. "Raider assholes are always following us."

"The guy I spotted, he's no rookie. I was a scout sniper in the Marines. I know training when I see it."

Another shrug. "So he follows us. Nothing to worry about until he or whoever he's working for tries something. They do, we'll end 'em."

"I don't like this, Spike. You should send your Blackthorns after him. Capture him. Find out who he's working for."

"I'm telling you Gabe, it don't matter. Look around. They'd need an army to take us on. These raiders on the plains, they're small time. They know better."

196

I let the matter drop, but resolved to remain vigilant.

My sense of unease grew until the seventh night out of Wichita. I spotted the guy following us again—at least I'm reasonably certain it was a guy and not a woman—about five hundred meters to the north. This time, there was someone with him. I stayed low and cranked up the magnification on my IR scope, and sure enough, they were watching us through a night vision spotting rig. No ordinary gear, that, and I sincerely doubted they had traded for it. Unless by trade, one meant demanding it at gunpoint or swiping it from an overrun military patrol.

I watched them for a couple of hours, but when it became clear they had no ambitions of approaching and whoever they were scouting for was nowhere in sight, I made my way back to the caravan. Once back at camp, I searched until I found Caleb and Eric and asked them to follow me back to the wagon.

"Why?" Eric asked, falling into step with me. "I know that look, Gabe. What's going on?"

"Later. Let's find the others."

We did and gathered everyone around the cook fire in the center of camp. Our wagon was on the inner perimeter just behind us. I checked the horses, made sure our gear was in order, sat down with the others, and motioned for them to listen.

"The caravan is being followed."

"No shit," Sabrina said. "Caravan this big, we probably had people dogging our trail since Hollow Rock."

"I'm aware of that. But this is different. The people following us are professionals. They have night vision gear and ghillie suits and they know how to avoid detection."

Elizabeth patted my forearm. "Not well enough, obviously."

"I'm pretty good at what I do. I doubt many other people would have spotted them. And that's exactly what has me worried."

"Did you talk to Spike?" Eric asked.

"Yes. He was his usual overconfident, dismissive self. No help there. Which is why I'm here talking to you right now. I know what happens when people get complacent, start to think nothing bad can happen to them. And I sincerely doubt those people following us are just doing it for fun. I think we're going to be attacked soon, and when it happens, we need to be ready."

"I'm always ready," Caleb said, his eyes shining in the firelight with the mad giddiness of anticipation.

"I know that. But I want us all to be ready. Stay close to the horses, and stay armed. I know it's a pain in the ass, but it just might save your lives. Even a failed attack can still get people killed. If the shooting starts, keep your head down. And if you have to shoot, don't hesitate."

The faces around me in the firelight nodded slowly, and I let out a relieved breath. For once they were taking me seriously and not simply indulging what they considered paranoia.

"You're seriously worried," Elizabeth said somberly, her fingers slipping into mine. "I've never seen you like this before."

I gripped her hand. "I've never had so much to lose."

*****

Eagle-eye Eric spotted them first.

"Contact, south side," he spoke into his radio, peering through a pair of field glasses. "Top of the green pre-fab metal barn, tin roof. Guy up there with a big-eye. Could be more."

"Copy," Spike said.

I had hounded Spike for two hours that morning until he finally agreed to give Caleb, Eric, and me a set of radios tuned to his encrypted comms channel.

"Keep eyes on 'em. Everyone else, maintain your AORs."

I raised my M-4 and peered through the VCOG sight. Sure enough, the same ghillie suited figure I had seen the night before was watching us through a large spotting scope. A rig that powerful could probably read the lines on my face. As I watched, he turned as if speaking to someone out of sight.

"Spike, Garrett. He's talking to someone up there. I think we're headed into an ambush. We better turn around."

"Negative. We've been through this, Garrett. All stations, proceed as planned."

I swore vehemently and debated what to do. With each passing second, we grew closer to the narrow road through the abandoned town of Haviland. Another ten minutes and we would be surrounded by buildings within which anything could be hiding. I cursed Spike for a fool and shouted for the people in my group to switch over to the channel I had pre-arranged so we could speak in private.

"What's up?" Caleb asked.

"We're breaking off. Sabrina, get the wagon turned around. Caleb, Eric, you take rear guard. I'll take point. Elizabeth, stay close to the wagon and be ready to bolt."

"Gabe," Eric said, "you sure about this?"

"No. But I'd rather be wrong and embarrassed than right and dead. Now get moving."

We left the column and began riding eastward, the confused faces of caravaners passing on our left. I felt my radio buzz to let me know someone was trying to reach me on the command net. When I switched over, Spike's voice buzzed angrily in my ear.

"The fuck you think you're doing, Garrett?"

"I'm doubling back, heading for Wellsford."

"What the hell for?"

"I already told you. I smell an ambush. I've got my wife and daughter with me, Spike. I'm not taking any chances."

"What about your trade?"

"I'll come back for it if you survive."

"Goddammit, there's not gonna be any ambush. You hear me? Get back here with my radios."

"If I don't come back, assuming you're still alive, take the cost of the radios out of my trade. You make it to the Springs ahead of me, turn my shipment in to the warehouse we talked about and tell them to take the monthly fee out of my salt. I'll collect the rest when I get there."

"I'm not waiting up for you, Garrett. You get left behind, it's on you. You'll be a sitting duck out here by yourself."

"Spike, if I'm wrong about this, I'll be happy to listen to you laugh at me and call me names and poke fun at me all the way to Colorado. But I don't think I'm wrong. Keep your head on a swivel, and good luck."

With that, I clicked off my transmitter.

"We need to move faster," I said, kicking Red's flanks. "If I'm right, we've got less than ten minutes. We need to put as much distance behind us as possible."

I looked and saw the others staring at me skeptically. A surge of irritation lent fire to my voice and I felt my eyes blaze with anger.

"What part did you not understand? You wanna die today? Move your asses!"

Their eyes went wide, their faces lost a little color, and I knew I would have to apologize later. Right then, I did not care. My outburst got them moving with a sense of urgency. For the moment, nothing else was important.

The oxen kept pace with the horses for all of about five minutes, but then began to slow. Sabrina snapped the reins and shouted and even resorted to the whip, but it was no use. The cart was too heavy.

"Hicks," I said over my shoulder. "Hop in back of the wagon and clear out the excess weight. Nothing stays but food, water, and munitions."

Elizabeth looked startled. "But what about-"

"We'll come back for it," I said, referring to her life savings and the comfort items we had brought along to make the journey less arduous. "If not...well, it won't really matter."

She started to say something else, then stopped. I had the feeling she was beginning to grasp the gravity of the situation.

Hicks, for his part, did not need to be told twice. In one motion, he tied his horse to the tailgate, dismounted on the move, and bounced into the rear of the wagon. A few seconds later, he had collapsed the canopy. No sooner had it settled onto the bench seat beside Sabrina than the first of Elizabeth's possessions sailed over the side. They came to rest in the long brown grass and spots of unmelted snow in the ditch beside the highway. When finished, Hicks jumped out, caught hold of his saddle horn, untied his mount, and was back in position. Total elapsed time: ninety seconds.

Three minutes until contact.

With less than half the load to draw, the oxen were able to pick up the pace. Sabrina pushed them hard, the animals' breath coming in labored huffs. The horses seemed to be holding up much better, but they had far smaller loads to haul.

"Keep it up, folks," I said. "Won't be long now. No matter what happens, don't stop. Just keep moving."

"What if there's no attack?" Eric asked, exasperated. "What then?"

"Then I apologize and we all have a good laugh at my expense."

The clock ticked down in my head. I found myself spending more time looking over my shoulder than watching where I was going. Ten minutes elapsed. I estimated in that time we had covered just over a mile. It did not feel nearly far enough. My shoulders felt tense and an itchy spot had started buzzing directly between my shoulder blades. I had felt it many times before, usually at the outset of a firefight when cover was scarce.

"Gabe, this is ridiculous."

"Just keep moving, Eric."

"Come the hell on, man. The caravan is moving through town by now. If those assholes on the rooftop were going to-"

A familiar sound echoed across the plains, stopping Eric midsentence. We both pulled on the reins to bring our horses to a halt.

"Was that…"

"RPG," I said.

The moment the word was out of my mouth, another *hiss-BANG* split the air. The chatter of guns beat mutedly in the distance, a disjointed staccato cacophony second in volume only to the pounding of blood in my ears. At this range, the sounds of combat were reaching us on a delay. The battle had actually been joined several seconds before.

"Shit!" Eric began wheeling his mount westward. "They're under attack!"

"Stop!" I shouted.

"What?"

"I said stop, you idiot. What do you think you're doing?"

For a few seconds, Eric was at a loss for words. "We can't just leave them."

"The hell we can't."

Eric stared incredulously. "Are you hearing yourself? We have to help them."

"No, Eric, we don't. What we have to do is get as far away from that fight as we possibly can."

Elizabeth rode closer and touched my arm. "But what about all those people?"

"There's nothing we can do for them. Listen, we didn't sign on as caravan guards. We signed on as passengers. I warned Spike there was an attack coming and he chose to ignore it. Hell, none of *you* even believed me." I pointed a finger westward. "Do you believe me now?"

No one spoke.

"This is not our fight. You said it yourself, Eric. There's over a hundred armed people protecting that caravan, two of them Blackthorns. If they can't handle what's coming at them, our presence won't make any difference. We'll just die with them. So what we're going to do is keep moving, far and fast. We're going to push through today and all of tonight if we have to. If need be, we'll abandon the wagon. The horses should be able to carry most of the gear. We can use the oxen as pack mules. But it hasn't come to that yet, and I'd rather it didn't. Now if it's all right with all of you can we please, for the love of Christ, get moving?"

"I'm with him," Sabrina said. "Anybody crazy enough to take on Spike's group is no one we want to fuck with. We should get out of here. Now."

Eric jumped a bit, as if he had forgotten Sabrina was there. We both looked at her. The gray eyes were cold and hard, the mouth a thin, sharp line. It gave me an eerie feeling, like peering into a distorted mirror.

"You're right," Elizabeth said. "Let's go."

The reins slapped and the wagon began moving again. Eric spurred his horse, as did Elizabeth. I cast a glance at Hicks and saw him staring back toward the embattled caravan.

"Hicks. You coming?"

The young soldier waited a few seconds before he responded. "Yeah. I'm with you."

"Look, man. I don't like it either."

His face cleared and settled into its usual emotionless mask. "Don't much matter what we like or don't like, does it?"

I watched him catch up with the wagon and felt a hollow pit where my stomach should have been. The gunfire to the west increased in frequency and volume. I heard a few explosions, grenades or pipe bombs, maybe. I told myself if was not my fight, but the old voice of survival informed me it was not a matter of personal choice. There was no doubt we had been seen fleeing the caravan. Raiders do not like witnesses.

Whether we wanted it or not, the fight was coming to us.

EIGHTEEN

"Riders coming," Eric said.

I keyed my radio. "How many?"

"Twelve."

"Disposition?"

"They don't look happy."

"Can the jokes, Eric."

"Yeah, yeah. Skirmish line formation, five meter intervals. Probably not expecting much resistance. Bunch of auto-rifles and one long gun. Oh, and one of them has an RPG launcher and at least one rocket."

"So he dies first, then the long gun."

"Want me to take 'em now?"

"No, not yet. I want them to stay bunched together. How long until contact?"

"They don't seem to be in a hurry, but you know how fast that can change. Current pace, about fifteen mikes. At a gallop, maybe seven."

I cursed under my breath. *Doesn't leave us much time.*

"All right, get back up here. Time to make a plan."

"On my way."

I looked ahead to the low rise of squat buildings that had once been Wellsford, Kansas. Now it was an overgrown tangle of weeds, sapling trees, dilapidated houses, crumbling shacks, and rusted-out vehicles sinking slowly into the soft earth. Not a great place for a farmstead, but an excellent spot to set up an ambush.

"What's the situation," Hicks said, riding next to me.

"Riders on the way. Twelve of them."

"That all?"

"For now."

Elizabeth's face was pale, her eyes bright and wide like a hunted thing. "How are we going to fight twelve of them?"

"*We* aren't doing anything. You and Sabrina are going to hide while the rest of us set up an ambush."

"But what if we-"

"It's the only way," Sabrina interrupted. "We're on the plains. There's nowhere to run. Our only chance is to turn and fight. And you don't know how to fight, so somebody has to look after you. These guys are trained for this military shit. I'm not. I'm trained to run and hide. It's how I've stayed alive for this long, so I'm the one who protects you. End of discussion."

Elizabeth started to say something else, but then put her hands over her face and nearly fell from her saddle. I grabbed her and held her with one arm, feeling her body tremble against me.

"I don't know what to do, Gabe. I've never been this scared before. Not even during the Outbreak."

"What you do is listen to me. Okay? Sabrina survived out here for four years. She's been in some tough spots and always come out alive. She knows how to keep you safe. Stay low, stay quiet, and do what she says. The rest of us will deal with those raiders. Everything will be fine, I promise."

I knew it was a stupid thing to say as soon as it came out of my mouth; one can never promise the outcome of a fight. There are too many variables, too many things to account for, too much that can go wrong. But Elizabeth was only a few seconds away from falling apart, and I had to say something to calm her down. The job ahead of us was going to be hard enough as it was, the last thing we needed was someone going into hysterics.

"I'm so sorry, Gabe. I don't know why I'm acting like this."

"You're afraid, Elizabeth. The last time someone came after you with a gun you almost died. It's okay to be scared. Hell, I'm scared. But you have to control it, you hear? You can't let it break you apart. You have to hold yourself together. I can't focus on fighting raiders and babysitting you at the same time. Right now, I need you to be strong for me."

I said it more harshly than I wanted to, but I had to get the message across. Elizabeth took a few deep breaths, wiped her face, and sat up straight.

"Okay. If you all can handle it, so can I."

I kissed her on the cheek and thought I had never been more proud of her. "Remember your weapons. You're not helpless. If it comes down to it, you fight like a crazy woman. Hear me?"

She nodded and gave me a weak smile. I kissed her again and turned to Sabrina. "Take her and go. Stay hidden."

A short nod. "Got my radio. Let me know when it's all clear."

"Of course."

As they rode toward the thickest tangle of crud Sabrina could find, my daughter shot a look over her shoulder and I knew she understood the unspoken context of the conversation. We had only talked of winning, of what to do while Eric, Hicks and I dispatched the enemy. What we had not discussed was what to do if we failed, and died, and Sabrina and Elizabeth were on their own.

Before leaving Hollow Rock, Sabrina and I had a discussion about what to do if something happened to me and she faced capture by raiders. True to her pragmatic nature, her response to the topic had been fatalistic.

"I won't let myself be taken," she had said. "There are fates worse than dying. I've seen it with my own eyes."

"And if someone is with you, facing the same thing?" I asked.

A shrug. "I'll put them down too."

"Even me?"

"Don't take this the wrong way, Dad, but especially you."

I took no offense. I knew what she meant. Better to let a loved one die quickly and mercifully by one's own hand than to leave them to rape, torture, despair, and a hopeless, agonizing death.

I watched Elizabeth and my daughter disappear into the long brown grass and green saplings bordering the cracked and split highway and felt an unlikely sense of peace. No matter what happened in the next few minutes, Sabrina would keep her pledge. Elizabeth may not understand it, may be enraged and betrayed in her last moments if it came down to it, but it beat the alternative. If I ever got another chance and pressed her on the subject, I was willing to bet she would agree.

*****

208

The grass did a good job of hiding the claymores, but I was worried about the tripwires. "It's fast work, but it'll have to do."

Hicks looked at me and smirked. "I've seen worse."

"Doesn't matter anyway. We're out of time. Let's get into position."

Eric and Caleb stayed low as they ran behind abandoned cars on both sides of the highway. I ran a hundred yards southward and climbed the stairs of a moldy, stinking house with several bleached skeletons lying amidst a wide black stain on yellow-brown carpeting that may have once been white. The stairs led to a bedroom with a window facing the highway. I bashed out the window with the stock of my M-40, pulled a nightstand in front of it, and piled dusty, rotting blankets from a closet until I had the right height for a rifle rest. Then I retrieved a chair from the next room, settled into it, and peered through the scope.

The raiders had given us more time than I would have hoped for. They had tracked us slowly, several of them scanning the periphery of the road to make sure we had not split up. Finding no such sign, they had remained in formation and were now coming fully into view. True to Eric's assessment, they were armed with a motley collection of Kalashnikovs, M-4s, and civilian AR-15-pattern rifles. One man had a long hunting rifle and another carried an RPG launcher, rocket affixed, across his lap. Their demeanor was confident, determined, the swagger of men who believe they are in charge. If the fight with Spike's caravan had been tough on them they gave no sign. I saw no injuries, no pained faces, no slumped shoulders or hands clutching bandages to bloody wounds. What I saw were grins, predatory eyes, the perverse anticipation of human animals on the hunt for others of their kind. None of this boded well for Spike and his people, or the fortune in cargo I had abandoned to their care.

Damn you and your arrogance, Spike. You should have listened.

I pushed the doomed caravan out of my head and thought about the wagon a hundred and fifty yards up the road. I thought of the explosives I had brought from Hollow Rock, hidden in our food supplies, wrapped in bundles surrounded by grain, beans, and dried peas. I thought about one of the wagon's wheels, how it had been deliberately removed, the oxen loosed from their yokes and contentedly chewing dry grass along the edges of the highway. I thought of the bundles of cargo still in the back of the wagon, easy pickings. I thought how all this might look to a raider: *They got spooked, cut their losses, took off on horseback. Probably scattered. Doesn't matter. We got the numbers on our side. We'll track them down.*

It would have been a logical assumption regarding most people. But as I had once told my daughter, I am not most people. Nor, for that matter, are Caleb and Eric.

I kept my breathing under control and positioned the reticle where I needed it. The riders were headed toward the trip wires. I had positioned the explosives to blast a semicircle straight back the way we had come. If the raiders hit the wires, that part of the job was done. If they did not, it was my responsibility to remote-detonate the claymores as soon as the wires were recognized.

And now, even though every instinct was howling for me to start carving some proverbial notches, I forced myself to wait. This attack needed to be perfect. We could afford no survivors. For this reason, Red waited around the back of the house tethered to a pine tree. If anyone rode off I would jump on my horse and give pursuit. That said, I sincerely did not want to jump on my horse and give pursuit. I wanted to do this quickly and efficiently and get back on the road to a more defensible position and use my satellite phone to call for assistance.

But that was later. Right now, I needed to focus on the threat at hand.

My earpiece crackled as I hit the transmit key. "Stand by. They're moving into position. Wait for the signal."

Two quick static chirps from each of my companions came by way of acknowledgment. The raiders drew to within fifty yards of the tripwires. A quick tug on the bolt of my rifle showed me there was a round loaded and seated. A twist of my hand confirmed the suppressor was on tightly. I listened to my heartbeat and slowed my breathing. The pulsing in my ears slowed with it. I leaned over the rifle, pulled it into firing position, and felt the old sense of calm descend.

Back in my Marine Corps days, I had once told my old friend Rocco that there were only two times in life I felt truly alive. When he asked what they were, I said, "When I'm in bed with a hot girl, and when I'm pulling the trigger."

At the time, he thought I was joking. I was not.

The two thrills, however, come from very different places within me and produce completely dissimilar effects. The rush I get from pulling the trigger is not sexual. It has no carnal implications. Rather, I feel as if I'm in an altered state of awareness, of calmness, like I'm reaching across some great abyss within myself and touching something at the center of who I am. It is quiet there. It is tranquil. And in this place, I feel nothing. I am a void.

And now, with the stench of moldering fabric in my nose and the rough texture of the trigger under my finger, the echoes of the void were heartbeats, its walls the parallax of the scope in front of my right eye. I sighted in on the man with the RPG. He was not tall, not particularly savage looking. He had long brown hair tied back with a piece of shoelace. His beard was reddish-brown with streaks of gray. I guessed his age at thirty-five to forty. Regardless

211

of the day's outcome, he would not see another sunrise. I wondered if he had known that this morning would be the last he would ever see, what would he have done differently? Not that it mattered. It was almost time.

My right hand rested lightly around the grip of my rifle while my left hand cupped the remote detonator, thumb poised over the switch. The raiders continued riding toward the wagon. The tripwire was now less than thirty feet in front of them.

And then a voice rose from the highway.

I could not make out what it said, but the effect was clear—the raiders halted. A man near the middle of the formation held up a hand, eyes fixed on the road ahead. His body language told me he was suspicious, the careful type, and had caught wind of something he did not like.

I heard static over the radio. "Gabe," Hicks said. "I got eyes on the leader."

"Copy. Maintaining visual on the RPG. Eric, you still on the long gun?"

"Got him. Just give the signal."

"Earplugs in?"

A round of affirmatives. I pulled out the small plastic radio earpiece and shoved a plug into my right ear, then keyed the radio.

"Stand by."

I watched the leader lower his hand. His eyes narrowed and swept the highway from left to right, pausing to examine the tangles of grass at the edges. For a moment, his gaze lingered on exactly the spot where I had placed a claymore and I felt my stomach clench. Then he turned his head and began speaking to the man beside him. The men around him were all watching him now, hands easing reins to one side or the other. They were going to split up.

I pressed the detonator switch.

The explosion was incredible. Two claymores went off simultaneously, hurling hundreds of little metal balls into the line of raiders at incredible speed. The eight men in the center virtually disintegrated in front of my eyes, limbs and heads and fractions of torso spinning madly through the air. Their horses fared no better and collapsed into barely recognizable lumps of shredded meat.

The four men on the periphery, however, were mostly unscathed. The breath had been knocked out of them and their ears were most certainly ringing, but they were alive. The skirmish line had been wide, and at the distance I had triggered the explosives, I knew would not get all of them. Worse, the RPG and the long gun were among the survivors. Two muted cracks rang out from Eric's side of the road and I watched twin blossoms of red mist explode from the long gunner's back. He slid from the saddle and was still.

Nice shot.

RPG was still on his horse, but disoriented. I let out half a breath, put the reticle center of mass, and fired. The rocket launcher fell from limp fingers as the man carrying it fell over sideways. His horse, spooked by the commotion, ran off to the north, its rider's leg stuck in the stirrup, body bouncing limply along the bumpy highway.

The last two men must have been well trained. They recovered from their shock and began firing in the general direction of Eric and the house where I was hidden. Bullets pocked through the wall to my left, forcing me to drop down and take cover. Another shot rang out and I heard a scream. Hicks had gotten one of them.

I risked a peek over the window sill and peered through the scope. No one there.

"Hicks, you got eyes on the last guy?"

Static. "He's riding away. I don't have a shot. Repeat, I don't have a shot."

"I'm on it."

I was up from the floor and bounding down the stairs in seconds, rifle slung over my back. Red was still tethered to the tree in the back yard, head high and tail twitching. He had been around enough gunfire to know something was amiss. Rather than waste time untying him, I cut the lead rope with my Bowie knife, climbed into the saddle, and kicked his haunches.

"Come on, Red. Let's go."

The big horse pushed off the ground with a tremendous snort and barreled full-tilt toward the highway. I kept my head low, hands loose on the reins, thinking how grateful I was I had trimmed Red's mane before leaving Wichita. If I had not, it would have been whipping me in the face.

I caught sight of the rider as soon as Red cleared the last building in Wellsford and eased the big fella to the right. Now we were in line with the fleeing raider, directly behind him. Red caught the gist of what we were doing and picked up speed, his long legs stretching out to catch the pavement in front of him, iron-shod hooves knocking up loose bits of asphalt. The rider ahead of me glanced over his shoulder, drew a pistol, and started squeezing off shots in my general direction. I could tell by the way he was holding the weapon he would not hit us, but that did not make getting chopped away at any more fun. I drew my own pistol, stood up a bit in the stirrups, and fired one handed. I knew I was unlikely to hit him at this range, but returning fire is almost always a better option than not doing so.

The rider fired three more times, then pulled the trigger on an empty magazine. He showed his discipline by holstering the weapon, seizing the reins with both hands, and urging more speed from his horse.

A few seconds later, Red had noticeably cut the distance between us. I was not surprised. Not only is my trusty steed big, strong, and fast, he was also fresh. The other horse had been on the road a long time, probably running sprints around Spike's caravan during the assault. I doubted the rider had let his mount take a drink or eat anything for a while. Red, on the other hand, had enjoyed a bucket of water and a few handfuls of oats while Caleb and Eric were helping me set up the ambush. With horses, such things greatly affect athletic performance. Humans too, for that matter.

The horse ahead of me ducked its head as it ran, froth flying from its mouth. I could tell by its body language it was exhausted. Red plowed steadily ahead, the two great bellows that were his lungs steadily pumping oxygen into his blood. When we were close to overtaking them, I aimed my pistol with one hand, breathed out slowly, held my shoulder loose like a gyroscope, and fired twice. The first round caught the edge of one of the raider's shoulders and ripped away a chunk of blood and fabric. As he shouted in pain and surprise, the second shot took him center of mass in the back. He went instantly limp and fell bonelessly to the ground.

Red overshot him, his attention on pursuing the horse, not the rider. I hauled on the reins and turned him around and stopped beside the fallen raider. To my surprise, he was still alive. I climbed down and stood over him to get a closer look. He lay on his back, eyes open wide, face bright with confusion and fear, lungs laboring, blood spraying from pale lips as he coughed, a bleeding exit wound in his centerline just below the sternum.

"Can't...can't feel my legs."

I fired a round into his thigh. He flinched, but his leg remained limp. His face registered no sign of pain.

"Must have got you through the spine. Can you feel your arms?"

"N…no."

"Then you've got a choice to make. You can lie here and wait to die, or I can end it quick and clean. What's it gonna be?"

"What…what do you want?"

"The raiders you're with. How many are there?"

His face split into a grin and he began to laugh. "Too many…for you…dead man."

I aimed the pistol at his head. "Quick or slow. Your choice. How many?"

"Doesn't…matter. They'll find you. Then you'll…know…when they kill you."

There was nothing more for me to do. I couldn't hurt him. Literally. The spinal injury took care of that. And if I left him alive, he might get a chance to tell his friends something to help them find me. I centered my aim and looked the dying man in the eye.

"You first."

NINETEEN

We rode east along the highway for as long as we dared, while Caleb and Eric hung back and took turns keeping an eye on our six. They saw no more pursuers. We covered twelve miles by nightfall and pushed on a few miles farther past the town of Cullison.

The plain was crisscrossed every mile or so by narrow service roads, most of them still more or less paved. This worked in our favor. Not only would traveling over pavement make us harder to track, assuming we cleaned up after the animals, but since there were so many roads we could have chosen, the raiders behind us would have to split their forces to attempt an effective search.

The path we chose took us over gently sloping terrain that rose up for close to a mile before sweeping sharply back down. When I figured we were close to the bottom of the shallow valley, I switched on my IR scope and looked behind us. I could not see over the ridge, which meant the raiders would not be able to see us from the road even in daylight. Another point in our favor.

Just after midnight I spotted the unmistakable cylindrical shape of grain elevators pointing toward the sky. I had the group halt and wait off the path while I rode ahead and reconned the area. It was quickly obvious the place was abandoned. Nothing had been disturbed for a long time, possibly since the Outbreak.

The grain elevators were still structurally stable, as were the ladders and catwalks leading to their peaks. There was a long cinder-block storage building at the elevators' base that was perfect for hiding the livestock and wagon. A little further down the road was a farmhouse and a barn. The roof of the house was half torn away, probably the victim of a high-plains twister, but the barn was intact. I thought about news reports of tornadoes back in the old days, of people describing how a funnel cloud would rip apart an entire town, and in the midst of it all, one house would be left standing unscathed. I had a feeling I was looking at the aftermath of just such an event. Then I had another thought and looked around the periphery of the house, and sure enough, I found the twin doors of a storm shelter.

The doors were padlocked, but a pair of bolt cutters has long been a staple of my survival kit. I cut the lock, activated the tactical light on my M-4, and opened one of the doors. The white beam cut deep into the darkness below, revealing a set of damp, green-tinted wooden stairs. A quick test with my foot determined the stairs were intact enough to hold my weight. I had a moment's indecision about how to proceed and decided it was best not to take unnecessary risks. I radioed for Eric to join me.

Static. "On my way."

When I heard the approach of hooves on soft grass I waved my tac-light in his direction. He saw it, dismounted, and tied his gelding to the same low maple branch I had tied Red.

"Whatcha got?"

I pointed down the stairs with my rifle. "Storm shelter. Stairs are in good shape."

"Let's clear it."

Eric switched to his pistol. I stuck with my rifle. We both took a moment to make sure rounds were chambered, suppressors were secured, and safeties were off. I went down first, leading with my rifle. The beam swept left, right, up and down. I saw no movement. The room smelled like mildew and old motor oil. To my right was a set of metal shelves with a collection of assorted engine parts, cans of bolts and screws, cracked radiator hoses, and other lumps of plastic and metal junk I could not immediately identify. To my left the space opened out to a bare concrete floor, cinder-block walls, and a metal door. Eric followed me down.

"Clear so far," I said.

"I'll take point in the next room."

"Yep."

Eric stacked up right, I took left. I gripped the door handle and turned it slowly. It was unlocked. I looked at Eric. He nodded. I pulled the door open wide, let him through, and followed close behind.

Eric's light tracked over one side of the room while mine shone on the other. On my side was a dust-covered couch, coffee table, and in the far corner of the room, a recliner with a table and lamp on one side. Next to me I heard Eric curse softly and I swiveled on my heels to see his side of the room. Where his light pointed, three ghouls were rising to their feet, still identifiable as the people they once were. One was a woman in a floral print dress, another a man in denim overalls and a blue pocket tee, and the last was a young boy in jeans and a short sleeved button-down shirt. Their skin was pale grey, eyes red in the glaring light.

Eric did not hesitate. He put two bullets in the head of the boy before he had even risen to his feet. It was a sound tactical decision, as ghoul children are significantly faster than their adult counterparts. As Eric fired, I canted my rifle, aimed through the back-up iron sights mounted forty-five degrees from my scope, and triggered two rounds. Both split the skull of the woman and painted the wall behind her with twin spots of crimson. Last was the man. He was lurching toward us by the time Eric drew down on him and fired. A single round took off most of the top of his skull. He collapsed, twitched twice, and was still. The entire incident took maybe five seconds.

We listened in silence, lights scanning the room. Other than the dead bodies, we were alone. I walked over and kicked the boy and the man over onto their backs. The boy had a small bite on his arm but no other injuries. The man and woman were covered in bites on their faces and arms, and much of their lower torsos had been ripped away. The boys mouth was a rictus of old, dried blood and black teeth. The other two showed no indication of ever having fed. From the corner of my eye, I saw a revolver lying on the coffee table. To my right, a small stairway led up to a heavy wooden door which I could tell was locked by the position of the deadbolt latch.

I lowered my rifle. "Not too hard to read this one."

"The kid gets bit," Eric said, "And the dad shoots the thing that bit him. I bet if you check that pistol there's rounds missing."

I did, and he was right. There were only three rounds in the cylinder. "And after he shoots the boy's attacker, they hunker down here." I pointed to the locked door. "Came in from inside the house, locked the door behind them."

Eric nodded. "So then they settle in and eventually the boy turns and his parents can't bring themselves to put him down and he kills them."

"One first, then the other. The second one had to watch. Probably too horrified to run away."

Eric wiped his face. When his hand came away, he looked a few years older. "Hell of a way to go. How long you think they been down here?"

220

"Clothes are still in okay shape. Maybe since the Outbreak."

"Jesus."

"You may notice they haven't rotted very much."

"Yep."

"And I'm willing to bet if they had fed enough, they'd be grays by now."

"Yep."

We turned and went back out into the open air. There was no discussion necessary. A night in the safety of a storm shelter would have been nice, but there was no way we were sleeping down there.

*****

Hicks volunteered to take the first watch. No one argued. We were all too exhausted. I gave the young soldier my IR goggles, admonished him not to hurt them, and watched him melt away into the night.

The rest of us put down our bedrolls in the barn's loft and lay down to rest. There was no conversation. No one had the energy.

The next thing I remember is a creak of wood and Hicks whispering to Eric the IR goggles still had three-quarters charge and to use them sparingly. It was full dark then. Another creak of wood came to me what felt like seconds later, but when I opened my eyes, the first gray shafts of dawn clutched the rim of the horizon.

"Last watch," Eric said, handing me the goggles. I took them and checked the battery. Half charged. I handed them back to Eric.

"Put them on a panel."

"Probably won't charge all the way. Too early."

"Do it anyway. Better than nothing."

"Sure."

I kissed Elizabeth on the cheek, smoothed Sabrina's hair away from her elfin face, told them both I loved them in a low whisper, and climbed down from the loft.

The sky was cloudy to the east and clear to the west, which did not really tell me anything. Kansas in late winter is a volatile place. Warm one day and cold the next. I would have to watch the skies carefully going forward, as storms can be downright deadly in this part of the world.

I walked to the storage building to check on the horses and oxen and found Eric had already fed them and put water in their buckets. The room reeked of piss and shit and filthy animals. I greeted Red and said a few kind words to him and promised better treatment once we were all out of danger.

Back outside, I walked to the pump Eric had used to water the animals and splashed my face a few times. The cold water revived me somewhat and shook a few of the cobwebs loose. I gazed at the pump for a moment, reminded myself to fill the gerry cans before we left, and desperately hoped we would be able to find enough water in the days ahead to keep the animals, and ourselves, alive.

A couple of hours later, when the sun was high over the horizon and I had walked and stretched and drank some water and was feeling something more like a human being, I headed back to the loft. The others were already awake and gathered in a circle on the dirt floor of the barn. They had collected chairs from inside the house and Hicks had scrounged a small charcoal grill from somewhere. He had a small fire going, a pot of dried potatoes, dried peas, and chicken jerky rehydrating in the hot water. The smell made my empty stomach groan.

"Got you a seat," Elizabeth said, patting a low camping stool beside her. I sat down and kissed her on the side of her neck. Her mouth turned up in a small smile and it made me feel better to see it.

"So what's the plan?" Eric said. His eyes, like mine, were fixed firmly on the cook pot. None of us had eaten since the previous morning.

"We'll talk after breakfast."

The food was done quickly but still took entirely too long. Hicks made plenty of it, and when we were done, there was nary a scrap left over. It was by far one of the better meals I have ever eaten. Cervantes was right. Hunger is the best sauce.

"For today," I said finally, "we stay put. We need to rest and so do the animals. That said, we'll make preparations to ride out of here on a moment's notice."

"I have a proposal," Hicks said.

"What's that?"

"How about I parallel our back trail and see if I can get a line on those raiders. Recon only. Be nice to know what we're up against."

I thought it over. The man had a point. "It'll be dangerous."

"What isn't these days?"

I nodded at that. "I'll go with you."

Elizabeth turned to me. "Gabe…"

"I don't want him going alone. It's too dangerous. We'll have our radios with us and we'll bring the horses. We've done this kind of thing before, Elizabeth. We know how to stay out of sight."

"I don't think either of you should go. What if someone sees you and follows you back here?"

223

"That's extremely damned unlikely. But regardless, it's a risk we have to take. Right now, those raiders are between us and Colorado. We have to find a way past them. If we don't, then sooner or later they're going to catch up to us. If that happens, I'd rather have it on my terms, not theirs."

"Exactly what I was thinking," Hicks said.

"There's also the matter of what happened to Spike's caravan," Eric said.

I scratched the side of my jaw, nails scraping the week-old beard. "Yeah. I'd like to know that too."

"You haven't said a word about your trade," Sabrina said. I glanced at her and she held my gaze with steady, implacable determination. "That was our meal ticket. Won't do us much good to reach Colorado flat-on-our-ass broke. I've heard about the refugee camps outside the Springs, and I gotta tell you, I'd rather take my chances in the mountains."

"What I brought with us was only about a third of my net worth," I said. "The rest is still back in Hollow Rock. I do business regularly with several merchants in the Springs, and at least a few of them will give me credit enough to get us set up. Not to mention I have a job offer from the largest mercenary outfit around. We'll manage."

"Except you don't have a job *offer*. You have a letter of interest. I might just be a poor uneducated Traveler girl, but I know they're not the same thing."

"I'll get the job, don't worry about that. But at the moment, that's of secondary concern. Right now we need to figure out how we're going to get to Colorado alive."

"And that's looking like a tall order," Eric said.

"Maybe not." I reached into a pocket on my vest and produced my satellite phone.

"That thing charged?" Eric asked.

"No. Can you take care of it while we're out?"

"No problem."

"Radios too. We'll take the fresh batteries while the others charge."

Eric nodded. "Hicks, did you throw out the deep-cycle battery?"

"No. 'Bout the only heavy thing I didn't throw out. Figured we'd need it."

"Good man."

I stood up. "Caleb?"

The young soldier grabbed his rifle and stood as well. "Let's get it done."

TWENTY

We tethered the horses in a small stand of trees a mile and a half away from the ambush site and proceeded the rest of the way in on foot. The tall grass concealed us as we traversed the last few hundred yards on our bellies.

When we reached the edge of the highway, I slowly raised my head and pulled up the hood of my ghillie suit. A slight rustle beside me told me Hicks was doing the same. I heard no sound above the wind and could see no movement in the town or on the road leading to it. We were on the east side of Haviland, looking westward, about two hundred feet from the first building lining the highway.

"Anything?" Hicks whispered.

"Not yet."

I carefully removed a small pair of binoculars from my belt and cupped my hands around the lenses to hood them from the sun. Doing so reduced the possibility of creating a flash in the sunlight. I watched the town for the better part of an hour, remaining as still as possible. Hicks watched the other side of the highway through a little hunting monocular he'd bought from Eric a few months ago. He made no sound, not even a rustle of grass from the movement of his lungs as he breathed. I would have been very interested to know who had trained Hicks, because it sure as hell was not the Army. The average grunt cannot do the things Hicks can do. Not with the same degree of casual skill, anyway. I had asked him about it before, and he had stonewalled me. Whatever mysterious forces had made him who he was, he wasn't talking. Not to me, at least. Which, of course, only made me all the more curious.

"I got nothing over here," Hicks said. "You?"

"Nada. Let's move in. See what we see."

And we did. Forty-five minutes later we had swept the town and found it empty of everything except tracks.

"We should go back and get the horses," I said. "Ride a circle around this place, mark each track we find. Maybe get an idea how many raiders there are."

"Gonna take a while."

"You got plans today?"

"Nope."

After retrieving the horses, I rooted around a small lumber yard on the edge of town and found a crate of rusted nails in an outdoor shed the Army must have missed when they scavenged the place. Hicks and I used the nails to mark each unique track we found by stabbing a nail into it and keeping count as we went. We started at just after ten in the morning, and by the time we finished, the sun was a low orange ball sitting in a pool of crimson and purple on the horizon.

"What do you have?" I asked.

"I count a hundred and fifty-two I'm sure of. Maybe ten or fifteen I can't tell for certain. You?"

"Hundred and forty-two confirmed. Thirty or forty might be different, might not be."

Hicks nodded silently. Some of the tracks were clearly from unique people, while others may have been repeated prints from the same tracks we'd already identified. Many of the tracks were partial, obscured by hoof prints and scuffs and such, making positive identification impossible.

"Lot of blood," Hicks said. "Lot of bullet holes and shell casings. Lot of streaks where bodies were dragged off."

I looked around and grunted. Hardly a window was left unshattered or a wall not riddled with bullet holes of various calibers. There was evidence of no less than two RPG blasts, and beneath the eaves of a house on the south side of town bordering the highway, I found the links left behind by the belt-fed ammo of an M-240 heavy machine gun and a slew of NATO 7.62x51 shell casings.

"Looks like they set up on both sides of the highway," I said. "Let the caravan get all the way into the zone of fire before they opened up. Hit them with RPGs at the head and rear to prevent escape. M-240 lit 'em up from the southwest while small arms fire strafed from two other directions."

"Takes control to set up a crossfire like that and not hit your own people," Hicks said. "Shows discipline."

"And training."

"Still risky for whoever did it. But done properly, highly effective."

I looked at the scorch marks to the west. "There's no bodies, no dropped weapons, no unwanted cargo. Even the wreckage of the destroyed wagons has been hauled away. The only indication anything went awry is the bullet casings, blast marks, and blood. And I'm willing to bet those were only left behind because we escaped and the people they sent to find us never came back."

"Which tells us they're a lot more concerned about getting caught than they are about finding us."

"And they're right to be," I said. "Probably think we're running scared and at least a week's ride away from Wichita. With all these service roads out here, they'd need to send hundreds of people to find us. Easier just to haul away the bodies, wagons, and cargo. If anyone comes to investigate, assuming rain and wind and whatever else haven't fucked things up too much, all the Army's going to know is a caravan came through, there was a fight, and the caravan disappeared. They're not going to waste their time marking tracks or counting bullet casings. They'll file a report, tell patrols to be on the lookout for a raider force of something more than a hundred, and maybe in a couple of weeks they'll get a cargo manifest out to the safe zones. Not that it'll do any good. These assholes will be long gone."

Hicks pulled a nail out of the ground and hurled it at a building. It hit the wall with a crack and fell to the ground. "Motherfuckers. This was a professional operation, Gabe. These guys knew what they were doing."

"And there's a lot of them," I said. "Take away the hundred and thirty or so tracks that belong to Spike's people, and we're probably looking at a force of at least two hundred. Ever heard of a raider band that big?"

"Insurgents, yes, back during the Alliance's heyday. But raiders? No. Too petty. Too contentious. Too likely to kill each other and break apart into smaller groups."

"Which means whoever is leading this bunch must be one ruthless son of a bitch."

"Yep."

I pulled a clean cloth from a pouch on my vest, poured some water on it, and wiped my face and neck. The cool air on wet skin

229

was refreshing. "Nothing more we can do here. It's getting late. We should head back."

"You go," Hicks said. "I'll camp here tonight, see if I can figure out which way they headed in the morning."

"You sure?"

"Yeah."

"Want us to come back for you?"

"No. I'll catch up. Be back before 1300 hours, rain or shine."

"Okay. See you tomorrow."

I climbed into the saddle and rode back to camp.

TWENTY-ONE

"Looks like it's rain."

Hicks wrinkled his forehead at me.

"You said you'd be back today by 1300, rain or shine."

"Oh. Right."

The young soldier dropped his rucksack and sat down in a wooden chair next to Sabrina. His Army-issue pancho was slick with water, his boots were muddy, and there were dark circles under his eyes. The skin of his face looked pale under a thin coating of week-old beard. The rest of us sat wrapped in blankets around a small fire in the barn. Outside, rain came down in sheets while the wind roared and moaned through the eaves above us and made the tin shingles on what was left of the farmhouse's roof clatter like metal bones. It was just past noon.

"Don't look like you slept much," Elizabeth said.

Hicks made a slight movement that may have been a shake of his head. "Didn't."

"Wanna tell me what you've been up to?" I asked.

He looked up then, blue eyes sunken from exhaustion. "Afraid I lied to you."

"I gathered as much."

Another slight movement. Maybe a nod this time. I could not be sure.

"Picked up the trail pretty easy. Followed it about eight miles before I found them. Dark by then. Backed off a ways, picketed my horse, and went in on my belly."

I had to bite down on an angry comment. Going after the raiders alone was a dumb move. He knew it, I knew it, and he knew I knew it. But that's Hicks for you. He does what he wants to do, and there's not much one can do to stop him. Reprimanding him after the fact would have been about as productive as asking a wave not to break itself against an ocean wall.

"Find out anything useful?"

"There's at least two hundred of them. Probably more."

"What about Spike's people?"

"I counted thirteen prisoners. All women and girls. No men, no boys."

Elizabeth closed her eyes and put a hand over her mouth. "Jesus."

"I ain't gonna lie," Hicks went on. "It was bad."

"What about the others?" I said. "Any sign?"

"Yeah. The bastards dug a mass grave, tossed 'em in like cordwood. Gave their own dead a proper burial. Looked like eight or nine of them."

"That's it?" Eric asked. "All those people in the caravan, and they only got eight or nine?"

Hicks nodded. "That's what it looked like."

"Mary mother of God," Eric whispered. "And we got twelve of them."

"Only because we took 'em by surprise," Hicks replied, "And only because we had those claymores."

"So Hicks has confirmed what we already suspected," I said, trying to keep everyone focused on the right part of the problem. "We're facing a professional band of raiders, skilled and coordinated enough to take out even large, well-protected caravans."

Eric stood up and began pacing. "Which means they'd crush us like fucking bugs."

"If they were worried about us, yeah," Hicks said. "But I don't think they are."

Eric stopped. "What makes you say that?"

No one moved for a few seconds. Hicks picked up a stick and poked at the fire. A few of the larger sticks on the pile broke and fell into the coals, new flames curling to life around them.

"They're headed south. Saw them leave this morning. Left behind about half of Spike's wagons, but no cargo."

"They didn't cache anything?" I asked.

"Nope. Looked like they got no plans to come back any time soon."

I mulled this news over. We were near one of the busiest supply routes between Colorado and the eastern settlements. If the raiders planned to come back this way, chances were strong they would have hidden a supply stash somewhere. It was what I would have done, anyway. If they didn't, it meant either they were very poor planners, which I doubted, or they were finished raiding in southern Kansas for the foreseeable future. I said as much.

"So we're in the clear," Sabrina said. "All we have to do it make it to Colorado Springs."

I nodded, but said nothing. I was thinking about those thirteen prisoners, all female. I was thinking about what would happen to them when the raiders got wherever they were going. I looked at Sabrina and Elizabeth and thought about what I would do if they were captured. Eric caught me staring and walked over to stand in front of me.

"I know what you're thinking, Gabe. And it's a bad idea."

I did not reply.

"It sucks. It's horrible. But we can't save them."

"You don't know that for sure."

A gentle hand settled onto my arm. "Gabriel, listen to me." Elizabeth said. "We need you. Now is not the time to go running off into a fight you can't win."

Sabrina looked at me, Elizabeth, and then Eric. "Somebody want to tell me what the hell you're talking about?"

"He wants to go after them," Eric said. "Like a fucking idiot."

I stood up quickly and got an inch from Eric's face. "What if it were Allison? What if it were your son? Would you call me an idiot for going after them?"

My voice echoed briefly in the barn. An impressive feat, considering the noise from the wind and rain. Eric's steady gaze wavered, then fell away.

"That's what I thought."

"Gabe," Elizabeth said. "What if they catch you?"

"They won't."

"You don't know that."

I turned to her and gave her the full weight of my attention. "One way or another, I won't let myself be captured."

She caught the meaning, stood up, and gripped the front of my shirt. "No, goddammit. Do you hear me? I'm telling you no. Do not go. I've lost too many people. I'm not losing you too."

I took her hands and gently eased them away. "Thirteen women and girls, Elizabeth. Thirteen. Do you know what raiders do to women? To children?"

Her eyes stayed fixed, but she said nothing.

"What if it were you? Or Sabrina? Would you want me to just abandon you?"

More silence. Her eyes grew watery and began to fill.

"I have to do this. I won't be able to live with myself if I don't. And then what kind of a husband will I be? What kind of father?"

"You can't," Elizabeth said, her voice a harsh whisper. "There are too many of them."

"Too many for me, yeah." I patted the pouch on my vest with the satellite phone. "But not too many for the Army."

Hicks cleared his throat and stood up. "Which brings me to the point I was about to make before things got all dramatic."

Everyone turned to look at him. Hicks' attention settled on Eric.

"Afraid I'm gonna have to tender my resignation, bossman. My first loyalty is to the Army. I can't let a threat like those raiders go unchecked, not after what they did. And God only knows what else they've done. Duty requires I follow them and report their movements at the earliest opportunity."

"That," Eric said flatly, "is the biggest crock of horse-shit I've ever heard."

A smile. "Maybe. Doesn't matter. I'm going after them. If Gabe is going too, we might as well work together."

"And what the fuck are the rest of us supposed to do?" Sabrina said. "Just sit here and wait for you two to come back?"

I looked at Eric. After a few seconds, he threw his hands in the air and let out an exasperated curse.

"Fine. I'll do it. But you owe me, Gabe."

"I know."

Sabrina picked up a stick and threw it at Eric. He swatted it away.

"Explain, fucker," she said. "I don't speak whatever silent, jackass language you two have."

"He wants us to go west. He'll catch up when he can."

Sabrina turned toward me. "Uh-uh. Not gonna happen."

"Sabrina…"

"No. Don't. Just don't. You might be my father, and I appreciate all you've done for me, but I do not answer to you. You don't get to order me around and expect me to just meekly go along with whatever you say. I'm not going anywhere without you. You go after those raiders, I'm going with you."

I took a step forward and very slowly reached up to touch her face. "Sabrina, you are a pain in the ass. But you're my daughter, and I love you, and I can't put you in the kind of danger I'm walking into. You're the only family I have left."

"Hey!" Eric and Elizabeth said at the same time. I held up a hand.

"Sorry. You know what I mean."

Their hackles went down.

236

"Did it ever occur to you," Sabrina said, her voice growing husky, "that you're the only family *I* have left?"

I let out a sigh and pulled her to my chest. She did not resist. "Yes, it did. But here's the thing: I can't leave those people to die. I have to do something because if I don't, no one else will."

Hicks pointed a finger at me and tilted his head. "Were you not here about ten seconds ago? You heard the part about me going after them, right?"

I frowned at him. "You know what I mean."

Hicks rolled his eyes.

"And I can't help those people," I continued, turning back to Sabrina, "if I'm constantly worried about you. I need you out of the line of fire. I won't be able to concentrate otherwise. You come along, I'm a whole lot more likely to get killed. I know it's a hard thing to hear, but it's the truth."

Sabrina grabbed the back of my jacket and squeezed. "Well, at least you didn't try to bullshit me."

"So you'll stay?"

"I thought you wanted me to go with Eric?"

Another sigh. "You know what I mean."

TWENTY-TWO

The first day on the trail I called General Jacobs' secure line with the satellite phone. A polite digitized female voice answered and asked for my authorization code. I gave it. The voice told me to stand by and someone would be with me momentarily. The someone turned out to be a lieutenant with a steady, bookish voice who asked me for my name, unit, and the reason for my call.

"My name is Gabriel Garrett," I said. "I'm not active-duty military, but I'm registered in the Archive. I'll wait while you look me up."

I could almost see the face puckering on the other side. "I'm sorry, sir, but if you're not active-duty military you'll need to-"

"I'm a contractor," I interrupted. "And I know contractors aren't normally given this number, but General Jacobs gave it to me personally. So trust me, you want to look me up before you blow me off. Might save your career."

The lieutenant was silent a moment, then told me to hold and he would be back with me shortly. He sounded angry. I did not care. Eight years in the Marines, a stint with the CIA, and several more years with the top-secret arm of a mercenary outfit sanctioned by Homeland Security—not to mention all the wetwork I've done for

General Jacobs since the Outbreak—has left me with very little patience for the self-importance of middle-management officer types. In fact, if I had wanted to, I could have taken a field commission as a colonel working directly for General Jacobs at Army Special Operations Command. Thing is, I didn't want to. Hence my status as a highly-valued civilian contractor with a direct line to one of the most powerful men in the Union.

"General Jacobs is away on assignment," the young-sounding officer said. "Can I take a message?"

"No. Whatever clearance you have, it's not enough. Put me in touch with Jacobs' chief of staff."

"I'm not authorized to do that, sir." The voice was downright lemony. I had, after all, called his boss 'Jacobs' and not 'General Jacobs'. He was probably not used to that level of familiarity pertaining to someone who could make or break his career with the stroke of a pen.

"Then find someone who is."

A pause. "Listen, sir-"

"No, you listen. I don't have time for this shit. I have a priority message to give the general and he needs it yesterday. If you can't get it done, go find someone who can. Because I guarantee you if he doesn't get my report very fucking soon, heads are going to roll. Starting with yours. Get me?"

Maybe it was my tone, or the confidence in my voice, but when the lieutenant spoke after an uncomfortable silence, he sounded subdued. "Of course, sir. I'll have to place you on hold, but I'll be back as soon as I can."

"You hang up on me and I'll have your liver on a platter."

"Yes sir." The line went silent, but I could tell by the static it was still open.

"Nice," Hicks chuckled. He sat astride his horse as we followed the raiders' trail southeast across the Kansas plains. "Not too subtle, but nice."

"I'm nothing if not effective."

"No argument there."

The line was quiet for nearly five minutes. Finally, a mature male voice picked up.

"This is Colonel Frank Stephens. State your name and make your report."

"My name is Gabriel Garrett." I gave the declaration time to sink in. The other voice did not reply for a few moments, which told me I had struck a nerve.

"Garrett, huh? Heard about you."

"I'm sure you have."

Stephens cleared his throat. "So what you got for me?"

"You stationed in the Springs?"

"I'm with ASOC, so yeah. Why?"

"Ever heard of a caravan outfit goes under the name of Morningstar Transport? It's one of the biggest outfits in the Springs, headed by a guy who calls himself Spike."

"Yeah, I heard of 'em. Why?"

"You might want to put in a call with the FTIC. They've been taken out by a band of raiders over two-hundred strong. Spike's dead, and so are most of his people. Raiders took the trade and thirteen prisoners, all female, and are headed southeast. I'm on their trail with Sergeant Caleb Hicks, First Reconnaissance Expeditionary out of Fort McCray. He's listed in the Archive among the same group of upstanding citizens as I am."

The sound of fingers clicking over a keyboard traveled across the line. I counted to six before Colonel Stephens spoke again.

"I'll need as many details as you can provide, Mr. Garrett."

So I did. When I finished, the colonel asked to speak with Caleb. His report was much the same as mine, although he punctuated his sentences with 'yes sir' and 'no sir'. Not unwise for a sergeant speaking to a colonel. When he was finished, he held the phone out to me.

"Says he wants to talk to you."

I took the handset and said, "Yes, Colonel?" No harm in being polite. My mother always told me one catches more flies with honey than with vinegar.

"For now I need you to continue reconnaissance," Stephens said. "Consider yourself on the clock. Full compensation per your usual fee upon completion of the mission."

"What constitutes completing the mission?" I asked.

"Honestly, I don't know yet. But I'm damned sure Phil ain't gonna be happy about this. He'll want retribution, and that right soon."

The fact Colonel Stephens had called General Jacobs 'Phil' without a hitch in his voice told me all I needed to know about him.

"I'm on it, Colonel."

"Call me with an update by 0900 tomorrow."

"Will do."

The line went dead.

"So?" Hicks asked.

"It seems we're sanctioned."

241

The young soldier's eyes brightened and narrowed all at once. "Perfect."

*****

My update the next morning, and for the next two days, was pretty much the same. The raiders were headed steadily eastward. During the day, we stayed out of sight and tracked them from a couple of miles back. At night, we moved in. The prisoners were under heavy guard and kept chained together in a pair of wagons. Thus far, as near as we could tell, they had not been abused. I figured their captors wanted to keep them looking healthy in case they ran across a federal patrol. However, the farther we traveled from Wichita, the sooner the prisoners' situation was likely to deteriorate. Raiders are not known for their profound sense of restraint.

On the fifth day Caleb and I ate the last of our rations shortly before I made my report. This time, when I called in, I finally got General Jacobs on the line.

"You certainly have a knack for finding trouble, Mr. Garrett," he said.

"Did Colonel Stephens brief you?"

"He did. Sounds like you're up to your ass in alligators again."

"Story of my life. Listen, we're in a bad spot here. We're out of food, and the guys we're tracking aren't getting any less horny. If we're going to do something we had better do it soon. The prisoners are running out of time."

"I can get you a supply drop by tonight, but sending troops will take a couple of days to coordinate."

242

"I don't need the Eighty-Second Airborne, General. A few skillful operators would do just fine."

The line was quiet for a few seconds. "What did you have in mind?"

"Four men, a Chinook, and some extra ordnance. When the caravan stops for the night I'll send in the drop coordinates. We'll go in, hit them hard, and get the prisoners to the chopper."

"That simple?"

"Of course not. But I don't want to bore you with the details."

"Call me back in twenty minutes."

He hung up. I waited twenty long, impatient minutes and called back.

"I can get you what you need," Jacobs said. "But you'll have to move tonight."

"That can be arranged."

"Any special instructions?"

"Actually, yes. Quite a few."

I laid out my plan in general terms and told Jacobs what supplies I needed and what I wanted from the soldiers he was sending me.

"Well, you've got balls. I'll give you that much. Can I assume you'll need operational control of the aircrew?"

"If you can swing it, yes."

"Done."

I let out a relieved breath. "Thanks for the assist, General."

"Thank me when those prisoners are out of harm's way. Anything else?"

"No. That's it."

"Good luck then."

The line went dead.

TWENTY-THREE

The Chinook flew in three hours after nightfall.

It landed in an unremarkable patch of field in a vast plain of unremarkable fields. I waited a short distance away while the twin rotors slowly spun to a stop before approaching with my hands in the air. Something moved in the darkness of the chopper's cargo bay and I knew I had no less than two rifles aimed at my chest.

"Arbiter," I called out, hoping whoever briefed these men had given them the correct code word.

"Mason," A voice replied. "Approach and be recognized."

I did as ordered, hands still in the air. A pair of darkly painted faces peered at me from within the Chinook. The soldiers wore black helmets, black fatigues, NVGs, and were heavily armed.

"You Garrett?" one of them asked.

"That's me."

"Name's Lanning. This is Greer, Clark, and the guy behind me is Duncan."

Now that I was closer, I could see the men clearly. Lanning was tall, lean, and appeared to be in his mid-thirties. Greer and Clark were both younger white guys of medium build. Duncan was black, stood about five foot six, and was built like a refrigerator. I estimated his biceps at roughly the diameter of my head.

"You in charge?" I asked Lanning.

"Ordinarily, yes. Colonel tells me I'm to follow your orders."

He did not sound happy.

"Have you been briefed?"

"Sure."

Lanning gave me the rundown. I had to correct a few details, but mostly the ops guys had gotten it right.

"Now we've got that straightened out," I said, "you have the supplies I asked for?"

"Yeah," Lanning said. "In the back."

I followed him in while Greer closed the door behind us. Lanning reached up and flipped a switch, bathing the interior of the Chinook in red light. A big, surly looking crewman stared down the barrel of a minigun aimed out a firing port and studiously ignored us. I returned the favor.

Two large green fiberglass crates sat strapped to the floor of the cargo bay. I undid the tie-downs on one and opened it. Inside were high-powered radios, six LAW rockets, two grenade launchers, a small box of fragmentation grenades, another small box of high-explosive point-detonation shells, two SAWs, a few boxes of linked 5.56 ammo, stick-on infrared patches, and most importantly, four GPS tracking devices. I rooted down to the bottom of the box and found four large duffel bags. The other box held water and provisions for Hicks, me, and our horses.

"Looks like it's all here."

Lanning grunted. I went to the front of the chopper and spoke to one of the pilots. "Can we get a message out to Wichita, make sure they have a fix on the transmitters?"

"Already done," the pilot said. "Been tracking since we left the FOB."

"Perfect."

I turned and motioned to the soldiers. "Just so I know, what outfit are you with?"

"Tenth S.F.," Lanning said. "You?"

"Marines. Scout sniper."

"You too old to be active duty," Duncan said. He had a thick southern accent, one of the Gulf Coast states by the sound of it. "No offense."

"None taken. And you're right. After the Marines I did some time in the intelligence community, then a merc outfit. Now I'm freelance."

"You a spook?" Lanning asked with more than a little distaste.

"Not anymore. Think of me as a concerned citizen."

A snort. "Yeah. Sure. A concerned citizen who just happens to be on a first name basis with the head of ASOC."

"Listen," I said. "Who I am is a lot less important than why we're here. There are thirteen prisoners being held by a group of raiders over two-hundred strong. And it's our job to get them out alive."

"No shit," Greer said. "Didn't we just review the briefing?"

I took a long breath and spoke evenly. Dealing with special operations types is always a pissing contest. Too many alpha dogs in too little kennel.

247

"I'm not trying to be patronizing. I just want to make sure we all stay focused on the mission, not the bullshit surrounding it."

"Right," Lanning said. His voice had taken on the tone of someone trying to be reasonable. "Speaking of the mission, weren't there supposed to be two of you?"

"The other guy is procuring transportation. Should be along shortly."

"Can you check in with him?" Greer said, pointing to the radio clipped to my vest. "See where he's at?"

"Sure. Be right back."

I walked outside, took a knee, and keyed my radio. "Hicks, you in range?"

No response. I waited a few minutes and tried again. This time, the earpiece buzzed to life.

"Copy Lima Charlie," Hicks said. "En route. Four mikes."

"How many did you get?"

"Enough for all of us."

"Bodies?"

"Dragging along."

"Nice work. See you soon. Out."

I went back inside the Chinook and waited with the four Green Berets until the crewman on the minigun said he had incoming. I fired up my IR scope, which I had attached to my rifle earlier in the night, and looked through a crack in the door. Sure enough, I saw the unmistakable outline of Hicks riding toward the Chinook with Red and four other horses in tow. Behind him, being dragged by lengths of paracord, were the slowly cooling bodies of four raiders. I went outside to greet him. The soldiers followed.

"Run into any trouble?"

248

"Nope. Caught these four bunched together on patrol passing a bottle around. You know what they say. Complacency kills."

I turned to Lanning. "This is Sergeant Caleb Hicks, First Reconnaissance Expeditionary. We work together from time to time."

Lanning nodded in Hicks' direction. "You ever been on a mission like this, Sergeant?"

"Yes sir."

Lanning did not correct Hicks for addressing him as an officer, confirming my suspicions about his rank.

"I heard of the First Recon," Duncan said. "Y'all supposed to be regular Army. The hell you doin' way out here?"

Hicks pointed a thumb at the corpses behind him. "Killing raiders."

Duncan grinned, his teeth white in the darkness.

"We need to get moving," I said. "Those raiders will be missed soon if they haven't been already."

"Right," Lanning said, all business. "Let's get the gear loaded on the horses."

After packing the duffel bags and securing them to the saddles with paracord, we cut loose the dead raiders, passed around the high-powered radios, did a quick comms check, and set off toward the raider encampment. Behind us, the Chinook's powerful engine whined to life, its rotors slowly beginning to spin as the pilots went through their checklists.

"Just out of curiosity," I said to Lanning. "Is horsemanship a part of S.F. ongoing training now?"

"Yep. Has been for two years. Rangers too, some of them. Heard a rumor the Joint Chiefs want to train five thousand mounted cavalry in the next four years, assuming the government can find enough horses."

"Interesting," I said, and meant it. The strategist in me saw the utility of mounted cavalry in a world with limited fuel and a dwindling stock of working vehicles. The business man in me, however, smelled an opportunity.

Get through tonight first, I told myself. *Stay focused.*

"What's that?" Lanning said.

I had not realized I was speaking out loud. "Nothing. Just thinking."

"Might want to do your thinking quietly from here on out."

I accepted the barb with a nod. "Sound advice."

*****

"All stations, alpha lead. Everyone in position? Over."

The two SAW gunners spoke up first, followed by the grenadiers, the aircrew, and finally Hicks.

"Acknowledged. Beginning approach. Stand by."

I raised my head just enough to survey the area with my IR goggles. *Now for the hard part.*

After leaving Haviland, the raiders who attacked Spike's caravan rode southward, turned east on Highway 160, then south again on an access road, and finally resumed an easterly path on Highway 44. They set a tough pace, sometimes covering nearly thirty miles a day, often riding long into the night such that Hicks and I had been hard pressed to keep up. Initially I had thought they were fleeing the possibility of federal pursuit. Now I knew better.

They were not worried about the Army. They had ridden as hard as they had because they were low on water.

The Chikaskia River ran north of my position and curved sharply to the south before turning southeast about a mile farther downstream. To the north, a thick stand of woodland ran along the northern bank of the stream and followed the curve of the river south and eastward. The raiders had stopped in a field close to the river.

Behind me to the west, two strips of woodland provided further concealment from the highway. One was a thin line of trees running along the ninety-degree angle of the field where the crop boundaries had once been, while the other meandered sinuously along a tributary that fed into the river further to the southeast. My grudging respect for the leader of this outfit went up a notch. This was a good place to make camp—hidden from the road, easily defensible, and near an abundant source of fresh water. Which also told me these men had been through here before. I wondered how long they had been at this game, and how many lives they had destroyed along the way.

I scanned left and right looking for signs of where I had ordered the others to take position. At my low vantage point, I could not spot them. If I had been up higher I might have had better luck, but lying on my belly in the grass, they were invisible. Which was good. If I could not see them, neither could the raiders. The possibility the scumbags camped along the river were equipped with NVGs was strong. There was also the possibility they had gotten their hands on FLIR equipment. A remote possibility, but a possibility nonetheless. I was taking no chances.

Satisfied there were no patrols between me and the raiders, I began the slow process of crawling toward them. I kept my head down, streamers of brush from my ghillie suit obscuring my vision, and let my ears guide me toward the camp. Every ten meters or so I looked up and evaluated my angle of approach. At the fifty yard

251

mark I was on a straight course to where the prisoners were being held.

I keyed my radio. "Eagle, Alpha Lead. Status. Over."

"Might want to hurry, alpha lead," Hicks replied. He was waiting with the horses to the south, hidden in the boughs of one of the trees bordering the field in that direction. I had lent him my IR scope, but kept my goggles. "Looks like the booze is flowing and I see a few men gesturing toward the prisoners. I think our luck is about to run out."

"Any sign they've noticed that patrol is missing?"

"No. But it's only a matter of time."

"Anybody goes to take the prisoners out of the wagon, put them down."

A pause. "Won't that alert the rest of the camp?"

"Yes, but at that point it won't matter because I'll give the signal and the raiders will have much bigger problems than their collective libido."

"Roger that."

I quickened my pace. The sounds of revelry from the camp were growing louder. The raiders were having some kind of celebration, probably figured they were out of danger from the feds. I tended to agree. The Army, for the most part, stayed close to the main trade routes, waystations, FOBs, and safe zones. It was unlikely they would venture this far south. And if I was honest, they had no reason to. Hardly anyone lived in this empty, remote part of the state. Not to mention the fact the farther south a person traveled, the more likely they were to run into infected. The men in the raider camp did not seem worried, which served as further evidence they were familiar with the area.

When I was within twenty meters of the prisoners I looked to my right and saw the edge of a cable fence within which grazed the raiders' livestock. Farther ahead, another fence surrounded half the caravan. The rest of the wagons were arranged in a defensive circle outside the fence. The prisoners' holding area was along this outer defensive layer. If I was careful and quick, I could climb into one of the wagons outside the fence and use it to get inside the perimeter. But then I had to figure out a way past the ring of cables.

One thing at a time.

I covered the rest of the ground without incident. A patrol passed by perhaps thirty yards behind me, but I was well hidden by my ghillie suit and the waist-high grass. When they were out of earshot, I crawled quickly toward the prisoners.

The women were within ten yards now. But before I could help them, I had one other matter to attend to. I crawled to the nearest wagon, took one of the GPS transponders from my belt, and stuck its magnetic side the top of the rear axle close to the wheel where it would be hard to spot even if someone were looking for it. If they were not, it would be invisible. Three wagons and three transponders later, I crawled back to where the prisoners were and examined one of the fence posts.

It was a cylinder of galvanized steel, four inches in diameter, driven into the ground and reinforced from the inside with a stanchion braced at a forty-five degree angle. I pushed on the post. It did not budge, so I tried pulling on it. To my surprise, it moved a centimeter or two in my direction. I smiled in the darkness. The fence was strongly resistant to anything pushing against it, such as a horde of ravening infected, but it was not designed to resist being pulled in the other direction.

Working quickly, I drew my Bowie knife and dug at the dirt around the base of the post. It was still soft from being tilled up earlier and packed in by hand. In just a couple of minutes I had removed enough dirt to destabilize the post if pulled toward me. I moved down the line and did the same with two more posts, staying low and keeping my head on a swivel. When I finished, I backed off and asked Hicks if there was anyone close by. He said there was not. I told him to keep his finger on the trigger, stood up, and hopped into the back of a wagon less than ten feet from the prisoners.

"Anything?" I asked into the radio.

"Nothing," Hicks said. "No one noticed."

I let out a slow breath. "Stand by."

The fabric of the wagon cover made a faint zipping sound as I cut a long vertical slash from the top of the canopy to the bottom. The material fell open, revealing the top of a fence post about chest level to me if I stood on a wooden crate along the wall of the cargo area. I stepped up onto the crate, grabbed the top of the fence, and leapt out and upward as high as I could. My left boot scraped the topmost cable as I cleared it and fell down the opposite side. It was a nine-foot drop, so rather than try to absorb the impact on a pair of knees nearing their forty-second year of service, I did a paratrooper's tumble and came up in a crouch, ears straining. My suppressed Beretta pistol was in my hand. I did not remember drawing it.

Seconds passed. I heard no one approaching. Behind me, I heard the prisoners speaking to each other in frightened whispers. Someone was weeping, but it was muffled, as if she were holding something over her face.

I keyed the radio. "Eagle, how am I doing?"

"So far, so good."

"Copy."

Now was the time for bold action. I slipped out of my ghillie suit, rolled it up, and lashed it to the back of my belt. That done, I went to work on the fence, first detaching the cables from their clips on two of the posts I had loosened and then pushing them over as much as I could. Once the posts were detached, I could plant a foot on one cable, pull up on another, and open it enough for a person to slip through.

It'll have to do.

I was about to move to the entrance of the one of the prisoners' wagons when my earpiece crackled.

"Alpha, you got inbound."

Shit. "How many?"

"Just one, but he's armed."

"Keep me posted."

I went to my belly, rolled under the wagon, and lay on my back with the Beretta clutched to my chest. The swish of legs pushing through grass grew steadily louder until a raider with a pistol in his hand came into view. The wagon creaked as he grabbed a handrail and stepped up onto the buckboard.

"Rise and shine," a rough voice said. "Vacation's over. Time to start the party."

I rolled out from under the wagon, stood, and holstered the Beretta. For what I was about to do, the gun was a liability. I could not risk shooting one of the prisoners. So I drew my knife, held it in a concealing grip along the back of my forearm, and stepped up into the wagon.

In situations like this I knew the key to success was acting as if I belonged, as if I owned the place, as if my actions were perfectly planned and logical and I had every reason to be where I was and to do what I was doing. I kept the knife hidden as I pressed my way into the wagon's narrow cargo hold. Inside, in the dim light from fires farther within the camp, I saw the bulky outline of a man crouched in front of me and the dirty, frightened faces of eight women of varying ages, each one bound hand and foot with ropes tied to iron rings driven into the floor of the wagon.

"Hey Smith, that you?" I said, gambling that out of two-hundred or so men at least one of them was named Smith.

The bulky form barely looked over his shoulder. "No. Smith is on patrol. What're you doing here?"

I pushed farther into the wagon until I was within arm's reach of the other man. "Somebody must have gotten their wires crossed. You here to get the girls?"

"Yeah, Carter sent me. How about you go to the other-"

He never got a chance to finish his sentence. I grabbed one of his shoulders, raised the Bowie knife, and plunged it into the base of his skull with all the force I could muster. The raider's body stiffened and twitched as I pulled him close to me, then I eased him to the floor and placed a finger over my lips. One of the prisoners opened her mouth to scream, but an older woman sitting across from her lunged forward, pressed a hand over her mouth, and hissed at her to shut the fuck up.

When the girl went quiet, the older woman looked at me. "Who are you?"

"I'm with the Army," I said. "I'm here to get you out of this place. But we have to move quickly."

"The Army?" another woman said. "Is this a rescue?"

"Yes," I said impatiently and looked to the older woman. "Can you get them moving?"

She nodded and began hissing orders. I cut loose her bindings and handed her a pocket knife so she could help me do the same for the others. In less than a minute, they were all free.

The women seemed to regard the older woman as a leader and did as she said. I cut a slit in the side of the wagon facing away from the campfires, hopped out, and began helping women to the ground. I told the first one of them to hold the cables open so the others could get outside the fence. She moved to comply. As each prisoner emerged I whispered to them to stay quiet, pointed out which wagon I wanted them to hide behind, and told them to stay there until I came for them.

The older woman came out last. "There are others," she said.

"I know. Let's get them."

TWENTY-FOUR

I led the way to the next wagon and kept a lookout while the old woman went inside. Hushed voices spoke in the darkness. I keyed the radio again.

"Eagle, Alpha Lead. How we doing?"

"Rider headed in from the north," he replied. "Might be pertaining to the missing patrol."

"Copy. Keep us covered. Just about done here."

"Roger."

Above me, the point of my pocket knife pierced the wagon's cover and traveled downward. The older woman leaned out and motioned to me. I moved closer and helped the women from the wagon and told them where to go. There were supposed to be only thirteen of them, but I counted eighteen. Most looked like they had not been used too badly, but a few were in terrible shape. Bruised, bloody, eyes sunken, faces gaunt with fear, the haunted look of people who have given up hope for anything but a swift death. It occurred to me the raiders may have taken prisoners before finding Spike's caravan. It also occurred to me what probably happened to them during that time.

Not now, Garrett. Focus.

I followed the last of the prisoners to the wagon where the others were hiding. To the old woman I said, "What's your name?"

"Lynn. Lynn Bristol."

"Okay, Lynn. Help me get these women into a single-file line."

She did as I asked. When they were lined up and hunched low in the grass, I took a handful of infrared reflective patches from my vest and put one on the first girl in line, the fourth, eighth, twelfth, and the last.

"What's this?" one of them asked.

"Reflector," I said. "So the helicopter can see us from the air."

"Helicopter? There's a helicopter coming?"

"Yes," I said, and moved on. The girl had more questions but Lynn hushed her.

"Stay quiet, girl. Do you want to get us all killed?"

The girl shut her mouth.

Finished with the patches, I pressed the transmit key. "All stations, Alpha Lead. Have eighteen souls. Repeat eighteen souls. We are outbound at this time. Alpha Strike, begin your approach. All other stations, wait for my mark."

To the prisoners, I said, "Time to go. Follow me, and make sure you keep a hand on the back of the person in front of you. If you get separated I won't have time to go back for you, so stay close. And for God's sake, keep your heads down. There's about to be a very large number of bullets flying around us very, very soon. So stay low. Let's move."

The woman at the front of the line grabbed the back of my belt and held on tightly. I pressed through the grass as quickly as I thought the prisoners could keep up. The grass around me was a washed-out shade of white through the filter of my IR goggles. The sky overhead was a yawning ocean of grayish-black. I saw a rider gallop into camp about seventy yards to my right. Bad news. The raiders would soon know about the missing patrol, and not long after, would probably notice the prisoners were gone.

"Come on," I hissed as loud as I dared. "We have to move faster."

To their credit, the women redoubled their efforts. As difficult as this was for me, it was undoubtedly twice as hard for them. They did not have the benefit of IR goggles and a radio. For them, the world was only darkness and grass pulling at them and pain in their legs and backs as they tried to run in a low crouch in a direction they could not see. I smelled sweat and heard harsh breathing behind me. The women were afraid, and were right to be.

Static. "Cat's out of the bag, Alpha Lead," Hicks said. "Over."

"Alpha Strike," I radioed, "tell me something good."

"Inbound, Alpha Lead. One mike. Over."

"Do you have us on FLIR?"

"Affirmative."

"Light up the target area as soon as you're in range. All other stations, commence attack when you see the tracers."

Lanning, Clark, Greer, and Duncan acknowledged. Hicks did not because he was too busy moving the horses to the rendezvous, as per the plan. Or at least I hoped he was.

I managed to drag the prisoners maybe forty more yards before the sound of rotors chopped the air above me. The whine and thump of the Chinook passed overhead, banked southward, and a second later, the light from the minigun's tracers flashed against the sides of my IR goggles' display. I heard a sound like a great angry insect pounding its wings impossibly fast from the direction

260

of the chopper, and an instant later, Lanning's voice came over the radio.

"Fire at will."

The command was unnecessary, but it probably made Lanning feel better to say it. I did not have long to dwell on the subject. Two grenades hit the raider camp with a pair of echoing *whumps* I could feel in the pit of my chest. Then two more came in the space of a few seconds, hitting a different part of the encampment. By the screams and hoarse shouts of panicked command, I guessed the raiders were now in disarray. The thrum of the Chinook passed northward and I heard the minigun let loose with another volley. The sound brought to mind a number of instances over the years when I had seen what miniguns could do.

The minigun on the Chinook was an M134 chambered in 7.62 NATO, the same round fired from most standard military-issue sniper rifles—a cartridge powerful enough to take a man's head off at well over six-hundred yards. And the M134 could pour them out at 3000 rounds a minute, or 50 rounds per second. Furthermore, because of its Gatling-style cyclical firing system consisting of rotating gun bolts and barrels, the M134 is highly stable and produces virtually zero recoil. The result of this is a relentless hail of lethally dense and frighteningly accurate fire with a hit rate nine times higher than that of most other forms of machine guns. And the results are nothing short of devastating. Miniguns can instantly turn vehicles into shattered, perforated wrecks, reduce human beings to puddles of red paste, and even worse, can quickly and easily transition from one target to another. Combine these capabilities with FLIR, an acronym for forward-looking infrared night-vision technology, and the raiders didn't stand a chance.

My radio crackled. "All stations, Alpha Strike. Be advised, hostiles are scattering. Some are headed toward your positions."

I activated the GPS transponder on my radio. "All stations, Alpha Lead. GPS is online. Repeat, GPS is online. Converge on my position. Alpha Strike, see if you can keep these assholes off our backs long enough to reach the extraction site."

"Roger that, Alpha Lead."

The Chinook moved ahead of us and began flying a wide, meandering circle, occasionally letting off small bursts of fire. To the raiders it probably looked like the aircrew was chasing down survivors. In reality, they were trying to cover us without giving away our positions.

The next ten minutes were a slog. The Chinook roared overhead, its noise growing and waning as it moved closer and farther away. Lanning and his men radioed to let me know they were on my flanks at twenty meter intervals, SAW gunners inside, grenadiers on the wings. I acknowledged and kept moving. The hand on my belt did not let go, and the labored breathing of the women behind me grew no less desperate. Twice I had to stop when I felt a tug and looked back to see that someone had fallen. The others had them on their feet in seconds and we continued on our way. Finally, the treeline at the edge of the field loomed ahead.

"Eagle, Alpha lead. You got a visual on us?"

"Affirmative," Hicks said. "Keep your heads down. Might have to shoot over top of you."

"Copy. What about the assault team?"

"Got them too."

"Any hostiles close?"

A short pause. "Not close enough to be a concern at the moment. Probably change when the helo touches down."

"Can you do anything about them?"

"Sure. Hug the dirt for a minute."

262

I stopped and ordered the prisoners to get down. For a moment, they just stared. I gestured emphatically and hissed louder than I felt safe doing.

"Get on the fucking ground!"

This time they obeyed. For a few seconds there was nothing. Then came a muted crack and a sharp cry in the darkness. Two more shots followed the first, but there were no more shouts.

"Let me guess," I said into the radio. "One center-of-mass and two head shots."

There was a smile in Hicks' voice. "You're in the wrong line of work, amigo. Should have been a detective."

"We clear?"

"For the moment."

Good enough. "Okay," I said to the prisoners. "On your feet. We're almost there."

The women rose, Lynn said something low and terse, and we got moving. I spotted the flash of Hicks' IR patch and pointed at him to let him know I had his position. He acknowledged by clicking his radio once. I headed to a spot of open ground roughly fifty yards away from him, told the women to lie down flat, and radioed the aircrew.

"Alpha Strike, Alpha Lead. We are go for extraction. Repeat, go for extraction."

"Copy Alpha Lead. En route, less than one mike."

"Roger."

And then I waited with my belly to the earth, the smell of damp vegetable rot in my nose, and thought how I had noticed over the years that the ground smelled differently in different parts of the world. In Iraq it had been dry and acrid, redolent with chemicals in places, and in others, tinged by the faint dust of things dead for millennia. In the Philippines, it had been hot and pungent. In Germany, cool and vaguely sweet smelling. Here in Kansas, the odor reminded me of corn chips, which I found very odd. And it made me want corn chips.

The sound of the Chinook grew louder until it was directly overhead. The pilot lowered it gracefully to the ground, the weight of its dark bulk settling gently onto the landing gear. I looked up and saw the cargo door open and the gunner beckoning at us.

"Time to go," I shouted above the roar of rotor wash. I stood up and pulled at the woman closest to me. She passed the message down the line, and in a few seconds, everyone was on their feet and running. There was no point in stealth anymore. Between the noise of the chopper and the wind tossing the grass like waves in a hurricane, anyone in shooting distance was going to know exactly where we were. Our best ally now was speed.

I led the way to the chopper holding the hand of the woman I had helped stand. She held the hand of the woman behind her, and so on and so forth. Someone in the chopper turned on a red light that was just barely bright enough to penetrate the gloom. The prisoners saw it and ran for it at a dead sprint. As soon as they were within ten feet of the chopper the light went out.

I took up position on the opposite side of the door from the gunner and urged the women into the cargo bay. Some of them had trouble due to injuries. The gunner helped me lift them bodily and set them inside where the others waited to haul them to a seat. When the last of the women were in, Lanning appeared behind me. I had not noticed him approach because I had been too busy with what I was doing, which I knew was a mistake.

Berate yourself later.

The gunner tapped me on the arm. "Give me a hand."

I nodded and grabbed Lanning by the arm. "Cover us for a minute."

He gave a thumbs up and began barking at his men. I followed the gunner inside.

"Gotta get these crates out of here," he said as loudly as he could. "Won't be enough room otherwise."

I held up a thumb and pushed my way to the back of the chopper. The gunner and I hauled the empty crates to the door and pushed them unceremoniously out onto the field. That done, the gunner motioned to Lanning.

"Let's go!"

Lanning touched his knuckles to my arm as I climbed out. When I looked at him, he nodded once. I nodded back and then sprinted toward the treeline. Behind me, the Chinook lifted off and carried its payload of damaged humanity off into the safety of the endless night sky. It was headed north. Any raiders in earshot would be looking in that direction, so when I reached Hicks and the horses, we rode west.

"Gotta put some miles behind us," Hicks said.

I looked back and saw the young soldier had released three of the captured horses and was using the fourth as a pack animal. "At least we're not on foot."

"Yep. There is that."

We spoke no more until dawn.

TWENTY-FIVE

Heinrich awoke soaking wet on the northern bank of the Chikaskia River. Maru sat nearby, rifle in hand, surrounded by six men Heinrich assumed were his inner circle, or at least part of it. He stood and approached them, one hand close to the handle of his pistol.

"Good to see you alive, Chief," Maru said. He kept his gaze steady to the west, a large pair of field glasses held to his eyes.

"What have you got?"

"Nothing good. Looks like it was the Army hit us last night."

Heinrich wanted to remain standing but found himself too tired to do so. *Fuck it*, he thought. *If they wanted me dead I would be.*

He sank into the grass by the riverbank. "Any idea how bad?"

"Pretty bad. After the attack everyone moved to the fallback position. What happened to you?"

Heinrich turned his head and glared at Maru. Any other day he would have shot the man for his impertinence. But this morning, with a hematoma pressing his temple, hunger gnawing at his gut, dehydration clawing his throat, and possessed of a healthy dose of gratitude that he was not dead, he let it go.

"Ran into a fucking tree in the dark. Knocked myself out."

Maru lowered the field glasses, looked at Heinrich's forehead, and made a face. "Christ. You look like a baby seal after the club."

"Feel like one too."

The men around Maru looked nervous. Heinrich took a few deep breaths, got his feet underneath him, and rose as steadily as he was able.

"What time is it?"

Maru looked at the sun and held up a hand. "About nine in the morning, give or take."

"How's the tribe?"

"Scattered. Lost a lot of men. We're the only ones crazy enough to still be near camp."

Heinrich pondered that. The Army did not usually move against raiders in half measures. They either attacked with overwhelming force and killed or apprehended everyone in sight, or they attacked not at all.

"So they came in, strafed us, and left."

Maru stood up. "More to it than that."

"I was in my command tent when the attack started. Fill me in."

"One of the patrols went missing. Found out about it maybe thirty seconds before that chopper tore into us. Rider came in to report, and the next thing I saw was tracers."

"So we were under surveillance."

"Seems so. And it gets worse. The women are gone."

"Gone?"

"No trace. Holes cut into the wagons, some of the fence posts on that side dug up and loosened." Maru gestured to a man sitting on his left. "This fella found one of our guys dead where the women were being kept. Looked like someone shoved a goddamn machete through the back of his neck. Nearly took his head off."

Heinrich felt his teeth clench and his fists ball up. "It was a goddamn rescue mission. They came for the women, probably sent a few spec-ops types."

Maru edged closer, his voice lowering. "We're compromised here, Chief. We should move on."

Heinrich shook his head. "If they could muster enough troops to show up here in force, they would have."

"They might be back. In fact, I'd say it's just a matter of time."

"Agreed. But we have to salvage what we can."

"What are you saying?"

"Round up the men. Get them back here. Do a damage assessment and regroup."

Maru sighed. "Hell of a risk. The Army comes back, we're dead."

"We're worse than dead if we don't. Lot of rivals in this part of the state."

Maru wiped a hand across the back of his neck. "Fair enough. So we regroup. Then what?"

"Scatter protocol."

The big Maori thought it over. "Okay. They won't all come back."

"Then they leave with nothing. They complain, kill them."

Maru looked at his men and gestured. They moved off toward the sound of horses clomping through grass. "I'll do a BDA and report back. Where should I look for you?"

"In the center of camp."

"Right, Chief."

*****

There was a small group of infected pushing ineffectively against the cable fence surrounding the livestock. The animals kept their distance, but otherwise seemed unperturbed. Heinrich felt around his torso and found his kukri and pistol were still in place. He tried to remember if he had grabbed his rifle before fleeing the hail of red fire pouring from the sky the night before, but his head was pounding so hard he couldn't think.

Focus on the task at hand.

He drew his pistol, removed the magazine, and worked the slide. It seemed to work fine. Looking ahead, he saw the infected were now less than thirty yards away around a curve of the cable fence. They had not noticed him yet, but would soon. They always did.

Heinrich replaced the magazine in the gun, chambered a round, and walked to within ten yards of the undead. There were eight of them. His weapon held fifteen rounds, plenty enough to get the job done. He assumed a firing stance, leveled the sights, and squeezed the trigger. The report echoed across the plains, startling the livestock. Oxen and horses bayed and snorted as the undead whipped toward the sound of gunfire. The ghoul in Heinrich's sights slumped to the ground in a limp heap.

The rest of the infected began shambling in his direction, mouths open, hands outstretched. Dimly, Heinrich noted that three of them were grays. They got off to a faster start than their still vaguely-human brethren and covered ground quicker. Heinrich shifted aim and dropped them before they were within five yards. Four left. Heinrich killed one more at point-blank range, then holstered his pistol.

His head hurt. His thoughts, much like his men, were scattered. He was in a bad situation. He had been caught by surprise and nearly lost everything and had been forced to flee in fear for his life like one of his victims. The sense of invincibility he had enjoyed the last few months was gone. In its place, buzzing angrily at the base of his skull, was the urge to kill something with his hands, an impulse that swelled and stretched and raked hot nails against the backs of his eyes. The ghouls were available. A living person would have been better, but Heinrich believed in making due with the resources on hand. He drew his kukri, the same one a Blackthorn had used to sever two of his fingers.

The first ghoul was a woman, middle aged when she died, probably turned at least a year ago. When she reached for him, Heinrich sidestepped, grabbed her wrist, and pulled her toward his outstretched ankle. She fell face first to the ground and was still for the briefest of instants. It was enough time for Heinrich to raise a boot and bring his heel down on the back of her neck with crushing force. There was a wet crunch and the ghoul went still.

The next one was there in an instant. Heinrich jumped a couple of feet backward to avoid its grasping hands. He was a strong man, but he had learned long ago not to test himself against even the smallest undead. Only a fool tried to overpower something that felt no pain. Instead, he rolled to his left, came up in a crouch at the ghoul's side, and slashed at the back of its knee. Tendons and ligaments parted like frayed cord and the ghoul fell over. A short, brutal chop to the side of its skull ended its struggles.

With the last infected, Heinrich took his time. The kukri was a big knife, easily capable of removing limbs in skilled hands. And Heinrich was certainly skilled.

First, he took the arms off at the elbows so the ghoul could not grab him. Then, he hacked at the creature's knees so it could not stand up. Satisfied it was no longer a threat, Heinrich stepped back and let it pull itself toward him on the stumps of its arms. He smiled as he watched and thought to himself he had to admire the thing's dedication. It knew what it wanted and pursued that goal with relentless determination. Something he knew a thing or two about.

When Heinrich grew bored teasing the pathetic monster, he put a foot on the back of its head, pressed its face into the dirt, and hacked at the creature' spine just below the base of its neck. The ghoul immediately went limp, but did not die. Heinrich backed off to admire his work. The creature's mouth twitched uselessly, its milky white eyes rolling in its head, limbs paralyzed.

"Have a nice eternity," Heinrich said, and walked away. On the way to his command tent he decided the exercise had done him good. He felt a little better now.

TWENTY-SIX

His pack, rifle, and other possessions were right where he had left them.

The tent had collapsed in the chaos, but the contents within were unharmed. Heinrich found enough unbroken posts to re-erect the command tent, and when finished, laid out the contents of his rucksack on his cot so he could check each item for damage. Everything was in good order, the most important item being his IR scope.

"Could have been a lot worse," Heinrich muttered.

He sat in the stillness of the abandoned camp a few minutes, eyes closed, forcing the pain in his head to recede and reorganizing his thoughts. The sound of helicopter rotors and the searing blaze of red tracers flashed in his memory. He remembered shouts of surprise and screams of fear, the braying and bleating of livestock, dozens of men running in all directions at once, most of them tripping and falling in the darkness outside the ring of campfires. He remembered footsteps pounding away into the night.

Heinrich struggled to establish a timeline. He knew he had stood in the entryway to his tent when he first heard the chopper approach. Whatever he was doing before that moment was a dim blur. He let it go. It was not important. The next thing he remembered was seeing the tracers arc downward and slice through his men like a great flaming scythe. There had been more than fifty troops congregated in the center of camp while the booze was being handed out. He remembered hearing Carter tell someone to go fetch the women. Was that before or after?

Doesn't matter.

Of the fifty or so men gathered around the liquor crates, perhaps five or six managed to escape. The rest had been reduced to parts and pieces, little more than mush. Heinrich had seen it happen before, but never so close. The bullets had hit his troops with unbelievable ferocity, flattening them like human nails being driven into the ground by a thousand falling hammers. Men one second, a mess of indistinguishable chum the next. Then he was running, pushing himself as hard as he could, a single word blaring like an alarm klaxon in his brain: MINIGUN!

While fleeing toward the river, he had seen a few brave, disciplined souls raise their weapons and attempt to return fire. They had not known how doomed they were. They knew nothing about miniguns, how fast they fired, how accurate they were, or how easily a gunner could shift from one target to the next. Firing their weapons had made them stand out brilliantly in the gunner's FLIR sights. A quick adjustment of the gunner's aim, and the raiders were dead before the last tracer hit the dirt.

Heinrich had seen it, registered it, and kept running. He had slipped in the thick mud near the riverbank and stood back up and groped his way forward in the dark. Then he was in the river, the water shallow, only chest-high at its deepest. He struggled across, and when his feet found grass on the opposite bank, he took off at a sprint. Then there was a flash of white, and the next thing he

273

remembered was waking up on the riverbank, soaked to the skin, with a hematoma the size of a walnut on his temple and his right eye swollen mostly shut. And now he sat in the same wet clothes looking at the only possessions he had owned before starting down the path that led him here, a path of blood and fire and pain, and wondered if he could mend what was left of the Storm Road Tribe.

Probably have to kill some people.

He thought about the first life he had ever taken, long before he joined the Marines. He had been twelve. The boy's name was Bennie Woodhouse, and he had been a bullying shit. Heinrich had always been big for his age, so bullies rarely bothered him. But Bennie decided one day to embarrass him by pushing him down from behind so that he fell into a mud puddle. For a moment, Heinrich had been merely confused. Then he heard the laughter.

It was the first time he was ever in a fight. He did not remember it well. He knew he went at the boy and that Bennie was bigger and grossly fat and hard to move around. So he'd gone for the eyes with one hand and the balls with the other. Both found their mark. Heinrich remembered Bennie's squeal, how he'd sounded like a pig being gutted alive. Then strong hands grabbed him and pulled him away and the burly history teacher who was also the football coach lifted him bodily and carried him to the principal's office.

Bennie had wept while they sat next to each other, one hand clutching a bruised testicle and the other covering a left eye with an abraded retina. The principal droned on about how fighting was irresponsible and they were both to be suspended and he would be calling their parents to pick them up immediately. Heinrich had not cared. He had stared at Bennie and smiled the smile of the converted zealot. The assistant principal standing in the corner watched Heinrich's face the whole time, head shaking, eyes sad. He knew what he was looking at. And for the first time in his life, Heinrich knew as well.

The fat fucker, as Heinrich always remembered Bennie, had spent the night in the hospital. Heinrich's mother had been distraught. How could her sweet little boy have gotten into a fight? His father assured her he would get to the bottom of things, took his son by the shoulder, and marched him upstairs to his room. The elder Heinrich then closed the door and ordered his son, who still went by Johnnie in those days, to sit down on his bed.

"So what happened?"

Heinrich told him. Truthfully, and in exacting detail. His father listened without comment or expression.

"Bennie Woodhouse, huh?"

"Yes sir." He always called his father 'sir'. One did not call a former Marine Corps officer 'daddy' if one wanted to keep one's teeth in one's head.

"I know his father," The old man said. "Used to work together at Tilbert Auto Supply. Want to know a secret about him?"

"Sir?"

"You want to know or not?"

Heinrich's father was smiling. He found himself smiling back. "Yes sir."

"Guy's a fucking fairy."

"You mean a fag?"

"Fairy, fag, same thing. Wife came home for lunch one day and caught him sucking some guy's dick in the living room. You believe that shit? Right in his own house."

"That's disgusting."

"Damn right it is."

Heinrich and his father stared silently a moment, both still smiling. Finally his father said, "So you put a hurtin' on that fat little shit he calls a son, huh? Good. He had it coming. Kid ever bothers you again, stomp him flat and tell him his old man's a cocksucker. See how he likes it."

"What about mom?"

"Let me worry about her."

As his father left the room he stopped, looked back, and winked. "Nice work, son."

Before that day, Heinrich never had any feelings at all toward his father. Not love, or hate, or anything else. He had never felt much of anything for anyone except a stirring in his genitals around pretty girls. But in that moment, he felt a connection with Harold Martin Heinrich. The old man had, just for a moment, pulled back his veil and let his son see the toothy monster beneath. Heinrich had done the same, and from then on, there was a connection between the two of them. Not love, necessarily, but an understanding. An acceptance of like-minded beings. As he got older, he and his father developed a silent shorthand, often glancing at each other with mute amusement at some stupid utterance from someone they knew or taking shared delight in someone else's misfortune. They never spoke of it, but they both knew it was there.

So two weeks later, when he caught up with Bennie and told him he was sorry and could the two of them go see a movie or something, and the boy accepted with the meekness of the beaten and humbled, and Heinrich stopped by his house to borrow money from his mom, his father had poked his head around the corner and given Heinrich a thoughtful look. He winked at his father and made a motion like breaking a stick. The old man's eyes twinkled with delight and he mouthed, *be careful*.

Heinrich gave a thumbs up.

They did not go to the movies. When they got off the bus, Heinrich asked if Bennie wanted a milkshake before they went to

276

the theatre. Of course, the fat little shit accepted. Heinrich said he knew a good place not far away. He then led Bennie into a dead-end alley between two empty buildings with boarded up windows. Bennie stopped, looked around, and asked where they were.

Heinrich answered by producing a hunting knife.

When he was finished, he left Bennie's corpse under a pile of garbage and walked to the theatre alone. Along the way, he stopped to drop the knife in a storm drain and washed the blood from his hands in the bathroom of a gas station. He had popcorn and a soda with his movie.

When he got home, he made sure to put his clothes in a trash bag, and the next day, he dropped the bag in a dumpster behind the school cafeteria. Later, sitting in class, he watched a garbage truck pull away from the cafeteria building and felt warm inside.

The police came the day after. He told them he'd gone to the theatre alone after he and Bennie had an argument over which movie to watch and Bennie said he was going home. The questions went on for an hour before his mother decided they had bothered her son just about enough, and if they needed anything else, they could direct their questions to the family's attorney.

It was another two days before a homeless guy found the body. Heinrich clipped the stories from the newspaper for the next couple of weeks and pasted them into a scrapbook and took them out at night and read them lovingly.

Afterward, every once in a while, Heinrich caught his father looking at him with an odd smile. His father knew what he had done, and wanted Heinrich to know he knew. They only spoke of it once, a year to the day after the murder. Heinrich and his father had been in the old man's car driving to visit his mother's sister in the hospital.

"So what was it like?" his father said.

Heinrich knew better than to play dumb. He scratched his cheek, looked out the window, and said, "It was a rush. Better than anything I've ever felt. Better than the time I talked Linda Welker into sucking my dick. It made me feel powerful. I think I want to do it again."

His father nodded. "Yeah. I know what you mean."

They looked at each other and shared a smile.

And now, in the ruins of his camp, Heinrich realized he'd violated the one rule of killing his father had always admonished him to keep.

Be careful.

He had not been careful. He had been sloppy, and now he was paying the price for it. *Chalk it up to a lesson learned,* he thought and stood up. Things weren't as bad as they could have been. He was still alive, after all. As for the men he had lost … well, they knew the risks when they signed on.

Heinrich changed into dry clothes and left his tent to find Maru.

*****

"I found Carter," one of Heinrich's sergeants said. "Or what's left of him."

Heinrich walked over and looked at the body. The head, part of the torso, and both left limbs were gone. The right arm was intact, however, and Heinrich recognized the tattoos. Maru walked over to stand next to him.

"Poor bastard."

Heinrich grunted and looked at the sergeant. "He was my friend. Grab five men and bury him."

278

"Yes sir. And the others?"

"Leave them. We'll come back when we have more time."

Heinrich turned and surveyed the bustle of men salvaging their caravan. At best count, there were sixty dead and four wounded. Two of the wounded were not expected to survive. Another twenty or thirty had either deserted or their bodies had not been found. That left Heinrich with just over a hundred and forty men. Not as strong as before, but still bigger than any other tribe Heinrich knew of.

"We got a status on the wagons?" he asked.

"We do," Maru said. "Only four destroyed in the attack. Managed to salvage most of the cargo."

Heinrich shook his head in amazement and pointed at the wagons. "A ten second strafe from that minigun and we'd be picking up splinters. But they didn't. Single-minded motherfuckers probably didn't even think to look at the wagons. Too focused on killing us and getting those women out of here. Could have crippled us, and yet here we are with our trade intact."

"We got lucky, Chief."

"Indeed." Heinrich crossed his arms did a few calculations. "From the standpoint of trade and supplies, we're no worse off than before."

Maru looked at his chief sharply. "No worse off? Are you blind? You see all these corpses around here? They used to be your men."

Heinrich returned the stare. Maru paled, closed his mouth, and took an involuntary step backward.

"Don't state the fucking obvious to me, Maru. I am not fucking blind. I know we lost men. It's not the first time and it won't be the last. They're gone, and we can't get them back. And in case *you* didn't notice, we're in one fuck of a bad situation here. So since I'm the chief and it's my job to focus on the men still alive and figure out how to keep them that way, I can't sit around crying over troops we can't save. If I seem callous to you, grow the fuck up. If my practicality offends your delicate little sensibilities, tough shit. It's a hard world, and if you want to stay alive in it, you better be a hard motherfucker. Understood?"

Maru looked at the ground. "Understood, Chief. Sorry."

"Forgiven. But that's the last time you take that tone with me, Maru. We clear?"

"Crystal, Chief."

Heinrich glared a few more seconds, then turned his gaze to the livestock pen. "The animals don't seem the worse for wear."

Maru let out a breath. "Yeah. Couple broke their legs panicking, but the rest are all right."

"Good. We're going to need them."

Heinrich began walking back toward his tent. Maru followed and asked, "So what's the plan now, Chief?"

"Same as it was before—we move on Parabellum. Only instead of heading straight in, we're going to split up into squads of twenty and meet at Brawley's Cove and regroup before we begin the assault."

"You mean…"

"Yes. Scatter protocol."

Maru went quiet, eyes down.

"I know what you're thinking," Heinrich said. "And you're right. This is a worst case scenario. None of us wanted this, but it's what we have to deal with. What we do now is get together with the officers and NCOs and remind everyone of their role and plot routes for all the squads to follow. I know it's dangerous traveling

280

in small groups, but it'll be even more dangerous if we stay together and the Army finds us again."

Maru nodded in acceptance. "Right, Chief."

"Find yourself a horse. It'll make things go faster. Get some people to help you, and bring everyone we need to the command tent. We have work to do."

"Right Chief."

TWENTY-SEVEN

Gabriel

"Phone's charged," Hicks said.

I sat up in my bedroll, poked my head out of the Army-issue tent, and looked at the sky. It was clear and sunny, which meant our electronics were now charged and ready for use.

"Anything on the tablet?"

"Yep. Got a solid GPS fix on all four transponders."

Hicks was sitting across from me. He had propped two MRE chemical heaters against a duffel bag so they could warm our breakfast. The duffel bag itself contained the remaining grenades, ammunition, and LAW rockets the Green Berets had not taken when they left. The horses were picketed not far away, munching contentedly at fresh sprouts of green grass. It was warm that morning, the first balmy stirrings of spring blowing on the breeze.

"Where are they?" I said.

"Looks like they split up. I got four different trackers following four different paths, but they all seem to be headed more or less in the same direction."

"Which is?"

"East."

I touched one of the MRE heaters with the back of my hand. It felt about right, almost too hot to touch. I removed a packet of corned beef hash, peeled it open, and took a few bites.

"Sounds like they've got someplace in mind," I said.

Hicks grabbed the other packet of hash. "And they're trying to avoid detection getting there."

"Dangerous strategy, splitting up. Might run into other marauders. Fuckers can get downright cannibalistic."

"No honor among thieves."

"None."

I took a few more bites of hash. It tasted exactly as I remembered from my days in the Marines: salty, mushy, and strangely delicious. Or maybe I was just hungry enough that anything would have tasted good.

"This whole thing might be a bigger deal than we thought," I said.

"How so?"

"They left Kansas with no intention of returning anytime soon. Do you remember when we were watching them by the river, how much water they were purifying?"

"I did. It was a lot. Looked like they weren't planning on stopping for water for a while."

"Exactly. Marauders have hideouts, hidden fortresses where they go to do business. So far, the Army hasn't had much luck

283

rooting them out. If we can find those places and shut them down, it'll put most marauders out of business. But the problem is finding them."

Hicks nodded. "And right now, we got a whole slew of raiders all headed in the same direction."

"Which tells us wherever it is they're going, it's important to them. I can only think of one kind of place that fits the bill."

"Sounds like you need to make a phone call."

"Not until I finish breakfast. Dealing with Army brass is a job best done on a full stomach."

"You're just saying that 'cause you're a jarhead."

"You want to make the call?"

"That would be a violation of the command structure. You're a civilian, so technically you outrank me. Also, General Jacobs put you in charge. I'm duty bound to defer such tasks to your superior qualifications."

I crumpled the empty MRE pouch into its box. "You know, for a guy who barely talks, you can really spin a line of bullshit."

Hicks grinned. "I am a man of many talents."

*****

"As always, you've done a great job," General Jacobs said. "Central Command is tracking the caravan as we speak. We'll watch them via satellite and find out where they're headed."

"And when you do?"

"If they stop at one of their hideouts, we'll monitor them. Observe the comings and goings, so to speak. See if we can track down more such places."

I tried not to grind my teeth. "Couple of problems with that, General."

"I know what you're going to say, Gabriel."

It irked me he had called me by my first name, something he only did when he was trying to appease me.

"While you're monitoring, they'll be raiding. People will die."

"More people will die if we don't. The goal is to shut them down for good, not swat mosquitoes in a swarm. To do that, we need intel."

"It doesn't matter how many marauders you kill, there will always be more. The best strategy is to save who you can, when you can. You want intel? Take prisoners and interrogate them."

"I wish I could. I really do. But most of the Army's forces are committed in the Pacific Northwest, or along the country's main trade routes and safe zones. And in case you forgot, we're still on the brink of war with the ROC. Hunting down marauders is not our top priority. I just don't have the assets in place to do what you're asking."

I held the phone away from my face, pinched the bridge of my nose between two fingers, and let out a long sigh. The flat Kansas landscape stretched out around me, broken only by the occasional copse of trees. I was standing in the shade of one such copse. There was a fallen maple on the ground about twenty feet away. It looked as though someone had felled it and cut the limbs away for firewood, but left the rest to rot. Probably marauders. No one else lived out here. I walked over and kicked the log. It was still solid. No ants came swarming out of the bark, so I figured it was safe to sit on, and did.

There was no use arguing with General Jacobs. If he could help, he would. I'd known him long enough to believe he was a good man trying to make the best of a terrible situation. He was not

285

indifferent to my concerns, he simply had other priorities. The world was at the beginning of a new dark age, and how dark that age would become depended largely on the actions of people like the general. And right now, with the fate of the Union—and the human race—on the line, hunting down roving bands of thieves and bandits just wasn't at the top of the list.

"I lost a lot of trade when they took the caravan I was with," I said.

"How much are we talking about?"

I told him. There was a long pause before Jacobs answered. "Can you get your hands on a cargo manifest?"

"It's registered with the FTIC."

"I'll get a copy. Beyond that, I'm not sure there's much I can do."

"If I'm right, and I think I am, the men you're tracking are headed for a large marauder settlement."

"I agree. But it doesn't change anything. I can't spare the resources to go after them right now."

"I'm not asking you to. Just let me know where to find them when they stop. I'll take care of the rest."

"Gabriel, I can't have you interfering with ongoing operations."

"And you can't stop me, either. You said it yourself, General. You don't have the people."

"I damn well can stop you. All I have to do is withhold the intel you're asking for."

"You do that, don't ever ask me for anything again. We're done."

Jacobs let out a frustrated hiss. "Fine. I'll give you the location when I have it. But Gabriel, I want you to keep me in the loop. Understood?"

"Understood."

"Anything else?"

"No. That's it."

"Very well. Your transportation is on its way. Should be there by tomorrow morning."

"Did you remember the horse trailer?"

"Yes, I remembered the horse trailer. I still don't understand why you don't just turn your horses loose and buy new ones. I could have a Blackhawk out there by midnight."

"My horse's name is Red, and I like him. He's a good horse. I'm not leaving him out here to fend for himself."

"Fine. Whatever you want. I'm sure you'll both have a wonderful new life in the Springs."

"If it's all the same, I'd rather get dropped off somewhere else."

"Where?"

"Place just outside of Haviland, Kansas."

"Can I ask why?"

"I need to find some people."

"Okay. That's not a problem."

"Thanks, General. For everything."

"I'll be in touch."

He hung up.

TWENTY-EIGHT

Eric

The lights of Dodge City floated on the horizon to the west. The three of us rode toward them in the last couple of hours before dawn.

"Be nice to get a room," Sabrina said. "Sleep on a real bed."

"You're going soft," I said. "Too much easy living."

Sabrina gave me a look. There was just enough moonlight I could make out the angular features of her face.

"Says the guy who took us four miles out of our way to search for toilet paper in a trailer park."

"And found it," Elizabeth said. "Personally, I think the trip was worth it."

"Thank you, Liz," I said. "At least someone appreciates my efforts."

Sabrina let out a snort. She did that a lot. I told her once she should not snort because it was unladylike. She responded by putting her middle finger an inch from my nose and asking, "Is it unladylike to call you a bag of diseased dick-tips? How about a flapping anus? By the way, what's the male equivalent of unladylike? If it's *not* scratching your balls in public, you have failed, Eric. You have failed."

I had made no such comments since.

We were quiet the rest of the ride into town. A week had passed since we left Haviland, and our progress had been slow. We had elected to abandon the wagon, deeming it unfit for stealthy overland travel, and set out with just the horses and oxen. Before leaving, we risked backtracking the section of highway where we fled the attack and found most of Elizabeth's trade still intact, as well as the other items Hicks had thrown from the wagon. Necessity forced us to leave quite a lot behind, but between what we had brought along and our food and water, we had enough cargo to load down two oxen. Fortunately for us, we had four oxen, so none of them were overburdened.

Nevertheless, the dumb, plodding creatures limited our pace to less than fifteen miles a night. And by night, I mean the hours between 10:00 PM and 4:00 AM. Traveling during those hours minimized our chances of running into marauders, but made encountering the infected a much more dangerous proposition. If we were anywhere but Kansas, I would have deemed the strategy too risky. But so far it had paid off. We had seen no infected.

During the day we rested well away from the highway we were paralleling. And now, less than a mile from what we hoped was civilization, the clomping of hooves took on a sharper note as we emerged onto the remnants of Highway 400 as it turned due north and became Wyatt Earp Boulevard. Beside me, Sabrina shifted in the saddle and scanned her surroundings more than she usually did, which was saying a lot.

"Something bothering you?"

"I don't like this," Sabrina said. "Maybe we should go around Dodge."

I let out a sigh. "Sabrina, we've been over this. We need water. *Clean* water. With our equipment, assuming the Arkansas River isn't a half-dry mud pit right now, which it very likely is, it would take us at least two days to purify enough water to get us to Colorado. And even then, we wouldn't be able to carry it all even if we loaded down the horses and walked, which would slow us even more."

"So we make do with what we have. We ration. We'll be all right."

"But the animals won't."

"We only need two oxen."

"Still won't be enough."

"Sabrina," Elizabeth said gently, "we have to stop. It's not just about water, it's about getting to Colorado Springs alive. Our best chance is to stay in Dodge City for a while and wait for a caravan to come through."

"Or find one of my business or military contacts," I said.

"Any of them live here?" Sabrina asked.

"No. But they travel a lot, and Dodge is on one of the most heavily used routes. Like Liz said, it's our best chance."

"I survived four years without relying on caravans."

"Yes," I said, "but you traveled in a pair or alone, which means you travelled light. We're not traveling light. We have trade, and livestock, and you and Gabe and Liz will need all of it if you're going to start over in the Springs. And all this baggage has the unfortunate effect of making us not only visible, but eminently trackable. So we do this my way. We're going to Dodge. End of discussion."

Sabrina lapsed into sullen silence. I could tell she wanted to argue further, but could find no logical basis for doing so. Everything I had said to her was true. Dodge City was our best option. She didn't like it, but she knew it.

The lights of the wall around the inhabited part of the city loomed above us as we covered the last few yards to the gate. The glare was painful after riding in the dark for so long. I put a hand over my face to let my eyes adjust, but before they could, a spotlight swung around and focused on us.

"The gate is closed," a voice called out through a bullhorn. "Come back at 0700."

"It's just three of us," I yelled back. "You sure you can't let us through?"

The spotlight swung away and tracked over the road behind us. I heard a hum of voices and then the crackle of the bullhorn.

"Approach."

I blinked against the green spots in my vision and urged my horse forward again. The lights from the nearby guard towers illuminated the wall and the main gate. Now that I was closer, I realized the wall was actually a triple-layered chain-link fence topped with concertina wire and fronted with a row of concrete highway dividers. Towers stood every hundred feet or so, and I could see the outlines of heavy machine guns in them. I was willing to bet there were snipers, grenadiers, and LAW rockets nearby as well. In the distance, I heard the steady thrum of a large generator.

"That's far enough."

I tugged the reins. Behind me, Elizabeth, Sabrina, and the oxen clattered to a halt. The gate was a heavy section of fence set on

291

rollers. At present, it was locked with a chain and heavy padlock. Three armed guards stood in front of us, flanked on either side by machine gun nests. The guard in the middle held a bullhorn and stood behind a tripod-mounted spotlight.

"Where you coming from?" the guard with the bullhorn asked.

"Wichita. Caravan got attacked by raiders. Been on our own for a while."

The guard walked closer. "We heard about an attack a few days ago. What was the name of the man in charge of your group?"

"Called himself Spike. Don't know his real name."

"How many people?"

"About a hundred and thirty or so."

The guard's gaze shifted and he nodded as if confirming a thought. "How did you get away?"

"Fella that was with us at the time spotted raider scouts following us. Figured Haviland would be a good place for an ambush, so we held back to see what happened."

"Guy who spotted the raiders warn the caravan leader?" Bullhorn asked.

"About fifty times. Arrogant jackass wouldn't listen. Thought he could handle anything."

"What happened in Haviland? How many raiders were there?"

I shook my head. "On both counts, I'm not exactly sure. We were pretty far away, but I could hear explosions and gunfire. Went back a couple of days later and the place was abandoned, all the wagons gone."

"Survivors?"

"You're looking at them."

"The raiders take any prisoners?"

"How should I know? I told you we were pretty far away."

It was not entirely the truth, but close enough. I saw no reason to involve the three of us in whatever fallout emerged from the attack.

The guard said, "What about the other guy you mentioned, the one who spotted the scouts. Who is he? What happened to him?"

I shrugged. "His name is Gabriel Garrett. As for what happened to him, he left. Said he wanted to catch up with the raiders and see if they had any prisoners. Maybe try to get back some trade he lost. Haven't heard from him since."

"And what was your relationship to this individual?"

"We ran a business together back in Tennessee. But he sold out and wanted to move to the Springs. I came along for my own reasons."

"Which would be?"

"None of your business."

The guard accepted the rebuke with quiet professionalism. "Anybody else in your group survive?"

"Yeah. Guy named Hicks. Army grunt. I hired him for his gun, but he quit on me and left with Garrett."

The guard thought over what I told him for a few seconds, and then turned and motioned to a soldier standing near the gate.

"Open it up. The Major will want to speak with them."

The soldier complied and rolled the gate open. The guard with the bullhorn, on whose uniform I could now read the name Reeves and saw the rank insignia of a lieutenant, motioned us through.

"You can stay in the caravan district tonight," Lieutenant Reeves said, motioning to one of his men who left his post and hustled over. "This is Sergeant Barnes. He'll show you the way."

293

"You said the major will want to speak with us. Who's he?"

"Major Santino, commanding officer here. He'll want a statement from you about the attack."

"I just told you everything I know."

"I understand, but we'll need an official statement anyway. From all of you."

"That's fine," Elizabeth said, ever the diplomat. "We'd be happy to help."

"Appreciated." Reeves nodded to Barnes. "Sergeant."

"Yes sir," Barnes said. He was a young black man, average height, athletic build, a long scar running from his cheekbone to his jawline. The scar diminished his youthful appearance, making him look tougher and more seasoned than he would have otherwise. Considering the state of the world lately, I had no doubt that was exactly the case.

"Please follow me," he said.

We did. He stayed ahead of us at a fast trot, seeming to have no trouble maintaining his pace. I had to tug the lead ropes a few times to goad the oxen to keep up. We passed a few blocks of dilapidated buildings, most of them dark, but here and there an orange glow of candlelight shining from a window. Now that we were past the gate, it was difficult to make out much detail in the darkness.

"Here we are," Barnes said, slowing to a halt. If running to this point had wearied him, he gave no sign. He pointed to an empty field that may have once been a park surrounded by a layer of fencing not unlike what I had seen at the gate. "There are no caravans camped right now, so you'll have the place to yourself."

"Thanks, Sergeant," I said. "Need anything else?"

He unlocked the gate and rolled it open. "Nope. I'll lock the gate behind you. Someone will be by in the morning to open it. Probably bring one of Major Santino's staff to take you to headquarters."

"What about our trade and livestock?"

"Not sure. Have to work that out in the morning."

I frowned. In my experience, trusting one's trade to the honesty of bored, underpaid infantry grunts was as good as giving it away. Elizabeth noticed my consternation and leaped in before I could say anything.

"Thank you for your help," she said. "We'll be all right from here."

She shot me a warning glare and rode into the caravan district. Sabrina and I glanced at each other, shrugged, and followed. The gate rolled shut behind us and I heard a padlock click and the rattling of chains.

"Tomorrow should be interesting," I said.

"I'm not a big fan of interesting," Sabrina replied. "Interesting usually means dangerous."

"Yes. It does."

TWENTY-NINE

In the clear light of morning, my first impression of post-Outbreak Dodge City was not a pleasant one. Sabrina tended to agree, and expressed her opinion with her usual delicacy.

"What a shithole," she said. "And I've seen some shitholes."

I looked up from the cook fire where I was preparing our first hot meal since leaving Haviland.

"In fairness, I would remind you that until about a year ago this place was overrun with infected, who are not known for their expertise at gentrification and urban renewal."

Elizabeth turned and looked past the fence at the broken windows, piles of rubble, and skeletal construction girders spearing toward the sky. "I'm afraid I have to agree with Sabrina's assessment," she said. "I've seen sewers that were more cosmopolitan."

I stirred the pot hanging over the fire. It was filled with water, potatoes, peas, carrots, and chicken meat, all of which had been dehydrated until a few minutes ago and were now swelling with reintroduced moisture. The brewing soup made me mourn the loss

296

of Gabe's trade. The blandness of the morning's repast would have been greatly mitigated by a prudent application of salt.

"Well, we're here now," I said. "So let's try to make the best of it."

Sabrina mumbled something under her breath. I made out the words 'horse shit', but nothing else.

Our trade and supplies were piled away from the fire near a set of wooden feed troughs. I assumed the troughs had been placed there by the city for the convenience of visiting caravans. When I finished breakfast I walked over, grabbed a bag of feed grain, and shook it loudly. A minute or so later I heard the approach of hooves and poured the feed evenly along a few feet of trough.

The night before, since there was little chance the animals would escape the fence surrounding the district, I had forgone picketing the animals. And so, untethered for the first time in weeks, they had happily wandered off to do whatever it is livestock do in their free time. Which, in my experience, mostly involved grazing, pissing out impossible quantities of foul-smelling urine, and fertilizing the soil with heaping mounds of fibrous dung.

Oh, the joys of owning livestock.

Presently, the animals came into view and headed straight for the smell of feed. I stood back and refereed as they stuck their long snouts into the trough and scooped up grain with prehensile mouths. The horses were more aggressive than the oxen and tried to edge them out and steal their breakfast. I did not let them. A few taps on the nose with a stick was enough to get them in line, a fact which I beheld with fascination. Horses are large, powerful animals. On average, they weigh upwards of a thousand pounds. They can bite with tremendous pressure and cave a man's chest or skull in with the flick of a hoof. But give them a light smack on the kisser with a soft willow twig, and they're putty in your hands. If only the infected were so easy to manage. Humans too, for that matter.

The drone of an engine picked up in the distance and gained volume as it grew closer. I walked back toward camp and arrived in time to hear the crunch of tires on crumbling asphalt and watch a man emerge from a Humvee in front of the gate. The driver stayed behind the wheel while the other man unlocked the gate and waved the vehicle through. Once it was in, he closed the gate without locking it.

"Looks like the welcoming committee has arrived," Elizabeth said.

"Indeed."

The man climbed back into the Humvee and it rolled sedately toward us. When they were twenty or so feet away, the Humvee stopped and three men in Army fatigues climbed out.

"Sergeant First Class Brian Thornberg," the tallest of them said, walking ahead of the other two. He had olive skin, brown eyes, and what I could see of his head beneath his hat looked shaved and was an even tone with the rest of his skin. He offered a hand. I shook it. "You must be Mr. Riordan."

"Yes, Eric Riordan," I said, surprised he knew my name already. "This is Elizabeth Stone and Sabrina Garrett."

"A pleasure. You in charge here?"

"When I'm allowed to be."

Thornberg kept his expression neutral, but I could tell he didn't think I was funny. "I need the three of you to come with me for just a little while. Major Santino has been informed of the attack on your caravan and would like to speak with you personally. Any information you might offer could be very helpful in tracking down whoever attacked you."

"Sure," I said. "Just as soon as we can hire someone to watch our trade and livestock."

"Already taken care of," Thornberg said, nodding to the two soldiers flanking him. I looked them over. Their rank insignia said they were privates, and I would have eaten my boots if either one was a day over twenty.

"You'll have to forgive me, Sergeant, but I don't much care to leave my life savings in the hands of people I don't know. I've noticed over the years that some soldiers have a tendency to avail themselves of other people's possessions when not properly supervised."

Thornberg's color darkened a bit. "I'm not stupid, Mr. Riordan. I know soldiers sometimes steal things. It's a failure of leadership. I do not tolerate such things from my men, and I will give you my personal guarantee that none of your possessions will be touched."

I didn't give the sergeant's personal guarantee much credence, but did not see as I had much choice but to take him at his word.

"Okay then. Let's get going."

The three of us piled into the Humvee. Sabrina and I took the back seat, Elizabeth rode shotgun, and Thornberg climbed in behind the wheel. The two privates walked behind us until we were through the gate and then closed it, locked it, and stood on either side with their hands resting casually on their rifles.

"Where we headed?" I asked.

"Headquarters," Thornberg said. "It's not far."

I looked at Elizabeth and Sabrina. They had nothing to offer. No one spoke for the rest of the ride.

*****

299

Headquarters turned out to be an elementary school that had somehow avoided the fires that leveled most of the city during the Outbreak. All around us, in the form of scorch marks and craters, was evidence of artillery shells dropped by the Army during Operation Relentless Force. The Army Corps of Engineers, or what was left of it, was hard at work bulldozing large sections of uninhabitable buildings. I wondered what they planned to do with the cleared land.

The Humvee stopped and Thornberg asked us to follow him. Lacking anything better to do, we did. The interior of the school was bare, clean, and orderly. Soldiers in uniform bustled around carrying out whatever tasks soldiers carry out when they are not killing people or destroying things. There were rows of desks in the student center, radios set up near windows with wires leading toward towers outside, and in a far corner by itself, what appeared to be a civilian owned food and beverage stand. The smell of fried eggs, pork belly, and roasted vegetables made my mouth water. There was a line of bored looking men and women lined up waiting on food orders, some in uniform, some not. I figured the proprietor of the little stand did pretty good business.

Thornberg led us past all of this to a hallway flanked on either side by what were once classrooms. The desks, decorations, computers, and other early-childhood accoutrements from a lost civilization had been removed and replaced with bunks, foot lockers, crates, and coat racks lined with dangling rifles—a sign of our society's shifting priorities.

One room had a couple of pool tables, a foosball table, and several dart boards mounted on a wall. I took note of the ranks on the uniforms we passed and realized we were walking through the senior NCO barracks. I was willing to bet the gymnasium housed the junior enlisted and the officers were quartered somewhere in town, probably in houses not yet rendered uninhabitable.

300

We rounded a corner and walked to the end of the hallway. To our left, an entire classroom seemed dedicated to a bank of file cabinets, a radio and associated equipment, and a lone Army officer sitting behind a desk who I could only assume was Major Santino. His door was open and he seemed busy with something on a ruggedized laptop. As we stepped into the entryway, on the far right side of the room against the wall, I saw a metal bunk, footlocker, and a massive cherry-stained wooden wardrobe. The wardrobe was ornate, beautifully constructed, and matched the dull austerity of the room about as well as a cherry blossom in a toilet.

Thornberg gently cleared his throat and knocked lightly at the door as we entered. Santino raised a finger and clacked away diligently at his keyboard. I took a moment to study him. He was medium height, had a strong build, reddish brown hair cut down to stubble, neatly trimmed moustache, black eyes, healthy-looking tanned skin, and strong facial features that suggested Spanish ancestry. He finished typing, closed his laptop, stood up, and came around the desk to greet us.

"Good morning," he said, offering a smile. "I apologize for asking you here so early. I'm Major Gerald Santino."

"Yeah, I kinda figured," I said.

The smile stayed in place. Major Santino inclined his head and gestured to the three chairs in front of his desk.

"Please, have a seat."

I thought about asking if we had a choice and decided against it. Thereby proving, at least to myself, that I am not always a loud-mouthed provocateur. I sat down. Sabrina and Elizabeth did the same. Santino grabbed a folder from the corner of his desk, opened it, and retrieved a recording device from a drawer. He clicked a button and told the device his name, our names (he mispronounced Riordan), the date and time, and the purpose of the interview.

"Starting from the beginning," he said, "please relate the events of the attack to the best of your recollection, Mr. Riordan."

"It's REAR-dun, not REE-or-dan."

"Sorry about that, Mr. Riordan." He said it correctly this time.

"It happens."

"Your statement please?"

I gave it, omitting the part where Gabe and Hicks rode back and read the raiders' tracks. If they wanted to include it in their official report, they would. I was not present for that part, and could offer no testimony as to the accuracy of their findings even if I had been. Despite Gabe's best instructional efforts, I am not much of a tracker.

When he was finished with me, he asked Elizabeth to go next. She told him I had covered everything. He asked her to give her version anyway. The only difference in her story was instead of lying on her belly in the dirt and shooting at the bad guys, she and Sabrina tied their horses to a telephone pole to act as a decoy if they were followed and then holed up in an abandoned tire shop until the fighting was over. Sabrina's version was more terse, but otherwise identical. Santino clicked off the recorder and made a few notes in his file.

"I appreciate your time," he said. "You never know what information will be helpful with something like this. Best to gather as many clues as you can and hope something shakes loose."

I knew at that moment Major Santino was not in the loop as to what Gabe and Hicks were up to. Gabe had probably contacted General Jacobs already, but I could not be sure. I had been hoping the major could tell me something about their progress, but if the information was available, it had not yet filtered down to his level, nor was it likely to do so anytime soon. General Jacobs likes to compartmentalize his operations, each player knowing only his

302

small role and operating with no concept of the larger picture. Dangerous for the people involved, but critical to operational security.

"Glad we could help," I said.

"How long will you be in town?"

"Why do you ask?"

"In case I have any more questions for you."

"Why would you?"

He shrugged. "I'm sending your statements to Central Command. They'll cross-reference them against what we already know to try and get a better picture of the incident. Could be something needs clarification, could be I need to notify you of something, could be you remember something you haven't mentioned yet. Purely precautionary."

"Sure," I said, sounding dubious even to myself. "I don't know for certain how long we'll be in town. It's not safe on the road for just the three of us."

"I understand. So you'll be looking to join a caravan or a convoy, correct?"

"Yes."

"Where to?"

"Same place Spike's caravan was heading. The Springs."

Santino leaned back in his chair. "We're rotating troops in the near future. Quite a number of people stationed here will be headed to Colorado."

"When?"

"In two weeks."

I looked at Elizabeth. She gave a small nod. Sabrina did the same.

"Think they'd take us on? We'll need to bring our livestock and trade."

Santino's dark black eyes shifted to Sergeant Thornberg. "Would you give us a moment, Sergeant? And shut the door."

"Yes sir."

The door shut. We sat in the quiet room for a few seconds and listened to the building's generator humming through the walls.

"Arrangements could be made, Mr. Riordan."

"How much?"

A small grin. "You cut straight to it, don't you?"

"This ain't my first rodeo."

"What do you have to offer in consideration?"

"Consideration? That word implies a contract, Major. Something tells me we're going to be keeping things off the record."

Santino made a flipping motion with one hand. "What would you like to call it then?"

"A bribe. Because that's what it is."

"I don't care for that term."

I let out a slow breath and rubbed my forehead. "Sure. Whatever. How much?"

"What do you have?"

"Tell me what you want, and I'll tell you what I can do."

The negotiation lasted perhaps five minutes. We settled on half a pound of sugar, a pound of dried beans, and a liter of Mike Stall's moonshine. It was far more than what I would have paid under normal circumstances, especially considering I was spending Elizabeth's trade, but we did not have much leverage to bargain with. With Liz's permission, I accepted the deal. We agreed to deliver the goods via third-party courier the day the convoy left. Santino tried to push for half in advance, but I refused flatly, telling him I wouldn't hand over a crumb until my gear was stowed in a truck, my livestock were loaded in a trailer, and I had personally confirmed all our names and possessions were listed correctly and in detail on an official cargo manifest with the proper seal. Santino said it would be difficult to get all that in writing. I told him I had faith in him. He smugly suggested his original designation of the bribe as consideration was accurate after all. I told him a bribe was a bribe, even with a pretty coating of semantic gloss.

"Are we all settled then?" Elizabeth interjected. She knew well my innate distaste for corrupt officials, even when I am the beneficiary of said corruption. The last thing we needed here was for me to start an argument. Knowing this did not make me want to start one any less.

"I believe so," Major Santino said. He stood and offered a hand. I shook it even though I didn't want to. Sabrina and Elizabeth did the same.

"Sergeant Thonberg will take you back to the caravan district."

I nodded once and we left.

THIRTY

The streets began coming to life as we bumped and creaked over the broken pavement of Dodge City. Sergeant Thornberg was much more talkative now that his official duties were concluded. At Elizabeth's prompting, he gave us a rough idea of the situation in Dodge. I had to admire the way Liz milked information out of the burly sergeant. She was pretty, and polite, and smiled in all the right places, and it was obvious Thornberg liked what he saw.

"So the military doesn't actually control this place?" Elizabeth said.

"No. We're not a safe zone or an FOB. Just a regular town."

"Could have fooled me with all the security," I said.

"We're on the biggest trade route going east out of the Springs. What you might call a high-value target. The joint chiefs designated the area as vital to economic recovery."

"So here you are."

"Here we are."

"If this place is so important," Elizabeth said, "where is everybody? We have the caravan district to ourselves."

"It's still early spring," Thornberg said. "You're in the off-season. In a month, this place will be a zoo."

"So if the military isn't in charge," Sabrina asked, "who is?"

"There's a mayor and a city council."

"Police?" I asked.

"Yeah. Chief is elected by the city council every four years."

"So you've had exactly one chief of police."

"Yes."

"Cops any good?"

"All right, I guess. Good as can be expected."

"What does that mean?" Elizabeth said.

"Let's just say the local business interests wield a lot of influence over what goes on around here."

The Humvee hit a particularly large bump that caused me to bite the tip of my tongue. I cursed softly and watched a man emerge from the doorway of a sporting goods store pushing a food cart. A gaggle of scrawny children dressed in rags turned a corner and went by at a dead sprint. One of them stopped to pick up a rock and throw it at the Humvee. The rock bounced off the driver's door with a resounding *whack*. Thornberg did not seem to notice.

"Vice?" Elizabeth asked. "Racketeering?"

"Probably," Thornberg said.

"And you don't try to stop it?"

"Listen, I'm a soldier, not a cop. It's not my job to police the civilians. Not without orders from on high, anyway. Our job is physical security. The Army doesn't get involved in local affairs unless the locals disturb the flow of trade."

"That ever happened?" I asked.

"Once."

"What did the Army do?"

Thornberg grinned over his shoulder. The curl of his thin lips over bare teeth had a nasty brutality about it. "We laid the fucking hammer down," he said.

The Humvee rolled to a halt in front of the caravan district. The only three buildings across the street that did not look like they were about to collapse were now occupied. I was able to determine by the wares on display that one was a bar and grill, one sold weapons and ammunition, and one was a brothel. Charming.

"Your kind of place, huh?" Sabrina nudged me with her elbow and tilted her head toward the whorehouse. I glanced at the underfed women slouching on the building's stoop with their crudely painted faces and tired, cynical eyes. Compared to Allison they looked like a gaggle of cow flops.

"Not even in the wild days of my youth."

"Hate to tell you," Thornberg said. "But the caravan district gave rise to sort of a red light district around here. The peddlers can't go through the gate—it's one of the few places we do control—but it's a short walk for anyone interested."

"Duly noted," I said.

As I got out of the Humvee, Thornberg rolled down his window. "Take a word of advice?"

"Sure."

He motioned me closer. "You want to get out of the caravan district. Ain't safe outside the gate after dark. I know a guy runs a tight business. Warehouse, livery, hotel, everything you need. He's not cheap, but you get what you pay for around here."

"I'm new in town. Got directions?"

He gave them to me and said, "Ask for Ross. Tell him I sent you."

I thanked Sergeant Thornberg and watched him drive away.

"If you think for one second that fucker isn't getting kickbacks," Sabrina said, "you're an idiot."

"I'd be amazed if he wasn't. Makes me wonder what other graft the Army has going on around here."

Elizabeth began walking toward the gate. "Let's hope we don't have to find out."

*****

Ross was a tall black man with a shaved head, graying goatee, and eyes just slightly less merciful than those of a great white shark. His face was smooth and unlined, and his age could have been anywhere from thirty to sixty. I told him Sergeant Thornberg had sent me. He nodded, finished polishing the glass in his hand, and sat down on a stool behind the bar. At the moment, the lobby of his hotel, which doubled as a restaurant and watering hole, was mostly empty. A couple of old men sat at a table in a corner playing cards and slowly sipping grain alcohol. A prostitute slouched in a chair near the stairway leading to the rooms upstairs. The place was newly constructed from raw wood and had a distinctly Old West feel to it. The only thing missing was a pair of batwing doors at the entrance.

"Have a seat." Ross waved a hand at row of bar stools. His voice was deep and resonant with a southern drawl that could only

309

have originated in the Mississippi Delta. I glanced out the front window to make sure no one was bothering Liz and Sabrina. They stood alone at the hitch rail with the livestock, people passing by indifferently on the street behind them. I took a seat.

"Care for a drink?" Ross asked.

"Sure. What do you have?"

"Anything you want, long as it's moonshine."

"Moonshine it is."

He poured me a drink. I took a sip. It wasn't as good as Mike Stall's, but it wouldn't blind me either.

"Not bad," I said.

He gave a slow nod and fixed the empty eyes on me. "What you need?"

"Room, laundry, stables, and a safe place to store my trade."

"Doin' business in town?"

"Not presently, no."

He glanced out the window and looked meaningfully at Liz and Sabrina. "You sure about that? Some good lookin' women with you."

The old familiar coldness rose in my chest and I felt myself go still. "They're not merchandise."

Ross smiled with all the warmth of an ice cube. There were a couple of teeth missing on the left side of his face.

"Don't be too sure," he said. "Every woman got a price."

"Anyone bothers them, it's their fucking life. How's that for a price?"

Another slow nod. The grin faded. "Pretty steep."

"Can you help me or not?"

He stood up and slowly wandered over to a cloth covered in wet, heavy-bottomed glasses, picked one up, and began drying it with a yellow towel. "Sure. What you got for trade?"

A negotiation ensued. I bought the three of us a room for a week, laundry service, stables for the horses and oxen, and a spot on the floor of a nearby warehouse. The price was much less than I would have expected. Maybe Thornberg had been telling the truth about this being the off season for Dodge City.

"I'll need to check out the warehouse before I render payment," I said. "Make sure the security is up to snuff."

"Sure. How 'bout you pay for the first night now, the rest when you're satisfied?"

"Fair enough."

Ross took a keyring out of his pocket, unlocked a panel behind the bar, and removed a room key.

"Number sixteen. Go upstairs and take your first left. Third door on your right."

I took the key. It was small, brass, and looked like the kind that opened a padlock. I dug four packets of instant coffee from a shirt pocket and dropped them on the bar.

"Thanks."

"No problem."

Ross continued drying glasses, holding each one up to the light through the window to assess its cleanliness. I stood up and walked toward the door.

"Hey," Ross called as I touched the door handle. I looked over my shoulder.

"Yeah?"

"You change your mind about them women, you let me know."

I stared at him for a long moment. Grown men had trembled under the weight of that stare, but Ross did not seem affected. I felt a strong urge to cross the room and back up the stare by putting a gun barrel under his chin, but didn't. Ross did not strike me as the kind of man who would be impressed by threats.

"Don't hold your breath," I said, and went out the door.

THIRTY-ONE

Room sixteen at the Sky River Hotel had two single beds, a dresser topped with a plastic pitcher, a large stainless steel bowl that would have been great for applying Buffalo sauce to chicken wings, and a small bathroom. The toilet was a crudely made wooden box containing a bucket of very dry dirt to which a cushioned seat had been attached. A smaller bucket with more dirt sat nearby. Sabrina peeked over my shoulder.

"I think we'd be better off shitting in a hole in the ground," she said. "At least then we could get away from the stink."

I glanced around the small room. "Sabrina, your eloquence and delicate mastery of expression never ceases to humble and astonish me."

"Fuck you."

"I supposed you and Liz will be taking the beds?"

"Yep."

"Good thing I have a well-equipped bedroll."

Liz smiled at me from one of the beds. She sat on it with her legs crossed, leaning back on a pillow propped against the headboard, a paperback copy of *A Farewell to Arms* in her hands.

"Just think what Allison would say if she knew you made one of us sleep on the floor," she said.

The mention of my wife sent a sharp jolt of pain through me. Her distance from me had been like a bone spur in the back of my mind, constantly grating, but until that moment I had kept it compartmentalized. Hearing her name, however, made the longing for her roar to life as sharp and merciless as a stomach cramp. I wanted to be close to my wife. I wanted to hold my son. It felt like a lifetime had passed since I had last kissed the little guy's face. I had been trying not to think of him, but now his absence was a physical thing, a pressure in my chest threatening to choke me. My jaw clenched and I felt the muscles along my cheek working under the skin.

"Hey," Elizabeth said. "I'm sorry. That was stupid of me."

I cleared my throat so I could speak. "I know."

"That I'm stupid or that I'm sorry?"

"You're not stupid, Liz."

"I'm sorry."

"No worries. I'm headed out. Walk the perimeter, look for trouble."

Liz did not speak for a few seconds, then said, "Be careful."

"Stay here. Both of you. Don't open the door for anyone but me." I looked at Sabrina. "You armed?"

She looked at me like I was an idiot. "Who the fuck are you talking to?"

"I withdraw the question. Be back soon."

Before I shut the door I stopped and leaned back into the room. "Hey Liz?"

"Yes?"

"The English nurse dies at the end."

She closed one of Hemingway's most distinguished works and threw it to the floor. "Asshole."

"Now we're even."

*****

The part of town I walked through was, according to the signs, the central business district.

Most of the place was a crumbling wreck, but some buildings had been repaired, others bulldozed and replaced with new construction. The streets were mostly clear of debris, and the most unstable areas had been cordoned off with signs and crude rope fences. By the inflow of people from the north and east, I surmised those directions harbored Dodge City's residential areas.

On the street I walked were two empty auction houses that had once been strip malls, the parking lots empty now, the gutted brick buildings uninhabited, the crudely-fenced livestock pens full of growing grass that would turn to shit-crusted mud when the caravan season started again. In the meantime, they looked disused and uncared for.

I passed the warehouse where I had stowed our trade and, upon assessment, agreed with Ross that it was highly secure. The building had once been a mixed-use office complex, but now the windows were boarded over and all but one entrance had been sealed with bricks and mortar. The only way in or out was a single

315

garage door in the back manned by heavily armed guards who all appeared to have been born without a sense of humor.

The streets themselves were cracked and broken like all pavement was anymore. Plants pushed through here and there where feet and hooves had not trampled them to death. Scorch marks and rust-brown streaks abounded, a mute testament to the scores of infected that once populated the town. And beneath the scents of living beings—wood smoke, dung, urine, rotting vegetables, and sweat—lay the unmistakable cloying scent of death. I wondered how long it would take for human habitation and the elements to cleanse the place.

A few filthy-looking restaurants served unappetizing food to grim faced customers, all of whom appeared to be locals. Everyone I saw was armed. They all seemed to know each other. And they didn't know me, a fact which became more acutely obvious the longer I walked the streets. The weight of the nine-millimeter pistol on my hip was comforting, as was the revolver against the small of my back, the fighting knife on my left leg, and the MK 9 ghoul-chopper strapped to my back. I kept my face blank and did my best to look like the kind of man one did not want to fuck with. I must have pulled it off, because no one did. But I got lots of looks.

As I walked back toward my hotel, I spotted a group of three men watching me. They were rough looking, like everyone else on the street, but there was a quiet menace in them I had not seen in any others. They sat in one of the few crowded bars lining the business district with no one close to them, a ring of empty tables insulating them from the rest of the crowd. I scanned their side of the street, not letting my eyes rest on the men for more than a moment. Two were bearded white men, very young. The third was older and had the kind of dark brown skin and sharp features that could have originated anywhere from southern Texas to Patagonia. By their posture, I could tell the two young white guys deferred to the dark-skinned older man. One of them leaned over and whispered something. The older man nodded once, his eyes steady on me.

One of the many talents I have developed since the Outbreak is the ability to tell the difference between casual distrust and outright hostility. There is a difference in the way a person looks at you when they mean you harm. It is a weight in the eyes, a stillness of the face, a tightness in the line of the jaw. And I saw it in the faces of the three thugs as they stared at me.

"Just what I fucking need," I muttered.

It occurred to me to avoid the hotel, but I decided doing so in a place like this was pointless. A simple inquiry would tell the three hardcases where I was holed up. If they wanted to make a run at me, they would. All I could do was remain vigilant, which was exactly what I was going to do anyway.

Back in my room, I informed Sabrina and Elizabeth of my findings. Liz looked worried. Sabrina looked angry.

"I told you we shouldn't have come here," Sabrina said.

"A few street toughs is nothing to get in a ruffle about," I said.

"What you saw is no indication of how many there actually are. Place like this, there's probably a syndicate running things. And here we are, a bunch of jackasses with plenty of trade and no backup. Sitting fucking ducks."

"You're making assumptions. Three guys in a bar gave me the mean mug. That doesn't mean we're about to be descended upon by an army of murderers."

Sabrina's eyes flashed. She never looked more like her father than when she was angry. "It doesn't mean they're coming by with flowers and fucking smiles either. They marked you. They're going to come for us. It's how things work on the road."

317

I sat down cross-legged on my bedroll and drew my pistol. Checked the chamber. Dropped the mag and popped it against my hand a couple of times. The rounds were seated. The gun was clean. I drew my dagger and checked the edge. It was just as sharp as the last time I'd tested it. I looked out the window at the tops of shattered buildings stretching into the distance under a cloudy gray sky. If they caught us in our room, we were done for. The only way to win was to ambush the ambushers.

"You're right," I said. "We need backup."

Elizabeth's gaze became very sharp. "What are you thinking?"

"Stay here."

I stood up, holstered my weapons, and headed downstairs.

THIRTY-TWO

Ross was still behind the bar, only now instead of polishing glasses he was thumbing through a faded copy of a pre-Outbreak men's magazine. The passage of years had not made the young actress on the cover any less beautiful, or any less scantily clad. I walked up to the bar and stood across from its owner.

"Got a minute?"

He did not look up. "Got lots of minutes."

"I'd like to talk in private."

"What about?"

"Like I said. In private."

He glanced up at me speculatively for a few seconds, then put down the magazine. "Let's go."

He lifted the folding divider so I could step behind the bar and I followed him down a short hallway and turned right into an open office. The space was about the size of my hotel room but much more nicely appointed. There were lanterns mounted in wall sconces in all four corners of the room, the soft yellow light creating a pleasant ambience in the windowless space. Richly stained bookshelves lined the walls complete with leather-bound tomes boasting such titles as *Robinson Crusoe*, *The Complete Works of William Shakespeare*, *The Sound and the Fury*, *The Three Musketeers*, *War and Peace*, and perhaps a hundred others I did not have time to scan. The desk was polished oak, the chairs were upholstered leather with little brass studs around the edges, and the floor was smooth and stained a dark walnut color. A dark brown leather couch lined one wall, supporting the considerable weight of a man whose skin tone nearly matched the flooring.

"This Terrell," Ross said, flicking a finger in the big man's direction as he walked behind his desk. Terrell stood up. He was not quite the size of a rhinoceros, but it was a near thing.

"Eric Riordan."

The big man nodded once. "Got to search you."

I glanced at Ross. His face remained impassive as he sat back in his chair. I looked back at Terrell.

"Okay."

Terrell was quick and professional. The Berretta and knife were out in the open, and he lifted them as light and quick as a talented pickpocket. His hands skimmed my arms, shoulders, waist, chest, stomach, legs, and he paid special attention to the ankles. When he was finished, he added my little revolver and a clip-point folding knife to the pile of weapons on the table next to the couch and flipped an enormous hand in Ross' direction.

"He safe."

"Thank you, Terrell." Ross motioned for me to sit down. I did.

"What's on your mind?"

The couch creaked as Terrell sat down behind me. I did not need to look in his direction to know he was watching me.

"I have a problem I need help with."

Ross spread his hands. "Everybody got problems. What yours got to do with me?"

"I may have attracted the unwanted attention of a few unsavory types."

"This Dodge City, baby. Unsavory the only type there is."

"There were three of them. Two young white guys with beards and an older Hispanic man. Older guy seemed like the one in charge."

"Where they at when you saw 'em?"

I told him the name of the bar.

"The old man be Lopez. You don't want no trouble with him. He bad news."

"I may not have much choice in the matter."

"You still ain't said what this got to do with me."

"I'm not a rookie when it comes to life on the road. I'm here with two women and some good trade. This Lopez guy thinks I'm an easy target and is looking to make a run at me. I would like to ensure he fails in this endeavor. With prejudice. You seem like a man who might know where I could enlist help in that area."

Ross grinned, once more exposing the two missing teeth. "I like the way you talk. Sound like you got some schoolin'."

"Princeton. Most people don't hold it against me."

"Ain't too many of you ivy leaguers around no more. Too spoiled. Too weak."

"There are outliers in any population."

The grin widened. "Say I help you. What you do for me?"

"What do you want?"

"I already told you what I want."

"No," I said firmly. "Not an option. What else?"

The grin went away. Ross' eyes glittered black in the dim light. "I could just kill you. Take those women for myself."

It was my turn to smile. "Good luck with that."

"I want you dead, white man, you dead."

"Isn't me you have to worry about. Those women are no wilting violets. They won't be taken alive, and even if you do, they'll spend every second of every day making you regret it. And if you give them half a chance, they'll kill you."

Ross crossed his legs and drummed his fingers on one knee. "They so tough, why you need me?"

"You're local. You know the score around here."

"You right about that."

I sighed. The conversation was starting to bore me. "So can we do business or what? If you can't help me, there are other people I can ask."

Ross stared a few more seconds, then opened a drawer and took out a ledger. "Lopez be a problem for me too. You see, after the Army clean up this town, we the first ones here looking to do business."

"What kind of business?"

Ross' face registered amusement "Way you say it, you think I be engaged in some kind of illegal activity."

"I think the hotel and livery and warehouse operations make an excellent front for a smuggler. And I can't help but notice the way the whores in this district never cross the street. I'm guessing you control one half of the vice trade around here and Lopez controls the other."

"And you only been in town one day. Maybe you smarter than you look, Ivy League."

"Maybe. Can we get to the part where you tell me what you want?"

Ross spun the ledger around. Inside were sheets of paper with small photos clipped to the upper left corner. I pulled the top photo from the folder and looked at it closely. It had been printed on photographic paper from an inkjet printer. The materials for making photos like this were rare and extremely expensive, not to mention the fact they required electricity to produce. I put the photo back in the file and read the papers attached to it.

"This is a dossier," I said.

"Got a file on everybody in Lopez's operation."

I closed the file and sat back in my chair. "Why me? You need a hit man, there's plenty of people around can do the job for you."

Ross shook his head. "Nobody who take on Lopez. Same reason he don't send no trigger man after me."

"Sounds like an uneasy truce. Maybe even a forced one."

"Might be."

"I'm guessing things haven't always been this peaceful between the two of you."

A laugh. "Hell no. We at it like cats in a bag till Major Santino show up."

I remembered what Sergeant Thornberg said about the time the locals disrupted trade, and how the Army had handled it. The picture was starting to come together.

"How deep does Santino have his hands in your pockets?"

Ross looked mildly impressed. "Deep. Same for Lopez. And he like us in competition with each other so neither one of us get too much power."

I nodded, one hand rubbing my chin. "Let me see if I understand the situation. You and Lopez show up here at the same time looking to establish a monopoly on the vice trade in Dodge City. You tangle. The locals get scared and complain to the Army, say all this fighting is bad for business."

Ross fluttered his hands in the air. "Think of the children!"

"Of course. So Santino shows up with Humvees and heavy machine guns and troops just itching to bust some heads, and takes the two of you somewhere private and tells you how things are gonna be."

A nod. "How I lost my teeth. Pair of pliers be a motherfucker on your dental work."

"And Lopez?"

"He got a bad knee won't never heal."

"And afterward, you and Santino build your headquarters on either side of the district from one another, close enough so your troops can glare and posture, and Santino dips from both buckets. Meanwhile, he forbids you from making a run at each other to keep you both in check."

"And if we try to take each other down legit, go to the cops or the city council, Santino hear about it."

"And maybe you end up with your own bad knee."

"At least."

I tapped my fingers on the arms of my chair. It was a very comfortable chair. "Which brings us to the crux of the conversation. You can't make a move on your own, can't go to the cops or the city leaders, and Santino has his boot on your neck. Which leaves you only one way out of this situation."

Ross pointed his thumb and finger at me like a gun and dropped the hammer.

"You need an outsider," I said.

"Got to make it look like Lopez made the first move."

"Self-defense."

"Exactly."

"What makes you think I'm up to the task?"

"You got no choice. Lopez coming for you."

"You sound awfully sure about that."

"I know Lopez."

"Still, for a guy with an operation like his, I'm small fry. What's he want with my trade if he's so big time?"

"Maybe he not as big time as you think."

"Meaning?"

Ross sat forward and steepled his hands in his desk. "We two different kind of squirrels, him and me. He a lazy squirrel. Greedy. Like to fill his belly and don't worry too much about the future. Not like me. I be a smart squirrel. Store my acorns for winter and make sure all the little squirrels got something to eat till springtime. Lopez, he all out of acorns. Got nothing to keep his men in line but promises and threats. He can't take from the locals 'cause Santino bust his other knee for him if he does. Can't take from me for the same reason."

"Caravans?"

"Not them either. He can sell 'em booze and women and whatever else they want, but it got to be voluntary. No highway robbery. And as you may have noticed, ain't no caravans right now. Even if there was, you ain't with no caravan, now is you?"

"I is not."

"There you go."

"So if he kills me and steals my trade and women and livestock..."

"Ain't no skin off Santino's back. Not so long as Lopez keeps it quiet."

"Sell the livestock, offload the trade, send the women out of town, bury the bodies, that kind of thing."

"Exactly."

I sat and observed Ross for the better part of a minute. He stared back placidly. I did not trust him. I did not believe he was telling me the truth, or at least not all of it. I had the feeling there was something I was missing, some piece of the puzzle he had laid out that I had not accounted for. The thing about him and Lopez being at odds was believable enough, but the rest of it smacked of contrivance. Whatever the missing piece was, I did not have time at present to dwell on it, nor did I have the luxury of refusing Ross' offer.

"So how do you want to play this?" I said. "You got a plan?"

Another smile. "Oh, I got a plan."

"Of course you do."

Ross slid the dossier closer to me. "You got some homework to do. Use my office. Terrell stay with you, keep you out of trouble."

With that, Ross stood up and left. He did not look back as he shut the door behind him. I looked at Terrell.

"Got anything to drink around here?"

He pointed at a cupboard behind Ross' desk. "In there."

I walked around the desk and opened the cupboard. "Chivas Regal," I said. "Not bad."

"Don't much care for it myself," Terrell said. "I'm a gin man."

"To each his own."

I poured myself a drink, sat down in Ross' chair, and started reading.

THIRTY-THREE

The day after meeting with Ross I sent a runner to a book store down the street. He came back with a box of paperbacks and a hardback copy of *For Whom the Bell Tolls*. I promised Elizabeth there would be no spoilers this time. I felt bad for ruining the ending of her last Hemingway novel.

We stayed in the room most of the day, only coming downstairs to eat in the lobby/bar/restaurant that comprised the ground floor. The food was simple but well prepared. We slept in shifts that night, someone always armed and watching the door.

The next morning I went out to check on the livestock. Ross said he would send a couple of guys to shadow me and make sure Lopez didn't move too early. The couple of guys turned out to be four. None of them was particularly good at tailing, but having so many following me told me I was a priority for Ross, which meant I was vital to whatever he was planning to do. This did not make me feel better. Ross did not know me and would not have given a damn about me if he did. To him, I was a pawn. Nothing more.

The oxen and horses were in good shape. They had been well fed and given plenty of water and allowed to exercise in a large corral. A stable boy brushed the horses down every night and gave extra hay to the oxen, per my instructions.

Done with that, I checked on the trade at the warehouse. The guards searched and disarmed me at the door. Two of them followed me and waited while I took inventory. They did not speak, not even when spoken to. When I was finished they showed me the door and gave me my weapons back. I left without comment.

Later that evening, I took the first watch. Liz and Sabrina bedded down and were snoring gently in less than twenty minutes. At the end of the first hour, as I lay on my bedroll, head propped on a hotel pillow and reading a copy of *A Catskill Eagle* by candlelight, I heard a soft knock at the door. My pistol appeared in my hand as if by magic. I did not remember drawing it or telling myself to do so.

"Just a second," I said.

Sabrina opened an eye to let me know she was awake. Her hands came out from under the blanket, one holding her Beretta, and the other holding a karambit. I turned to Elizabeth. Her eyes were wide and nervous. I placed a finger over my lips and she nodded. A sun-browned hand went under her pillow and settled on the grip of the pistol waiting there.

The door to the room was secured by a padlock that fastened to a sturdy latch on my side of the door. When the room was unoccupied, the padlock went on a latch on the outside. It occurred to me when I rented the room if anyone wanted to imprison me all they had to do was put a lock on the outside latch, so I had used my multi-tool to remove it. The last couple of nights, rather than lock the door, I had left the padlock open and tucked the shackle through the eye of the interior latch. This kept the door locked

329

from the inside, and if I had to open the door, anyone outside the room waiting to take a shot at me would not hear me fiddling with the lock.

I removed the shackle quietly, stood aside from the door, and placed the pistol against the wood about where I figured center-of-mass would be for anyone in the doorway.

"Come in," I said. "It's unlocked."

It was dark in the room, a pale glimmer of silver moonlight the only illumination. Someone pushed the door open and said in a low voice, "Ross need to talk to you."

I pulled the door open the rest of the way. Terrell stuck his head in. "You coming?"

"In a minute."

"I'll wait in the hall."

The door shut and several footsteps creaked in the hallway. The creaking stopped and I felt a slight tremor against my shoulder. I knew if I looked around the corner I would see Terrell leaning against the wall, arms hanging loose so he could get to his weapons quickly.

I evaluated my position. There was no choice but to go down and talk to Ross. But there was the very real possibility things were going to get rough. I had dealt with men like Ross in the past, and I knew how they operated. At some point he was going to establish dominance, or attempt to. People like him can't stand to let someone be on equal footing. They always have to have leverage, some kind of button they can push to obtain compliance. Ross knew Sabrina and Elizabeth were exactly the kind of thing he could use to manipulate me, but there was also the threat of physical violence. The former concerned me very much, whereas the latter merely made me angry. I had a feeling the next few minutes were going to decide if Ross viewed me as someone working *with* him, or *for* him.

Before I left I dug in my pack and removed a homemade sap. It was made with two thick strips of cow hide, thin hemp twine, and the contents of several shotgun shells containing number 8 bird shot. If the meeting with Ross went south, I wanted a non-lethal option. The sap went into my left hip pocket.

Terrell was waiting around the corner. "Leave your weapons here," he said.

"No."

"Boss's orders."

"He's not my boss. I don't take orders from him."

"You do when I tell you to."

"No. I don't."

My right hand hung near my Beretta. Terrell's eyes shifted to it, then back to my face.

"Have it your way. Come on."

I followed him downstairs at a safe distance. We emerged into the lobby and Terrell proceeded toward the back room. I stopped and took a seat on a stool facing away from the bar. The tables were empty, the door was barred, and only a single lamp above the liquor bottles provided illumination.

"You coming?" Terrell asked, holding up the bar divider.

"Ross wants to talk, we can do it out here."

"He want you to come to his office."

"Too bad."

Terrell stared a few moments, his breathing growing a little heavier. "You walking a thin fucking line, white man."

"Story of my life."

The big man turned away and disappeared down the hall. He came back a minute or two later with Ross and two other men. The two newcomers were both large and visibly armed, one white and one Hispanic.

"Nice to see you're an equal opportunity employer," I said.

"This here business be a meritocracy," Ross said. "I promote based on talent."

His voice was jovial, but his eyes were steady and cold. Terrell stepped around the corner and began walking toward me. There was purpose in his stride and a gun in his right hand. I slid off my stool.

"Sit down," Terrell said, still closing the distance.

I knew the big man was fast; he had demonstrated that when he had searched me. But doing so had been a mistake on his part. If he had taken his time, I might have underestimated him. One should always attempt to seem less dangerous than one actually is. But evidently no one had ever bothered to inform Terrell of this rule. So when I drew my Beretta and pointed it at his head faster than he could bring up his own weapon, the surprise on his face was highly satisfying.

"That's far enough, big guy. Put the gun on the ground and kick it away."

He stood and stared. There was motion to my right. In a practiced move, I dropped the Beretta, caught it with my left hand, and whipped the little revolver from the small of my back.

"Ah-ah," I said to one of the thugs behind Ross. "Hands where I can see them. All of you."

No one moved. I fired a round from the revolver between the heads of Ross' two thugs, splintering the wooden wall behind them.

"Do it now!"

Their hands came up slowly, as did Ross'. The veneer of amusement on his face had disappeared.

"You're buying yourself a world of trouble," Ross said. The Southern accent and ghetto diction was suddenly gone from his voice. I'd figured it for an affectation, but its absence was still a startling contrast.

"Don't bullshit me, Ross," I said. "Want to explain why you closed the bar, locked the place up, and told Terrell to bring me down to your office, unarmed, in the middle of the night?"

"Maybe you worry me."

"That what the two goons are for? Figured you needed to make it four-on-one for a fair fight? And I can't help but notice you're all armed."

"You readin' too much into it. Put the guns down and we talk."

The accent was creeping back in, telling me Ross' anger was fading and he was attempting to reassert control. He was used to being in charge, to giving orders, to intimidating people. He was not used to being outmaneuvered. I could kill him if I wanted to, and he knew it. I had shown him I was not someone to be trifled with. I had shown him how badly he had underestimated me. I had shown him he wasn't necessarily the most dangerous man in the room. And while these were all good things, my problem now was to find a way to bring this confrontation to a peaceful resolution that allowed Ross to save face, and allowed me to retain him as an ally.

"So let's examine the situation," I said. "You send Terrell up to my room and he tells me you want to see me. Tells me to leave my weapons. I bet that works most of the time, doesn't it? Terrell is a scary man. Most people probably fall all over themselves to do what he says. But then I tell him no, and he sees he can't scare me, and he sees I'm willing to do violence against him. So he does what any good soldier does when he's faced with a situation he doesn't know how to handle—he reports back for further orders. Only he was expecting me to come to your office like a good little lamb. Both of you were. Why wouldn't I, right? You already said you were going to help me. What reason would I have to be suspicious?"

Ross remained silent.

"And the moment I walked through the door your men were all set to jump me, rough me up, point some guns at me, threaten me, tell me how things were going to be. And after that you were going to take my trade, take the women with me, and use them against me as leverage to get me to do what you wanted. And afterward, I wouldn't be much use to you now would I? How am I doing so far?"

A shrug. "Pretty good, actually."

"You must think I'm pretty fucking stupid."

"Till now."

"Glad to hear it. Because you see, I've been doing some thinking since our little meeting. I've been thinking about you, and Lopez, and Santino, and Thornberg. I've been thinking about how convenient is was that Lopez knew exactly where and when to look for me, and how he seemed to recognize me on the street. I've been thinking how quickly you were willing to tell me about your troubles with Lopez and offer to help me deal with him. What do you think about all that, Ross?"

"I think you reachin'. I think you be paranoid."

"Sounds that way doesn't it? I was thinking the same thing until something occurred to me and I had what you might call a minor epiphany. Know what that was?"

No answer.

"The morning Thornberg first came to see me," I said, "he knew my name. He knew who I was. And being on Santino's staff means he has security clearance, which means he has access to classified files in the Archive. He would have had plenty of time to read up on me before bringing me to Santino. What exactly did he tell you about me, Ross?"

Another shrug. "Few things. You work for the government some. You a trigger man. Shit like that."

I felt the connotation 'trigger man' was an unfair misrepresentation, but decided now was not the time to discuss it.

"So the two of you got together and discussed me. Figured I might be the man to help you solve your little territorial dispute without arousing the ire of Major Santino. And if I couldn't, no big deal. A small group without a caravan is like chum in a shark tank. I wouldn't be missed, and neither would my trade or the women traveling with me. Still tracking?"

"You smart, Ivy League. I'll give you that."

"Thanks," I said. "Now as I'm sure you've figured out, there are three ways this can play out. First, and easiest for me, is I kill the four of you and claim self-defense. Santino will probably give me a medal. Lopez moves in and takes your territory. Probably forgets all about me."

I let the comment hang and watched Ross' expression. The gears turning behind the coal-black eyes were well-tuned and finely-made. This was his chance to save face—and his life—and he was acutely aware of it.

335

"Or maybe he don't," Ross said. "Maybe he be mad you stole his thunder. Maybe he don't like some lone wolf did what he couldn't. Make him look bad. Maybe he kill you on general principle."

"You missed one."

Ross raised an eyebrow.

"Maybe he wants to clip you himself. Maybe he wants it so bad he'd kill me for getting to you first. It wouldn't be unprecedented in the annals of criminal lore."

Ross laughed quietly. "You talk a good game, Ivy League. But tell me something. Your arms gettin' tired yet?"

"Hell no," I said. "Between all the time I spend shooting and working the speed bag and sparring and everything else, I can hold my guns like this all day."

"Good to know."

I saw movement in the shadows near the staircase. My face threatened to peel back into a smile, but I resisted the urge. It was time to bring this thing to a close and provide Ross with another demonstration of prowess. Ordinarily I would have considered my next move a dumb one, but I knew Ross was a hard man to impress. Either I instilled a healthy fear in him now, or I would have to spend the rest of my time in Dodge City watching my back.

"So we've established why you're still alive," I said. "The second way this plays out is I leave you all here, unarmed and incapacitated, go to the cops, and take my chances with Lopez. If any of you give me trouble on my way out, I kill you."

"You gonna do that," Ross said, "you do it already."

"Yes. I would have. Which leads us to the third possibility."

"The one where I kill yo' cracker ass?" Ross said.

"No. The one where we sit down together and figure out how to take down Lopez *and* Major Santino."

Ross was already standing still, but the stillness took on a depth and resonance that was nearly palpable.

"And how you gonna do that?"

"Lopez is up to you. You're the local authority. As for Santino, leave that to me."

Ross shook his head. "Ain't buyin' it, Ivy League. How you gonna bring down the major?"

"Ever heard of General Phillip Jacobs?"

A blink. Ross swallowed and looked down for just a moment. "Yeah. He the director of ASOC."

"You're familiar?"

"Used to run guns for the Alliance."

"Found yourself on the receiving end?"

"More than once."

"Jacobs is a friend of mine."

Ross snorted. "Bullshit."

"Thornberg was holding out on you, Ross. I've worked for Jacobs on several occasions. We're on a first name basis. I put in a call, and there'll be an investigation in less than a week. Jacobs will hang Santino by his balls when he finds out what's going on around here. You know anybody other than Thornberg with access to the Archive?"

"'Course."

"Have me checked out."

"That take time. Don't do us much good right now."

"No, it doesn't." I nodded my head toward the far end of the room. "But I know something that does. Ladies?"

Elizabeth stepped out of the shadows on the side of the room closest to Ross. She was holding an M-4 and aiming it at Ross and his two goons. Sabrina crossed the room in a flash and had her karambit to Terrell's throat before he had a chance to move.

"Drop the gun and kick it away," she hissed. "Now." She punctuated the sentence by shoving her Berretta into the small of his back. Terrell dropped the gun and kicked it toward me.

"Here's how we're going to do this," I said. "Ross, you and Thing One and Thing Two are going to come around here and put your hands against the bar. Terrell, you do the same. Ladies, they make one wrong move, kill them."

Ross and his men did not make a wrong move. Neither did Terrell. I made sure they had their weight back with their feet spread so they would not be able to lunge at me, had Sabrina and Liz cover them from both sides, and searched the men thoroughly. By the time I was finished there were eight guns and six knives in a pile at the end of the bar.

"Now," I said, motioning to one of the larger tables. "Have a seat and we can talk like civilized people."

Ross sat down first, followed by the rest of his crew.

"Anybody want a drink?" I asked.

"Cabinet under the bar," Ross said. "It's locked. Key the last one on the bottom right."

I opened the cabinet and took out a bottle of Woodford Reserve. "This okay?"

Ross nodded. I poured five doubles and carried the glasses to the table. After distributing them, I sat down in a chair a few feet away. The last thing I wanted was for them to make a grab at me.

338

We all sipped our drinks and stared at each other. Which is to say, I stared at Ross and everyone at his table stared at me.

"It seems what we have here is a failure of trust," I said. "Ross, you don't trust me to keep my word. I told you I would help you with Lopez and I meant it. But that's not good enough for you, is it?"

"Afraid not."

"If I decided to walk out of here right now, who would you send after me?"

He did not hesitate. "Terrell."

"Figured."

I took another sip of the bourbon. The burn settled my nerves. I let it do its work for a moment and then stood up and walked to the bar. The knife I had taken from Terrell was a black tanto-style blade manufactured by Cold Steel. I picked it up, put my own weapons down except for the sap, walked back to where Terrell was sitting, and threw the blade at his feet. It flipped twice in the air and stuck into the floor next to his boot. I said a silent prayer of thanks; I would have looked like a fool if the knife had hit wrong and gone skittering across the floor.

"Pick it up."

Terrell looked at me, then at Ross.

"Your women gonna interfere?" Ross said.

"No."

Liz eyed me anxiously but remained silent. Sabrina's expression was blank. Terrell pulled the knife out of the floor and stood up.

"Anytime you're ready," I said.

In the movies, when people fight each other, they square off, exchange some threatening banter, and then perform a choreographed sequence of flashy movements that would get them killed in a real fight. Terrell was under no such illusions about the true nature of combat. Neither was I.

He crossed the distance quickly, but I was ready for him, hands empty, stance wide with my weight on my toes. Terrell feinted once with the knife and then lashed out with a kick aimed at my groin. I dodged the kick by turning sideways and slipped Terrell's follow-up left. The force he put behind the punch left him momentarily open, and I nailed him on the chin with the hardest overhand right I could muster. The shock of the blow traveled down my arm and across my back all the way down to my kidneys. I am not an especially big man, but I know how to throw a punch. Terrell took a step back.

With my opponent temporarily stunned, I knew it was time to make my move. I stepped in front of him to present an open target and dropped my shoulder like I was going to throw a straight left. Terrell took the bait and slashed at me with the tanto. I let the blade pass in front of me, drew the sap from my pocket, and when Terrell followed up with a backward slash, I whacked him on the back of the hand as hard as I could. There was a sound like carrots snapping, and the knife clattered to the floor.

Terrell still had one good hand, and he was a tough bastard. He took a swing at me, but his technique was off. I let it glance off my shoulder, dropped my weight, and snapped a left cross into his groin. The big man grunted and countered with a push kick, but I was already out of the way. The kick threw him off balance. I grabbed one of his arms with my free hand and yanked him sideways, forcing him to his knees. Out of instinct he put both hands down to catch himself and cried out in pain as the broken bones in his right hand ground together.

Now I smelled blood in the water. The sap seemed to switch from my left hand to my right hand of its own volition. I brought it down hard on the back of Terrell's head. He went wobbly, but was

340

still trying to stand. So I hit him again. And again. And again. On the fifth blow, he rolled onto his side and stayed down, his breath coming in great snoring gasps. I stood up straight, tucked the sap back into my pocket, let out a deep breath, and turned to Ross.

"Who you got better than him?" I said.

"Just me," Ross said.

"Want to try it?"

He shook his head slowly, the broken, shark-tooth grin reappearing. "Probably not."

I sat down and picked up my drink. Sipped it. Looked at Ross. "Can we talk business now?"

He thrust his chin at the two thugs sitting with him. "Y'all take off. I send for you if I need you."

The two men looked at me.

"Let 'em go," I said.

Liz covered them as they walked out the door and then barred it behind them. Sabrina kept her aim steadily on Ross.

"You can stand down now," I said. Sabrina lowered her weapon and took a seat, but did not look away. Liz did the same.

"Lopez won't come for you here," Ross said. "You have to draw him out."

"Got any ideas?"

"A few. How you gonna handle Santino?"

"Can you get me access to an encrypted satellite phone?"

"Government phone?"

"Yes."

"Be expensive."

"For you."

Ross shook his head. "I ain't paying for it."

"You're the one who wants Santino out of the picture. Personally, I don't give a shit if he stays or goes. Your call."

"Fine."

I stood up and didn't bother offering to shake hands. "We're going back upstairs. I trust we won't be disturbed any further?"

"I think we past that."

"Good. See you tomorrow."

Ross' eyes tracked over to Terrell's prone form. "Yeah. See you."

Back in the room, I lay down on my bedroll and tried to ignore the pain in my right hand. The first two knuckles were already beginning to swell. The ache made me long for the days of ice machines. Liz and Sabrina sat down on their beds and watched the door nervously.

"You really think he'll leave us alone?" Liz asked.

"Yes."

"What makes you so sure?"

"Because he wants Lopez and Santino out of the way. That's his top priority. He knows we can help make that happen, now. He'll want to keep us alive for the time being."

"Then why all the theatrics?" Sabrina said. "I mean, was all that shit really necessary?"

"No," I said. "It wasn't. But men like Ross live by their own rules. In Ross' world, there's only room for one top dog. Everybody else has to know their place."

"So that's what he tried to do tonight," Liz said. "Put us in our place."

"Yep."

Sabrina smiled. She looked impish in the pale light filtering through the window. "Didn't work out too well for him."

"No, it didn't."

I took off my boots and laid my weapons on the ground beside my bedroll. The adrenalin from the fight had worn off and sleep was pulling at me hard. I climbed under the covers and felt myself beginning to drift.

"That man, Terrell," Liz said. "You made beating him look easy."

"Glad it looked that way."

"You could have killed him."

"Yes."

"He didn't even get in a punch. Never hurt you at all."

"Nope."

"If you'd had a knife..."

"It would have been a much shorter fight."

Liz did not speak for a few seconds. I sat up so I could look at her.

"You okay?"

"Yes. I've just never seen anything like that before."

"How does it make you feel?"

Her dark brown eyes were earnest when she looked at me. "It makes me glad you're on our side. But..."

"But what?"

"I saw a side of you tonight I didn't know was there. All this time we've known each other, I had no idea what you were capable of. When Terrell picked up that knife, I was afraid. I thought he was going to kill you. But then…I've never seen anyone move that fast. I feel like I'm looking at someone I don't know."

"Liz, I'm the same person I've always been. What I can do with a blade or a gun or my fists doesn't change who I am. I'm your friend. And I plan to stay that way."

"Of course."

"You should get some sleep. Both of you. Be a long day tomorrow."

"Sure."

I lay down and closed my eyes and thought of Allison. She had never seen me fight before, and if the fates were kind, she never would. The last thing I wanted, ever, was for her to look at me the way Liz had looked at me tonight.

It was the last thought I had before I fell asleep.

THIRTY-FOUR

One of Ross' couriers showed up the next afternoon with a satellite phone.

"You got ten minutes," Ross said. "This thing ain't cheap."

I gave him my best glare. "Seeing as you're the one responsible for my current situation, I think I'll take as long as I need."

"I told you, I didn't sell you out to Lopez. That was Thornberg."

"You going to punish him for it?"

Ross stood still behind the bar in the mostly empty lobby. He did not reply.

"You benefitting from it?"

More silence.

"That's what I thought. Mind if I use your office?"

"Go ahead."

I followed the hallway back, shut the door behind me, and dialed Jacob's number. After giving my identification code and navigating through a swarm of lackeys intent on not letting me waste the general's precious time, Jacobs finally came on the line.

"Riordan, thank God," Jacobs said. "Glad to hear you're still alive. Have you heard from Gabriel?"

I felt a heaviness in my stomach. I had done a good job over the last week of not thinking too much about my old friend. But hearing Jacobs say his name reignited the slumbering anxieties.

"No," I said. "You?"

"Anything I tell you is classified. Not to be repeated to anyone. Clear?"

"Clear."

"He and Hicks were successful. They rescued the hostages and our people did a number on the raiders that took them."

"You wipe 'em out?"

"No. About a hundred or so survived, but we're tracking their movements. They're headed for the Arkansas border as we speak."

"Marauder settlement, you think?"

"It's a distinct possibility."

"Gabe recover his trade?"

"No. In fact, he didn't even mention it until the mission was over."

"Sounds about right. Where is he now?"

A sigh. "I wish I knew. I offered him air transport to Colorado Springs, but he refused. Said he didn't want to leave his horse behind."

"Figures."

"Last I heard, he was dropped off near where the attack occurred. Haviland, I believe it was."

"How long ago was that?"

"Two days."

"Is Hicks with him?"

"No. He's on his way to Colorado Springs."

"Any special reason?"

"Need to know, Mr. Riordan."

I took a deep breath and let that one go. Doing the occasional job for General Jacobs did not entitle me to infinite operational intel. And besides, I could always ask Hicks later.

"So Gabe picked up our trail in Haviland," I said. "And is probably on his way here right now."

"How would he know to come to Dodge City?"

"I left markers for him as a precaution. He'll know what they mean and follow them here."

"Smart thinking."

"Thanks. Listen, General. I have a problem I need help with."

I explained to him my difficulties with the local organized crime leaders and Major Santino's involvement. Jacobs listened quietly. When I finished, it was a long few seconds before he spoke.

"Can you prove Santino is on the take?" Jacobs asked. He sounded tired.

"I already bribed him for passage to Colorado Springs in a couple of weeks. And I imagine Ross would be willing to testify, although I'm not sure how much good a racketeer's testimony will do. But I think others will come forward if they sense Santino is on the way out."

"In that case, I'll talk to CID and ask them to send an investigator."

347

"Think they'll do it?"

"If I ask them to. I'm not without influence around here."

"Okay. I'll take care of the rest from my end."

"You have a plan?"

I told him. He laughed and said, "Bold. Stupid, but bold. Think the other two will go along?"

"Yes."

"Be careful, Riordan."

"I always am. Thanks for the help, General."

"Call me Phil. And you're welcome."

I hung up, walked back into the bar, and gave the satellite phone back to Ross.

"So what's the deal?" he asked.

"Jacobs is going to talk to someone at CID, have them send an investigator. Probably be a week or two before they get here."

"CID federal?"

"Yeah. They handle criminal investigations for the Army and Department of Defense. Local cops give them any trouble, they'll call in the FBI."

Ross accepted the news calmly. "And in the meantime?"

I told him how I planned to deal with Lopez and what I needed from him. He smirked and said, "I can swing that."

"Good. Have your men ready to go in an hour."

"Sure."

I felt Ross' eyes on my back as I walked upstairs to talk to Elizabeth and Sabrina.

THIRTY-FIVE

There were a couple of options for dealing with Lopez.

One was to take my women and trade and leave town and wait for Lopez to come after me on the road. Ross' men would follow at a distance and help us take them out. If Lopez himself was not with the attacking party, we could simply drag the dead bodies back to town and drop them at the feet of the Chief of Police who would then have no choice but to investigate. Santino would have to cooperate with the investigation, and his best bet for covering up his involvement would be to arrange Lopez's untimely demise. This would put Lopez on desperate ground, where his best option would be to leave town at his earliest opportunity. Either way, Ross would win and take over Lopez's territory, and gain enough power and influence to stand against Santino until the CID investigation got off the ground.

My problem with this approach was it assumed Ross and his men would not simply shoot me the moment Lopez's crew was taken care of. It also required using Sabrina and Elizabeth as bait, which was something I was not willing to do. If they were going to be involved—which they would have to be since Ross could not

349

take direct action—I wanted to make damned sure they were on offense, not defense. So I asked myself a familiar question: What would Gabriel do?

The answer fell under Gabriel Garrett's Fourth Rule of Combat:

Defensive positions are made to be overrun, so stay mobile. Surprise attacks are always your best option.

And his Seventh Rule of Combat:

When you're enemy thinks he's holding all the cards is when he is at his most vulnerable.

So I had a talk with Sabrina and Elizabeth and told them what I needed them to do. I told them Ross' men would follow them and watch their backs until it was time to carry out the plan. And once the fighting started, Ross' men would make sure no one interfered. Sabrina agreed readily. She'd had to fight and kill before, and was confident in her abilities. Liz was not so certain.

"I don't know if I can do this," she said as we were preparing to leave.

We were in the lobby of the hotel, Ross' men lounging at the bar waiting for us to depart. Ross himself was nowhere in sight. Liz was armed with her Beretta, M-4, and a backup pistol, the same as Sabrina—who I was certain was also carrying enough knives to outfit a cutlery store—whereas I had only my pistols and combat knife. Both women wore the Kevlar vests we had brought with us from Hollow Rock. I had forgone wearing mine, as what I had planned for Lopez hinged on him believing I was helpless and unable to defend myself.

"You know what to do," I told Liz. "We were both trained by the same guy. Stay out of sight until you hear the fighting start, and then move in. Standard room clearing procedure just like at the CQB course at Fort McCray. We've done it a hundred times."

"Never with people shooting back."

"Listen," I said, turning to look at her. Her face was pale, her lips drawn and white. "At least you'll have a gun. I'll be unarmed in there, and I'll be counting on you. You freeze up, and you'll get me killed at the very least. At worst, you'll get all of us killed. But that's not going to happen. You know why?"

"No."

"Because you're going to remember your training. When the bullets start flying, you'll know what to do. You won't think, you'll just act. Believe me. I know."

With that, I turned and walked out the door. Sabrina followed immediately, Liz doing the same after a moment's hesitation. I hated being abrupt with Liz—she had every right to be scared—but the more she dwelled on it the worse she was likely to react when the bullets started flying.

If they start flying, I reminded myself. *Big if.*

We did not have far to walk. Lopez's headquarters was a tavern directly across the street called *El Presidio*. A fitting name, considering its purpose. It was the place I had first noticed Lopez and two of his lieutenants watching me. I headed straight for the tavern while Sabrina and Liz broke off to circle the block and come in from the east.

As I approached the entrance I called to mind all the faces from Ross' dossier on Lopez's men and wished like hell I had Gabe's eidetic memory. I recognized two men sitting on the porch rail, nonchalant as could be, doing their best to look like a couple of out of work caravan guards spending what little trade they had on booze and women. I strode toward them purposefully, and like the amateurs I figured them for, they focused their attention on me and did not watch the street. From the corner of my eye, I saw Liz and Sabrina round separate corners and casually move into position.

The two men on the porch followed my progress as I went past them toward the bar. The bartender's face was familiar. According

351

to Ross' file his name was Rodrigo Salazar. He was short, bald, sported a patchy black beard, and was covered in tattoos from neck to knuckles. Three crudely drawn teardrops adorned one side of his face just below the eye. I approached him and laid my hands on the bar.

"What can I get you?" Salazar said. His eyes shifted to a trio of men seated at a table nearby. I glanced at them and recognized their faces as well.

"I'm here to see your boss," I said.

"You're looking at him," Salazar said. "I own the place."

"Is Lopez here or not?"

The beady black eyes narrowed. "Who?"

"Lopez. You know, Hispanic fella, walks with a limp, owns this side of the district, tells you who to shoot and who to beat up when you're not pouring drinks. That guy."

He put down the glass he was holding and leaned over with his fists on the bar. The finger tattoos on one hand spelled EVIL and the other spelled WAYS. Very intimidating.

"I don't know what you're deal is, gringo, but you're about to get yourself fucked up."

"Just let him know I'm here. Tell him it's about Santino. I have some information for him."

Salazar glared another moment, trying to terrify me. I stared back.

"Wait here," he said finally, and walked the other end of the bar. One of the men at the table stood up and walked over. There was a whispered exchange. The guy from the table looked me over and then walked toward a narrow hallway behind the bar. Salazar made his way back.

"Might be a while. Want a drink?"

352

"No thanks."

I sat down and looked around the room. Perhaps a minute later Sabrina moseyed in and took a seat at the end of the bar closest to the door. She glanced at everyone in equal proportion, me included, and put on a face that said she was not impressed. Salazar walked over to her and offered her a drink. She asked for moonshine. Salazar asked what she had for trade, and Sabrina asked if bullets were okay. Salazar said they were and poured her a drink. Sabrina downed half of it in one gulp and sat back to enjoy the burn. No matter how many times I saw it, watching a fourteen-year-old girl drink like a soldier on a weekend pass made me feel like a bystander at a crime scene.

Past Sabrina, out the front window, I saw Elizabeth stop outside a food stand and pretend to study the offerings on display. From where she stood, she could hit anywhere in the tavern except behind the bar. That was Sabrina's area of responsibility. All I could do now was wait and hope Ross kept his word.

While I waited, I thought of what to say to Lopez. So far, he had made no overt moves against me, which was more than I could say for Ross. The only evidence I had that Lopez was hostile toward me at all was a dirty look, a hunch, and Ross' say so. And Ross was not exactly an unbiased party. My instincts, however, told me something was wrong. That Lopez was planning something, and he did not have my best interests at heart. I have not survived as long as I have by ignoring my instincts.

Still, I had to know for sure. So I sat, and waited, and after what felt like about ten minutes, a man poked his head around the corner and nodded at Salazar. Salazar turned and jerked his head toward the hallway.

"That way," he said.

I stood up and walked to the end of the bar. Salazar lifted the divider to let me through. I proceeded down a narrow, dim hallway built of wood planks cut a little wider than my hand. At the end of the hallway a bruiser about Hicks' size waited in front of a heavy-looking door.

"Arms up," the bruiser said.

I raised my arms. He searched me and took both pistols and my knife. Quick, efficient, no nonsense, the kind of thing he had done a thousand times. When he was finished he opened the door behind him.

"Go in."

"Sure," I said, and entered. The bruiser followed me.

Inside the office there was another man leaning against the wall to my right. He was tall, lean, bearded, dark skin, and watched me with a pair of merciless brown eyes. His shirt had no sleeves, revealing a pair of hard, heavily tattooed arms.

Bruiser and Sleeveless, I thought. *Those are your names.*

The office was a little bigger than Ross', and like Ross', it was windowless and lit by oil lanterns made from scrap metal. But that was where the similarities ended. There were no shelves, no books, no couch for Lopez's men to sit on. Just a desk at the far side of the room, a couple of impressionist paintings most likely liberated from some rich collector's abandoned home, and the hard-faced Hispanic man who had glared at me on the street a couple of days ago.

"Have a seat," Lopez said.

His accent was heavy and his tone brooked no argument, the voice of a man used to being obeyed. There were two straight-backed wooden chairs in front of his desk. No leather, no brass studs, no plush upholstery. Unlike Ross, Lopez did not seem to care if his guests were comfortable or not. It made me think a little more highly of Ross. He may have been a lowlife and a back-stabbing hoodlum, but at least he had taste.

354

I sat down in one of the chairs and found it every bit as uncomfortable as it looked. But it felt solid enough. The other chair was within arm's reach. I glanced behind me and saw Lopez's henchmen standing shoulder to shoulder a couple of feet behind me. As good a setup as I could have asked for.

"Was he armed?" Lopez asked Bruiser.

The man walked around me and set my weapons on Lopez's desk. *Dumb*, I thought. Lopez looked at the guns and knives, then at me. His eyes were narrow and black, his lips drawn down in a thin line, jaw outthrust, nostrils flared. I wondered how many hours he'd spent practicing that look in a mirror.

"You come here armed, to my place, looking to see me?" Lopez said. He made it sound like a challenge, as if I'd committed some great offense. Five years ago, in a situation like this, I might have been frightened. But now, I wanted to laugh.

"Anybody comes into this place unarmed," I said, "and I'll eat my boots."

Lopez held the angry look a few more seconds, and then his mouth split into a smile and he laughed.

"You see that?" Lopez said to Bruiser as he walked back behind me. "He ain't scared. I like that. Surrounded by a bunch of stone-cold motherfucking killers, and he ain't scared."

"Should I be?"

"Yeah, you should. If you were smart. But hey, you come to talk to me, right? Said you got some information about Santino."

"I do."

"Well, let's hear it."

"Santino's days are numbered," I said. "An investigator from Army CID is going to come out here in a week or so and start digging. I'm going to cooperate with them, and so is Ross."

355

"Who?" Lopez said.

I went on as if he hadn't spoken. "I'm telling you this so if you have any operations running you don't want the feds to know about, you'll have time to wind them down. You're going to have to go legit for a while. But when Santino is out of the way, and he will be, it'll just be you and Ross."

Lopez stared quietly for a few seconds. The fake tough-guy look was gone, replaced by an empty-eyed calculation that seemed far more genuine.

"How you know all this?" Lopez asked.

"Because I'm the one who notified the Army official who's requesting the investigation."

"No, I mean how you know about me and Ross and Santino?"

"I asked around."

"Who told you about us?"

"I don't see how that matters. What's important is you know what's coming so you can prepare."

Lopez leaned back in his chair and propped his feet on his desk. His cowboy boots were of pre-Outbreak manufacture and looked expensive.

"And you telling me this...what, out of kindness?"

"No. I'm telling you this because I don't want to have to kill you."

Lopez laughed again. He looked at the men behind me, each in turn, and his eyes crinkled with amusement.

"Man, you got some *huevos*, I'll give you that."

"Ross thinks I'm here to take you out."

The laughter faded. Lopez's expression went suddenly blank. "That so?"

"Yes."

"And how he think you gonna do that?"

"He may have had some idea of me coming in here with guns blazing."

"You a trigger man?"

"Something like that."

"And you told Ross you gonna come in here and shoot the place up?"

"I may have mislead him a bit."

Lopez crossed his hands over his stomach and tapped one finger a few times. "Ross ain't the kind of man you want to be messing around with, homes. He ain't gonna be happy you didn't do what you said you were gonna do."

"Ross can eat a bag of syphilitic dicks," I said. "I don't much give a shit what he likes or doesn't like."

Lopez's grin returned. Only this time, it actually reached his eyes.

"Makes two of us. Anything else you want to tell me, trigger man?"

"That's it."

"So what now? You just walk out of here?"

"That was the plan."

"And go where?"

"Back to my hotel room."

"And then what?"

"Wait around until the CID investigator gets here. Then I imagine I'll have to make a statement. Once that's done, I'll sign on with the first caravan headed toward the Springs and you'll never have to see me again."

The two paintings on the wall behind Lopez had glass-covered frames. The light from the lanterns fell so I could see the reflections of the two goons standing behind me. I glanced at their reflections and saw them watching Lopez, arms loose at their sides, the stance of men preparing for action.

"Afraid that's not gonna happen," Lopez said.

I tensed my legs beneath me. "What's not going to happen?"

"That whole thing you just said about leaving and going back to your hotel and all that shit."

"Why?"

Lopez shrugged. "Two reasons. One, you know too much. Can't have a loose end like you running around. Two, I need trade. You got a lot, and ain't nobody but you and those two women with you to know you was ever here. And I like those women. Especially the girl. She's nice and young, the way I like 'em."

Lopez looked at the men behind me. I watched their reflections in the glass picture frames. Sleeveless reached behind his back.

Now or never.

Lopez had a small smile on his face. He was still smiling when I grabbed the chair next to me, stood up, and swung it at him. The flat edge of the seat bashed him square in the mouth and sent him tumbling over backward.

The men behind me were stunned for the briefest of moments. It gave me the precious time I needed to kick the chair I had been sitting in and send it into the legs of Sleeveless. He stumbled backward, got his legs tangled in the chair, and fell down. Bruiser dodged sideways and avoided the chair, but he did not avoid the jab-cross-hook-uppercut combination I pounded into his jaw. The force of the blows knocked him back against the wall, eyes vacant and unfocused. A step forward and a hard knee to the balls sent him crumbling to the floor.

Behind me, I heard Lopez cursing in Spanish. To my left, Sleeveless had gotten his feet under him and came up with a knife in his hand. He feinted a slash at my face and lunged forward, intent on burying the knife in my gut. I parried the knife with a cross block, head-butted Sleeveless in the nose, and used the moment he was stunned to drag his arm across my chest and flip him over my shoulder with an old Judo throw called *ippon seoi nage*. Sleeveless landed flat on his back on Lopez's desk, the force of the impact driving the air from his lungs. Despite this, he still had the presence of mind to reach for the weapons Bruiser had taken from me and placed on the desk. His hand curled around the butt of my Berretta, pointed it at me, and squeezed the trigger. The gun did not fire. While he was doing this, I stripped the knife from his hand, flipped it so I was holding it in an underhanded grip, and buried the blade in his heart. His finger twitched spasmodically on the trigger a couple more times. Still, nothing happened.

"You forgot about the safety," I said as I disarmed him. "And you forgot to chamber a round."

I worked the slide on the Beretta. Sleeveless had seconds to live. A glance behind me revealed Bruiser was still down, and still dazed. I turned back to Lopez and saw him on his knees digging a revolver out of a desk drawer. Four of his front teeth had been knocked out and his mouth was a bloody mess.

"*Hijo de la chingada!*"

He started to point the revolver in my direction. I aimed the Beretta at his head and pulled the trigger. A neat hole appeared above Lopez's left eye and the contents of his skull painted the wall behind him in a splash of crimson. The roar of the weapon was deafeningly loud in the small space. If the guys in the bar hadn't been aware of what was transpiring in Lopez's office before, they were now.

With my ears ringing, I grabbed Bruiser by the scruff of his neck, hauled him to his feet, pressed the Beretta against the small of his back, and shoved him toward the door.

"Move!"

He moved.

Come one, girls, I thought. *Don't let me down.*

THIRTY-SIX

I rounded the corner into the bar with Bruiser still in front of me, my gun pressed against his back.

"Nobody move!" I shouted.

Everybody moved.

In moments of high stress, I sometimes experience a strange slowing of perception. My heart pounds loudly in my ears, all tactile sensations become hyper-sensitive, each sound takes on its own individual resonance, every one separate and distinct and all moving together in a harmony of awareness. I heard the thunder of my pulse, felt the texture of my pistol's grip, the rough fabric of Bruiser's collar, the warm air against my skin. The room seemed to turn a light shade of gray, all color fading.

To my right, Salazar reached down as though to grab something from a low shelf. Sabrina pulled something from under her shirt and threw it at him. I watched it spin for a few hours until it came to rest point-first in Salazar's shoulder. There was a scream and Sabrina leapt over the bar, a karambit in each hand.

At the same time, the three men at the table stood up and moved to draw weapons. The men who had been sitting outside the bar on the porch railing rushed through the doorway, guns in hand. I saw Elizabeth behind them, raising her M-4.

Still holding onto Bruiser, I kicked his feet out from under him and went over sideways. I landed on my back and Bruiser landed on his side, his body shielding mine. I knew it probably would not do much good—a body isn't much of a barrier to a bullet—but it was better than nothing.

Liz opened fire, two short bursts. The two men on the porch arched backward and fell. The three men at the table turned toward Liz. I raised my pistol and fired twice into one body, shifted aim, and fired twice again. Liz squeezed another burst from her rifle and dropped the third as he pulled the trigger. The round hit the doorframe at the bar's entrance, splintering the wood. Otherwise, it did no harm.

I sat up and looked at the bar. In the time it had taken to kill the gunmen, Sabrina had reached Salazar. I watched him pull the throwing knife from his shoulder as Sabrina launched her attack. He dodged backward from a slash aimed at his face and countered with a front kick. Sabrina tried to jump out of the way, but the kick caught her on the hip and drove her back a step.

Salazar waded toward her, the blood on the throwing knife splashing the polished wood around him as he attacked. Sabrina weaved left and right, avoiding two slashes at head level, and then Salazar dropped and tried to cut her legs. Sabrina stepped in, caught Salazar's wrist with the outside of one forearm, and used a karambit as a hook to trap Salazar's hand. At the same time, she whipped her other blade in a quick up-and-down motion, severing the muscles and tendons in Salazar's forearm like thin cables. Salazar screamed again and dropped his knife. The scream became a gurgle when Sabrina cut both his carotid arteries with two lightning-fast slashes. Salazar's good hand went to his throat as he

362

stumbled backward and ran into the wall. Sabrina stared coldly and watched the light go out of his eyes until he tipped forward and landed face-first with a floor-shaking thump.

I heard whimpering and looked at Bruiser. He had curled into a ball, arms shielding his head and face.

"Get up," I told him as I struggled to my feet. The room was beginning to regain its color and the pounding in my ears was fading.

"Don't shoot me," Bruiser whined. He sounded like a schoolboy begging a bully to leave him alone.

"I said get up."

Bruiser got up, hands in front of his face.

"Please…"

"Get the hell out of here," I said.

"What?"

I put the Beretta's barrel against his nose. "You want to live?"

"Yes."

"Then get the hell out of here. Ross owns this district now. He knows who you are. Show your face here again and you're a dead man."

Bruiser nodded vigorously. "Okay, okay."

"Go!"

He went, tripping over a dead body on his way out the door. I followed him out and watched him run away, then turned to Elizabeth.

"You all right?"

"Yeah," she said, breathlessly. "Are you okay?"

"I'm fine. Give me your rifle."

"Why?"

"Just do it."

Sabrina came around the bar, knives in hand, arterial blood staining her shirt. "You two still alive?"

"More or less," I said. I walked back into the bar, asked Sabrina for one of her knives, and used it to cut a strip of cloth from a dead gunman's shirt.

"Get out of here," I said to Liz as I wiped down her M-4.

"You sure?"

"Yes. Go now."

She gave a single nod and walked briskly back toward the alley she had come from. In seconds, she vanished into the gathering crowd. Ross' men emerged from their hiding spots and began circulating, giving terse orders, and generally ensuring that everyone present knew if anyone asked, they hadn't seen a damn thing.

When all traces of fingerprints were gone from Liz's M-4, I threw it into the street. I doubted it would stay there long. Guns are valuable things, and Dodge City was not the most affluent town I had ever been in. I motioned to Sabrina and stepped away from the entrance to the bar.

"Lot of good trade in here," I shouted to the crowd. "Free for the taking."

There was a moment of hesitation as a few people poked their heads through the doorway and one of the open windows. When they saw everyone inside was down and no one was moving, the crowd surged through the entrance and the feeding frenzy began.

Sabrina and I walked down the street and sat down against the side of a building and waited for the police to arrive.

*****

The Dodge City Police Department was a newly constructed building on the north side of town. It reminded me of the concrete and steel structures at Fort McCray—big and imposing with all the charm of a shipping crate. Government construction at its finest.

My holding cell consisted mostly of bars with a bare concrete wall in the back. There was a toilet and a sink and running water and a flat metal shelf to lie on. The lights were electric and the constant hum of a large generator buzzed through the walls and bars. I imagined Sabrina arriving at her own cell, looking around, shrugging, and thinking to herself, *Hey, I've seen worse. At least I'm indoors.*

After being taken into custody, the cops had kept us separate for two days. Both mornings someone brought me a plate of beans and eggs and a cup of water and the Chief of Police. His name was Stanford Ellis. He was about my height, lean, iron gray mustache, and had flat black cop eyes that had seen everything, heard all the lies, and found nothing terribly impressive anymore. He would sit in a chair across from me and ask me the same questions over and over again in the presence of Elizabeth Stone, my attorney.

I had known for a long time that Liz had a juris doctorate, but I had not been aware she had spent four years with the Metro Public Defender's Office of Nashville and Davidson County before moving back to Hollow Rock and running for mayor. She was not barred in the state of Kansas, but that didn't matter. In the post Outbreak world, anyone with a law degree could act as a defense attorney.

So the chief would ask questions and I would answer some of them and Liz would tell me I didn't have to answer others. The chief was sharp. He tried to poke holes in what I told him. But I stuck to my story. On the first day, before Liz arrived, Chief Ellis

365

had tried the old trick of lying and saying Sabrina was selling me out and had confessed to murder, and I had laughed and told him nice try, buddy. Not buying it. After that we seemed to understand each other.

"There's something still bothering me," Chief Ellis said on the morning of the third day. "Those two men you say were outside the building. You sure you didn't get a look at who shot them?"

"My client has already answered that question," Liz said.

Ellis glanced at her with his blank eyes and nodded. "Sure he has. All the same, I'd like to hear it again."

"Like I told you," I said. "No, I didn't."

Another nod. Ellis looked at his notes and flipped a few pages. "So let me make sure I have the story straight. You came to see Mr. Lopez because Demetrius Ross, owner and proprietor of the Sky River Hotel, said you might could hire Lopez and his men as caravan guards. Is that right?"

"Yes."

"Right. And so you go there, and make him an offer, and he tells you he's gonna steal your trade, and the next thing you know his men are trying to kill you."

"Yes."

"Except you somehow managed to get the better of three hardened criminals, all armed, and you unarmed."

"Yes."

"You must be tougher than you look."

I said nothing.

"And when you went to exit the building," Ellis continued, "there were three men in the bar brandishing weapons and two more trying to enter the premises."

366

"Right."

"So you hit the ground, and someone outside starts shooting, and the two men on the porch go down."

"Yes."

"And you see the three armed men turn toward our mystery shooter, and you decide to intervene."

I shrugged. "Whoever they were, they were on my side. I wasn't going to just lay there and let those guys shoot at them."

"Right. And after you and the mystery shooter dispatched five gunmen, the guy behind the bar grabs a shotgun and instead of pointing it at you, he goes to point it at your friend, Sabrina."

"Yes."

"And before you can say spit, the girl throws a knife at him. Then Salazar, the bartender, drops the shotgun, pulls the knife out of his own shoulder, and attacks the girl with it."

"Yes."

"And this little fourteen-year-old slip of a girl, armed only with a knife, kills a man with a record of felonies a mile long and ten years of federal prison under his belt."

"Actually, she had two knives."

"Mm-hmm. I'll tell you something else that's bothering me, Mr. Riordan. I tried looking you up in the Archive, and I found your name, social security number, where you went to school, who your parents were, and a whole lot of files I couldn't access because they were classified. So I contacted Major Santino and asked him if he could help me out. You know what he told me?"

"No."

"He said, and I quote, 'I'm not at liberty to disclose Mr. Riordan's files.' Just like that. No explanation, no apology. I've known Santino since I took this job. We've always cooperated, always helped each other out. But you come along, and all of a sudden I get stonewalled by a man with whom I share a mutual respect. Any idea what would motivate him to do that?"

I shrugged and said nothing.

"Any idea why a police chief would be unable to access information about a suspect in a murder investigation involving multiple homicides?"

"I couldn't imagine, Chief."

Ellis looked at Liz. "Can we speak off the record for a moment?"

"Of course."

Ellis dropped his notepad on the ground and let his pen fall on top of it. Then he sat back in his chair, crossed his arms, and stared at me.

"I notice you have blue eyes, Mr. Riordan. I find that surprising."

"How so?"

"Because you're so full of shit they ought to be brown."

Against my better judgement, I laughed. "You sound hurt, Chief."

"I'm not. Between you and me, I ain't gonna lose any sleep over Lopez and company. They were a bunch of scumbags, and the world is a better place without them in it."

"I tend to agree."

"But still, I'd like to know what really happened in that bar. I'd like to know why you went there and took on a bunch of armed criminals and how the hell you managed to get out alive. But I don't think that's going to happen. Thing is, we can't get any witnesses to come forward. Street full of people and nobody saw anything."

"Sad times we live in."

"Yes they are. And what's worse is the looters tore the crime scene up so bad I got no way to prove or disprove what you say one way or the other."

"Those filthy animals."

Ellis leaned forward and put his elbow on his knees, hands clasped. "Here's the thing, though. I don't much care for people who think they can operate outside the law. I don't much care for mystery men with classified files under their names. I don't much care for being lied to. And I sure as hell don't much care for shootouts in my town. Shootouts have a way of killing innocent people. You catch my meaning?"

"I think I do."

"Good." Ellis stood up and nodded to a uniformed officer standing outside the cell. The officer produced a set of keys, opened the door, and stepped aside. Ellis stood still a moment, and then said, "I can't pin nothing on you, Mr. Riordan. As far as the DA is concerned, it's a clear-cut case of self-defense. But just because I can't put you in jail don't mean I got no recourse. You got any sense, you'll get your ass out of my town at your earliest convenience and stay gone. We clear?"

"Crystal."

Ellis motioned to the door. "You're free to go."

"And Sabrina?" Liz said.

"Her too."

A female officer brought Sabrina to us in the lobby. She smiled when she saw us and gave Liz a hug.

"Let's get the fuck out of here," she said.

369

As we walked out the front door, Sabrina slipped her hand into mine and gave it a squeeze.

THIRTY-SEVEN

Three days after I got out of jail, Gabriel walked into the lobby of the Sky River Hotel and joined me at the bar. He smelled like a sweaty horse, his clothes were stained and filthy, and there was dirt caked in his beard and creased into the lines of his face.

"'Bout damn time," I said.

"Would have been here two days ago if you'd left me a few more markers."

"Excuses, excuses."

He shook his head. "Asshole."

"I heard Hicks had to go to the Springs. Some kind of special assignment."

Gabe turned his head. "Where'd you hear that?"

"General Jacobs."

"When did you talk to him?"

"Long story. Tell you later. Any idea what Hicks is up to?"

"No. I don't think Jacobs told him much. Generals aren't usually in the habit of explaining themselves to sergeants. They give orders and expect them to be followed."

Ross came over and poured him a drink. Gabriel downed it in one swallow and pushed the glass across the bar. Ross poured him another and set the bottle in front of him.

"Let me know when you done," Ross said, Southern drawl firmly in place. He glanced at me briefly before walking to the other end of the bar. I took the bottle and refilled my glass.

"Took me a few hours to find you after I got into town," Gabe said. "Had to ask around. Talked to a few cops. Sounds like you've had some trouble."

"Nothing me and the girls couldn't handle."

"How are they?"

"Tired. It's been a rough week. Liz is a little traumatized. Sabrina's worried about you."

"Where are they?"

"Upstairs in our room. You should take a bath before you go see them. Maybe put on some clean clothes."

"Don't have any."

"I'll get you some."

Gabe looked me with one eyebrow raised.

"We went back for Liz's trade before we left Haviland," I said. "Brought some of your clothes along. I'll leave an outfit with Ross while you clean up."

"Sounds good. You manage to save any of the livestock?"

"All alive and well."

Gabe nodded. "You made out better than I'd hoped for. Want to tell me what happened since you got to town?"

372

"Later. Go get cleaned up. My eyes are starting to burn over here."

Gabe nudged me in the shoulder with an elbow as he stood up. When I looked at him, he was smiling.

"Good to see you alive, old friend," he said.

"Bath. Now."

"Yeah, yeah. I'm going."

Ross guessed Gabe's intentions and rang a bell above the bar. One of the hotel employees came out and asked Gabe if he would please follow her. They went through a door and out of sight. I went upstairs to pick out an outfit for Gabe.

"What are you doing?" Sabrina asked as I rooted through our luggage.

"Getting some clothes for Gabe."

She and Liz both sat bolt upright. "He's here?" they asked simultaneously.

"Yes. Just got into town today."

"Where is he?" Liz asked.

"Taking a bath. You want to let him clean up before you see him. Trust me on that one."

"Is he okay?"

"He's fine. Smelly, but fine."

The relief on Liz's face was heartbreaking. "Thank God."

"Tell him to hurry up and get his ass up here," Sabrina said.

I faked a truly terrible British accent. "I shall relay the message, my good lady."

Ross was still at his usual perch behind the bar. I handed him Gabe's clothes, which he passed off to another hotel employee.

"Going to need another room," I said.

"One next to you open."

I thought about Gabe and Liz, and how long they had been apart, and had a vision of Sabrina holding pillows over her ears to block out the grunts, moans, thumping of bedframe against a wall, and creaking of strained mattress springs.

"Maybe something down the hall," I said. "Or on another floor."

"No problem."

"Still on the house?"

Ross put down the glass he was polishing. "I told you. You in Dodge City, this where you stay. You eat free, your room be free, you drink free. You and everybody with you. Just so long as you don't abuse the privilege."

"Never would have pegged you for the grateful type, Ross."

A shrug. "Depends on the favor rendered."

The bottle Ross had left for me and Gabe was still on the bar. I retrieved it and sat down in front of Ross. He handed me a clean glass.

"How go the, ah, acquisitions?" I asked.

"They going fine. Had to bust a few heads, get some folks used to the new regime. But things be linin' up good."

"Have any trouble buying up Lopez's properties?"

Ross looked at me with a blank expression.

"Right. Dumb question. How's Terrell? Haven't seen him around."

"Terrell be on the mend. And you won't be seeing him around no more."

"You fire him?"

Ross shook his head. "He quit. Say he going back to work in the residential district."

"Doing what?"

"Bodyguard for some rich cat."

"And you just let him walk?"

Another shrug. "Plenty more where Terrell came from."

I poured myself a drink. "What about Santino. Any trouble out of him?"

"He mad as a rattlesnake in a sack, but there ain't shit he can do with CID breathing down his neck."

"The investigator is in town?"

"Yep. Him and a whole posse. Got here yesterday."

"He talk to you yet?"

"No. But I figure he be here soon."

I finished my drink and got up to leave the bar. As I was walking toward the stairs, the front door opened and two men walked in. One of them was Chief Ellis. He pointed toward me and said, "That's Riordan. The man behind the bar is Demetrius Ross."

I stopped and stared. The man Ellis spoke to wore Army fatigues and the rank insignia of a sergeant first class. He took off his hat as he entered the building and approached me.

"Hello," he said. "I'm Sergeant Jeff Barnes, Army CID. I believe you've been expecting me."

Ross and I shared a glance. "Yes, Sergeant. We have."

*****

375

Two weeks later, Major Santino was relieved of duty and detained at the Dodge City Police Department. He was not alone. Most of his staff and nearly a dozen enlisted men were detained with him. A grizzled-looking captain, who had been a master sergeant before being given a field commission, took over his duties. I did not envy him the job. And I almost felt sorry for Santino and his cronies. They were crooked as the Appalachian skyline, but what they were doing was no worse than what was going on all over the country. They had just been dumb enough to get caught. That said, I didn't lose any sleep over it.

With Santino out of the way, the deal we had struck to get a spot on the Army convoy headed for the Springs was null and void. But as it turned out, the deal was unnecessary. Gabe used his ever handy satellite phone to call in a favor with General Jacobs, and we got to ride along for free.

The day we left, I stood with Gabe, Liz, and Sabrina outside the city gates and waited for a red-cheeked lieutenant to tell us which truck we were assigned to. A long line of APCs, Bradleys, trucks, Humvees, and HEMTT transports sat on the broken pavement like a long green snake, fumes pouring out of blackened stacks and staining the air with the reek of exhaust. Our livestock was out there somewhere, occupying a large horse trailer Liz had rented for the journey, and our trade was in a locked crate in one of the HEMTTs. The sky was clear and sunny and bore down on us with the heat of the oncoming summer.

"How long do you think we'll be on the road?" Sabrina asked.

Gabe scratched the scars on his clean-shaven jaw. "About three days, maybe four. It's only a little over three hundred miles, but the convoy has to make a few stops along the way."

I wiped sweat from my forehead and adjusted my hat. "Be glad to get out of this place."

Gabe grunted. No one spoke for a while. The lieutenant got a message over her radio and directed us to a deuce-and-a-half in the center of the convoy. We walked over to it and took seats next to a couple of squads of soldiers. The troops were in good spirits and spoke loudly of how much they were looking forward to getting back to the Springs. If their boasts were to be believed, the state of Colorado would soon be experiencing a shortage of alcoholic beverages and an unprecedented baby-boom. Gabe glanced at them, gave a short laugh, and shook his head.

"Some things never change," he muttered.

I looked at Gabe, and Sabrina, and Liz, and felt a sudden weight in my stomach. One of the things I had been working hard lately not to think about came to the front of my mind, and I had to face the fact that things were ending. Three of the most important people in my life were starting over in a new town, and I would not be a part of it. I would spend a few weeks with them while I handled some business matters, but then I would have to say goodbye and head back to Hollow Rock, and our lives would continue on separate courses. It was a rotten feeling. The thought of going back home without Gabe living next door, and Liz as mayor, and not being around to watch Sabrina grow up, and Gabe not witnessing my son become a man, and how different things were going to be without my friends close by made me feel bereft and empty inside. Sabrina must have guessed what I was thinking because she reached out and took my hand.

"Hey," she said.

"Hey."

"It's gonna be okay."

"Yeah. I know."

Her eyes tracked to Gabe. "Doesn't matter the distance between you two. He'll always be your friend."

"More like a brother."

The hand in mine squeezed. "Family is family. Nothing's going to change that."

"I know."

Family is family, I thought, and decided it was a good summation. *Family is family.*

I kept telling myself that all the way to Colorado.

THIRTY-EIGHT

Heinrich crouched in the darkness and thought things had turned out as well as they could have since the Army attacked his tribe.

Most of his men had made it to Brawley's Cove just north of the Arkansas border. A few had been lost to accidents and encounters with the infected, but not enough to make a difference. Once reassembled, they had taken on supplies and begun the journey south to Parabellum.

The map he'd purchased from one of Necrus Khan's men had turned out to be accurate. He and Maru and a few other of his lieutenants had split the tribe's forces and led them through a series of underground tunnels into the heart of the settlement. And now, Heinrich stood beneath a hatch leading straight into the Khan's private chambers.

"I hear the Khan's voice," a sergeant whispered, his ear pressed to the hatch. He moved his lantern in Heinrich's direction. "Guess the map was good."

So it is. Almost makes me regret killing the man who gave it to me. "Keep it down," Heinrich said. "Don't want them to know we're here yet."

"Right, Chief."

Heinrich checked his watch in the dim light. Thirty seconds to go. He holstered his pistol, wiped his sweaty palm on his shirt, and then redrew the weapon. Twenty seconds. Ten. He held up his diminished left hand where his men could see. The remaining fingers counted down three, two, one.

"Go."

The sergeant under the hatch raised a breaching shotgun and pressed its barrel to the latch.

"Fire in the hole!"

The boom echoed deafeningly through the tunnel. Heinrich had his earplugs in while his men stood with hands pressed over their ears. The sergeant dropped his shotgun, threw the hatch open, and went up the ladder as fast as his feet would carry him.

"Move!" Heinrich shouted. It was the only shout to be heard as he and his raiders pushed upward through the opening. He had admonished the men before entering the tunnels to be quiet, not to scream and yell and call challenges to their enemies. In a building this size, a shotgun blast would sound like it could have come from anywhere. The sound of raised voices, however, would be easy to track.

Heinrich blinked in the bright light cast by nearly a dozen lanterns as he scrambled up through the hatch. He was in a large bedroom, the rug covering the trap door flung aside by his men. To his right was a desk, wardrobe, macabre paintings, and sculptures on the floor and shelves. To his left was a bed currently occupied by two naked women and the man himself, Necrus Khan.

"Cover the door," Heinrich said, pointing at a squad leader.

380

The man motioned to his squad mates and did as ordered. The two remaining squads trained their weapons on the Khan as Heinrich approached him.

"On your feet," he said.

Necrus did as he was told, his expression blank as he stood naked before the armed raiders.

"You're a fucking dead man, Heinrich."

"Hands over your head. Do it now."

Necrus' hands went up. "You have no idea what you just stepped into. You just signed your own death warrant, small-timer."

"No. I just signed yours." Heinrich covered the distance between them in one swift step, drew his knife, and plunged it upward just below the tip of Necrus Khan's sternum. The blade sank deep into the doomed man's heart, blood pouring out over Heinrich's hand. He twisted the knife and shoved upward again. Necrus' eyes went wide, his mouth a rictus of pain. Then the muscles in his face went slack and he slumped to the floor. Heinrich removed his knife as the body fell. The men began to cheer, but Heinrich hissed them to silence.

"You," he said, pointing to one of his men. "Give me those bolt cutters."

"Yes sir."

Heinrich used his knife to cut the tissue around the Khan's neck, then crunched through the spine with the bolt cutters. There was no hair to hold onto, so he held the head up with both hands until the blood finished draining. And as always, when he decapitated someone, he was amazed at how much scarlet liquid came out.

"I need something to stick this on," Heinrich said. One of his men unslung a short spear from his back and offered it to him.

"Perfect," Heinrich said, and had the subordinate hold the spear while he stuck the head onto it. The blade held firm as it pushed upward into the dead man's brain. Necrus' jaw flopped open and the eyes rolled backward. Heinrich found the expression comical and smiled.

"Clear the building," he said to his men. "Spare the women and servants if you can. Everybody else dies. Rourke, you're in charge of the assault."

Rourke grinned at the unexpected honor. "Yes sir. You heard the man. Let's move."

As the men poured through the doorway and the gunshots and screams started, Heinrich looked at the two girls on the bed.

"Don't go anywhere."

The girls nodded, eyes bulging with fear. Heinrich hoisted Necrus' head, drew his pistol, and followed the last of his men out the door.

The main objective had been accomplished, but there was still work to do.

*****

Before the attack, Necrus Khan's guardsmen had numbered somewhere between seventy and eighty, depending on how many he killed from one week to the next over violations. As Heinrich watched, the last surviving dozen of them were marched into the town square, the hulking form of Ferguson among them. The moon was bright overhead, and torches had been arranged and a bonfire set to provide onlookers with a clear view of the proceedings.

"That's the last of them," Maru said, standing beside Heinrich. His second in command had a shiner under one eye and a blood-soaked bandage on his right bicep. If the injuries caused him any pain, he did not show it.

"Bring Ferguson up here."

Maru walked down the steps of the building Heinrich had already renamed the Governor's Mansion and proceeded across the dusty square where nearly a third of the Storm Road Tribe stood in a semi-circle around the last of Necrus' troops. The rest of the raiders were still patrolling the streets, putting down small pockets of resistance. Most of the people who lived in Parabellum had given his men no trouble. This was not the first violent regime change they had lived through. But some, for reasons that defied explanation, were loyal to their dead tyrant leader and chose to fight. This did not concern Heinrich. His raiders knew how to deal with them.

The citizens of the encampment stood in doorways, looked out windows, and gathered in clusters in the streets. Ragged, barefoot children clung to their mothers' legs. Hard-faced men looked on in stoic silence. Some of the women seemed worried, others indifferent. Slaves clutched their collars and gravitated close to their owners as if hoping they could shield them from danger. Heinrich found this ironic, slaves seeking protection from the very people who held them in bondage. But, if he was fair about it, it was not as if they had a plentitude of options.

Maru ordered Ferguson to his feet and motioned to two of his raiders. The four of them walked toward the steps where Heinrich waited. When they reached the base of the stairs, Maru ordered Ferguson to a halt.

"Good to see you again," Heinrich said.

"Wish I could say the same," Ferguson rumbled. Despite the fact he was on the ground and Heinrich at the top of the stairs, the giant's head was still nearly level with the raider chief's. Ferguson had been stripped to his underwear, but appeared uninjured.

"You give up without a fight?"

Ferguson shrugged. "Caught me fucking one of my slaves. Wasn't much I could do, staring down eight barrels with my dick in my hand."

Heinrich laughed. "Were you mistreated?"

"No. Your boys were downright polite."

"As they were ordered to be."

Ferguson nodded as though confirming a thought. "So what do you want?"

"You told me once you don't much care who you work for as long as you're allowed to do your job as you see fit. You worked for Necrus' predecessor, and then for Necrus."

"You want me to work for you?"

"If you're willing."

"And if I'm not?"

"I respect you, Ferg. You've always dealt straight with me. If you don't want to work for me, I'll have my men escort you to your house. You can gather your things and leave town at first light. When it comes to my tribesmen, I want volunteers. Not slaves."

Ferguson looked dubious. "You for real?"

"What reason do I have to lie? It's not as if you're holding any cards, Ferg."

The giant nodded and considered the offer. Finally he said, "What the hell. Man's gotta make a living somehow."

"Glad to hear it," Heinrich said, and nodded to Maru. "He's free to go."

Maru holstered his pistol. "Welcome aboard."

Ferguson grunted and began walking away.

"Hey Ferg," Heinrich called.

"Yeah?"

"Come by the mansion tomorrow around noon. We'll talk then."

"Sure."

As Ferguson departed, the remaining prisoners stared at him with manic hope in their eyes. *Maybe they think I'll hire them too,* Heinrich thought, and chuckled.

"What about the rest of them?" Maru asked.

Heinrich let out a long breath. He had planned to make a spectacle of the execution, something to let the townsfolk know exactly who they were dealing with. But the journey from Brawley's Cove had been arduous, the night's work had been stressful—albeit enjoyable—and Heinrich was tired down to his bones. He wanted a stiff drink, a hot meal, a blow-job, and ten hours of sleep. In that order.

"Shoot 'em and hang their bodies from the walls."

"Right, Chief."

Maru pointed his thumb and forefinger at the squad leader in charge of the prisoners and let his thumb drop. The squad leader shouted an order and raiders stepped forward with guns in hand. Each man put his weapon against the back of a prisoner's head. The doomed men closed their eyes and muttered prayers, begged for mercy, and in many cases, simply wept. A few cried out for their mothers. The squad leader shouted again and the reports of pistols echoed in the town square. The prisoners slumped forward.

385

"Mandatory curfew tonight," Heinrich said to Maru. "Make sure the civilians stay indoors until told otherwise. Anyone caught breaking curfew is to be shot."

"Will do, Chief."

Heinrich thumped his second in command on the shoulder. "You did good work tonight, Maru. Tomorrow, we'll go down to the auction house and you can pick your reward. Horses, guns, ammo, booze, anything. And you can pick any five girls from Necrus' harem you want. My gift to you."

Maru's eyes lit with an acquisitive gleam. "Thank you, Chief. You honor me."

With that, Heinrich headed back into the mansion, his personal guard in tow. His next order of business was to see how many servants he had left. Someone had to cook his dinner and fetch his drinks, after all.

*****

Half a kilometer from the walls of Parabellum, Tyrel Jennings took his right eye away from a night-vision spotting scope and turned his gaze to the man lying in the dirt two feet away.

"Well that was unexpected," he said.

"No shit," Mason Harker replied. He was a former SEAL, like Tyrel Jennings. Both men were dark of hair and eyes and sported short beards. But that was where the physical similarities ended. Where Tyrel was medium height and compactly built, Mason was tall, broad shouldered, and strongly muscled.

"Had to be tunnels," Tyrel said, looking down the hillside at the marauder settlement in the valley below.

Mason turned the spotting scope his way and looked through it. "I think you're right. No other way they could have disappeared like that and then reappeared in the middle of town. I think one of the tunnels led into the leader's compound."

"That would explain why we didn't see anybody go in but saw a shitload of raiders come out. I'm pretty sure that's the former leader's head on a pike in the town square."

"Must not have been well liked."

"Evidently not." Tyrel keyed his radio. "Hawk, Eagle. You get all that?"

"Affirmative, Eagle," a voice replied. It belonged to Andy Turner, team leader of one of Tyrel's elite Blackthorn units known as Raptors. He was on a hillside on the opposite side of town snapping photos with a long-range digital night-vison camera and recording video from a stealth drone flying high enough not to be heard by anyone in the encampment below.

"General Jacobs is gonna shit a brick when he sees the footage," Mason said.

"I don't know. The general's seen some things. Doubt anything shocks him anymore."

"Probably right. Should we do anything about the supply train?" Mason asked, referring to the long line of wagons the conquering raiders had hidden in the hills near the fortified settlement. The two Blackthorns had been watching the raiders for the last couple of days.

"Not yet. Let them move their supplies inside. People with FTIC claims on that cargo are going to want some of it back."

"Sure they will," Mason said lightly. "I've seen the manifests. But they don't need all of it, right?"

Tyrel grinned. "Of course not. Without us, they'd get nothing back at all. Entitles us to a small finder's fee."

The two men shared a quiet laugh. It was both illegal and against their government contract to pilfer from trade recovered from marauders, but what the government did not know couldn't hurt them. Tyrel lived in the real world. He understood he had to keep his men happy, and happy meant well paid. Unlike the regular military, Blackthorns were not bound by contracts of enlistment. They could quit anytime they wanted. If Tyrel wanted to keep them, he had to give them a reason to stay.

"Fun fact for you," Mason said.

"What's that?"

"One of those FTIC contracts you mentioned is in the name of Gabriel Garrett. Ring a bell?"

Tyrel turned his head. "The guy we're bringing out from Tennessee? The new trainer?"

"The very one."

"Hunh. So that means he was with one of the caravans that got hit by those Storm Road assholes."

"Yes. Want to know which one?"

"Sure."

"Spike's."

Tyrel was silent a few seconds. He remembered hearing of Spike's demise and being angered by the news. Not just because he had lost two of his Blackthorns, but because Spike had been a regular customer. And as founder and CEO of the Blackthorn Security Company, Tyrel hated to lose a good client.

"So Garrett's the one who survived and went after the prisoners. The one who led the rescue mission."

"General Jacobs will never admit it," Mason said, "but yeah. I think so."

Tyrel went back to looking down the hillside. "Must be one tough son of a bitch."

"We'll find out soon enough."

"Makes me wish I could be there for the interview."

"Not me," Mason said. "I'm happy right where I'm at. I'll take field work over administrative bullshit any day of the week."

"Amen to that," Tyrel said.

The two men lay silently in the darkness until dawn, watching. The settlement went quiet after a while, the gunfire and screams ceasing. Men patrolled the streets with naked aggression, daring anyone to step outside. Tyrel figured they had the place on lockdown. It was what he would have done, given the circumstances. It raised his estimation of the leader of the Storm Road Tribe, and his desire to kill him, that much more.

Enjoy the spoils, you son of a bitch, Tyrel thought. *You won't have them for long.*

THIRTY-NINE

Gabriel

It's always a wonder to me how easy it is to get used to one's circumstances. Doesn't matter how jarring the transition; give yourself enough time, and you can adjust to anything.

Leaving Kentucky for Paris Island was tough at first. It was hot, and there was a lot of yelling, and running, and pushups, and I remember being confused as hell the first week or so. Then things sort of fell into a routine, and I grew accustomed to the heat, and the yelling, and the bugs, and the constant use of physical training as punishment, and I got to know the men around me, and we came together and things weren't so bad. By the time boot camp was over I thought I would kind of miss the place.

The years spent in Iraq and Afghanistan were no different. At first there was confusion and fear and a lot of mistakes, and then I got a handle on things. And while none of it was exactly pleasant, I learned to deal with the daily challenges, indignities, and

390

difficulties. Even the constant danger of being killed eventually became background noise.

Kansas had been a bad experience, but there was one positive out of the whole mess—I had not seen a single infected during my tenure there. It was a departure from life in Hollow Rock, where the moans of the undead and the staccato crack of distant gunfire were an ever-present miasma. After a while, I reached the point where I noticed these things only vaguely, much the way I noted sunshine or cold or the smell of wood smoke on the wind. A perfectly natural and expected occurrence.

Consequently, the weeks spent in Kansas spoiled me. The absence of wailing ghouls was akin to the cessation of a pain I didn't know I was feeling. I started sleeping better at night. My overall mood improved. Food tasted better. Sex was more enjoyable. The brilliant play of colors along a morning horizon once again held the hopeful majesty I remembered from my younger days.

And then we reached the Colorado border.

The first indication of trouble was a young sergeant in our deuce-and-a-half transport truck pressing his fingers to his ear and motioning for his squad to stop talking. He said something into the mic I could not hear and then stood up.

"Got a horde inbound," he said. "Big one. Back on the clock, ladies."

The convoy halted, the brakes on our transport squealing. A cloud of dust swirled around the truck as troops filed past us and hopped to the ground. I looked across at Eric.

"What do you think?" I said. "Lend a hand?"

Eric grabbed his rifle and stood up. "Why the hell not. Got nothing better to do."

"I'm coming too," Sabrina said.

"Long as you stay with me or Eric," I told her.

"Fine."

I glanced at Elizabeth. "You staying here?"

She responded by laying down on the bench and putting a rolled blanket under her head. "I have faith in the might of our armed forces. Think I'll take a nap."

"Too bad the bench isn't wider. I might join you."

She smiled languorously. "You'd be welcome."

Sabrina made a gagging noise and jumped down from the truck. Eric put on his MOLLE vest, checked his rifle, made sure his canteens were full, and went after her. I went down to one knee and kissed the woman I loved, taking my time about it.

"Wow," she said when I came up for air.

"Wow yourself."

"What was that for?"

"Because I wanted to."

The smile became carnivorous. "What else do you want to do? I can't help but notice there's a canvas over the door and it's just the two of us."

I kissed her again, lightly this time. "Later. Somebody's got to keep those two out of trouble."

Her hand cupped my cheek. "Be careful."

"Always."

The morning had been sunny and clear, but there was weather moving in. A wind had picked up from the east and brought with it the howling, keening cry of the approaching horde. Thunderheads gathered in the far distance, a line of towering gray behemoths looming over the plains. Looking westward along the convoy, I caught sight of Sabrina and Eric talking to a young woman with

392

captain's bars on her uniform. Eric said something to the captain which prompted her to shake her head and point back toward our truck. Eric said something else, looking frustrated. I quickened my pace.

"Listen, we don't need civilians getting in the way. Just wait in your truck and let us handle this," the captain said as I reached them. A rocker patch on her left shoulder identified her as part of the Army Expeditionary Corps, meaning she had been a Marine until just over a year ago when the Marine Corps was disbanded and absorbed into the Army, along with the Air Force.

"Everything okay, Eric?" I asked.

The captain shifted her irritated gaze over to me. Her nametag read Silverman. She was medium height and build, probably in her early thirties, had dark curly hair under her cap, a pair of large brown eyes, and was not at all unattractive.

"I'm trying to explain to the good captain here that we can help her," Eric said. "But like most people in uniform, she's under the mistaken impression that civilians are useless. It's almost as if she's incapable of realizing we've survived the Outbreak just as long as she has, only without the benefit of the Army's resources. Which, in a backwards twist of logic I cannot claim to comprehend, somehow makes us less than qualified to kill ghouls."

Captain Silverman's fists balled up at her sides. "Who the hell do you think you're talking to, asshole?"

I let out a sigh. Eric was getting angry, and that wasn't going to help anything.

"It's not his fault," I said. "He went to Princeton."

Silverman looked at me in surprise for a few seconds, then burst out laughing. Her fists became hands again.

"Well that explains a lot," she said.

"Your alma mater?" I asked.

"Villanova."

"Ah. Understood."

"You?"

"University of Hard Knocks, otherwise known as the Marine Corps. Started out in infantry, then scout sniper school and Force Recon the last few years."

"No shit. What units?"

I told her. The smile faded, her expression growing respectful. Silverman tilted her head toward Eric. "He with you?"

"Yep. Spent the last few years training him. The girl too." A small lie, but the captain didn't need to know that.

"I'm his daughter, by the way," Sabrina said irritably.

Captain Silverman smiled at her. "Yeah. I can tell."

"We're not trying to cause trouble," I said. "We have our own weapons and ammo, and we're willing to lend a hand."

Silverman scratched the side of her neck and glanced at the soldiers taking position atop trucks, Humvees, and HEMTTs. A few Bradleys and an Abrams were breaking off from the column and heading toward the approaching infected.

"If I'm honest," she said, "we could use the help. I just don't like endangering civilians. Goes against the job description."

"We can handle ourselves."

The captain looked us over, reassessing in Eric's case. She seemed to note the way he wore his gear and the casual way he held his sniper carbine, a sure sign of long practice. "Yeah, I guess you can. Hang out here for a minute."

Silverman walked farther west toward the front of the convoy where another, more senior captain stood. She said a few words to

394

him and pointed in our direction. The older captain shrugged and said something back. Silverman gave him a thumb's up and returned to speak with us.

"You see that HEMTT?" she asked. "Guys with long guns on top of it?"

I looked where she pointed. A knot of troops armed with bolt-action rifles and sniper carbines were climbing atop the truck she indicated.

"Yeah," I said.

"Snipers and designated marksmen are going out to provide overwatch. You can ride with them."

"Will do." The three of us headed over to the truck.

"You ready for this?" Eric asked Sabrina. "Been a while since you shot a rifle."

"You're always telling me I need more practice. Is this not a chance to practice?"

"It certainly is."

A sergeant stopped us when we reached the HEMTT and asked us what we wanted. I invoked Captain Silverman's name and said I was a Marine scout sniper the other two were skilled shooters. He gave us a funny look, but let us climb the ladder. Once on the roof, we received more funny looks, but no one bothered us.

The HEMTT was a flatbed carrying a cargo container. We rode atop the container, and I was pleased to discover some enterprising soul had welded galvanized steel bars to the outer edges to form low hand rails. By the scorch marks and obvious scoring of angle grinders, I guessed the rail had been welded on and cut off several times.

The driver leaned his head out the window. "We got everybody?"

395

A master sergeant turned to the driver. "Yeah. Everyone who's coming, anyway."

"Tell everybody to hang on."

"Roger that." The master sergeant turned to address the assembled troops. "You heard the man. Stay low and hang the fuck on."

The driver put the HEMTT in gear and the engine roared as we began trundling over the countryside. I kept one hand on my rifle and one hand on the rail as we bumped and heaved along. The height of the cargo container beneath me allowed me to see into the far distance where thunderheads were moving straight at us, and swiftly. The storm's shadow fell over what looked like an undulating black carpet pouring slowly over a hillside perhaps a mile away. It covered about a quarter of a mile running north to south, and had morphed into the now-familiar teardrop formation. Across from me, a soldier came up on one knee and peered at the horde through his scope.

"Damn," the young man said. "Big one. Gotta be two thousand or more."

"Don't sweat it," the soldier next to him said. "This container we're sitting on is full of ammo. Over a million rounds."

I blinked. If he was right, we were sitting on a staggering amount of wealth.

"Might need it before the day's over."

The soldier sat back down and gripped the rail. A flash of blue and orange lightning moved among the approaching clouds, bringing with it a peal of thunder. The wind from the east picked up, blowing dust and debris into my eyes. I put on my goggles, checked my rifle, and waited for the fight to begin.

The storm held its rain for the moment, but the wind had kicked up a hazy cloud of dust, casting the sky in turbulent shades of yellow and orange. To the north, an Abrams tank that had disappeared behind a hillside a few minutes ago reappeared on the horde's left flank. It stopped on the top of the hill and turned its turret toward the horde. The tank was perfectly silhouetted against the sky, an ugly lump of death-dealing machinery juxtaposing with the calm, gently rolling countryside.

Sensing a photo opportunity, I took out a small digital camera with rechargeable batteries I often keep with me. It took a moment to get the zoom and focus right and press the button, and by some stroke of improbable luck, I captured the very moment the tank fired. The sound and concussion startled me. Not because I've never been around tanks firing, but because it was as if pressing the button on the camera had been the catalyst that made the cannon go boom. I lowered the camera, let out a breath, and looked at the image I'd captured.

"Holy shit," I said.

Sabrina leaned over. "What?"

"Look at this." I turned the camera in her direction.

"Wow," she said. "That's pretty damn cool."

The tank squatted black and featureless against the amber burn of the northern horizon, a ball of smoke and expanding gasses bursting from its cannon like a silent scream. The bullet-shaped projectile emerging from the exploding cloud floated in perfect stillness in the fraction of a second before it rocketed downhill. Dimly, I noted the sound of it detonating over the heads of a few thousand infected, leaving a circular crater of pulped corpses in its wake.

"Whoa," Eric said. "Must be using frag rounds."

I looked where the shell had hit and agreed with Eric's assessment. A few seconds later, six Bradleys opened up with their 25mm chain guns, sending parts and pieces of ghouls flying into their undead compatriots. The Abrams continued firing, its crew sending ordnance downrange with the speed and accuracy of experienced troops. Each shot created a circular clearing that was quickly swallowed up. The Bradleys kept their strafes at roughly head level, steadily whittling away at the ghouls' flanks. The chattering of M-240s joined the cacophony of chain guns and artillery.

The HEMTT continued toward the horde until we were less than a hundred yards away. The tank crew and Bradleys noted our position and adjusted their fire accordingly. I was willing to bet they had done so without being told.

On our HEMTT, the sergeant in charge unslung his rifle and assumed a seated firing position. "We ain't here to look pretty. Get to work."

The other marksmen moved to the edge of the cargo container and began taking firing positons. I came up on my right knee, squatted on my back leg, and rested my elbow on my left knee. The rifle slid into position like a key in a lock, the reticle lining up just where I wanted it to. I made a small range and windage adjustment to my scope, sighted in, and started firing.

To my left, Sabrina lay in the prone position. She had taken a wad of clothing out of her pack, balled it up, and laid it over the handrail, her rifle resting atop it. While I worked I counted the shots she took. When she had expended fifty rounds I stopped what I was doing and asked her how many she'd taken down.

"Forty-two," she said, not looking away from her point of aim.

I did the math. Eighty-four percent kill rate. At this range, that was four percent higher than what the Army expected from infantry grunts. However, her rate of fire was less than half what Eric and I were capable of.

As I watched her, I noted small mistakes she was making. My instinct was to make in-the-moment corrections the way my instructors had done at Quantico, but I resisted the urge. The context of our current situation was a world away from my days at sniper school. Sabrina was not trying to pass a course of instruction, she was killing walking dead people swarming toward us with unnerving, single-minded persistence. Best just to let her practice and trust my memory to catalogue all constructive criticisms for another day.

Ten minutes later, my rifle was starting to burn my hands through the barrel shroud. The wind was still blowing strongly, so I stood up and held my weapon in the air to let the wind help cool it down. Looking around, I noticed several of the troops with us doing the same. Two men had laid down their guns and were busy reloading magazines. A hatch in the top of the container lay open, several green ammunition boxes on the roof next to it. The soldiers reloading magazines were working furiously, but not fast enough to keep up with demand.

"Looks like they could use a hand," Eric said. He had stopped firing and stood next to me.

"Maybe you should show 'em how it's done."

A sigh. "Looks like someone needs to."

Eric fished a magazine loader from his MOLLE vest, grabbed a box of ammunition, and sat down cross-legged. He then took off his boonie hat, laid it upside-down in his lap, and poured four boxes of 5.56 rounds into it. A soldier brought him a stack of magazines. He took one, affixed the loader, and went to work. It was a thing to behold.

Eric has square hands with long fingers. He is the most skilled guitarist I have ever met. The deftness with which his fingers pluck notes from a guitar is only one example of his remarkable dexterity. I am firmly convinced it is this dexterity, this awareness of his body and its component parts, that makes him such a deadly marksman and an uncommonly skilled fighter. It has been three years since the last time I actually enjoyed a sparring session with Eric. These days, it just hurts.

But in this instance, he was not fighting. He was reloading magazines, specifically standard-issue metal STANAG magazines. The fastest I've ever managed to reload one was eighteen seconds. Eric could do it in twelve, and demonstrated as much to the soldiers in attendance. The other two men reloading noted this with no small amount of jealousy and redoubled their efforts.

I turned, peered through my scope, and examined what was left of the horde. The artillery from the tank and relentless assault from the Bradleys, combined with the efforts of those of us on the HEMTT, had reduced them by maybe forty percent. The teardrop formation had stalled due to the long line of corpses piled at the front of the horde's ranks, a pile formed deliberately by the marksmen, tanks, and Bradleys. It was a ghoul-slowing tactic known technically as a revenant berm. Or, as most troops called it, a shitpile.

The infected coming toward us had bunched up at the shitpile, clustered together as close as sardines in a can. Unable to move forward, they stood stomach to back, hands reaching toward the sound of living flesh ahead of them. Some of the ones on the flanks began to envelope the sides of the pile and push past it. An officer standing on the roof of a Humvee saw this and said something into his radio. Moments later, more Humvees came pouring over the hill behind us, laden with troops. The soldiers formed up into squads and moved into position on the left and right sides of the horde. I heard the squealing of treads and the roar of engines as the Abrams and Bradleys backed off. Machine-gun crews took position on hillsides, grenadiers following along. The marksmen around me on the HEMTT continued firing over their heads.

The Abrams pointed its gun upward and fired. There was a sound like a rocket passing close by, a high whistle, and the round detonated a few feet above the horde's rearmost ranks. At a signal from the officer on the Humvee, the reinforcements opened fire, further containing the undead with the bodies of their own brethren.

The rest was clockwork. The ground troops kept the horde contained and bunched together while the Abrams decimated them with methodical precision. The marksmen on the HEMTT with me ceased fire and settled in to watch the show. I sat down next to Sabrina, who had also stopped firing, and now sat quietly as the tank did its work.

"Forty," I said.

Sabrina turned to me. "What?"

The tank fired again. I pointed at it. "Forty-one."

"How can you keep track?"

Another boom. "Forty-two. Time to reload."

As if on cue, the tank commander spoke into his radio and the officer on the Humvee waved in response. The Abrams backed off down the hill.

"How'd you know that?" my daughter asked.

"Abrams M1A2. Max loadout is forty-two rounds for the 120mm cannon. Glad these guys were by the book. Would have looked silly if I were wrong."

Sabrina smiled at me and nudged me with her elbow. "Nobody likes a know-it-all."

"Time to head back," the HEMTT driver called through his window. "Infantry's got the rest of 'em."

I slung my rifle across my chest and held on as the HEMTT did a U-turn and headed back toward the convoy.

FORTY

The storm flew right over us, turned abruptly south, and dumped its contents on the communities along the Arkansas River southeast of Pueblo. The convoy headed steadily westward on Highway 94, beset on all sides by the flat brown plains underlining the distant towering peaks of the Rocky Mountains.

Sabrina had never been this far west before, and found the prospect of seeing it through the window of an automobile fascinating. Consequently, she talked our driver, a young private named Wilson, into letting her ride shotgun. Wilson was perhaps nineteen years old and looked like he was about twelve. I smiled to Sabrina's face and told her it was a great idea, give her a chance to see the countryside. And as soon as she was out of sight, I pulled Wilson aside and informed him that if he so much as dreamed of laying a hand on my daughter he would die choking on his own testicles. He offered no argument.

The last night before arriving in the Springs, the convoy stopped a few miles outside of town. There were a few convoys and trade caravans ahead of us, all of which had to go through mandatory processing, so the captain in charge had elected to camp overnight to let the traffic die down before we approached the city gates.

The vehicles in the convoy formed a circle, Bradleys and Humvees and the Abrams positioned to lay down fire while infantry and support troops erected modular watch towers, fired up generators, and set up spotlights. Watchmen checked out NVGs from a supply sergeant and went out on patrol. Those not on working or on watch sat down in clusters and ate good-naturedly from field rations. I talked a friendly HEMTT driver into parting ways with a few wooden shipping palettes and built a small cook fire in the center of camp. Eric cooked us a meal from our dwindling supplies and we ate quietly, trying to ignore the elephant in the room. After a while, Elizabeth stood up and said she was going for a walk.

"Want me to come with you?" I asked her.

"No," she said. "I need to be alone for a while."

"Okay."

She walked toward the perimeter. I stared down at the remnants of my meal and felt my appetite fade.

"You should go after her," Sabrina said.

I looked at her. Her fork moved rapidly from her plate to her mouth, steady as a metronome. The hard years she had spent on the road had taught her to eat as much as she could, when she could, and to eat it quickly. She had probably spoken without pausing. I wondered if she would ever learn to slow down and enjoy her food.

"She said she wants to be alone."

Sabrina glanced up. "You really don't know much about women, do you?"

I set my plate on the ground and looked at Eric. "You?"

"It's what I would do," he said.

I took a deep breath. "Okay then."

I walked toward the perimeter, following Elizabeth's tracks. Near the perimeter, spotlights lit up the night outside the circle of vehicles, but on my side, it became too dark to make out footprints. So I stood and closed my eyes and listened. A crunch of gravel sounded off to my left. I moved toward it and spotted her staring at the ground next to a Humvee with a flatbed trailer attached to it.

When I was close enough so she could hear me, I said, "Hey there."

Elizabeth jumped and rounded on me. "Jesus Christ."

I held up my hands, palms out. "Sorry. Didn't mean to scare you."

She came forward and slapped me on the chest. "Goddammit Gabe. What have I told you about that?"

"I said I was sorry."

"You almost gave me a fucking heart attack."

This was not going the way I had hoped. "I'm sorry. Really. Come on, let's sit down."

We took a seat on the empty flatbed trailer. It had been carrying a pair of ATVs until a couple of hours ago. I heard their engines revving as soldiers rode by on patrol. Elizabeth took a seat next to me, still trying to get her heart rate under control.

"It's not right," she said.

"What?"

"Nobody your size should be able to move that quietly."

I smiled and shrugged. "Saved my life a few times."

She looked at me from the corner of her eye. I figured it was a good segue to the heart of why I had followed her.

"You've been awfully quiet yourself lately," I said.

She looked down at her hands and twisted her fingers together. A few seconds went by.

"Eric told me what happened."

A small nod, but that was all. I knew what was bothering her. My instinct was to think of something to say to fix the problem, to make Elizabeth feel better about what she had done, but that would have been the wrong tactic. Trying to fix it would have made the problem about me, not her. And this was definitely not about me. Women and men are different. Men see a problem, and the first thing we want to do is get rid of it. But when women experience trouble, they have a more internalized response. Not in all cases, but enough to make it statistically significant. So I reached out and laid a hand on Elizabeth's shoulder and said the best thing I could think of.

"I'm sorry that happened to you."

I felt her start to tremble. She scooted closer to me, wrapped her arms around my chest, and the dam finally broke. We held each other in the darkness, the sound of engines and generators buzzing around us, spotlights streaking through the night, alone together on the high plains of Colorado. I looked up at the brilliant stretch of stars overhead, the hanging road of the Milky Way contrasting against the dark indifference of the universe, and wondered if there really was anything to look forward to after this life. If I had my choice, I would spend my eternity reliving moments like this one. I could think of no better heaven.

"I know I shouldn't feel bad about it," Elizabeth said after a while.

"Doesn't help."

"No, it doesn't. I keep seeing it over and over again. Lining up the sights, pulling the trigger, the blood, the screams. I dream about it."

"I know."

She untucked her head from my chest, wiped the tears from her face, and looked up at me. Her eyes were wide, dark pools under the moonlight. "Do I talk in my sleep?"

"Sometimes. Mostly you just thrash and moan. I've done my fair share of that."

"You still do."

"I know."

Her head resumed its place against my torso, face nuzzled close to my heart. I wondered if she could hear it beating.

"Does it ever get easier?"

"Yes," I said. "It takes time, but it does."

Elizabeth let go of me and stood up and walked a few steps away, face turned upward to the night sky. "Do you still remember the first one?"

"In my case, it was more like eight. Happened in Afghanistan. Militants put a few women and children on the hood of a truck and charged us. I was on a fifty-cal."

Elizabeth looked over her shoulder. "So what did you do?"

"What I had to."

"Dear God. I'm so sorry, Gabe."

"It was a long time ago. I've killed a lot of people since then."

She came over and sat down again. "I know that. I've always known that about you. But seeing what it's like for myself ..."

"Makes it more visceral."

407

"Yes."

"Here's the thing about killing," I said, turning so I could look her in the eye. "There's two kinds of people. People who've taken a life, and people who haven't. These days there are a lot more of the former than there used to be, but the dividing line still exists. Killing goes against our instincts. Most people just aren't built for it. But therein lies the problem. When you cross the killing line, it's only difficult the first time. And like all lines, the more you cross it, the easier it gets. After a while, you forget why the line was ever there to begin with. It's when you reach that point you have to be very, very careful. You have to make sure your reasons are justifiable. If you don't, if you fail to examine closely why you choose to end a life, each and every time, it gets too easy. And that's when you stop being a defender and start being a monster."

Elizabeth wrapped a gentle hand around the back of my neck and pulled until our foreheads touched. "You are not a monster, Gabe."

"No, I'm not. But I speak the language."

A smile. "And that's why you're so good at what you do."

"Yes."

We sat together a while longer, then headed back toward camp. Elizabeth's step was lighter and she was holding her head high again.

As we walked I said, "For what it's worth, I'm proud of you."

Elizabeth looked owlish. "Proud?"

"It took a lot of courage to do what you did. Most people couldn't have done it. So yeah, I'm proud of you. You're as tough as you are beautiful."

She slipped her fingers through mine, raised my hand to her lips, and kissed one of my knuckles.

"You're not the most sensitive man I've ever met, Gabe. But sometimes you know exactly what to say."

FORTY-ONE

Our first order of business in Colorado Springs was to secure lodging.

On the way in, I talked to a few soldiers familiar with the area and they recommended the Mountain View Hotel. It was on the south side of town, well away from the crime-ridden refugee districts. The southern part of town had been rebuilt since the Outbreak and boasted the city's best restaurants, safest streets, and cleanest hotels.

Once lodging was taken care of, Eric arranged livery services for our livestock while I rented space on a warehouse floor for our trade. By the third morning, we were settled in, fed, bathed, our animals well cared for, and wearing new, non-travel-stained clothing.

Eric and I woke up early and made our way to the complex of government buildings near the former shopping mall that was now the Colorado Springs Federal Refugee Intake Center. We stopped by the Intake Center, stood in line with travel-weary new arrivals for the better part of an hour, and paid five .308 rounds—the equivalent of twenty federal credits, according to the clerk—to send a message to Hollow Rock that we had arrived safely in Colorado Springs. The message would be put on the board at city hall, which Eric knew Allison would be checking on a daily basis. It occurred to me it had been nearly three months since Eric had seen his wife and son, and I felt like a sorry bastard because I had not once thought to thank him for all he had done for me. On the way out of the Intake Center I corrected that mistake and apologized for taking so long to get around to it.

"Don't mention it," he said.

"Fuck that. You've done more for me than I can ever thank you for."

"You'd have done the same for me."

I started to reply, hesitated, and decided to shut my mouth. Eric was right. I would have.

Our next stop was the Federal Militia and Contractor Liaison Detachment (otherwise known as MCLD), a squat cinder-block building with as much charm as a case of foot fungus. I told the guard at the entrance our names and registration numbers in the Archive. He called them in and told us to wait while someone inside checked us out. A few minutes later, he checked us for weapons and let us into the building.

The interior was austere and white with bare concrete floors and scavenged pre-Outbreak furniture. The receptionist, an attractive brunette in her late twenties, asked us our business. We informed her we were there to collect payment for services rendered. The young woman clicked and clacked at her computer for a few minutes while the two of us stood and waited. I didn't mind. The building was air conditioned, a pleasure I had not enjoyed since the Outbreak.

411

"Second floor," the receptionist said finally. "Stairway is around that corner over there, first door on your right. Go to the front desk and ask for Mr. Belson. He'll settle your accounts."

We went up the stairs and down the hallway toward the front desk. On the way, I said, "What are you collecting for? You earn a reward for killing that Lopez guy?"

"No. The job in Illinois," Eric said.

I stopped walking. Eric went ahead a few steps before looking over his shoulder. "What?"

"You never collected on that?"

"No."

"Why not?"

"Didn't need it. Figured I'd save it for a rainy day."

I shook my head. The reward I had been paid for my part in bringing down the Alliance had been substantial. I could not imagine Eric's was any less.

"Why are you collecting it now?" I asked.

"So I can give it to Sabrina."

I stared at him a few seconds, then couldn't hold back a laugh. "You son of a bitch. You knew I wouldn't take it."

"Nor Elizabeth."

"And you know Sabrina doesn't share our pre-Outbreak sensibilities."

"She's a practical girl. Must get that from her mother's side."

I walked closer and put my hand on my friend's shoulder. "In that case, maybe I'm not so impractical after all."

"You sure?"

I shrugged. "I lost a lot of trade on this trip. I have a family now. And besides, you can take what I owe you out of my trade once you get back to Hollow Rock."

"Sure I can."

I gave him a searching look. "But you won't."

Eric tilted his head and said nothing.

"Fine," I said. "Let's get this over with."

We filled out the paperwork and both of us signed a form assigning Eric's reward over to me. When we were finished, I went to hire a wagon while Eric went back to the hotel. I watched my old friend walk away and felt a sharp pain in my chest and wondered if I had made the right decision coming here.

Nothing for it now. Done is done.

I ended the day richer by six M-4 rifles, ten Beretta M-9 pistols, two thousand rounds of 5.56 ammo, a thousand rounds of .308, a thousand rounds of nine-millimeter, fifty one-liter bottles of grain liquor, ten pounds of sugar, thirty pounds of salt, and enough federal credits redeemable at the local exchange to keep my family fed for three months. If I traded two of my oxen, a few of the pistols, and maybe five or six hundred rounds of ammo, I could buy a place in a nice part of town. Maybe even a little plot of land. Not a bad prospect.

And there was still the job interview to consider.

*****

The headquarters of the Blackthorn Security Company occupied a set of buildings that had once been a pair of motels across a parking lot from the local IRS office. It was bordered on the north and east sides by Fountain Creek and the Pike's Peak greenway

413

trail. I heard the sound of cadence being called on the trail and saw men in the distinctive dark uniforms of Blackthorns running behind a tall, lean trainer. If everything went the way I was hoping it would, it might be me leading those recruits on their next run. The prospect made me quicken my pace.

A very attractive receptionist met me at the front entrance. I gave her my name and my reason for visiting and she directed me toward a set of comfortable chairs. I sat down and listened to the drone of generators and enjoyed the cool bite of air conditioning as it pulled away the light sweat I had broken on the mile and a half walk from my hotel. A few minutes passed before the receptionist told me Director Flint was ready to see me. She led me down a long corridor and stopped at a corner office. At her knock, a deep voice said to come in. The receptionist opened the door and went away.

Hadrian Flint, Director of Operations for the Blackthorn Security Company, sat behind a mahogany desk. I walked in and looked him over. He was almost my height, lean and trim, with dark brown skin, a shiny bald head, neatly shaved goatee streaked with gray, and black eyes about as forgiving as the edge of a knife. The smile he showed as I approached did nothing to soften his countenance.

"Mr. Garrett, a pleasure to finally meet you," he said.

I shook his hand. "Likewise."

"Please, have a seat."

I sat. Flint opened a laptop computer and typed what I assumed was a password to unlock it. The laptop's power cord ran to a plug in the floor next to the desk. Overhead, fluorescent lights had been removed and replaced with LEDs. The air conditioning was cooler here than in the lobby, which meant Flint had his own thermostat. Very posh indeed.

"I assume you received my letter?" Flint asked as he sat down.

"That's right."

He leaned back in his seat. "Well, you're here, so you must be interested."

"I am."

A few clicks on the computer. "You came highly recommended from one of our top clients. Unfortunately, he wasn't able to divulge much about you other than your service record in the Archive. That said, I have to say I was impressed. Graduated top of your class at Quantico, five deployments, two bronze stars, a silver star, more confirmed kills than malaria." He chuckled at his own joke. "Your country owes you a debt of gratitude."

I didn't laugh, but it was a near thing. "Thank you."

A nod.

"Let me guess," I said. "General Jacobs."

The smile was genuine this time. "Not too hard to figure out, was it?"

"Considering our history, no."

"How did you come to know the general?"

"Well…you might want to ask him about that."

"Classified?"

"Why I defer to him on the subject."

Flint crossed his feet in front of him. "Fair enough. So tell me about what you did after the Marines."

I took a breath and let it out. Tapped my fingers on my legs a few times. I'd known this was going to be hard, but now that it was in front of me, it was like I had a clamp holding my mouth shut. I told myself to get over it. The world had changed and not for the better. There were not many places for people like me in the civilian world, and if I wanted this opportunity, the time for

415

keeping my sins to myself was over. My life wasn't about me anymore.

"Did some time with the CIA," I said. "Black ops, mostly contractor stuff. Had a bad mission in Baghdad and got shown the door."

"How come?" Flint said.

"Bad intel. It was a rescue mission. People we went in for got killed. Asshole who sent us in wasn't about to ruin his career over a trifling thing like the truth."

"So he pinned it on you."

"Enough to get me rolled out, at least."

"I don't find that surprising."

"Oh?"

"I've had a few encounters with Christians in Action myself."

I nodded and waited.

"So what about after the CIA?"

"Went to work for a merc outfit," I said. "Aegis Incorporated."

"I'm familiar with them as well. What division?"

"Global rapid response."

Flint let out a whistle. "How long did you last at that?"

"Long enough to stack my chips and retire."

"I see. So what got you back in the game?"

I shrugged. "Same thing as most other guys like me since the Outbreak. Gotta earn a living somehow."

Flint steepled his hands and tapped his index fingers together. "General Jacobs told us you did some work back east training volunteers."

"Yep. Ninth Tennessee Volunteer Militia."

"I read a few reports on them. Seems you trained them well."

"That's the rumor."

Another smile. "Confidence. Assurance. I like that. It's what we look for in our trainers."

"As well you should," I said. "Do you mind if I ask a question?"

"Please."

"What is it you want me to do? I mean, I know you want me to train your men, but specifically, are we talking firearms, wilderness survival, intelligence gathering, fieldcraft, sniper training …" I held my palms up.

"All of the above. Assuming you're up to it."

"I am. And then some."

"You'll have to prove it."

"Be glad to."

Flint regarded me thoughtfully for a long moment. The generators hummed. The air conditioning continued to feel wonderful. A door opened and shut somewhere down the hall. There was a faint buzzing in the room, the sound of electricity coursing through wires and pre-Outbreak devices. It had been a long time since I had heard it, and it was comforting. I felt like a middle-class merchant in the lavish manor of some obscenely rich feudal lord learning what real wealth looks like. Flint rose to his feet and offered me a hand. I stood up and shook it.

"I think I've seen enough. Welcome aboard, Mr. Garrett."

EPILOGUE

General Phillip Jacobs' office was a spartan affair with white cinder block walls, metal shelves, gray file cabinets, a few plaques and framed college degrees on the walls, pictures of his family from before the Outbreak, and an ugly metal desk with a green formica top. The only luxury he allowed himself in the small space was a window-mounted air conditioner, which rattled gently, the temperature set just short of maximum cool and the fan set to medium. He had removed his ACU jacket and sat behind his desk in his moisture wicking undershirt. A few years ago he would have considered the office uncomfortably warm. Now, with the thermometer on his desk reading seventy-nine, he felt pleasantly cool.

He stared at the manila folder in front of him. He had read it several times and committed most of it to memory. His memory had always been sound, allowing him to recall details and minutia that had been critical to his ascent through the ranks. Now, as the director of Army Special Operations Command, his sharp mind was indispensable to carrying out his duties, and he knew it. Consequently, he exercised daily, ate a healthy diet whenever possible, indulged in alcohol rarely and only in small quantities, and did everything he could to get at least seven hours of sleep a night.

He looked up from the manila folder to a simple wooden plaque above the entrance to his office. It was a piece of oak stained a rich dark brown with three words carved in black. The words comprised the mantra Jacobs repeated to himself every day when he woke up.

Hold the Line.

And he had. It had cost him dearly, but he had helped orchestrate the organization of what was left of the US Army, implemented new training to deal with emerging threats, convinced frightened politicians to commit resources to provide the Army with much needed new technology to fight the revenant scourge, and was the mastermind behind the downfall of the Midwest Alliance.

It was this last accomplishment that caused him to lose the most sleep at night. The conflict with the Alliance had been nothing short of civil war. The fact the Alliance had been in league with an invading foreign military force did nothing to change this reality. Jacobs had been forced to plot against people he had once sworn to protect, and he had not flinched. But for all that, he had not acted with ruthless abandon either. He had planned carefully and avoided loss of life whenever possible. But war is war, and in war people die. He had sent good people to their deaths, even non-combatants. His actions haunted him, but he knew deep down it had to be done. And in the end, the Alliance had crumbled and a much larger, more destructive conflict had been avoided. He often wondered if the men who had ordered the destruction of Hiroshima and Nagasaki had used the same rationalization.

The general returned his attention to the folder on his desk. He opened the front cover and looked again at the young man in the photo. He was in his early twenties, sandy blond hair, blue eyes, a scattering of scars on his cheek and the side of his neck just behind the ear. According to his service record, the scars extended from his face all the way down to his left hip. Jacobs had never asked the young man about it, but he had a good idea of where the scars had come from.

When an explosion goes off close to a person, their natural reaction is to close their eyes and turn away. Jacobs guessed this had happened to the young man, and a flight of shrapnel had peppered the left side of his body as he turned. It would have been a painful and traumatic injury, requiring medical treatment and weeks of healing. This by itself was not odd. Life in the Army was dangerous. What *was* odd, however, was the fact the scars had already been there when the young man enlisted.

A knock sounded at his door.

"Yes," Jacobs said, closing the folder.

The door opened and a lieutenant on his staff stood in the entryway. "He's here, sir."

"Send him in."

The door opened wider and Sergeant Caleb Hicks entered General Jacobs' office.

"Have a seat, Sergeant," Jacobs said.

The young man complied. Jacobs looked him over. Hicks looked much the same as he had the last time they had met, tall and lean and probably weighing around two-hundred and ten pounds or so. Judging by the width of his neck and the diameter of his wrists, Jacobs guessed the kid was a lot stronger than he looked. But his physique was not Sergeant Hicks' most striking feature. It was the eyes that held Jacobs' attention. Most kids Hicks' age would have been shuffling and nervous in the presence of a general, but Hicks did not look perturbed in the least. His eyes were steady and attentive, taking in everything and giving away nothing. Nevertheless, the general detected a hidden danger there, an understated ruthlessness. From what he had learned about the young sergeant and his performance thus far, Jacobs did not find this surprising.

"I trust you've settled in all right?" Jacobs asked. "Quarters, laundry service, new uniforms, all that?"

"Yes sir." The sergeant's voice was a mild tenor. He spoke quietly, but somehow his tone still held a strong resonance.

"That was good work you did in Kansas. You and Mr. Garrett both."

"Thank you, sir."

They sat for a moment in silence. *Kid doesn't give you anything*, Jacobs thought. *Just sits there and stares.* The general leaned back in his chair and crossed his hands over his stomach.

"You're wondering why I asked you here," Jacobs stated.

"Yes sir."

"Let me ask you a question, Sergeant Hicks. How do you like it with the First Recon?"

There was a flicker behind Hicks' eyes that Jacobs took for mild surprise. "All right, I guess. Got a good squad, good platoon. Good bunch of guys."

"You've made friends?"

A small smile. "Yes sir. Like I said, they're good guys."

"How hard would it be to take on a new assignment?"

Hicks' eyebrows came together. "Sir?"

"What I mean is," Jacobs explained, "how hard would it be for you to walk away?"

The young sergeant thought it over for a moment. "Well, sir, I guess that depends on what I'd be walking away for."

"How about something that gives you more autonomy. Something larger and more important than killing ghouls and hunting raiders in an FOB on the frontier. Something that gets you away from all the mickey-mouse bullshit a regular soldier puts up with and allows you the freedom to exercise your own judgment and carry out missions as you see fit."

Hicks' eyes glittered. "What did you have in mind, sir?"

Time to show my hand, Jacobs thought. "First, let's go over your history." He opened Hick's personnel file. "Your father was Sergeant First Class Joseph Hicks, a former Delta operator."

Jacobs glanced up to see what effect the pronouncement had. Hicks' face remained impassive. *Probably knew we'd figure that out sooner or later.*

"Judging by your birthday," Jacobs went on, "you were born late in his career, shortly before he retired. We have no records of you or him for a few years after your mother passed away. According to her death certificate, she passed during childbirth."

Another check for reaction. Hicks showed none. *Figures. This is all stuff anyone could find in the Archive with a little digging.*

"At the age of five, you showed up in Houston, Texas. Your father remarried and took a job at a company called Black Wolf Tactical. Your parents home schooled you. You finished your high school requirements two weeks before the Outbreak."

"That's correct, sir."

"After the Outbreak, you showed up again in Colorado Springs. Worked for the city for a while, then took a job with a salvage outfit. Seems you amassed quite a little fortune for yourself. But then it all went bad. Your common law wife, Sophia Holden, passed away due to complications from childbirth. The child didn't make it."

Finally, Hicks' façade cracked. He swallowed and looked down for a moment. When his eyes came back up, there was a hint of anger. "There a point to all this, sir?"

"I'm getting to it, Sergeant. Afterward, you had several arrests for vagrancy and public intoxication. There was an altercation with a rather famous individual, Mr. Tyrel Jennings, founder and CEO of the Blackthorn Security Company. Didn't go too well for you. Says here you had to be treated for a mild concussion. Then, a few months later, you were arrested and charged with felony assault. Put a man in the hospital. Messed him up pretty bad."

Hicks stared and said nothing.

"Judge gave you a choice. Labor camp, or the Army."

A nod.

"And you chose the Army. Smart decision, if you ask me. I've seen those labor camps. Wouldn't wish that on my worst enemy."

No response.

"There are a few other things I've pieced together," Jacobs continued. "According to the M&D list, there were three people associated with you that passed away between you leaving Houston and arriving in Colorado Springs. Blake Smith, a co-worker of your father's at Black Wolf Tactical, your father himself, and your stepmother, Lauren Hicks."

"That's correct, sir."

Hicks' anger had passed like a cloud's shadow on the plains. His face was once again calm and impassive. Jacobs was impressed. He thought again about what his job required of him, and what he was about to say to this young man, and felt a surge of regret.

423

"For what it's worth," he said with genuine sympathy, "I'm sorry about your wife and child and your parents. And anyone else you lost, for that matter. My wife and my daughters…"

Jacobs suddenly found he could not speak.

"The Outbreak," Hicks said.

Jacobs nodded.

"We have that in common, then."

"Us and the whole damn world," Jacobs said, his voice rough.

They sat together in silence a few moments, an understanding passing between them. Jacobs cleared his throat and closed Hicks' file.

"I'm no detective," the general said, "but I'd like to run a few theories by you."

Hicks stared.

"It has occurred to me that you possess skills far in advance of any infantry grunt I've encountered in my long career in the Army. And I'm not the only one who has noticed this. Yet you seem to go out of your way to downplay your abilities."

A shrug.

"Any reason why?"

"I don't like to make waves, sir. There's an old Japanese saying: *The nail that sticks out gets hammered down.*"

Jacobs chuckled. "If only more people followed that wisdom. Son, I'll level with you. I don't think you're lying to me, but I think there's more to it than that."

He waited for Hicks to respond. And, of course, he didn't. So Jacobs forged ahead.

"The first thing that stands out to me is the list of people your father worked with at Black Wolf Tactical. Tyrel Jennings and

424

Blake Smith, for instance. A former SEAL and a Green Beret, respectively. Jennings arrived here at the Springs in an Army convoy two weeks before you did and filed a notice with the registry at the Intake Center. Put down a deposit to have a runner notify him if the names of you, your father, Sophia Holden, Blake Smith, or Michael Holden showed up there or on the missing and deceased list. Not long after that, Michael Holden left town and you and Tyrel Jennings became coworkers."

He gave Hicks a searching look. Still nothing.

"Obviously, none of these things are coincidence. So here's what I think happened. You knew Michael Holden, Tyrel Jennings, and Blake Smith since you were a little boy. Your father worked with them and they became close friends. You were home schooled, which left you with plenty of free time and gave your parents a great deal of flexibility as to how you spent that time. Furthermore, from what I understand of the training facilities at Black Wolf Tactical, they were the best a person could hope to find outside the special operations community. How am I doing so far?"

Hicks shrugged. "All factually correct, sir."

"Indeed. Now, what I'm going to say next is pure conjecture, so I don't expect you to confirm or deny it. But here's my theory. I think you were trained by some of the best special warfare operators the military ever produced. I think you started that training before you were old enough to read. If I'm right about that, then you spent your formative years with a gun in your hand and with access to top notch training facilities and instructors the envy of any spec-ops program. You learned marksmanship, unarmed combat, explosives, edged weapons, tactics and strategy, fieldcraft, infiltration and evasion, close quarters combat, and God only knows what else."

Jacobs paused. Hicks' blue eyes were as cold and empty as a winter sky. The only sound in the room was the gentle rattle of the air conditioner.

"I've heard people spout conspiracy theories about the government kidnapping orphans and training them to be super solders. All ridiculous, or course, but a fascinating concept nonetheless. Except I don't think you're a concept, Sergeant Hicks. Nor do I think you're a conspiracy theory. I think you're the real thing. A man trained virtually from birth to be something extraordinary. And as impressed as I've been with what I've seen from you so far, I think we've only scratched the surface."

Hicks took a deep breath and tapped his fingers on the arms of his chair. "What does any of this have to do with my new assignment, sir?"

Redirection. Smooth. Kid was well taught. "Everything," Jacobs said.

He opened a drawer in his desk, put away Hicks' file, and removed another one. He laid it on his desk and put a hand on top of it. Hicks glanced at it briefly.

"You're familiar with the problems we've been having with the Republic of California?" Jacobs said.

"Yes sir. Everyone is."

"No, they're not. They know what they've been told. They don't know the whole story."

Jacobs paused a moment to let that sink in. There was a flicker behind Hicks' expression. To Jacobs, it looked like curiosity.

"So what's the whole story?" Hicks asked.

"Ever wonder why the ROC hasn't mounted an offensive?"

"Sure. Wonder about it every day."

"Why?"

426

"Because it doesn't make any sense. When the Alliance fell, it seemed obvious they had only one course of action—attack. Only they haven't. No one seems to know why."

Jacobs smiled. "Seems like that should beg an obvious question, doesn't it?"

"Yes sir."

"And that would be?"

"Why hasn't the Union attacked the ROC?"

Jacobs nodded. "Any theories?"

Hicks looked down, brow knitting thoughtfully. His fingers tapped on the arms of his chair. Jacobs noted the action. When the kid was thinking, he tapped his fingers. The clock on the wall counted fifteen seconds before Hicks spoke.

"There are only a few reasons I can think of."

"Such as?"

"The Union wants to preserve resources, seek a diplomatic solution. But that doesn't seem likely."

"Why not?"

"The ROC is not a bloc of anti-Union Americans like the Alliance was. The American citizens in the ROC have all been subjugated. The government there is a bunch of puppets under the control of North Koreans and whoever else they brought over with them. And North Koreans are not known for their diplomatic proficiency. If they were the only obstacle, we'd have invaded months ago."

Jacobs held in is reaction, but it wasn't easy. The kid had cut straight to the heart of the matter. "What else?"

"Another possibility is they're stronger than what the government's been letting on. Maybe the ROC can't launch an invasion, but they're dug in deep enough we'd be crazy to try and root them out. Kind of like what happened in Vietnam. But again, I doubt that's the case."

Jacobs rolled an index finger in a 'go on' gesture.

"Well," Hicks continued, "for starters, they're on unfamiliar ground. The Viet Cong was on land they knew like the back of their hand. They had sympathizers everywhere. Places they could hide, people they could rely on to help them. I doubt too many Americans in ROC territory are happy with being under the rule of foreign invaders. On the other hand, the Union knows ROC territory better than its occupiers and would be welcomed as liberators by the locals. So that really only leaves two possibilities. The first is mutually assured destruction, but I don't think that's the case either. If the ROC had any nukes, they'd have used them by now, consequences be damned. We don't use ours because we'd be blowing up our own country, and Union citizens would probably revolt. So that narrows it down to one."

"I'm listening," Jacobs said. He did his best not to smile, but was not entirely successful.

"Same reason anyone would hesitate to go after an enemy," Hicks said. "It's ages old, been around forever. Same way a lot of kingdoms used to keep other kingdoms from invading them, how nations mutually assured each other they were serious about peace. Took the consent of the royal families involved, but it worked."

Jacobs knew the answer, but he asked anyway. "And that is?"

"Hostages," Hicks said flatly. "Way it worked was one kingdom's royal family would give a few key hostages to a rival nation, and the rival would do the same. The other country invaded, the hostages died. And vice versa. Shitty way to do things, but it kept the peace. I think that's what's going on here, only one sided. The ROC is holding the Americans in its territory hostage. We invade, the hostages die."

General Jacobs sat up, pulled his chair closer to his desk, and leaned forward on his elbows. "You know, there's a lot of folks in our intelligence community who would like it very much if you kept those assessments to yourself."

"Then they'd better figure out something quick," Hicks said. "I'm not the first person to come up with the idea. People aren't as dumb as the government thinks."

"No, they're not." Jacobs removed his hand from the file on his desk and opened it. "And you're right about the hostages. Tens of thousands of American citizens are being kept in internment camps in deplorable conditions. We intend to free them, not get them killed. However, there are other reasons why we haven't attacked the ROC. Reasons you haven't thought of because you don't have all the facts."

Hicks tilted his head like a curious dog.

"First, there's dissention in the ranks among the ROC's leadership. We have agents close to them who've given us solid evidence of a forthcoming coup. And at the center of that coup is someone you know very well. He, more than anything, is the reason I want you for this mission. You are in a unique position to help him, and by proxy, help the Union."

Jacobs spun the file around and moved it closer to Hicks. The young man stared in confusion for a moment, then his expression cleared and understanding dawned in his eyes.

"The man you're looking at," Jacobs said, "is the leader of a large contingent of resistance fighters in California and Oregon that have been making life a living hell for the ROC. I believe you know him."

Jacobs waited. Hicks stared at the photo and did not speak, so the general spoke for him.

"He's an old friend of yours. Your father-in-law, once upon a time."

Hicks leaned back in his chair and looked Jacobs in the eye.

"It's Mike," he said. "The leader of the resistance is Mike Holden."

Jacobs took the file and closed it.

"Any questions?" he asked.

"Two," Hicks said.

"Go ahead."

"I can leave my unit behind. It'll hurt, but I can do it. But…" Hicks struggled to speak.

"There's a woman." Jacobs said knowingly.

Hicks nodded.

"Will she relocate?"

"I don't know, sir. I'd ask her, but she's in Hollow Rock."

Jacobs sat up. "That's not a problem. I'll help you get a message to her. If she says yes, we'll have her airlifted out here and set the two of you up on base."

"Thank you sir."

"However, Sergeant, you have to account for all possibilities."

Hicks ran a hand over his mouth and let out a breath. "I know, General. If she says no…I don't know. I'll just have to figure something out. That said, I want the assignment."

Jacobs gave a grunt of approval. "Glad to hear it. What was your other question?"

Hicks' eyes grew cold and sharp, and General Jacobs, despite his long experience, felt a small tremor of fear when he looked into them.

"How soon do I leave?" Hicks asked.

Despite his involuntary trepidation, Jacobs had to struggle to keep a triumphant smile to himself.

"Soon, Sergeant. Very soon."

About the Author:

James N. Cook (who prefers to be called Jim, even though his wife insists on calling him James) is a martial arts enthusiast, a veteran of the U.S. Navy, a former cubicle dweller, and the author of the Surviving the Dead series. He hikes, he goes camping, he travels a lot, and he has trouble staying in one place for very long. He lives in North Carolina with his wife, children, a vicious attack dog, and a cat that is scarcely aware of his existence.

34005960R00246

Made in the USA
Middletown, DE
05 August 2016

6. . . . A typical series of defendants' requests and plaintiffs' responses is as follows:

Request No. 6

[Admit or deny that] The name SUN INSURANCE AGENCY INC. is currently in use for an insurance agency located at 1131 East Highland, Phoenix, Arizona 85014.

Response

In response to Paragraph 6 of defendants' Requests, plaintiffs show that a company with the name and address shown in said paragraph is listed in the Dun & Bradstreet Dun's Market Identifiers data base and that such data base shows the business of the company as "insurance agency." Plaintiffs have no knowledge as to whether such name is, in fact, in use as a trade name or service mark in connection with any business of the purported company identified in this request.

Request No. 7

[Admit or deny that] The business of SUN INSURANCE AGENCY INC. is the sale of life, health, home, and automobile insurance.

Response

Denied.

Request No. 8

[Admit or deny that] The name SUN INSURANCE AGENCY INC. has been in use in connection with the sale of insurance since approximately 1962.

Response

Denied.

***

7. The responses of plaintiffs identified above 5 fail to satisfy the requirements of Rule 36, which states in part:

An answering party may not give lack of information or knowledge as a reason for failure to admit or deny unless the party states that the party has made reasonable inquiry and that the information known or readily obtainable by the party is insufficient to enable the party to admit or deny.

8. It is well settled that the "reasonable inquiry" mandated by Rule 36 requires effort by the answering party to obtain information beyond that

already known to it and contained in its files. *Brown v. Arlen Management Corporation,* 663 F.2d 575, 580 (5th Cir. 1981) (requests ordered admitted where respondent failed to make reasonable inquiry of former employees); *Asea Inc. v. Southern Pacific Transportation Co.,* 669 F.2d 1242, 1245 (9th Cir. 1981) (answering party must obtain information that is reasonably available); *Ranger Insurance Co. v. Culberson,* 49 F.R.D. 181, 183 (N.D. Ga. 1969) (reasonable inquiry includes verification of information by telephone, etc.); *Cada v. Costa Line, Inc.,* 95 F.R.D. 346, 348 (N.D. Ill. 1982) (answering party must make a "reasonable effort to acquire the information sought"); *Lumpkin v. Meskill,* 64 F.R.D. 673, 679 (D. Conn. 1974) (answering party required to conduct independent research to verify survey data); *E.H. Tate Co. v. Jiffy Enterprises, Inc.,* 16 F.R.D. 571, 574 (E.D. Pa. 1954) (answering party must make inquiries beyond party's knowledge). Rule 36 requires that the answering party make efforts *to obtain* information by consulting with employees, third parties, and other reasonably available sources. *Anderson v. United Air Lines, Inc.,* 49 F.R.D. 144, 149 (S.D.N.Y. 1969) (responses under Rule 36 require inquiry to third persons). As stated in *Al-Jundi v. Rockefeller,* 91 F.R.D. 590, 594 (W.D.N.Y. 1981):

> Because Rule 36 admission requests serve the highly desirable purpose of eliminating the need for proof of issues upon trial, there is strong disincentive to finding an undue burden where the requested party can make the necessary inquiries without extraordinary expense or effort—i.e., if consultation with the third party is "readily obtainable," in the words of Rule 36(a). Blanket assertions that it is excessively burdensome to have recourse to third persons in preparing responses to admission requests, as made by some of the movants here, are not acceptable. The proper course is to make reasonable efforts to obtain the requested information. . .

9. Here, reasonable inquiries by plaintiffs would include, at a minimum, inquiries to (1) the list of third-party users provided to plaintiffs by defendants; (2) employees of plaintiffs located in the area of the third party user; and (3) relevant state and federal agencies responsible for registration of names, marks, and businesses.[3]

***

12. Plaintiffs erroneously contend that defendants are improperly seeking to shift the burden of discovering facts by requiring "admissions of facts which cannot be determined or verified without conducting third party discovery." As discussed above, defendants have made investigations to verify the facts, have provided plaintiffs with the means to easily make the same verification, and plaintiffs have the duty under Rule 36 to make their own reasonable inquiries rather than subject the parties to the time and cost of expensive depositions.

THEREFORE, plaintiffs have failed to comply with the requirements of Rule 36, and defendants are entitled to an order that the matters set forth in Response Nos. 1–3, 6–8, 11–13, 21, 22–24, 2–30, 33–35, 3–40, 43–45, 48–50, 5–55, 58–60, 69–71, 74–76, 7–81, 8–86, 90–92, 95–97, 100–02, 10–07, 17–64–66, 110–12, 116–118, 121–23, 126–28 are admitted, and that the genuineness and authenticity of Exhibits 1–5 be admitted in answer to Request Nos. 14, 25, 61, 87, and 113. In the alternative, defendants are entitled to an order requiring plaintiffs to make reasonable inquiries to obtain information and serve amended answers. Defendants are also entitled to an award of expenses incurred in relation to this motion in accordance with Rules 36 and 37(a)(4).

In the United States District Court for the Northern District of Georgia Atlanta Division

SUNAMERICA CORPORATION (formerly) SUN LIFE GROUP OF AMERICA, INC.),) a Delaware corporation, and *SUN)* LIFE INSURANCE COMPANY OF AMERICA,) INC., a Maryland corporation,	)
	)
Plaintiffs,	)
	)
v.	) CIVIL ACTION FILE
	) NO. 1:89-CV-1315-JTC
SUN LIFE ASSURANCE COMPANY OF CANADA, a Canadian corporation, and SUN LIFE ASSURANCE COMPANY OF) CANADA (U.S.), a Delaware corporation,	)
	)
	)
	)
	)
Defendants.	)
	)

Plaintiffs' Response to Defendants' Motion for Order Admitting Requests for Admissions and Alternative Request That Certain of Defendants' Responses to Plaintiffs' Requests for Admissions Be Held to be Insufficient

***

Background

Defendants served their Requests to Admit (Set II) (the "Requests") on September 13, 1990. The Requests sought plaintiffs' admissions concerning a variety of third-party "uses" of the word "Sun." After receiving the Requests, Plaintiffs served interrogatories and document requests seeking the backup material relied on by Defendants in support of the Requests and Defendants agreed to provide such material.

Defendants supplied a package containing a printout listing a variety of businesses that in some way incorporated the word "Sun" in their name along with several envelopes, letterheads, and business cards, which Defendants have managed to collect containing the names of some of these businesses (Exhibit A). The printout described the businesses in only the most general terms and did not contain most of the information Defendants requested Plaintiffs to admit. When Plaintiffs inquired as to whether or not any other information was available, Defendants' counsel indicated that its investigation consisted of nothing more than having a paralegal call the businesses and verify the information in the printout with some unidentified individual (Exhibit B).

Based on this cursory investigation, Defendants requested Plaintiffs to broadly admit that the businesses listed in the Requests "used" various corporate names, trade names, service marks, or trademarks including the word or element "Sun" in connection with various specified business activities. Defendants did not define the terms "use" and "used," which are terms of art in trademark and trade name law.

After receipt of the printout supplied by Defendants, Plaintiffs' counsel undertook to investigate of the business names listed in the Requests by obtaining printouts of the Dun & Bradstreet information available regarding those businesses through the DIALOG® DUN'S MARKET. IDENTIFIERS® computerized database. Much of the information supplied by Defendants or requested to be admitted was inconsistent with the information supplied by Dun & Bradstreet, especially with regard to the dates that the various businesses were started and to the nature of the business activities of the companies listed in Defendants' Requests. Based on this information, and in some cases, references to other sources such as telephone directories and documents produced in this case, Plaintiffs admitted those portions of the Requests that appeared to be true and denied the portions which could not be determined to be accurate or which were clearly false.[1] Plaintiffs denied a number of requests relating to the specific dates and to products or services sold by the businesses listed in the Requests as well as to the legal conclusion as to whether the names listed were "used" as marks as that phrase is defined in the Lanham Act as amended. 15 U.S.C. §1127. Plaintiffs believe the only means of obtaining reliable information about the names and marks used by third parties, the duration, nature and extent of such use, and the goods or services for which the names or marks in question used would be to take Rule 30(b)(6) depositions of each of the third parties listed and appropriately objected to the Requests to the extent obtaining this information would require such extensive discovery from numerous third parties throughout the United States.

Argument and Citation of Authorities

A. Rule 36 of the Federal Rules of Civil Procedure does not require Plaintiffs to conduct third-party discovery.

Federal Rule of Civil Procedure 36(a) provides :

> A party may serve upon any other party a written request for the admission, for purposes of the pending action only, of the truth of any matters within the scope of Rule 26(b) set forth in the request. . . . An answering party may not give lack of information or knowledge as a reason for failure to admit or deny unless the party states that the pjarty has made reasonable inquiry and that *the information known or readily obtainable by the party* is insufficient to enable the party to admit or deny. . . .

(Emphasis added). "Reasonable inquiry" under Rule 36(a) is a "relative standard depending on the particular facts of each case," and its meaning is within the sound discretion of the Court. *Dubin v. E.F. Hutton Group Inc.,* 125 F.R.D. 372, 374 (S.D.N.Y. 1989). Such inquiry typically requires making a good faith effort to ascertain information "within the immediate reach of an answering party." *Criterion Music Corp., v. Tucker,* 45 F.R.D. 534, 536 (S.D. Ga. 1968) (adopting "majority" view subsequently espoused in 1970 amendment to Rule 36(a)). It does not, however, require a party to discern information "where sources of corroboration are [not] at hand," *see id.,* nor does it require seeking information from an unaffiliated non-party *unless that party's sworn deposition testimony is already of record, see Dubin,* 125 F.R.D. at 374. *Accord Pearce v. General American Life Insurance Co.,* 637 F.2d 536, 544 (8th Cir. 1980) (refusing to award requester's expenses of taking non-party depositions; answering party had "good cause" to deny requests to admit because information was not readily available); *Dallis v. Aetna Life Insurance Co.,* 100 F.R.D. 765, 766 (N.D. Ga. 1984) (refusing to award expenses of non-party deposition), *aff'd,* 768 F.2d 1303 (11th Cir. 1985).

In *Dubin v. E.F. Hutton Group Inc.,* 125 F.R.D. 372, 374 (S.D.N.Y. 1989), for example, the plaintiffs sought admissions as to matters within the knowledge of a former employee of the defendants. When the defendants denied the requests to admit without having interviewed their former employee, the plaintiffs moved to compel discovery pursuant to Rule 37(c). In denying the plaintiffs' motion to compel, the court noted the futility of requiring the defendants to interview the non-party:

> Thus, even if defendants did interview [the former employee], the most they could gain would be his personal recollection [of events in issue]. This is an insufficient

> basis upon which to require [defendant] affirmatively to admit or to deny the truth
> of plaintiffs' characterizations of the [the events] in the absence of sworn
> deposition testimony by [the former employee].
>
> Plaintiffs nevertheless contend that defendants are required, under the
> "reasonable inquiry" standard of Rule 36, to interview [the former employee].
> However, plaintiffs have not brought to this Court's attention any authority
> demonstrating that a party's obligation to make "reasonable inquiry" entails
> seeking information from a third party *absent sworn deposition testimony*. . . .
> Accordingly, plaintiffs' motion to compel answers to the requests for
> admissions. . . is denied.

Dubin, 125 F.R.D. at 374–75 (citations omitted) (emphasis in original).

Contrary to Defendants' contention, the issue of the existence, duration, nature, and extent of "use" of certain words, trade names, corporate names, trademarks, or service marks by third parties could not be determined by simply placing a telephone call and relying on a hearsay conversation with whoever answered the telephone. The discrepancies between the Dun & Bradstreet data obtained by Plaintiffs and the purported "facts" in Defendants' Requests and in their paralegals' list demonstrate the lack of reliability of any information sources other than sworn testimony in verifying "use" of a name or mark, the duration, nature, and extent of such "use" and the goods or services involved.

Defendants place great reliance on *Ranger Insurance Company v. Culberson,* 49 F.R.D. 181 (N.D. Ga. 1969), in support of their Motion. However, this reliance is misplaced. In *Ranger Insurance,* there was no holding as a general principle that a "reasonable inquiry includes verification of information by telephone, etc." as Defendants have represented in their brief. Rather, the court merely indicated that the potential expense to the party should be taken into consideration in determining the reasonableness of the investigation. *Id.* at 183. Furthermore, the court in *Ranger Insurance* did not order the relief sought by Defendants in this action. Rather, the court first ruled on the defendant's objections to the plaintiff's requests. Only *after* the court considered and dismissed the defendant's objections did the court direct the defendant to either admit or deny plaintiff's requests or set forth specific facts as to why the defendant could not admit or deny the requests. The court did not order the defendant to supplement her answers or order the request for admissions admitted.

Plaintiffs assert that the only method of obtaining sufficient information to respond more fully to the Requests would be to conduct extensive third-party discovery, an inquiry not required under Rule 36 of the Federal Rules of Civil Procedure. Plaintiffs, in their responses, properly objected to the Requests to the extent the Requests require such discovery. Therefore, Defendants' Motion should be denied.

***

Plaintiffs, having fully responded to Defendants' Request for Admission (Set II) to the extent such responses do not require third-party discovery, assert that Defendants' Motion should be denied. In the alternative, if the Court should grant Defendants' Motion and Order Plaintiffs to supplement their responses, Plaintiffs respectfully ask the Court to also Order Defendants to supplement their responses to Plaintiffs Request for Admissions.

In the United States District Court for the Northern District of Georgia Atlanta Division

SUNAMERICA CORPORATION (formerly) SUN LIFE GROUP OF AMERICA, INC.),) a Delaware corporation, and SUN) LIFE INSURANCE COMPANY OF AMERICA,) INC., a Maryland corporation,)	
Plaintiffs,)	
)	
v.)	CIVIL ACTION FILE NO. 1:89-CV-1315-JTC
)	
SUN LIFE ASSURANCE COMPANY OF) CANADA, a Canadian corporation,) and SUN LIFE ASSURANCE COMPANY OF) CANADA (U.S.), a Delaware) corporation,)	
)	
Defendants.)	
)	

Plaintiffs' Renewed Motion for a Protective Order With Respect to Defendants' Notice of Deposition of the Chief Executive Officer of Plaintiffs' Parent Company

I. Introduction

Plaintiffs, SunAmerica Corporation and Sun Life Insurance Company of America, hereby renew that portion of their "Expedited Motion for a Scheduling Order" (filed September 21, 1990) that requests entry of a protective order with respect to Defendants' efforts to depose Mr. Eli Broad, the Chief Executive Officer of Plaintiffs' parent company Broad Inc., a large, publicly traded company headquartered in Los Angeles, California.[1]

In the course of discovery in this case, Plaintiffs have made available and Defendants have deposed virtually all of the present and many of the former high-level management employees of Plaintiffs. For example, Defendants deposed Plaintiffs' President and three Vice Presidents during the week of October 8, 1990. Defendants also have deposed numerous other present and former officers of Plaintiffs and the Chief Financial Officer of both Plaintiff SunAmerica Corporation and its parent, Broad Inc.

When Defendants first advised Plaintiffs of their desire to depose the Chief Executive Officer of Plaintiffs' parent company, Plaintiffs objected to the proposed deposition because Mr. Broad had far less involvement in matters related to the litigation than did the management personnel and corporate officers already made available for deposition. Discovery similarly demonstrated that Mr. Broad does not participate in the day-to-day management of either of the Plaintiff corporations. Plaintiffs advised Defendants, however, that they would consider withdrawing their objection if Defendants would identify any relevant subjects uniquely within Mr. Broad's knowledge and as to which his testimony would not be merely cumulative of that provided by other witnesses. Despite the diligent efforts of and Defendants' counsel have stated their intent to depose Mr. Broad during the week of December 3, 1990.

Regarding Defendants, the depositions failed to establish any unique knowledge of Mr. Broad regarding significant issues in this litigation, and Defendants have entirely failed to identify any specific information that they have not obtained through the extensive discovery already conducted. Nonetheless, on November 16, 1990, Defendants transmitted to Plaintiffs a "Notice of Depositions" of seven individuals, including Mr. Broad, for the week of December 3, 1990 (Exhibit A).[2]

Mr. Broad is the Chief Executive Officer of a multibillion dollar publicly traded corporation that serves as the ultimate parent corporation of Plaintiffs. He is an extremely busy corporate executive whose time is subject to numerous demands. Defendants' failure to identify any reasonable basis for believing that Mr. Broad has knowledge of facts not already provided by other witnesses thus evidences that the sole reasons for their insisting on Mr. Broad's deposition are to harass and, possibly, retaliate against Plaintiffs for instituting and prosecuting this litigation.

II. Statement of Facts

Plaintiffs' Expedited Motion for a Scheduling Order recites in detail the status of the discovery period through September 21, 1990. During the discovery period, Plaintiffs have

---

2. The Notice of Depositions was transmitted by telecopy, contrary to Federal Rule of Civil Procedure 5(b), made available, and Defendants have deposed at length 12 present and former top management officials of Plaintiffs and their affiliates, including

Robert Saltzman	President
Gerhardt Hoffformer	President
Martin Dannenberg	former Exec. Vice President and Chairman Emeritus
Scott Stolz	Sr. Vice President
Frank Mahoney	Sr. Vice President
John O'Leary	Sr. Vice President
Jana Greer	Sr. Vice President
Norman Metcalfe	Chief Financial Officer and Exec. Vice President
Thomas Daniel	Sr. Vice President
Robert Kubicki	Vice President
Ken Mlekush	former Sr. Vice President
Dave Leonard	former Vice President and General Counsel

Defendants also have deposed (or have noticed and plan to depose) present and former employees from virtually every aspect of Plaintiffs' operations, including another former Senior Vice President, a former in-house attorney, a paralegal, a customer service manager, three persons involved in producing promotional and advertising literature, two mail room supervisors, two mail room employees, and two receptionists.[3]

Defendants have deposed numerous non-parties as well. In a fruitless attempt to attack the rights to the name and mark "SunAmerica" acquired by Plaintiffs, Defendants deposed three.[3] Plaintiffs have not objected to any of these depositions other than that of Mr. Broad and in-house counsel, as discussed in the Expedited Motion for a Scheduling Order, officials of Chemical Banking Corporation and its affiliates, and intend to depose yet another officer of a Chemical Banking Corporation subsidiary next week. Defendants also have deposed the warehouse manager of a fulfillment house under contract with Plaintiffs, two employees of a corporate identity firm formerly engaged by Plaintiffs, and a representative of a public relations firm engaged by Plaintiffs for a short period. Defendants have noticed depositions of three others associated with a public relations firm previously employed by Plaintiffs' parent company Kaufman & Broad, Inc. (now Broad Inc.), and have noticed but not deposed more than ten other individuals during the course of discovery. Plaintiffs have expended substantial sums in defending and attending cumulative depositions conducted by Defendants in Los Angeles, San Francisco, Baltimore, New York City, Cleveland, and Atlanta.

On September 10, 1990, Defendants noticed the depositions of, inter alia, Plaintiffs' present in-house counsel and Mr. Broad. Plaintiffs objected to these notices and other improper discovery conduct of Defendants, ultimately filing the Expedited Motion for a Scheduling Order on September 21, 1990. The motion included a request for an order prohibiting depositions of Plaintiffs' counsel who had never communicated with Defendants and of Mr. Broad, the Chief Executive Officer of Plaintiffs' parent corporation. After the motion was filed, Defendants agreed not to depose Mr. Broad as noticed, and the parties resolved the other issues addressed in Plaintiffs' motion, with Plaintiffs contacting the Court by telephone and requesting that the motion be held in abeyance pending further negotiations between the parties. Defendants then proceeded to depose the remainder of the top management of Plaintiffs and their affiliates.

On November 13, 1990, Defendants wrote to Plaintiffs and "renewed" their request to depose Mr. Broad (Exhibit B/under seal). Defendants attached to the letter excerpts from several depositions in which Mr. Broad's name was mentioned. The letter provided no reference to information which could not be and had not already been obtained through other discovery means. Plaintiffs, therefore, responded to the letter by stating:

> We believe your clients have had more than adequate opportunity to explore the issues relevant to this litigation. If, however, you can identify specific information regarding Mr. Broad which you neither have obtained through other sources nor had the opportunity to obtain, we would appreciate receiving such information and discussing the matter with you thereafter.

(Exhibit C). Rather than responding to Plaintiffs' reasonable request, Defendants invited Plaintiffs "to move for a protective order if [they] continue to adhere to [their] present position" (Exhibit D). Defendants also retelecopied a "Notice of Depositions" to Plaintiffs on November 20, 1990, noticing Mr. Broad's deposition in Los Angeles for an unspecified time during for the week of December 3, 1990.

III. Argument and Citation of Authorities

Federal Rule of Civil Procedure 26(c) provides:

> Upon motion by a party or by the person from whom discovery is sought, and for good cause shown, the court in which the action is pending or alternatively, on matters relating to a deposition, the court in the district where the deposition is to be taken[3] may make any order which justice requires to protect a party or person

---

3. This Court, as that "in which the action is pending," may properly decide the issue raised in this renewed motion. *See* 4 J. Moore, J. Lucas, and G. GDefendanter, *Moore's Federal Practice* 5 26.68 at 26-429. Plaintiffs' initial Expedited Motion for a Scheduling Order was filed in this Court more than two months ago, this Court executed the Joint Motion for a Scheduling Order resolving the other issues raised in the initial motion, and no other court has issued process in connection with Mr. Broad's proposed deposition. Cf. *Lampshire v. Procter & Gamble Co.*, 94 F.R.D. 58, 59 (N.D. Ga. 1982) (indicating that protective orders involving non-party depositions normally should be filed in the district where the deposition is to occur; when the court where the action is pending "has the necessary background information to rule on the motion," however, it may do so even for non-party depositions).

from annoyance, embarrassment, oppression, or undue burden or expense, including one or more of the following: (1) that the discovery not be had; (2) that the discovery may be had only on specified terms and conditions, including a designation of the time or place;. . . (4) that certain matters not be inquired into, or that the scope of the discovery be limited to certain matters. . .

Under Rule 26(c), "the extent of discovery and the use of protective orders is clearly within the discretion of the trial judge." *Lewellinq v. Farmers Ins. of Columbus, Inc.,* 879 F.2d 212, 218 (6th Cir. 1989).

In *Salter v. Upjohn Co.,* 593 F.2d 649 (5th Cir. 1979), the Fifth Circuit affirmed an order vacating a notice of deposition of the president of a corporate party. According to the district court, the president could be deposed only if other corporate employees lacked personal knowledge of the facts in issue or "if the testimony of the other employees was unsatisfactory." *Id.* at 651. In upholding the district court's order, the Fifth Circuit stated:

> The judge's attempt to postpone or prevent the necessity of taking [the president's] deposition was within his discretion in light of. . . reasonable assertions that [the president] was extremely busy and did not have any direct knowledge of the facts. Thus, the judge's issuance of the protective order vacating [the] notice to take [the president's] deposition was not error.[4]

Other courts similarly have prohibited a party from deposing top management officials of its adversary. *See, e.g., Lewelling,* 879 F.2d at 218 (precluding deposition of opponent's Chief Executive Officer); *Hughes v. General Motors Corp.,* 18 FR Serv.2d 1249, 1249–50 (S.D.N.Y. 1974) (prohibiting deposition of party's President); *M.A. Porazzi Co. v. The Mormaclark,* 16 F.R.D. 383, 383–84 (S.D.N.Y. 1951) (vacating notice to depose).

> No good cause exists to require [a party] to submit its president for a deposition when it is clear that the information [the adversary] wants is available through other employees. . ., and such employees have been questioned or on. . . request can be questioned. The request borders on harassment and would at best result in a duplication of testimony.

---

4. Although the Fifth Circuit also implied that "extraordinary circumstances" were required to prohibit the taking of a deposition altogether, the court's language subsequently was interpreted by the Eleventh Circuit to mean nothing more "than the accepted abuse of discretion standard." *Lombard's, Inc. v. Prince Mfg. Co.,* 753 F.2d 974, 976 n.1 (11th Cir. 1985), *cert. denied,* 474 U.S. 1082 (1986) (adversary's Vice President). In *Hughes,* 18 FR Serv.2d at 1250, the court remarked

The *M.A. Porazzi* court, noting that the sought-after testimony could be gleaned from others, held that good cause had been shown to vacate the deposition notice of the opponent's Vice President. According to the court, the party seeking the testimony bore the burden of subsequently establishing its need for further examination of the company through its officers. *See M.A. Porazzi Co. v. The Mormaclark*, 16 F.R.D. 383, 384 (S.D.N.Y. 1951).

Here, Plaintiffs have provided Defendants with every opportunity to obtain information concerning facts relevant to this litigation, making available for deposition more than 20 present and former employees from virtually every aspect of Plaintiffs' business. Defendants have conducted substantial non-party discovery as well as that concerning the issues mentioned in their November 13, 1990, letter (Exhibit B). In accordance with *Salter and M.A. Porazzi*, Plaintiffs requested in writing that Defendants specify what information uniquely known by Mr. Broad they had not previously had the opportunity to obtain from the myriad of witnesses previously deposed or from the other discovery conducted (Exhibit C). Defendants refused Plaintiffs' reasonable request, merely reiterating their intention to depose Mr. Broad (Exhibit D) and noticing his deposition at a location of counsel affiliated with Defendants (Exhibit A). Such conduct further establishes Defendants' intent to harass Plaintiffs and subject them to undue burden and expense rather than conduct meaningful, noncumulative discovery. Under Rule 26(c)(1), therefore, Plaintiffs request that the Court vacate with prejudice the Notice of Depositions of Exhibit A to the extent it seeks testimony from Mr. Broad.

IV. Conclusion

For the foregoing reasons, Plaintiffs respectfully request that their request for a protective order be granted.

****

In the United States District Court for the Northern District of Georgia Atlanta Division

SUNAMERICA CORPORATION (formerly) *SUN* LIFE GROUP. OF AMERICA, INC.),) a Delaware corporation, and SUN) LIFE INSURANCE COMPANY OF AMERICA,) INC., a Maryland corporation,))) Plaintiffs and) Counterdefendants,) v.) *SUN* LIFE ASSURANCE COMPANY OF) CANADA, a Canadian corporation,) and SUN LIFE ASSURANCE COMPANY) OF CANADA (U.S.), a Delaware) corporation,) Defendants and) Counterclaimants.)	Civil Action File No. 1:89-CV-1315-JTC

Defendants' Memorandum in Opposition to Plaintiffs' Renewed Motion for a Protective Order With Respect to the Noticed Deposition of the Chief Executive Officer of Plaintiffs' Parent Company
I. Introduction

Plaintiffs, SunAmerica Corporation and Sun Life Insurance Company of America, Inc., ("SunAmerica") have moved to prevent defendants from taking the deposition of their chief executive officer, Mr. Eli Broad, on the grounds that "he is an extremely busy corporate executive" and there would be overlap with the testimony of other members of plaintiffs' management. These are clearly not the standards to be met under F.R.C.P. Rule 26 (c). As is shown below, Mr. Broad has, in fact, played an integral and vital role in the issues of this action and indisputably is subject to deposition. Defendants, Sun Life Assurance Company of Canada and Sun Life Assurance Company of Canada (U.S.), therefore respectfully request that the Court deny plaintiffs' motion. Because plaintiffs seriously misstate both the facts and the law in their "renewed" motion for a protective order, defendants additionally ask that the Court impose sanctions on plaintiffs for having caused needless increase in the cost of this litigation.

II. Statement of Facts

The infringement and unfair competition claims in this case center around names and marks containing SUN and SUN LIFE, as well as "S" Logos used by the parties. Defendants allege, inter alia, that plaintiffs' claims are barred by gross laches, since the parties have coexisted under their SUN LIFE names and marks for 75 years, and that if problems now exist, it is plaintiffs who are liable because they admittedly are second users of a SUN LIFE name and mark and recently have dramatically changed their business to bring it into conflict with defendants' business. Defendants also claim that any alleged rights in the marks SUNAMERICA, SUN FINANCIAL SERVICES and plaintiffs' "S" Logo, which form the basis of some of plaintiffs' claims, were abandoned.

A. Mr. Broad's Integral Role

Defendants first notified plaintiffs of their intent to take the deposition of Mr. Broad by letter of April 23, 1990. (August Decl. 1 2, Exh. A-1). When plaintiffs objected to producing Mr. Broad, defendants proceeded with the depositions of numerous other plaintiff employees over a period of months. Those depositions confirmed Mr. Broad's integral involvement in the decision-making process of his companies and the key issues of this case. For example, Gerhardt Hoff, speaking of operating procedures while he was president of Sun Life Insurance Company of America, said of Mr. Broad:

> We discussed all important policy decisions. I could not hire new people or replace people with salaries of, say $50,000 or more [without his consent]. . . I could not make changes in the corporate structure, I could not enter into new lines of business or discontinue old lines without his approval.

(Hoff Dep., pp. 15–16). Similarly, an "Internal Management Study" based on interviews of nine members of plaintiffs' top management stated:

> Most people felt the company's short- and long-term business goals will be determined by one person, Eli Broad.

> "The company is guided and directed by Eli Broad. It may be a public company, but the decision-making process both begins and ends there."

Kaufman and Broad, Inc. Internal Study; Greer Dep., Vol. III, p. 9, Exh. 4). Mr. Broad, in fact, apparently was the one who decided to file this lawsuit against defendants. (Greer Dep., pp. 189–90).

Based on the repeated confirmation of Mr. Broad's key role in the issues of this litigation, as more fully described below, defendants formally noticed Mr. Broad's deposition on September 10, 1990. (August Decl. 12, Exh. A-2). Plaintiffs objected, and defendants agreed not to take Mr. Broad's deposition on the noticed date but specifically reserved the right to take the deposition at a later date.

By letter of October 10, 1990, defendants reiterated their intention to take Mr. Broad's deposition, but plaintiffs again resisted. On November 13, 1990, *defendants sent opposing counsel over 80 pages of extracts* from depositions and other materials showing Mr. Broad's integral role in every important issue in this case, including the selection and use of corporate names and marks that are at the heart of this controversy. (August Decl. 14, Exhs. C, D). On November 20, 1990, plaintiffs were served with a new notice of Mr. Broad's deposition, in response to which they have now moved for a protective order. (August Decl. 14, Exh. E).

B. The Changes in Plaintiffs' Business

It "is, in fact, Mr. Broad who dictated the changes in plaintiffs" business during the 1980s that changed them from a small home-service debit insurance company to a broad-based financial services operation. These changes, inter alia, brought them for the first time into direct competition with defendants, after little or no competition for more than 50 years. (Hoff Dep., pp. 63–65, 87–89). During that time SunAmerica greatly increased its emphasis on the sale of annuities, underwent a substantial acquisition program, made fundamental changes in its methods of product distribution and sale, and decided to stop selling life insurance altogether.' (Saltzman Dep., pp. 9-29; Hoff Dep., pp. 23-89). The genesis of these changes—and plans for the future orientation of plaintiffs' business—are the

'Curiously, the decision to stop selling life insurance was made shortly before plaintiffs brought suit over use of the name and mark SUN LIFE.

exclusive province of Mr. Broad. As one of his executives put it: "I think the owner of the company had a vision of the future that called for the resources to be committed in a whole different direction—the vision of the owner was to change the nature of the company in such a way where the total emphasis would be on the sale of investment oriented products. . . and. . . get out of the sale of life insurance." (Mlekush Dep., pp. 104–06).

C. Mr. Broad's Recent Attempts To Alter Plaintiffs' Tarnished Corporate Image

Mr. Broad also has been integrally involved in plaintiffs' recent attempts to alter their tarnished corporate image. He was one of nine management interviewees for the above-referenced 1986 corporate image Internal Study. While plaintiffs have alleged that defendants have been trading upon the goodwill of plaintiffs' as symbolized by their SUN LIFE name and mark, that study confirms the opposite. It reports the interviewees' perception that "The general public often confuses Sun Life of America with Sun Life of Canada— a company with a strong, stable, 'somewhat stodgy' reputation. To a certain extent this is helpful: it allows Sun Life [of America] to benefit from Sun Life of Canada's solid reputation. Most [of the nine members of SunAmerica management interviewed for this study] felt that Sun Life [of America]. . . is not well regarded within this industry group."[2]

[2]That same study reported the top executives as stating,"we have a very rough reputation: that we're tough to deal with; that our word is not our bond; that you never know when a deal that you thought was done and settled with will be reopened through a lawsuit. I'd say once someone's done a deal with us they don't do a second one." (Internal Study at p. 5).

Mr. Broad's testimony about that study is not only relevant, it is vital to this litigation.

Plaintiffs dismissed Hill and Knowlton shortly after Mr. Broad read the results quoted above, and the research for a new corporate identity was taken over by Landor Associates.[5] Landor conducted its own interviews of plaintiffs' management, including an interview of Mr. Broad himself on November 20, 1987. Notes on those interviews reveal that the interviewees, including Mr. Broad, openly discussed Sun Life of Canada and its renown in the insurance industry, as contrasted to Sun Life of America's lesser reputation. For example, at one point those notes read: "Chairman likes Sun derivative names, Sun Life of Canada one of largest insurance [*sic*] in the world." (Mlekush Dep., Confidential pp. 135–41, Mlekush Exhs. 3 and 4.)

D. Mr. Broad's Decision To Purchase The SUNAMERICA Name And His SUNAMERICA Negotiations

Plaintiffs assert that they purchased the name and mark SUNAMERICA in 1988 in order to distinguish plaintiffs' names and marks from those of defendants. (Complaint 1126–28). They also claim that defendants should pay them damages for that purchase. (Complaint, Prayer for Relief 13). Defendants have counterclaimed

There is conflicting evidence as to whether or not SUN- AMERICA was in current use by Chemical Bank and had any real value at the time of its purchase by plaintiffs. (Contrast, e.g., Greer Dep., Vol. II, pp. 181-183 with Greer Dep. Exh. 183i). It is Mr. Broad himself who personally conducted the negotiations for the purchase of SUNAMERICA. As testified by Mr. Broad's vice president for public relations: "the first discussion of [Chemical Bank's

---

5. Plaintiffs' corporate image has continued to suffer since the Hill & Knowlton study. On November 26, 1990, the Los Angeles Times reported that plaintiffs' parent is "in the ranks of alleged bombs that have yet to go off," due to the fact that "about 9.6% of Broad's portfolio [is] invested in more speculative assets, including junk bonds and real estate. If that $911 million chunk of the portfolio were to become completely worthless, it would more than wipe out Broad's capital, leaving the firm bankrupt." (August Decl., 15, Exh. F). that any rights in the name SUNAMERICA were abandoned by plaintiffs' predecessor prior to the purchase. (Amended Answer and Counterclaim, Count V).

use of SUNAMERICA] would have been—I believe there was a meeting that was set up or a correspondence between Eli Broad and Walter Shipley." (Greer Dep., p. 105). In his letter of June 14, 1988, to Walter V. Shipley (Chairman of Chemical Bank), Mr. Broad states: "You and I spoke many months back. .. We understand that you haven't been using the name actively since 1985. . . ." (Greer Dep., pp. 181-183, Greer Exh. 183i). In that same letter Mr. Broad made an offer on behalf of plaintiffs to purchase the SUNAMERICA mark. Plaintiffs' vice president later testified that her impression as to whether or not Chemical Bank had abandoned SUNAMERICA prior to its purchase by plaintiffs came largely from conversations with Mr. Broad. (Greer Dep., p. 112).

E. Mr. Broad's Role In Other Key Issues

Mr. Broad also has made himself of record on a number of other key issues in this case, including plaintiffs' abandonment of its "S" Logo and the mark SUN FINANCIAL SERVICES ("We have no intention to abandon either the 'S' Logo or any of our Sun names and marks, all of which will continue actively to be used in our life insurance operations,"March [4], 21, 1988, Broad letter to Thomas M. Galt, at that time defendants' CEO; August Decl. 13, Exh. B); the selection of the new Sundial logo for SunAmerica, which defendants believe was selected to replace plaintiffs' "S" Logo (he was one of the three people most involved in that selection, Greer Dep., pp. 55, 58 and 68); and the confusion alleged by plaintiffs, ("The most recent example of the confusion. . . is a letter I received from a business colleague. . .," March 21, 1988, Broad letter to Thomas M. Galt, supra), among many others. (See, August Decl., 54, Exh. D).

III. Legal Argument

Plaintiffs argue that Mr. Eli Broad is entitled to a protective order because (1) he is busy, (2) he is the top officer of plaintiffs' organization and (3) there will be overlap with the testimony of other members of plaintiffs' management. These allegations do not begin to support an order preventing the taking of a deposition. The law requires that truly extraordinary circumstances be present before such an order can be issued. As stated in Salter v. Upjohn co., 593 F.2d 649 (5th Cir. 1979), the case upon which plaintiffs principally and erroneously rely (593 F.2d at 651):

> It is *very unusual* for a court to prohibit the 4Plaintiffs' life insurance operations have since been sold off. (Daniel Dep., pp. 17-20; Saltzman Dep., pp. 9-122, 22, Exh. 2). taking of a deposition altogether and absent *extraordinary circumstances* such an order would likely be in error. [Emphasis added, citations omitted].

Obviously being "busy" or "a top officer" does not constitute extraordinary circumstances. Nor does overlap with previous deposition testimony constitute such "extraordinary circumstances," as explained in Moore's Federal Practice:

It is fairly rare that it will be ordered that a deposition not be taken at all. All motions for protective orders must be supported by "good cause" and a strong showing is required before a party will be denied entirely the right to take a deposition. The mere fact that the information sought by deposition has already been obtained through a bill of particulars, interrogatories, or other depositions will not suffice. . . .

4 J. Moore, J. Lucas and G. GDefendanter, Jr., Moore's Federal Practice 1 26.69 (3d ed. 1989), (citations omitted). Wright & Miller similarly explain:

It is even more difficult to show grounds for ordering that discovery not be had when it is a deposition that is sought, and most requests of this kind are denied . . . .

Reasons that have been advanced for an order that a deposition not be taken, and that have been disposed of by the court—and usually denied—on the facts of the particular case, are: that the information sought has already been obtained by prior depositions or other means of discovery . . . .

8 C. Wright & A. Miller, Federal Practice & Procedure: Civil § 2037 (1970).

Plaintiffs' principal case, Salter v. Utriohn Co., 593 F.2d 649 (5th Cir. 1979), rather than supporting plaintiffs, actually squarely supports defendants on this issue. In Salter extraordinary circumstances were shown where the plaintiff had been required by court order to depose first the employees that defendant indicated had more knowledge than its President. The appellate court upheld the preclusion of the president's deposition only because plaintiff failed to take the depositions of the other employees and then to renew properly its request to take the deposition of defendant's president (592 F.2d at 651-652):

[I]t is clear that the [protective] order merely required plaintiff to depose the other employees that Upjohn indicated had more knowledge of the facts before deposing [Upjohn's president] . . . . of course, if after taking the other depositions, plaintiff was not satisfied and again properly gave notice of or requested taking [the president's] deposition, the judge probably should have allowed the deposition. After the first protective order, however, *plaintiff never again properly raised the issue in the trial court* . . . . because plaintiff did not properly reassert the request, the district judge did not abuse his discretion by preventing the deposition . . . . [Emphasis added].

Here, in contrast, defendants have taken depositions of numerous plaintiff employees and top management, and those employees have repeatedly pointed to Mr. Broad as knowledgeable on the issues. Defendants, furthermore, having first notified plaintiffs of their intention to take Mr. Broad's deposition in

April, 1990, have properly renewed their request after taking the other employee depositions. Under *Salter*, therefore, defendants clearly are entitled to take Mr. Broad's deposition.

The other cases relied on by plaintiffs are simply inapposite. For example, in *Lewelling v. Farmers Insurance of Columbus, Inc.*, 879 F.2d 212 (6th Cir. 1989), a protective order was issued *for reasons other than the corporate status of the deponent*. The Court there explained (879 F.2d at 218):

> Plaintiffs filed a notice to take the deposition of. . . (the] Chief Executive Officer of Farmers Group, Inc. Farmers sought a protective order, and plaintiffs responded that they would cancel the deposition requests if [the CEO] would agree to meet with plaintiffs regarding possible settlement of their action. *Based on this fact and Farmers' representation that [the CEO) had no knowledge as to facts pertinent to plaintiffs' action*, the district court granted defendants' request for a protective order. [Emphasis added.]

Contrary to plaintiffs' assertions, it is, in fact, it is well- settled that when a party's president or chief executive officer has direct and personal knowledge relating to the issues of the action, he or she is subject to deposition by the opposing party. *See, e.g., Scotch Whiskey Association v. Majestic Distilling Co., Inc.*, 14 F.R. Serv. 3d 940, 947 (D. Md. 1988) (citing the *Salter* decision); *Amherst Leasing Corp. v. Emhart Corp.*, 65 F.R.D. 121, 123 (D. Conn. 1974). Even Presidents of the United States have been subject to deposition when they have had direct and personal knowledge relating to the issues in a lawsuit. See, *U.S. v. Poindexter*, 732 F. Supp. 142 (D.C.C. 1990), in which former President Reagan was ordered to appear for a testimonial deposition, including that court's listing of deposition appearances by other former presidents. While Mr. Broad may be "busy" and "a top executive officer," surely even plaintiffs' exalted opinion of Mr. Broad cannot place him in a class above our country's president.

IV. Defendants are Entitled to Sanctions

Because plaintiffs have filed a patently baseless motion, defendants ask that the Court award to defendants their costs, including attorneys' fees, incurred in responding to it. Rule 11 of the Federal Rules of Civil Procedure provides:

> The signature of an attorney or party constitutes a certificate by the signer that the signer has read the pleading, motion, or other paper; that to the best of the signer's knowledge, information and belief formed after reasonable inquiry it is well grounded in fact and is warranted by existing law or a good faith argument for the extension, modification or reversal of existing law, and that it is not interposed for any improper purpose, such as to harass or to cause unnecessary delay or needless increase in the cost of litigation.

In view of the extensive evidence of record that Mr. Broad has direct and personal knowledge relating to the key issues of this case, and plaintiffs' clearly inappropriate reliance on the *Salter* decision, this is a motion that, after reasonable inquiry, should never have been filed. Prior to plaintiffs' filing of this motion, in fact, defendants provided plaintiffs with over 80 pages of extracts from depositions and other materials demonstrating that Mr. Broad indisputably was subject to deposition. Plaintiffs nevertheless elected to increase the cost of litigation by filing this motion.5 In addition to incurring costs responding to plaintiffs' baseless motion, furthermore, defendants were unable to take the deposition of Mr. Broad along with other depositions scheduled in Los Angeles during the week of December 3, 1990.

[5]Plaintiffs also allege in their Motion that defendants have harassed Mr. Broad by noticing his deposition to take place at law offices five minutes from plaintiffs' Los Angeles headquarters. Plaintiffs conspicuously fail to mention that every time plaintiffs have requested that an employee deposition be relocated to plaintiffs' offices, defendants have complied. Defendants are willing to do so again for the deposition of Mr. Broad

Sanctions therefore are warranted. *See, e.g., Ortho Pharmaceutical Corporation v. Sona Distributors*, 847 F.2d 1512, 1518–19 (11th Cir. 1988); *Donaldson v. Clark*, 819 F.2d 1551, 1556–58 (11th Cir. 1987).

V. Conclusion

Plaintiffs have failed to show any support for their contention that a chief executive officer with the type of direct and personal knowledge evidenced here has the right not to be deposed by reason of his position, his busy schedule or any alleged overlap with the testimony from other employees of the corporation. Plaintiffs' allegations do not even begin to demonstrate the "extraordinary circumstances" necessary for such a protective order, and the principal case on which plaintiffs rely, *Salter*, actually confirms the absence of any valid basis for plaintiffs' motion.

Defendants have satisfied *Salter's* requirements by first taking the deposition of the other employees of plaintiffs who are alleged to have more knowledge of the relevant facts than Mr. Broad. It is those very employees who have pointed to Mr. Broad as the one person who is best situated to testify as to the issues at the heart of this litigation. The record is replete with evidence demonstrating Mr. Broad's integral involvement with those issues, and there simply can be no question that defendants are entitled to take his deposition in defense of this action and in support of their countercomplaint. Defendants therefore respectfully request that the Court deny plaintiffs' motion for a protective order and order plaintiffs to pay defendants their costs, including attorneys' fees, incurred in responding to this motion, in accordance with rule 11 of the Federal Rules of Civil Procedure.